Pengarron's Children

Gloria Cook

CANELO

First published in the United Kingdom in 1993 by Headline Book Publishing

This edition published in the United Kingdom in 2019 by

Canelo Digital Publishing Limited
57 Shepherds Lane
Beaconsfield, Bucks HP9 2DU
United Kingdom

A CIP catalogue record for this book is available from the British Library.

Print ISBN 978 1 78863 407 6
Ebook ISBN 978 1 78863 071 9

This book is a work of fiction. Names, characters, businesses, organizations, places and events are either the product of the author's imagination or are used fictitiously. Any resemblance to actual persons, living or dead, events or locales is entirely coincidental.

Look for more great books at www.canelo.co

Printed and bound in Great Britain by Clays Ltd, Elcograf S.p.A.

This book is dedicated to my mum, Betty

Chapter 1

Jessica Trenchard forced her way to the front of a crowd which was circling a large area of grass where two brawny men were about to begin a wrestling match. There had been a recent shower of rain, and straw had been spread in the ring to prevent the wrestlers from slipping. Philip Trenchard, one of Jessica's twin brothers, was in the ring and as he glimpsed her head of long golden curls he gave her a confident grin. The other twin, David, squeezed himself in behind her and held out his arms to protect her from the press of excited spectators or from furtive assault.

'Where on earth did you get to?' he shouted in her ear. 'Phil was getting worried. He's just stepped into the ring and is about to shake hands. Wouldn't be like you to miss him wrestling.'

'I was looking for Olivia and Cordelia, they said they would be at the market today. You needn't worry about me,' Jessica told him haughtily, her large blue eyes bright with the prospect of the coming match. 'I can look after myself.'

'I know that, but you don't have to with your menfolk about.'

'Tush!' Jessica said impatiently. 'How much money have you put on Philip?'

'Nothing,' David answered patiently.

'Of course, I forgot you don't bet,' she said as they were jostled about. Jessica dug her heels into the wet ground and wished that instead of looking for her friends she had put the two shillings she had saved up on a wager that Philip would win.

There was a bigger crowd than usual for this match because Philip, who was gaining a reputation as a first-class wrestler, was to compete with the current Mount's Bay champion, a huge fisherman, Matthew King, known as the Barvah Giant, and both the men were local. They had won their two earlier matches, contended the day before against different opponents, and now as 'standers' they were wrestling in the last rounds of the championship.

The crowd was thickening and the tension was growing steadily. The match promised to be one of the most skilful and tightly contended. Matthew King had many years of experience to go with his ox-like strength but Philip Trenchard had youth and speed on his side and the toughness of being a hard-working farmer's son. The match was reckoned to go either way and the betting was feverish.

There were cheers and a surge of excitement as the wrestlers shook hands and sized each other up, circling round, knees bent, eyes locked.

Jessica listened to the opinions of the crowd, made up of men, women and children, both working class and gentry.

A pockmarked man who was jammed in next to her, remarked to his bull-necked companion, 'Trenchard may be a fast mover but he'll have to be pretty damned quick to get a hitch in first on the Barvah Giant.'

'Aye, but I don't reckon much to that cocky young clod-shifter's chances anyway,' the bull-necked man replied scornfully.

Jessica turned sharply with her mouth wide open but David clamped his hand over it. 'You're not to say a word, Jessie!' he warned her. 'Just watch the match.'

She struggled and mumbled angrily under his hand but David would not give way. His sister's tongue ran away all too often and he wanted to watch Philip peaceably.

'Olivia and Cordelia are ladies. If they're about here somewhere you'll show yourself up by wagging your tongue,' he scolded her. 'If I let you go, do you promise to keep quiet?'

Jessica nodded but once freed she shot him a reproachful look and elbowed him viciously in the ribs.

The crowd fell silent and the rustling of the straw in the ring was the only sound to be heard as the wrestlers and the sticklers, the three men chosen from among well-known former wrestlers to referee the match, moved about.

Jessica watched with bubbling excitement, proud of her tall, well-built brother's expertise in the ring and proud of herself for the work she had done on his wrestling jacket. She didn't take kindly to the supposed feminine art of sewing but had taken hours to stitch the short, tight-fitting garment from tough, untearable linen for the wrestling moves called the hitches, which were made by gripping and then pulling on an opponent's jacket.

Philip tucked his jacket up at the bottom to prevent Matthew from getting a good purchase. Matthew, who preferred to wear a sash worn over one of his massive shoulders and across his barrel chest to rest at his side, was known to take up to half an hour to make his first move, and had then often won a match outright. They wore nothing else but their breeches and thick stockings and Jessica knew her brother liked to show off his muscular physique and handsome limbs. She saw Matthew's patient expression and she chewed her full red lips, hoping Philip would not attempt his first hitch too soon.

Minutes ticked by. The two wrestlers were content to bide their time and raise the tension of the onlookers. The crowd began to mumble but every eye stayed rooted inside the ring.

Jessica clutched David's coat sleeves in her fists, willing Philip to be careful, to remember all he had learned over the thirteen years he had been wrestling since a boy.

In a sudden rapid movement Philip reached out with his right hand and gripped a hitch on the sash on the Giant's right shoulder. Then he passed his left hand under Matthew's arm, gripping the sash at the back of Matthew's neck. It was a good move and would have resulted in a winning throw on a lesser man but Philip couldn't get control of Matthew's heavy body to lever him off balance. Before Matthew could grab him and turn the hitch to his advantage, Philip released his hold and stepped quickly backwards. But Matthew had got a tight hitch on Philip's jacket and the crowd broke out into roars of encouragement for whichever of the men they favoured. With a tree-trunk leg bending the backs of Philip's knees, Matthew attempted to lever Philip over his hip to the ground in a 'back heave'.

Jessica squealed. If Matthew brought off this throw and got any three of Philip's two hips and shoulders on the ground and one of the sticklers considered it a 'fair back', then Matthew would win the match outright.

Matthew succeeded in lifting Philip off his feet to hit the ground.

Shouts of 'Get his pins down, Matt!' or 'Wrastle un off, boy!'; and 'You have him there, King!' or 'Get up, I say, Trenchard!' rang out, according to the spectator's station in life and on whom he had placed his money.

Jessica screamed, 'Get up, Phil, get up!' and cheered wildly as Matthew only managed to get two of Philip's 'pins' down on the ground and a stickler signalled for the contenders to break, get up and resume as before.

Further round the front row of the ring of eager spectators, Kane Pengarron was watching the wrestling with a nostalgic smile warming his face and lightening the dark shadows of pain under his eyes. He was twenty-four now. It was two years since he had stood in this marketplace, gripped with the same fervour.

The preceding match had been contested by two very young standers, boys of no more than twelve years, intent on going on to win the youths' championship. Kane Pengarron had recognised only one boy as the son of a local man; he hoped he would be able to watch the remainder of the matches without being recognised himself. He was the adopted son of the Lord of the Manor of the next parish. His presence would cause a stir among the spectators and he wanted to savour this match and the other familiar sights, sounds and smells that a market day at Marazion could offer at his leisure. People looked at him often; he cut an impressive figure in his army officer's uniform, but so far he had managed to keep his head down and stay unrecognised.

Kane had put ten guineas on the Barvah Giant. He had watched Matthew King wrestle from childhood and every time the amiable giant had won. Kane knew the Trenchard twins well; many years ago he had played with them and had retained their friendship. He knew of Philip's strength and desire to become the Mount's Bay and then the Cornish champion. Kane was impressed today at the way he had kept both hips off the ground and foiled Matthew King's winning throw.

The wrestlers were bending forward now, eye to eye, feet wide apart for balance. Expectation rippled through the crowd. Then Matthew sprang up and at arm's length grasped the cords on the front of Philip's jacket. At the same moment he pivoted his left leg and turning to face Philip's direction he pulled the younger, lighter man along, four, five, six, seven paces, speeding up the forward movement as he went for a 'flying mare'. When Matthew had gained satisfactory momentum he stopped running abruptly, arched his back and tried to pull Philip over his buttocks. But on the halt Philip had dug his feet into the ground and with straining muscles pulled back hard and his jacket was wrenched from Matthew's grasp.

Despite having his money on the Giant, Kane cheered at Philip's display of brute strength. Jessica squealed in delight and jumped up and down, and her golden mane of curls caught Kane's attention.

'Jessica Trenchard,' he muttered under his breath and laughed. 'You haven't changed a bit and still as pretty as a picture.'

Instinct told Jessica she was being watched and she swept her head around the crowd until her shining blue eyes caught sight of the noble figure in the red tunic with white facings. Kane nodded his head and lifted his hand. Jessica stared back, raised her stubborn chin, pouted her lips into a cupid's bow and refused to return the acknowledgement.

So you're still a haughty little madam, Kane thought, much amused, before returning his attention to the match.

Jessica kept her eyes fixed on Kane's dark face and leaned back to whisper in David's ear, 'Look over there, see what the cat's dragged back into Marazion.'

David saw Kane at once and grinned heartily and waved to his old boyhood friend.

'What are you bothering to do that for?' Jessica cried crossly. 'He's as horrid as his rotten brother.'

David ruffled her hair and shot his eyes back to their own brother. Jessica glared at Kane who put his hands round his lips and mouthed the words, 'I'll see you after this.'

'Not if I have anything to do with it!' Jessica returned hotly.

At that moment a cheer went up and the crowd surged forward. Jessica was pushed round into David's chest and when she'd struggled to face the ring again she saw with horror that Philip was on the ground and one of the sticklers was holding up the Barvah Giant's arm in victory.

'Ahgg!' she screeched. 'That Kane Pengarron's made me miss the end of the match! What happened? How did the Giant win?' she demanded, doing a little dance with her heels.

'With his favourite throw, a forehip,' David said with a sigh. 'It was all over in a moment. You should have been watching, Jessie.' Then grabbing Jessica's arm he dragged her along to join the supporters who were giving Philip their commiserations.

'Well done, Phil, you did your best,' Jessica said.

'Aye, I did, but the best man won,' Philip said sportingly, while enjoying the adoration he was getting anyway, and particularly from a gaggle of interesting-looking young females. 'But I'll beat the Barvah Giant one day, I swear to that.'

Matthew King extended his congratulations to Philip on a well-fought match and took his army of little children off to enjoy the sideshows before his next match. Philip was exchanging his wrestling jacket for his usual shirt when a voice, this one edged in a cultured tone, hailed him from behind.

'You wrestled well, Philip. It was a pity you didn't meet the Giant in the final round, then you would have been the runner-up. I don't believe any other man is capable of beating you.'

'I know that voice!' Philip whirled round. 'Kane Pengarron!' He shot out his hand in greeting. 'Bloody hell, man, it must be all of two years!'

Kane pumped the proffered hand while Jessica looked on, scowling. 'It's good to see so many old friends in one place,' he said, passing his hand on to David and then to Jessica. He held her reluctant hand, and when he tried to raise it to his lips she snatched it away. Kane laughed and looked at the twins. 'I see you've done nothing to tame this little one.'

'I would be grateful, Captain Pengarron, if you would not refer to me on such terms,' Jessica said tartly.

The group was asked to leave the ring so the next match could begin and Kane suggested they all retire to a refreshment tent – 'For good ale and pasties as my treat.'

'How are things in the Thirty-second Foot?' David asked Kane when they were standing in a corner under the dirty canvas, chewing on enormous pasties.

'The regiment is fine. I'm home because I had an… accident out in the Caribbean,' Kane replied, then went on quickly, 'This is good, you don't taste anything like this when you're away from Cornwall and I didn't realise I was so hungry.'

'Hurt bad, was you?' Philip asked. 'Now I've had the chance to study your face, I can see pain written all over it.'

Jessica looked up from sipping water from a small tankard. Kane Pengarron had changed a good deal in the last two years. He may have suffered somehow but he had a more confident air about him. His hair, which had been red from childhood, had a dark brown tint to it now; his face, which had always been worth a woman's second look, was thinner, almost gaunt, and his strong chin was covered with a shadow, needing a razor's attention. But his eyes were the same, a warm dark brown yet somehow permanently startled, and they begged a woman's constant attention.

Kane caught her examination and grinned and raised his ale tankard to her. Jessica put the last morsel of crimped pastry into her mouth, eyed him solemnly as she swallowed it then thrust her tankard at one of her brothers.

'I'm off to find me friends,' she said loftily, and made to exit the tent.

'Don't be late getting back to the wagon, Jessie,' Philip ordered at her back, 'or I'll tell Father and you'll have him after you. And don't get into any trouble.'

Jessica let out an impatient sound and flounced away.

Kane took his eyes from her pleasingly rounded form and turned to the twins. 'Trouble? Who are Jessica's friends?' he was curious to know.

'They're nothing to worry about, Kane, they're your sister and your cousin,' David replied.

'Olivia and Cordelia? I'm pleased to hear Jessica still gets along with them at least,' Kane said.

'Aye, Jessie's an awful worry to us sometimes,' Philip remarked, swiftly finishing off his ale then slapping his tankard down on the trestle table for a refill. 'But at least she'll be all right with your womenfolk for company.'

Kane nodded, reflecting light-heartedly to himself that the Trenchard twins' rebellious younger sister had indeed not changed one little bit.

Jessica swept herself, cloaked but hatless, through the busy market crowds. There was always a bigger crush when the two-day wrestling championships were being held but her demeanour helped her to pass through easily, her long fair curls bouncing down to her waist over the hood of her cloak. She was disappointed Philip had lost his match but she'd known he was unlikely to beat Matthew King, and she grudgingly shared a viewpoint of Kane Pengarron's – that it was a pity they couldn't have met in the final round.

'Oh well,' she mused out loud, 'there's always next year.'

'There's always now if you'd like, Jessica.' A young man, whom she had not seen making a beeline towards her, stood directly in front of her.

Instantly in a fury, Jessica made to bawl the man out but when she saw it was Simon Peter Blake she flashed a huge smile instead. 'You nearly got your ears bitten off then, you dolt, Simon Peter.'

'For a moment I thought you were going to beat me into the mud.' He offered her his arm.

''Tis a good job for you that I've known you all my life and I know you're only jesting with me,' Jessica replied, taking his arm and using it as a lever to leap over a pile of sheep droppings.

'You know I meant more than that, Jessica,' Simon Peter said seriously. 'I'd marry you tomorrow if you'd have me. I've told you often enough.'

'I know, and I'm flattered for all that, but I don't see myself as an itinerant preacher's wife and besides, I'm only eighteen years old. I don't want to get tied down yet. Folk don't expect it from a man and I don't see why I have to be any different.'

'You break my heart, Jessica Trenchard,' Simon Peter said wistfully, 'don't you know that?'

'Oh, Simon…' Jessica was two inches taller than Simon Peter. She looked down at his pale face and planted a kiss beside his delicately chiselled nose. ''Tis a pity that my brother David's not a woman. With his plans to be the same as you with the Methodists you would have made a happy couple.'

'But you are a Methodist,' Simon Peter pointed out.

'Aye, but not in the same way as you and David and your mother are. And anyway, you're gentry and I'm working class, it wouldn't work.'

'My mother was working class, she still considers herself working class.'

'Simon Peter!' Jessica's voice rose with exasperation. Somehow this gentle young man's romantic talk made her feel guilty that she could never reciprocate his feelings. 'Do you want me to walk off and leave you this very minute?'

'No, don't do that,' he answered, looking at her contritely, then changing his expression to one that pleaded for understanding. 'But you can't blame me for trying. I'm sorry that Philip didn't win his match, he put up a good show.'

'Thank you, but he'll beat Matthew King one of these days, you see if he don't.'

Simon Peter allowed Jessica to propel them in the direction of a high-quality milliner's shop where she stopped and put her pert nose to the window.

'Are you going in there, Jessica? Must I be forced to leave you so soon?'

'Course I'm not going in there. I haven't got money falling out of my ears to spend on fancy hats and suchlike.' She tossed her head and her curls swirled. 'Not that I'd wear such things anyway. I'm looking for Olivia and Cordelia, I've got some news for them.'

'Oh, something of importance, is it?' Simon Peter asked, turning crimson as a gentlewoman inspecting the wares hanging on a row of hooks looked out and frowned heavily at him.

Jessica saw her and tossed her head away. 'She'll be wondering what you're doing with me, dressed up in your fine clothes.'

'My father insisted I dress like this today. He hates to think I'll meet up with someone influential while wearing what he calls my "Methodist" clothes, which he says are too plain and not of high enough quality.'

Jessica looked at Simon Peter sympathetically. 'Your father does try to force his own ideas on you, doesn't he? Well, never mind, 'tis better than being accused of being a scruff like me. I don't think Olivia and Cordelia sure in there. They'll be some excited when they hear the news I've got to tell them.'

'Oh, and what's that?' Simon Peter asked, deeply curious.

'Well, 'tis nothing that interests me of course, but Kane Pengarron's suddenly come home.'

–

Kane was on his own again and he meandered through the hustle and bustle with the same intention as Jessica, to locate his younger sister Olivia and their cousin Cordelia Drannock who lived with the family at Pengarron Manor. He was unconcerned at being recognised now and was greeted and gossiped at continually. He mingled with east coast fishermen who had come down to the region for the mackerel, and with pious faces heading for sight of St Michael's Mount on their pilgrimage route which followed the steps of Cornish saints. Also milling about were sailors, soldiers, farmers and livestock holders and quite a few women of the street.

Kane felt sorry for a youth locked in the pillory. He was obviously an imbecile and whatever his crime had been, it was certainly one that he should not have been held responsible for. He watched angrily as folk threw rotten vegetables at the prisoner, and when a gang of youths lurched up and started throwing stones Kane chased them off. He crouched down and wiped the youth's face clean then paid a brutish-looking young miner to protect the boy until his release, which he was told would be in an hour's time.

Moving away from the main area of the market stalls, he made for a quieter part of the town. He headed towards the sea and stopped to breathe in a sudden waft of salty air. He felt a burning urgency to get a closer look at St Michael's Mount, half a mile out in the waters of the busy sea port.

When he got to the beach he found the tide was out and he climbed to the top of the single outcrop of rocks there. From here he gazed at the castle which gave much to the magic of the Mount's reputation as an important trading place and port on the ancient tin route to the Mediterranean. St Michael's Mount castle had seen a lot of changes: it had been a priory and a fortress protecting the coastline, and a beacon had been lit on top of its church to warn of the approaching danger of the Spanish Armada. Now an aristocratic family owned and lived in it.

Kane put his face to the chilly wind and surveyed the sea to his right, busy with the fishing craft of Newlyn, Mousehole and Penzance. These were sights he had been looking forward to seeing again for a long time. He jumped down from the rocks, holding a protective hand to his stomach where he had been wounded, and made his way quickly over the grey sand, littered with seaweed and pebbles, tramping in the direction of the fishing boats. He passed a row of cottages built close to the beach edge where folk were about seeing to their boats and nets. The tide was an exceptionally low one and he walked seawards to look over the black stumps of what remained of an ancient petrified forest. It wasn't a particularly still day, but Kane listened hard, as he had done as a child, in case he could hear the church bells of the legendary land of Lyonesse, said to lie submerged just past the horizon.

He considered walking on to Penzance, a few minutes away at the other end of the gently curving beach, but sight of his family beckoned stronger and he turned round. Back in the main street again, it wasn't long before he saw one of his relations.

Two young gentlemen were leaving an exclusive coffee shop and coming towards him. Both were impeccably dressed in the latest fashion. One was tall, dark and broadly built with an arrogant bearing and a stiffly held right arm. The other was fat and dandy-like. The tall dark man was Kane's brother. But instead of making himself known immediately, Kane slipped into a doorway to listen in on their conversation.

Luke Pengarron was saying in a harsh voice, 'If anyone is going to seduce Jessica Trenchard, it's going to be me!'

The fat dribbly lips in Sebastian Beswetherick's florid face smirked at the corners. He was trying not to laugh but did not succeed and out came a muted titter. 'I only said she's a fine little piece, Luke. A bit too wild and common for my tastes.'

Luke wasn't convinced his friend was not interested in the subject under discussion. 'You may have been fortunate at my expense at the card tables last night, Bessie, but don't you ever forget, when it comes to that little creature, she's mine!'

'Jessica Trenchard may have other ideas,' Sebastian said, unperturbed by Luke's ill humour, which he was quite used to. He rubbed his wobbly stomach through his yellow and brown striped waistcoat. 'I don't think she ever mentions you in those little tête-à-têtes she shares with Olivia and that other little interesting piece, Cordelia Drannock, when they get together.'

Luke Pengarron prodded the other man's arm. 'How could you possibly know what those girls talk about? Jessica would hardly speak about me to my own sister. And you can keep your eyes and paws off Cordelia too. Do I have to remind you that she's my cousin?'

'I know one thing,' Sebastian said, his fleshy cheeks going red with exertion as he searched in his pockets in the hope that he'd missed a piece of liquorice in his earlier delvings. 'Jessica Trenchard hates you, Luke.'

'I don't give a damn about that.' Luke sniffed. 'I've promised myself that one. And when I've been successful, I'll take one of those golden curls as the proof of it.'

'Would you consider marrying her, I wonder? I do admire the menfolk in your family, like your father, for marrying outside their class. My family have intermarried so much with the county's gentry that the only ladies who would have me, with me being only a fifth son, are my damned awful second cousins. It's a good thing to bring some new blood into a family. I wonder if the old pater would consider—'

'What I intend to do with Jessica Trenchard is my business,' Luke said, under his breath, paying no attention to Sebastian's ramblings on his marriage prospects.

Sebastian knew he was being ignored and sighed. 'I wonder if the wrestling has finished. Someone said that Philip Trenchard is challenging the Barvah Giant this afternoon. Trenchard is good but I've got fifty guineas on the Barvah Giant.'

'I've put double that amount on the Barvah Giant. A Trenchard doesn't stand a cat in hell's chance against anyone, let alone the Barvah Giant. And never mind the wrestling now, our conversation has given me a certain appetite. If we've got any winnings, we can pick them up later.'

Kane didn't care for the talk about Jessica Trenchard but he was pleased to see Luke again. He stepped out of the doorway and said, grinning broadly, 'As I recall from our last meeting, little brother, you owe me a drink and I'm happy to inform you that you can count on having good winnings to buy it with.'

Luke Pengarron was agog for a moment or two, then his dark features broke into a blissful smile. With sight of the elder brother who could usually be guaranteed to go along with his wishes and schemes, Sebastian Beswetherick was immediately forgotten. Luke rushed forward and greeted Kane with a hearty hug.

'Heavens above, you're a sight for sore eyes, dear brother! Come along with me back to the coffee shop or, if you've a mind, let's go into the very house you've just stepped away from.' Luke winked crudely. 'There's good sport to be found within, but first I want to hear all your news and tell you what I've been—'

'Slow down, Luke,' Kane laughed, putting up his hands and acknowledging Sebastian with a polite nod. 'I'd be most interested to hear what you've been doing with yourself since I last saw you, but first I'm for going home, unless you can tell me that Mama, Father and Kelynen are to be found in town today. I have heard that Olivia and Cordelia are about the locality.'

Luke looked sulky and turned his back to Sebastian Beswetherick to block him from Kane's view. 'But I haven't seen you for years and have so much to tell you. And I thought you wanted a drink.'

'That can wait until later. Come with me and let's find the rest of the family and you can tell me your news then,' Kane said.

Luke had wanted Kane all to himself, but he sensed his brother would not be moved. His mouth took on a cruel line. He was slightly taller than Kane and he straightened to his full height intimidatingly. 'As you please. Father may be about somewhere, he mentioned he was to call on Sebastian's grandfather, and of course Kelynen will be at his side. Mama did not come into town today.'

Kane asked, 'How are they?'

'They're all very well. Mama and Father are as much in love as ever.'

'I think I will ride straight for home. It's only right that our parents know I'm here before gossip of my arrival is spread from a coffee shop.' Kane looked with distaste at the doorway he'd vacated. 'And Mama would be most upset if she thought I'd prefer to patronise a place such as this before seeing her.'

Luke scowled, but seeing the darkness under Kane's eyes he said on a softer note, 'I'll see you at home in an hour or two then.'

Kane moved off to the hostelry attached to Angove's blacksmith's shop where his horse was stabled. As he drew closer he realised that the ever-increasing noise reaching his ears was not the natural hum of the busy market town. A fracas was in progress. He started to edge round the outskirts of the commotion but a shrill scream sent him plunging into the middle.

Several men were fighting amidst some overturned stalls. It was more than a fracas, it was a full-blown brawl. Kane saw that most of those fighting were sailors and he assumed an old rivalry between two ships moored up at the Mount had turned sour. He was in time to see Simon Peter Blake, who presumably had been trying to placate the warring factions, being punched into the midst of a heap of scattered apples and the girl who had screamed about to throw herself on the neck of a bare-backed olive-skinned sailor.

The sailor growled in his foreign language but then grinned lecherously. He could see different sport here. Kane rushed forward and pushed the sailor heavily aside and back into the thick of the brawl again. Then he gathered Jessica up in his arms and walking backwards as she struggled against him, he clutched Simon Peter's coat collar and hauled them both away from further danger. Jessica became still when she realised who was holding on to her. She was quiet for once and looked into Kane's soulful dark eyes.

'What do you think you were doing?' he asked her severely. 'Didn't I hear your brothers order you not to get into any trouble?'

Chapter 2

Three other members of the Pengarron family were arriving in the next parish of Perranbarvah, having ridden there from Pengarron Manor. Facing the little fishing village that nestled at the foot of the steep hill below the church, they dismounted at the lychgate. Kerensa, Lady Pengarron, gazed for a moment at the fisherfolk moving about down in the village then glanced at the small granite church which was silhouetted against a murky May sky. Finally her grey-green eyes rested mournfully on the graves.

'I'm glad the rain has held off,' she said solemnly, as her husband, Sir Oliver, passed her an armful of flowers.

'I'll take your pony round to the Parsonage stables, my dear,' he said gently, regarding Kerensa with concern in his dark eyes. He bent from his great height to kiss her affectionately. 'Shelley and I will come back another time to pay a visit. Will you be all right?'

'Don't worry about me,' Kerensa replied, hugging his broad body. 'I'm always all right when I come here. It's just that I like to be alone with him for a little while… I'll see you and Kelynen at home later. I think Luke is bringing Sebastian home for supper tonight and Olivia and Cordelia were going to ask Jessica if she can come.'

Oliver grinned. 'A houseful of children, eh? And Hezekiah said he will be calling on us tonight. Should make for a noisy and boisterous evening.'

'Not me though, Father,' Kelynen said, winding her arms round Oliver's waist and holding on to him possessively. 'You promised me a game of chess, remember?'

'I haven't forgotten and I'm looking forward to it, sweeting,' Oliver said indulgently to the fourteen-year-old daughter he adored, whom he always called Shelley, a derivative of Michelle, the name he had chosen for her.

He gave her a leg up on to her pony and swung up on his big black horse, a fine specimen called Gereint. Then Kerensa stood back to wave them off for their ride to Marazion to visit Sir Martin Beswetherick.

The flowers Kerensa was holding were mostly of wild varieties and divided into three bunches. She passed by the paupers' graves and those mainly of the fishermen of the village and made straight for the Pengarron plot where she stopped in front of a tiny grave. Laying two of the bunches carefully on the ground, she put the third bunch, the smallest, into a little black granite pot. Then standing back and wiping tears from her eyes she read, as she always did on this weekly pilgrimage, the inscription on the headstone: 'Here lieth Joseph Henry Charles Pengarron. Beloved infant son of Sir Oliver and Kerensa, Lady Pengarron. Born 26.1.1773. Died aged 1 Month 2 Days. In God's Keeping.' Losing her baby Joseph was the only bad thing that had happened for many years in the marriage Kerensa shared with the tall, aristocratic man she loved passionately.

She stayed there for ten minutes, bending to tidy the grass that covered the small mound and polishing the headstone with a cloth. Then she rose for one last look, pushing back a loose strand of her glossy auburn hair under her wide-brimmed hat, blinking away the tears that told of her grief.

She moved on to a nearby grave and placed another of the bunches of flowers at the bottom of the headstone inscribed to the memory of the Reverend Joseph Ivey who had been parson of the parish and who had died in the same year as her child. Holding the last of the flowers, she rounded the side of the church and saw someone was already at the last grave she had come to visit.

There stood a tall, lean man with blond hair, his head hung down as if deep in thought, his hands pushed lightly into his coat pockets. Kerensa moved silently up beside him and slipped her hand into his. Surprised but pleased to see her, he smiled from behind deep, summer-blue eyes.

'Hello, Clem,' Kerensa said softly. 'You must have arrived after me because I didn't see your horse tied up outside the churchyard when I came in. I've brought some flowers for Alice.'

'I brought some myself,' Clem Trenchard, who was Jessica's father, murmured. 'I put them in the pot – not very neatly I'm afraid.'

Kerensa looked down at the grave. A knot of emotion caught in her throat at the higgledy-piggledy arrangement hanging over the side of a simple brown vase on Alice Trenchard's grave.

'You still miss her, don't you?' she remarked as she bent and tidied Clem's flowers and added the ones she had brought.

He bent down beside her. ''Tis two years but it only seems like yesterday.'

'I still miss her too. Alice was the best friend I've ever had. The pain never goes away, does it?' she asked, thinking back to the little grave she'd just left.

'No, Kerensa, it doesn't,' and he knew who she was thinking of. 'I never saw your baby. Alice did, she was full of the news the day he was born… She always wanted another baby herself after Jessica, did you know?'

'Yes, she talked about it often.'

Clem picked up a lump of earth and rubbed it between his fingers, staring at the powdered soil he made. 'She was so proud to be asked to be your baby's godmother. "Fancy that," she'd say proudly. "Me, plain and ordinary Alice Trenchard, farmer's wife, former lady's maid, ex bal-maiden at a tin mine, godmother to a Pengarron, no less."'

'Dear Alice, I felt it an honour to ask her to be one of Joseph's godmothers. I'll never forget the look on her face when she handed him over to the Reverend Ivey to be baptised, standing there among the gentry. She was so nervous but I thought she was going to burst with pride.'

'Aye, and 'twas said so would the Reverend Ivey having the baby named after him.'

Kerensa's eyes filled with tears again. 'And then… the typhoid outbreak… and in a week they were all taken from us. But at least I feel Alice and the Reverend Ivey are looking after little Joseph.'

Clem glanced about the churchyard to ensure they were alone, then he put his arm round Kerensa's shoulders, the beautiful young woman he had once nearly married. 'I'll never forget that time, so many folk died. How's Kelynen today? She was so ill back then... I was so frightened, looking on her as I do as our child, Kerensa.'

'Well, thank God she recovered fully.' Kerensa smiled on this happier note.

'She's like one of my own. 'Twas me who delivered her, who first saw her,' Clem said, adding in his thoughts, and your damned husband hates all that I've had to do with her. 'I suppose Sir Oliver spends so much of his time with Kelynen because he feels he has to make up for not being around at her birth, and calls her Shelley because he won't use the name I suggested for her.'

Kerensa was used to the fact that the two men who loved her hated each other. And she still cherished Clem. She put her face against his shoulder for a moment. 'Kelynen's not as highly spirited as her brothers and sister, she can be quiet and moody at times, just like you are.'

'Can she really?' Clem looked delighted.

They looked into each other's eyes and the twenty-two years that had passed since circumstances had forced them not to marry seemed to disappear. For a long stolen moment they were two young people betrothed and in love again.

Then Clem moved away and stood at the foot of his wife's grave. 'I really did love her,' he whispered, his voice choked. 'Not in the way that I loved you, and still do, but I loved Alice very much.'

'I know you did, Clem.' Kerensa brushed fresh tears away and forced a smile. 'You can walk with me to the Parsonage, if you like. I'm taking tea with the Reverend Lanyon and Miss Lanyon.'

Clem walked close but, for propriety's sake, slightly behind Kerensa, flexing one of his hands.

'What's the matter with your hand?' Kerensa asked, eyeing it before he could hide it away. She knew Clem didn't like unnecessary fuss.

'Oh, 'tis nothing much. I was in Marazion a short time ago and saw a stray dog attacking a rabbit and fowl stall in the market. I went to help and the dog turned on me. I chased it off but not before it nipped me. 'Twas a good thing I left my dogs with Kenver to keep him company back on the farm. Would have had a proper fight on my hands.'

'You need to get that hand looked at, Clem.'

''Tis nothing to fuss over,' he said dismissively.

'I'll have none of that, Clem Trenchard,' Kerensa said with mock sternness. 'You don't want to risk blood poisoning, do you? You can come into the Parsonage with me. I'm sure the Reverend Lanyon won't mind if I clean the bite and spread a salve over it for you. What would Jessica say if you were laid up and she had to nurse you? She has enough to do as it is, being the only woman on the farm.'

'I would enjoy you nursing me, my little sweet,' he returned, using the term of affection he'd first called her in their courting days. 'Jessica will never have need to be concerned over me but she worries the life out of me.'

'Oh, Clem, I am sorry. What is it this time? Can I help?'

'Jessica's always been wild and reckless but she's practically out of hand now. She thinks she's like the twins, free to go where and when she likes and do what she likes. But Philip and David can look after themselves. David never mixes with the rougher element and Philip's got his strength to rely on. Since Alice died, Jessica's got no mother to turn to, to teach her the finer things of life, to show her how to be feminine, to do the things women should do. I don't know about that sort of thing, Kerensa, I don't know what to do.'

They had reached the Parsonage back door where a wide porch led into the kitchen. Kerensa stopped walking. 'Where is Jessica now, Clem? Presumably at Marazion with her brothers for the wrestling championships.'

'Aye, that's right. I left her in the twins' care. I'm supposed to be on my way home to get on with the chores but I felt compelled to stop in here and… well, speak to Alice about Jessica. Alice adored her, I know she'll be relying on me to look after Jessica and see she comes to no harm.'

'Alice wouldn't expect you to look after Jessica all by yourself, Clem. She knew what Jessica's like, she used to confide in me. I believe Alice would have expected me to look after her too. The next time she's over at the Manor with Olivia and Cordelia, I'll have a little chat with her.'

'Well, if you can find out what goes on inside her head and tame her down a bit, I'd be eternally grateful. It's made me realise that I've never known much about women.'

'Yes,' Kerensa said softly, looking into his eyes. 'I believe you are a little shy of them.'

'Not with you,' he said, touching her shoulder. 'You look no older than Jessica and you're as beautiful as the girl I fell in love with. 'Tis hard to believe in a few months you'll be—'

'Clem Trenchard! It's bad manners and tactless to mention a woman's age!' Kerensa said, laughing as the warmth and love on his face turned to horrified embarrassment. 'I'll be forty and it's no one's business but mine to mention it.'

'Sorry,' he muttered, and Kerensa loved it when his fine, fair features turned into their usual expression of moodiness.

'You're right,' she said, nodding at him, 'you don't know much about women, and you probably don't know either that your hand-some, moody face holds a great attraction for them. Well, I suppose we'd better go inside. If Miss Catherine is watching us she'll be wondering why we're taking so long coming in.'

Kerensa had only entered the Parsonage by its front door once, on the day she had been brought here to reside until her enforced marriage to Sir Oliver Pengarron. While she'd stayed here she'd made a point, out of stubbornness and to emphasise her working-class background, of entering only by the kitchen door and had always continued to do so.

The Reverend Timothy Lanyon was languishing in a chair at the kitchen table. He jumped up to greet his two visitors. With his long arms waving furiously, he welcomed Kerensa and Clem in the animated fashion his parishioners were still trying to get used to. 'Come in, come in, sit down and join us, that is Nancy and me, Catherine doesn't approve of me drinking tea in the kitchen. Nancy has just baked a batch of her delicious scones.'

'I thought you might be in here, Timothy,' Kerensa said, allowing him to sweep her into a chair. 'I believe the kitchen is your favourite place.'

'Place. Aye, it is that.' Nancy Wills, who had the habit of repeating the last word of another's sentence, chuckled. She stood up with the stocking she·was darning and bobbed a curtsey to Kerensa. 'He's under my feet all the time, m'lady,' she added fondly, glancing at the young parson who'd returned to his chair.

Miss Nancy Wills was the Lanyons' housekeeper. An agreeable little woman in her early fifties, she moved about silently and one could quickly forget she was there. She manoeuvred Clem, who was obviously feeling uncomfortable, to a chair close to the parson.

It had proved a difficult task to replace the virtues of the Reverend Joseph Ivey in the parish of Perranbarvah and no one had expected a man like Sir Oliver Pengarron to install a purely conventional incumbent. But the parish had not been prepared for any part of the Reverend Timothy Rawlyn Lanyon. They had expected a parson of mature years and much experience. The Reverend Timothy Lanyon had neither. He was expected to be modest of stature and ill-favoured in face. He was neither.

He did come from a genteel family but he did not possess the usual qualities. He cared nothing for etiquette and saw no reason to treat women in a more respectful manner than men; in fact it was soon discovered he could be singularly rude to them. But he had the redeeming features of a small scar in the middle of his chin which formed a most interesting cleft, humorous grey eyes, and his straight earth-brown hair allowed wispy bits to escape along his forehead and in front of his ears. The number of women who came to listen to his no-nonsense approach in the pulpit had markedly increased.

'Put your feet up, man,' he exhorted Clem, 'make yourself at home. No need to stand on ceremony in this house.'

'Clem is in need of medication, a dog bit his hand,' Kerensa explained, as Clem looked stunned at the parson's mode of communication. He had rarely seen and never spoken to the Reverend Timothy Lanyon.

'Nothing serious, I hope,' Timothy said, springing up and almost knocking a plate of scones from Nancy Wills's hands. He grabbed the plate and put them under Clem's nose, which stopped him rising as a mark of respect. 'Smell these. Delicious, aren't they? I'll get my medicine box. You sit tight and have a cup of tea, have a scone, have one with jam and cream on it. I think you must be Clem Trenchard of Trecath-en Farm. Have a well-running concern on the Pengarron estate. Well, good for you, man, I like to see people getting on in life. Got two sons and a daughter, haven't you? One son who likes to wrestle, so do I,' he pointed to his chin, 'that's how I got this little scar, took a bad fall. Your other son's interested in becoming an itinerant preacher like the Blakes' son, so I've heard, but I'm glad to say he comes to church. I tolerate this Methodist thing but don't entirely approve of it. I'll expect to see you and the rest of your family back in church where you belong. I hear your daughter's a parish beauty but a bit of a tomboy. Haven't caught sight of her yet, the parish had a long interregnum, only been here a few months.' Timothy Lanyon finally thrust his hand out for Clem to shake.

Clem looked thunderstruck and only managed to nod back.

'I'll see to the medicine box,' Nancy said firmly, taking the plate of scones and conveying them safely to the table. 'Reverend Tim, sit down and sit still. Lady Pengarron has just come from the churchyard.'

'My apologies, m'lady,' Timothy Lanyon said humbly, noting she was clad mainly in black clothes. Kerensa always dressed this way when bringing flowers to the churchyard.

'Please be yourself, Timothy. There is a time to be sad and a time for good humour, and I have to say I rarely leave your company without being greatly cheered.'

'You are too kind to him, m'lady,' Nancy said, keeping up the teasing that the young parson enjoyed as she poured out fresh tea. 'Though I do believe the old Reverend would have approved of him, he still needs to learn to keep still.'

'He reminds me of my son, Luke. He's another one who's continually on the move,' Kerensa said.

Clem sat stiffly, feeling out of place and wishing he had not allowed Kerensa to talk him into coming into the Parsonage. She was the only person in the world who could have done so.

'Do you take tea, Mr Trenchard?' Nancy asked him kindly.

'Um… oh, yes please, thank you.'

'Nice and strong I expect. Most gentlemen like their tea strong.'

Clem watched Nancy as she placed the tea on the huge table. He stared suspiciously at the china cup and saucer. What made her say he was a gentleman? He'd never been called that before. Was it because he had entered the room with Kerensa? He suddenly wondered if the new parson knew of his and Kerensa's past love and that there were still feelings between them. It was common enough knowledge and folk were always ready to gossip. Clem relaxed. He was taking tea in the Parsonage with the parson and the Lady of the Manor, and it occurred to him that Sir Oliver Pengarron, who did not trust him where Kerensa was concerned, would be angry and jealous. Clem smiled warmly at the little housekeeper and its rarity and masculine beauty sent her into a fluster.

'I… I must go and fetch the Reverend's medicine box!'

Kerensa smiled to herself and wondered how Nancy Wills would look upon Clem if she was ten years younger.

Timothy Lanyon cut scones, jammed and creamed them for all without asking, and they were silently being savoured when the medicine box was brought in. It was carried by Timothy's older sister by three years, a lady with milk-white skin and a straight carriage, Miss Catherine Lanyon.

She greeted Kerensa then spoke to her brother. 'Nancy is at the front door receiving the couple from Rose Farm who enquired about having their baby baptised, Timothy.'

'I'm on my way.' Timothy shot up from his chair, stuffed half a scone into his mouth, swilled it down with a gulp of tea and sped out of the kitchen under one of Catherine's disapproving frowns.

'There goes the whirlwind,' Kerensa said.

'Yes,' Catherine said dryly.

Then Timothy's head flashed back round the doorway. 'If you'll excuse me, m'lady.'

'Yes, of course,' Kerensa laughed.

'And you, Clem?'

Surprised to be included in the delayed show of manners, Clem nodded over his teacup and the young parson was finally gone. Clem put his cup down hastily when he realised he was under the scrutiny of Miss Catherine Lanyon who was probably wondering why her brother had spoken so intimately to him.

'I understand you have received a dog bite on your hand, Mr Trenchard,' Catherine said in her clear and distinctly feminine voice. Clem had expected her tone to be reproving but it was cordial.

''Tis nothing,' he said, and he was cross that his words came out meekly and made Kerensa titter from her chair behind Catherine.

The next instant he was horrified when Kerensa said, 'Men always say things like that, Miss Catherine. They're such babies when they're hurt.'

Catherine placed a small towel on the table. 'Put your hand on there, please, Mr Trenchard.'

She moved about lightly as she unpacked some of the small bottles and ointment pots from the medicine box. Clem had never seen her up close and was surprised to see her face was rather childlike and that she was not unattractive, as he'd taken it for granted an unmarried woman of her age would be. Her hair was the same colour as her brother's but pulled back too severely. Her eyes were a lighter grey, enhanced by slightly curving dark brows. She was the same height as Kerensa, which Clem thought was the right size for a woman, comfortable for a man to relate to.

Kerensa got up and watched as the three deep teeth marks on Clem's hand were cleaned and covered with an ointment.

'That smells quite pleasant,' she said to Catherine.

'It's got sage in it, m'lady,' Catherine replied.

Clem sat rigid, determined not to wince, which he was sure Kerensa expected, as the ointment stung the open wounds.

Catherine glanced at Clem often. Kerensa noticed this and knew Clem had too and was unhappy about it.

When she was satisfied that the bite was thoroughly cleansed, Catherine looked Clem in the face and said in a soothing voice, 'If you'll just keep your hand on the towel, Mr Trenchard, I'll fetch a clean bandage for it.'

Clem would have protested but he wanted this woman, whom he was finding disturbing, out of the room.

'Better now?' Kerensa asked sweetly when Catherine had gone.

'I don't know why you have to make fun of me,' he said sulkily, and looking mournfully at his hand added, 'I'd rather you had bathed this. She acted very strangely. I'd have thought she'd look down on the likes of me.'

'I don't know why you're so surprised at Miss Catherine's attitude towards you, Clem,' Kerensa said, half in teasing. 'You're a very handsome young widower.'

'Eh? What are you saying? She can't possibly be interested in me. She's gentry, I'm just a—'

'A handsome widower only one year past forty who's a successful farmer and a man of some substance. Miss Catherine's ten years younger than you, not old by any means – unless you're an unmarried woman. And the Lanyons are regarded as minor gentry; they won't be setting their sights too high in the marriage stakes.'

'I believe you're gone quite mad, Kerensa! Me and that woman have nothing in common! I'm a Methodist, she's a diehard Anglican. That makes a big difference even if the new parson is tolerant like the Reverend Ivey was, and you heard the Reverend Lanyon just now, he's not that tolerant anyway. You've got it all wrong!'

Kerensa tapped his shoulder. 'Shush, she'll hear you. And don't be such a crosspatch.'

'Well, I still wanted you to bathe my hand. You ought to kiss it better for saying such a ridiculous thing to me.'

Kerensa gave him a superior look. 'Too late, she's coming back.'

They were silent with straight faces when Catherine came back. She looked at them both curiously, as if she knew they'd been talking about her.

'Not got your dogs with you today, Mr Trenchard?' Catherine asked casually as she bandaged his hand.

'I've been visiting my wife's grave,' Clem said shortly, emphasising the word 'wife'. 'Hardly the place to bring dogs to.'

'Oh, yes, of course. I… um… like dogs. Yours are fine animals. I often remark to my brother that we ought to keep a dog. If we do decide to have one, perhaps we could ask you for some advice on the matter.'

'I'm usually very busy.'

'Oh, I see.' Catherine's face gave no sign of how she felt about Clem's bluntness, but Kerensa was sure she'd been cast down inside.

'Kelynen knows a lot about dogs, Catherine. You've seen her dog Rex. She'll be happy to tell you all you'd need to know.'

'That would be very kind of her,' Catherine said, packing up the medicine box. 'I hope your hand will give you no further trouble, Mr Trenchard. Now if you'll excuse me I have something I must attend to. I expect my brother will return shortly.' Without looking at Clem again she left.

'You didn't have to be so rude to her, Clem Trenchard.' Kerensa pounced on him at once. 'You didn't even thank her.'

Clem had the grace to blush. 'No, I didn't, did I.'

'Well, you'll just have to do it some other time, won't you?'

Before Clem could answer, there was a sudden flurry and Nancy Wills came rushing in in a state of elation. 'Oh, m'lady, you're going to be so thrilled! Sir Oliver and Miss Kelynen are riding up to the front door and they have someone with them. It's Captain Pengarron!'

Kerensa clutched Clem's arm. 'Kane? What's he doing home?' She hurtled out of the kitchen and rushed out of the front door. Kane threw himself off his horse and swept her off her feet.

'We saw him coming towards us on the outskirts of Marazion, my dear,' Oliver said, dismounting and joining them. Kelynen followed and hugged her brother.

Kerensa lifted her head away from Kane's chest and sought his eyes. 'What's the matter, Kane? Are you well? Why are you home so suddenly? You didn't write to say you were coming.'

Kane kissed her cheeks and laughed. 'Why do mothers always assume something is wrong with their children?'

But Kerensa had seen the dark shadows under his eyes. 'There is something wrong, isn't there? You don't look at all well and you've become so thin!'

'I agree with your mother, Kane,' Oliver said firmly. 'What's happened to you?'

Kane sighed light-heartedly in submission. 'I was badly hurt in the Caribbean.'

'Oh, Kane, you never told us!' Kerensa gasped. 'You've been back in England for months. Why didn't you send word to us when it happened?'

'I didn't want you to worry, Mama. I was incapable of writing for a long time and I forbade anyone else to write with the news. When I got back to England, there didn't seem any point in mentioning it.'

'Well, that explains one of your long silences,' Oliver said.

Kane grimaced at the slight reprimand. 'I've spent a long time thinking over the future. I decided not to go to Ireland with the regiment and resigned my commission. I've been in the regiment for five years now and I want to set up my own farm, to see how things work out in my life.'

'You mean you're home for good? That's wonderful! But where were you hurt, Kane? Has it left you with lasting effects?' Kerensa next wanted to know.

Kane looked across to the doorway where a group of people had gathered. 'I'll tell you everything there is to know later,' he said. 'I'd like to say hello to Nancy and Clem and it seems I have a new parson and wife to meet.'

'Miss Catherine is the Reverend Timothy Lanyon's sister,' Kerensa said, reluctantly letting her eldest child go.

'What's he doing here?' Oliver demanded, his face as black as thunder as he glared at Clem.

'He was visiting Alice's grave,' Kerensa said soothingly, her eyes still on Kane. 'He was bitten by a dog and Miss Catherine bathed it for him.'

'I hope the dog recovers,' Oliver said acidly, under his breath. He caught Clem's eye and they glared at each other in mutual despite.

'Oliver,' Kerensa said chidingly, but she was too happy to let her husband's chagrin upset her now.

Oliver was pleased that Kelynen had stayed beside him and was holding his arm. He wanted to show Clem Trenchard that his daughter was totally his and nothing of her belonged to the other man just because he happened to have delivered her. He had wished often over the years that he could have put a stop to their wives' idea of their children mixing and playing together, then the rapport Kane and his other daughter, Olivia, had with the Trenchards would never have occurred.

Kane had made his introductions to the Lanyons, delighted Nancy Wills by kissing her fondly and turned to Clem when his parents and sister joined the group on the doorstep.

'I saw Philip, David and Jessica in Marazion, Clem,' Kane said, shaking the farmer's hand. 'I watched Philip's wrestling match with Matthew King.'

'Who won?' Clem asked eagerly. 'I had to leave to get back to the farm – in fact I should be home now.'

'Then don't let us keep you, Trenchard,' Oliver interrupted.

Clem ignored him and Kane looked slightly shocked. The animosity Clem and his father shared over the love they had for his mother obviously hadn't lessened. He knew his father felt it was wrong that Clem Trenchard should be sharing in their reunion.

'I'm afraid the Barvah Giant won. He pinned Philip down with one of his famous forehips,' Kane said quickly, hoping Clem would take his leave and they could resume their friendship at some later date.

Clem had no wish to stay. He knew Kane would call at Trecath-en Farm sooner or later and as he had now left his regiment, there was no hurry. 'I didn't expect Philip to win,' he said. 'I'll be off now.' He bade Timothy goodbye and wanted to do the same to Kerensa and rectify his bad manners with Miss Catherine, but Oliver put himself in the way. Clem would never ask this man to do anything for him, even a little thing like excusing him so he could pass by. He hardened his fair features and walked away to his horse.

Kane watched Clem thoughtfully. He was back home for good and had seen most of his family today. But the thing he would remember most was Jessica Trenchard's hostility.

Chapter 3

Several days later Simon Peter Blake was sitting at breakfast with his parents in their small but grandly built house at Trevenner on the outskirts of Marazion. The family were close and enjoyed spending mealtimes together. Despite the fact that Simon Peter knew the reason why his father was despised and shunned by the county's gentry, namely his dishonourable discharge from the 32nd Foot and his underhand business transactions, he loved him as much as he did his gentle mother. But this morning a secret part of his father's behaviour was giving Simon Peter much pain.

'You're quiet this morning, my dear,' Rosina Blake said softly to him. 'You haven't touched your oysters and they're your favourite. Is something wrong?'

'Oh…' Simon Peter sighed, and his father, Peter, looked up expectantly from the newspaper he was reading. Simon Peter had to think of something quickly to say. 'It's Jessica, I asked her to marry me again and she refused… again.' He didn't like to talk about his love and heartbreak over Jessica Trenchard but he had to ward off his mother's interest in his low spirits.

Because Rosina had come from working-class mining people, and knowing that despite his wealth few of the gentry would consider his son for their daughters, Peter Blake did not disapprove too much of Simon Peter's interest in Jessica Trenchard. If his son wanted the wayward beauty then that was what Blake wanted for him too. Jessica Trenchard could be tamed and dressed up and would provide agreeable company for Rosina.

'Faint heart never won fair lady,' he said, turning the pages of the latest London gossip. 'I had to fight for your mother's hand.' He smiled at Rosina, the faithful wife he loved as much as ever after twenty-two years of marriage.

'Why don't you invite Jessica over to tea, Simon Peter?' Rosina said, rubbing his hand affectionately.

'She wouldn't come, Mother.' Simon Peter squirmed inside and wished he'd thought of another reason for his tenseness this morning. 'Jessica's made it quite clear she sees me only as a friend.'

Peter Blake folded his newspaper and put it down on the table. 'It can't be that difficult to get the girl to take an interest in you, my son. You have much to offer her.'

'I haven't got your good looks,' Simon Peter said sulkily, looking into his father's face, who in his early forties was considered by women to be still beautiful. Then into the pale, ethereal quality of his mother's face, noting again her cornflower-blue eyes the same as his father's, and wishing his own weren't a wishy-washy sky colour. 'Or the height or broad shoulders of the Trenchard and Pengarron menfolk. I wish you both didn't think it was so easy.'

'Nevertheless, you are a most attractive young man,' Rosina said. 'You have a lot to offer a future wife. You really must stop putting yourself down all the time, Simon Peter.'

Rosina felt for her son. She knew he'd found his childhood lonely, not having received the many brothers and sisters she and her husband had hoped to give him. Now he was finding his youth difficult. He wasn't accepted by the gentry, except for Olivia and Kane Pengarron, and although he had a mother of humble beginnings, he didn't feel comfortable with his working-class peers either.

'You will inherit this house and my property at Marazion one day, and my business interests, the renting of fishing boats and the mining speculations. You have an exceedingly generous allowance now and you are respectable and intelligent. The Trenchard girl will come to her senses, you'll see. You even follow the same faith as her.' To Peter Blake it was beyond belief that any girl of Jessica Trenchard's background and expectations would continue to spurn his son.

'I'll have another try,' Simon Peter said, brightening up his face for his parents' sake. 'I'm hoping to see Jessica later in the day. Olivia

Pengarron has been allowed to plan her own twenty-first birthday party and I'm to be included in those plans. I'm hoping Jessica will be with Olivia.'

'You can always try a prayer, son. I don't believe in them but you do. One just might work,' Peter Blake said, rising from the table.

'Are you well enough to go out today, my dear?' Rosina said, tilting her face so her husband could kiss her. 'You're only just over that stomach fever.'

'As much as I'd like to spend another day under your tender care, my beloved, I must see what has been happening out in the big wide world.'

As Blake asked her what she intended to do with her day, Simon Peter got up and tried to think of a reason to ask to speak to his father alone; his was a family that shared most things with each other and his mother would be curious.

The clatter of a falling tray, a loud shriek followed by hysterical wailing in the passageway outside hastened Rosina's departure from the room. 'I wish Mrs Blight would admit she's too old to work and take things easy in her room,' she said mildly and limped out on her one good and one lame foot to the aid of their highly strung, ageing servant.

As Blake made to follow her, Simon Peter took his arm. 'May I have a word, Father?'

'Yes, of course, Simon. I think I know what this is about,' Blake said smiling knowingly. 'Shall we sit down again?'

'I don't think you have any idea of what I'm about to say,' and Simon Peter stood his ground.

'You want some advice on how to treat the gentler sex, do you not?'

'I do not. I don't want any advice, Father. I'm afraid I have something to tell you, something really terrible, and now that Mother's out of the room…' He stopped to listen to Rosina's soothing voice as she led a wailing Mrs Blight upstairs.

'We ought to get rid of that damned woman,' Blake said under his breath, low enough for Simon Peter not to hear. Louder, he said,

'You have me concerned. You haven't been with a woman and caught something, have you?'

'This concerns you, not me, Father.' Simon Peter blushed and looked away. 'It wasn't easy to face your father with the sort of news he was about to impart. This is difficult for me to say. Normally I'd never have mentioned it... but I think you ought to know that... that...'

'Spit it out, for goodness' sake, son, or you'll give me an attack of the vapours like that hysterical woman.'

'Last night I was over at the Assembly Rooms at Penzance. There was talk, the whole place was buzzing with it, of a woman being brutally murdered in the next street... Father, her name was Dinah Tredinnick.'

Peter Blake paled to a ghastly white, a gurgling noise came from his throat, then he choked and gagged. His knees buckled under him and Simon Peter caught him and led him to a winged chair next to a tall window.

'Dinah...' Blake gasped and choked again. 'Dead? Murdered?' His mouth fell open and saliva dribbled onto his tasteful clothes.

'I'll get you some brandy,' Simon Peter said softly.

'No! No, stay with me, son... How did you know that I...?'

'That you had an interest in Dinah Tredinnick? I've known about your association with Dinah for many years. You took me there once, when I was about two and a half. You probably thought I'd forget all about it, but when I got older and walked past the house, I realised it was familiar to me. Then I saw you going in there... and people do talk. Your name was mentioned last night. I expect you'll be questioned, Father.'

Blake wiped at his chin and ran his shaking hands down his coat front. He looked anxiously at the door, fearful that Rosina was returning or one of the servants would come in and see his distress.

'I'll close the door,' Simon Peter said, 'and we can tell Mother we're having a man-to-man talk, like you thought we were going to.' He fetched his father a glass of water from the table.

Blake sipped from it then gasped out, 'Simon, you've known about Dinah and me all this time. Don't you hate me?'

'I may be religious and prefer to keep myself chaste but in every other respect I am a man of the world. I am aware that a lot of gentlemen keep a mistress, Father.'

'But they are usually men who don't love their wives. But you know that I worship the ground your mother walks on. Doesn't that make you feel differently, Simon Peter?'

'I prefer not to know your reasons, Father. And I'm sorry about Dinah. I know... well, I'm sure she was the only one you... went with.'

'She was, I swear to you, Simon.' Blake was more himself now. He drank down the water and handed Simon Peter the glass. 'Is it known who did it? Who murdered Dinah? How she died?'

It was Simon Peter's turn to gulp and become shaken. He squeezed the glass between his palms and took his time putting it down on a side table. 'It seems that from the condition of the body she had been dead for about a week. She was... she was mutilated. I'm sorry.'

'Like all those other people? Oh God,' Blake moaned. 'These murders have been going on for years... and now poor Dinah. They say whoever does it likes to kill slowly...'

'Don't, Father,' Simon Peter said, putting his arm round his father's shoulders. 'Don't torture yourself. Look, you are not fit to go out today. I'll tell Mother you've come over with the stomach cramps again, that you need to lie down quietly.'

'I'll be grateful to you if you would do that,' Blake said vacantly, his senses numb. 'What about Amy?' he asked, gazing into Simon Peter's eyes.

'Who's Amy?'

'Dinah's maid. She's been with her for years, she's a sweet girl, kind and totally loyal.'

'I heard the maid has disappeared but there was no sign of her being hurt.'

'He may have taken her away,' Blake moaned. 'People disappear and they're found days later hacked to pieces.'

'Try not to think about it,' Simon Peter counselled, but he knew that would be impossible. He could hear his mother coming back. 'Mother's coming. Will you be all right?'

'Yes, yes, I think so. I'm sorry that you knew about Dinah, Simon.'

'We all have our weaknesses, Father, and I'd rather this awful news came from me than someone else.'

–

That afternoon Jessica Trenchard was sitting at the bottom of the valley of Ker-an-Mor Farm, the Pengarrons' home farm. She was sharing a picnic with Olivia Pengarron and Cordelia Drannock and because Ker-an-Mor bordered Trecath-en farmland, she'd only had to climb over a hawthorn hedge to reach her friends. She sat with her back against the hedge watching the river a few inches away sparkle under the sunlight. The sun was strong today and the three young women wore protective hats and light dresses with floral patterns. Jessica's was faded through constant wear. They were sitting on a blanket discussing Olivia's forthcoming birthday.

''Tis a pity your birthday's on the twenty-sixth of June and not on midsummer's eve,' Jessica said, nibbling on a juicy green apple and studying her teeth marks. 'Just think of the fun we could have – we could build an extra big bonfire.'

'Yes, but this means we can have the fun of midsummer night's eve and of celebrating my birthday,' Olivia replied, picking at the blanket she lay sprawled on.

'Aye, that's a point,' Jessica said brightly, tossing the flame-haired Olivia an apple. 'Two lots of fun within a few days. What do you think, Cordelia?'

Cordelia was sitting with her back against the picnic hamper, daydreaming, as she often did. With the dark hair and eyes of her male Pengarron relatives, Cordelia made a perfect contrast to Olivia and the fair-haired Jessica. Olivia was slender, Jessica had a shapely figure and Cordelia was small and finely-boned and, despite being twenty-two years old, was considered 'a wisp of a girl'. She brought out the protective feelings of her family and friends.

Jessica carefully threw an apple to land on Cordelia's lap. 'Hey, I was talking to you, Dolly Daydream. Are you thinking about Philip again?'

Philip Trenchard had been showing a lot of interest in Cordelia. She was flattered but he made her nervous. Her little sparrow face turned an embarrassed pink and she was annoyed because she had actually been thinking about Ricketty Jim, a one-time rover who seemed to have made a permanent home in a shack at the top of Trecath-en's valley.

'I was thinking about Ricketty Jim,' she said. Because she had started life as a poor fisherman's daughter, until Sir Oliver had found out that he and her father, Samuel Drannock, were half-brothers and shared the same father, her accent was nearly the same as Jessica's. 'I was just wondering if he is going to stay living in his little hut on your father's land for good now, Jessica, that's all.'

'Why were you thinking about him?' Olivia asked, completely puzzled. 'He's got nothing to do with my birthday party and we agreed to make up our minds exactly how it would be celebrated today.'

'You said just now that you'd like to invite no one but unusual people and I thought about Ricketty Jim. Would you invite him?'

'Well, that's an idea,' Jessica said thoughtfully. 'He tells some wonderful stories. What do you think, Livvy?'

'Mmmm, I'll think about it,' Olivia answered, brushing away a fly intent on sharing her apple. 'It will definitely be a costume affair. Nymphs, elves, that kind of thing. What do you two think? Will you be all right at getting a costume, Jessie? We haven't got much time left.'

'Oh, I'll arrange something, don't you worry. Can't see my brothers agreeing to dress up though, that's if they can be persuaded to come in the first place,' Jessica replied.

'But they must come, they're more our friends than any of the gentry folk, especially that disgusting Sebastian Beswetherick creature who drools over every girl he comes across.'

'He don't bother me none, he knows what he'll get if he ever tries to lay a finger on me,' Jessica said, then changed tack to tease the other girl. 'Bet you can't imagine Philip dressed up as an elf, eh, Cordelia? I bet he wouldn't do that, even for you.'

Olivia took up the theme but turned the tables on Jessica. 'But Simon Peter would for you, eh, Jessie? He would dress up as Old Nick if he thought it would impress you.'

Jessica looked crossly at the two cousins as they laughed at her. 'It's not at all funny. The poor boy's besotted with me and he makes me feel guilty because I don't feel the same way. I wish he'd forget me before he gets even more hurt.'

'Pity you don't like him though, Jessie,' Cordelia said. 'He's kind and gentle and is a good catch.'

'Why don't you give him the glad eye then?' Jessica said bluntly then turned her attention to parting tiny clover leaves in an attempt to find one with four leaves.

'I don't want to get married. I am quite happy to stay with Uncle Oliver and Aunt Kerensa for the rest of my life,' Cordelia answered.

'And then with Luke when he inherits after Father,' Olivia put in. 'You've always been happy to trot round after him and pander to his every whim, even when he's being beastly.'

'And that's practically all the time,' Jessica said at once. 'You've got no adventure in you, maid, none at all.'

'I'm perfectly content as I am, and that says a lot in life,' Cordelia replied musingly, gazing at her apple.

'Oh, eat the wretched thing, don't start daydreaming all over again,' Jessica muttered at her.

'We could dress as people from mythology, get some books out of Uncle Oliver's library and copy their clothes,' Cordelia said. 'The men could come as ancient heroes.' Then she closed her eyes to picture herself in a costume.

'I think that's the best idea yet, dear cousin,' Olivia said excitedly, 'but only us younger people must dress in costume. Can you imagine the dreadful sight of Lady Rachael Beswetherick, Sebastian's mother, dressed as a siren or something similar? And we'll have the food banquet style, lots of fruit and grapes.'

'Don't make it sound too naughty or that new parson will have something to say,' Jessica said, giggling.

'He can mind his own business!' Olivia said with a snap. 'I haven't received a civil word from that man since I was first introduced to him. I can't think why Father chose him to take over from the dear old Reverend Ivey.'

'He's good-looking though,' Cordelia remarked dreamily.

'So what if he is? A parson's got no right to be good-looking!'

Jessica and Cordelia were so surprised at this outburst they both gave a little scream and rolled about laughing.

'Shut up, the pair of you!' Olivia ordered.

'Hark at Master Luke Pengarron talking through his sister's mouth,' Jessica said, wiping tears of mirth from her eyes. 'You sounded just like your stuck-up brother then. What on earth made you say a thing like that, about a parson being good-looking?'

'It's something old Beatrice says about him,' Olivia said irritably, pursing her red lips. 'Let's get back to my party arrangements and then we'll paddle in the river. It's so hot today I can hardly breathe.'

'I'm not surprised if you can get so hot under the collar so quickly over a parson,' Jessica said, putting her tongue against her cheek.

'You're far too outspoken, Jessica Trenchard,' Olivia said, throwing her apple core at her friend in an affectionate gesture. 'Just like your dear mother was. You're so like her at times, she used to have me in fits of laughter over the way she used to tease Beatrice.'

'Yes, and just like my mother, there's always a mountain of work waiting for me back on the farm so I won't be taking a paddle.'

'Oh, what a shame,' Cordelia said. 'We get so much more free time than you do. But we won't spend our time idling it away, we'll collect some comfrey leaves along the river bank for Beatrice.'

Jessica gazed at the dense colony of the stout plant, its thick foliage growing up to four feet high, its bell-shaped flowers adding a dash of colour, reddish-purple, dull violet, creamy-yellow and a dirty white. Small bees and bumble bees were busy pollinating the flowers, the smaller ones by crawling up the corolla, the bumble bees by biting a hole near the stem to reach the nectar.

'Oh, well,' she said nonchalantly. 'We each have to work in our own different ways. When you've gathered enough of that "knit-bone", there's some herb robert here you could take to Beatrice,' she offered, twiddling the red-tinged stem of a delicate wild flower growing against the hedge. 'Funny though,' she said, returning to her earlier mood, 'it seems we all have a man interested in us at the moment but we don't return his feelings.'

'How do you make that out?' Olivia asked, but not really sure she wanted to hear what would come out of her friend's pouting lips.

'We know Simon Peter Blake is in love with you, Jessie,' Cordelia said, waking up from another daydream. 'But how does what you just said involve me and Livvy?'

'As I said before, Philip likes you, my dear Cordelia, and I've noticed you never stay around for long when he's about. And Livvy of course has her parson.'

'I have not!' Olivia almost screamed. 'I've told you, Jessica Trenchard, he's nothing but rude to me. How does that mean he likes me?'

'Men are often rude to the women they've taken a fancy to, 'tis how some of them behave, didn't you know?' Jessica said in a superior voice.

'But the Reverend Lanyon's rude to everyone, including Cordelia. You tell her,' Olivia implored her cousin.

'But I've heard he's rude to you in a particular way,' Jessica persisted.

Olivia got up and knelt before Jessica, clutched her by the shoulders and looked into her eyes. What she said next wiped the satisfied smile clean off Jessica's face.

'And in the three weeks since my brother Kane has been home I could say that you have been rude to him in a most particular way too.'

Chapter 4

Jessica scrambled over the manmade hedge, built by Ker-an-Mor labourers and heightened by Clem after his father died, leaving him with the title of Trecath-en Farm's tenant. The heightened barrier was a statement from Clem, signifying the distance between himself and Sir Oliver, and he was relieved that it was Matthias Renfree, Ker-an-Mor's steward and his brother-in-law, who called at Trecath-en Farm on behalf of his landlord. Clem and Jessica were both glad that Luke Pengarron, who was superior and spiteful, had refused to step over the barrier from the age of twelve.

During their childhood, when they had played together at the wish of their mothers but the disapproval of their fathers, Jessica and the twins and the Pengarron children had made a sizeable gap in the hedge that divided their properties. The gap had not been built up. Despite the difference in their class and advantages, the children had usually got along well, with only Luke's behaviour upsetting their unusual friendship. The three girls had ended up as firm friends.

Jessica began to run; she had a good deal of work to get through before cooking the evening meal and she kept her mind on what she had to do, temporarily forgetting the promised events of Olivia's birthday party. She had butter to churn, bacon to put to smoke and washing to be taken off the line. She was half across the bottom of Trecath-en valley where a clump of elm trees grew on the river bank when she saw something that brought her to a halt.

Someone was lying on the ground against the trunk of one of the trees. Jessica could see that it wasn't Ricketty Jim, asleep after a morning's work on the farm, or anyone else she knew. The still figure didn't look like a vagabond but Jessica approached it cautiously.

She bent down beside the unconscious body of a young woman. The woman was dressed in better-quality clothes than Jessica's own but she didn't look like a lady. She was dirty all over, her hair was matted, her skin scratched and bruised, her stockings were torn and spattered with dried mud and there was no sign of her shoes.

'What's happened to you?' Jessica whispered, gingerly touching the woman's cheek. It was cold and lifeless and Jessica thought for a moment she was dead but then she saw her chest was faintly rising and falling. The woman couldn't have been there long; Jessica had only passed through the valley about an hour ago, but the woman's face was sunburned on the side that was turned to the sun.

Jessica pulled off her tucker, the piece of frilled muslin worn round her shoulders and covering the greater part of her bosom, and went to the river and soaked it. Wringing it out, she returned to the woman and wiped it gently over her face. The woman did not move, not even a twitch. Jessica next wrung water over the woman's face but still she remained lifeless.

'You're either totally senseless or completely wearied out,' Jessica muttered sympathetically.

She studied the woman, considering her weight and size to see if she could carry her to the farm or would have to run and fetch one of her menfolk. The woman was short and thin with no figure and Jessica thought she could manage on her own. She put out an arm to slide it under her shoulders when the woman sprang up and screamed in terror, 'Don't you touch me! No! No!'

Jessica stopped a scream of her own by clutching her hands to her mouth, but she quickly got a grip on herself. 'It's all right! I won't hurt you. I only want to help.' She had to shout to get through the woman's abject fear.

The woman suddenly went quiet. She stared at Jessica from terrified glassy eyes, her mouth sagging open.

'I won't hurt you,' Jessica repeated in a clear, calm voice. 'You are safe now. Let me help you. I live not far away. Let me take you there and help you to clean up. Then you can have a proper rest on a bed.' Jessica wasn't sure if she was being understood.

'Don't let him hurt me, will you?' the woman said, whimpering.

'I won't let anyone hurt you.'

The woman kept her eyes rooted to Jessica's face and in a daze she allowed her to help her to her feet.

'Lean on me,' Jessica said. 'I'll help you to the farm where I live, 'tis not far away.'

The woman clutched Jessica tightly and peered all around then seemed to be trying to hide herself behind Jessica's body. Jessica looked up and down the valley. 'There's no one here but me. Can you walk? If not, I think I could carry you.'

The woman's head came up to Jessica's shoulder; she laid it there and wound her arms round Jessica's waist. Jessica could see she wasn't going to get an answer and took a tentative step forward. The woman moved forward and after a shaky start matched Jessica's slow, careful steps. It was going to take a long time to get to the farm.

–

Clem was in the farmyard leaning over the pigsty fence, fully involved in a friendly discussion with Kane Pengarron. 'So you're planning to set up your own farm then?'

'That's right. I learned a lot from my visits here as a boy as well as from Ker-an-Mor,' Kane replied, sounding nostalgic. 'It's something I've wanted to do since I was a child.'

'You sound as though you're really glad to be home.'

'I want to do as you, and your father before you, have done. Build up a profitable farm from a scrap of land. It's a constant struggle. You always have uncertainty ahead of you, but you always have a challenge too.' Kane glanced around the yard. 'I can see the changes you've made since Morley's death and I took the liberty of riding around your fields before I came here. If the weather is on our side this summer, you should get good yields from your fields. I'll be glad to help you with the harvesting, Clem, just like I did in the old days.'

'I'll be glad to have your help.' Clem looked at him thoughtfully. 'So all those years away in the army, you didn't really have your heart in it then?'

Kane reached over the fence and patted the back of one fat white pig. 'I didn't mind it for a short spell but I was never really keen. I suppose I did it for my father. He wanted to see his sons follow him into the regiment but of course Luke wasn't fit for service with his frozen arm. He had his heart set on a long and distinguished army career but then came the accident...'

"Twadn't your fault, Kane,' Clem said, stroking the head of one of his three dogs which had nuzzled his knee. 'You were only boys when that happened and Luke has always been headstrong.'

'But I was the elder. I should have stopped us going riding that day.'

'Some people do exactly what they want to and your brother will always be one of them. I've got one just as stubborn in my family.'

'Yes, I know,' Kane said, smiling, thinking back to the day he'd arrived home and rescued the other man's daughter from a brawl.

'So what made you finally decide to leave the regiment then?'

'It was because of something that happened out in the Caribbean. When the unit left St Vincent in seventy-three I was flat on my back recovering from a serious sword wound. It nearly cost me my life. Only my father knows that. I didn't tell Mama, I don't want her worrying and I'm asking you to keep silent about this too, Clem.'

'You have my word not to say anything to Kerensa.'

Kane knew about Clem's love for his mother and that they were still close, but such was his friendship with Clem that they could talk about Kerensa unselfconsciously.

'It was a long time before I got back to England,' Kane continued, 'and a long time after that before I could run or sit astride a horse.'

'So what happened to you, boy? Sounds ominous, if you ask me, and you have the look of pain still about you.'

'I was wounded helping a fellow officer. He was having an affair with a foreign official's wife. The official found out and it got back to me via a worried servant that my colleague was about to have his throat cut. I went to his aid and probably saved his life but ended up spiked through the stomach for my trouble. The whole thing was sordid. The officer wasn't even in love with the wife concerned, it

43

was no more than mutual lust, and he got away without a scratch. The incident being of a sensitive nature we couldn't tell the truth, of course, so we said we were attacked and robbed.

'The wound became poisoned and I spent weeks in delirium. The officer wrote to my parents and told them I had a tropical fever. After that, when I wrote, I thought up excuses as to why I was so long in coming home. When I finally did get back to England and was fit again, I took my time thinking over what I wanted to do, which way I wanted my life to go. In the end there was only one choice. I'm a man of the earth and fields, so I won't be going to Ireland with the regiment this year.'

Clem shook his head in wonder. 'You were away for nearly two years all told, Kane. Kerensa told me she was worried about you.'

'Well, I'm home now and Mama and Father know of my plans. They want me to take my time adapting to civilian life again, before I decide on which piece of land to buy. I've got my own money and I'm raring to go.'

'You sound like Jessica, but she can't keep still for even a minute.'

Kane looked up and his eyes became more startled-looking than they usually were. 'Talking of Jessica, what's she doing?'

Jessica had entered the farmyard with a woman clinging to her.

Clem swung round and gave out an exclamation. 'Jessica, what's happened? Who's she?' He surged towards them and Kane followed but when the woman saw the two men, she screamed and clung to Jessica's body, twisting a fold of Jessica's flesh on her back and making her cry out.

'Stop! Don't come any closer!' Jessica shouted, then lowered her voice to ease the woman's distress. 'Stay there. She's frightened of you.'

The dogs were bounding towards Jessica and the woman, and Clem commanded them to lie down. They obeyed immediately and lay in a scattered line between him and Kane and Jessica and the woman. The men stayed their ground but Jessica had to edge back from them, dragging the woman with her until she stopped blubbering.

'What's wrong with her? Where did you find her?' Clem called out.

'Down by the river, she was lying under one of the trees. She's in some awful state, something terrible must've happened to her,' Jessica explained.

'What can we do to help?' Kane asked, his body, like Clem's, alert and ready to move.

'Just stay completely still. She seems to be scared of you both.' Jessica edged the woman slowly, a few steps at a time, towards the farmhouse. She fought back tears of pain as the woman seared her back with an ever-tightening grip. When she tried to move to lessen the pain, the woman panicked and the cycle of grip and pain was repeated.

Thankfully the farmhouse door was open wide to let in the summer's fresh air and Jessica stumbled through it with her burden and made straight for the parlour. Once inside its cool confines, she struggled hard to disengage the woman's hold on her and pushed her into a lumpy stuffed chair. The woman grabbed her dress and Jessica stood still, close in front of her, breathing in relief and giving comfort by putting her hands on the woman's shoulders.

'You're safe now,' Jessica said tenderly. 'I've brought you home.'

'No! Not home! I don't want to go home!' the woman shrieked, and her hands flailed out and tried to grasp Jessica's body again.

'I mean I've brought you to my home,' Jessica said loudly above the hysteria. 'You're all right now, you'll be safe here, you can trust me.'

The words got through the fear and the woman went quiet. Jessica had forgotten her own pain and bent and gently stroked her face. 'I won't leave you, I promise.'

Realising Clem and Kane were hovering outside the parlour, being careful not to be seen, Jessica said without turning round, 'Can someone fetch me a bowl of warm water and a cloth and leave it in the doorway?'

'I'll get it,' Kane said quietly, knowing Jessica would prefer her father stayed close by.

'Are you all right, Jessica?' Clem whispered worriedly when Kane had gone to the kitchen.

'Aye, I'm fine. If I can just get her out of these dirty clothes and cleaned up a bit she'll feel more comfortable.'

'Have you any idea who she is?' Clem asked.

'I've never seen her before,' Jessica said, pulling strands of the woman's hair aside and checking to see if she had lice. There were none and her scalp was clean so she had kept herself washed before arriving at the condition she was now in.

'Ask her her name,' Clem said.

Jessica smiled at the woman. 'What's your name? Can you tell me?'

The woman just stared back and Jessica realised that something in her head had switched off. She had found a safe haven and her brain was not registering any feelings or responses.

'She's gone quiet,' Jessica told her concerned father.

'Well, that's a relief.'

Kane brought the water. With the woman in a stupor, Jessica was able to leave her to pick it up from the doorway. 'Go fetch one of my dresses, will you, Father?' she said softly.

'Where do you keep them?' Clem hissed back through his teeth.

'In my room of course. You'll find one hanging over the back of a chair.' And Jessica had to smile at the irony that no matter how strong and tough her father was, he was almost helpless at doing anything as simple as fetching a dress. He brought it downstairs and carefully laid it in the doorway.

Jessica stripped the woman of her dirty dress. She could see no marks on her body that suggested she had been beaten as Jessica had suspected. The woman allowed herself to be washed clean of mud and dirt and have Jessica's dress, a castoff from Olivia, put over her head. She made no attempt to put her arms through the sleeves or pull it down and Jessica had to do it for her. By the time she was fully clothed again, the woman had drifted from the stupor into a deep, exhausted sleep. Jessica put a cushion behind her head and, confident she would not wake for a while, tiptoed out of the room.

A moment later she was sitting on the settle in the kitchen, shaken and relieved with Clem's arms round her. 'It was like tending to one of Aunty Rosie's little ones,' she told him and Kane.

'What on earth could have happened to her?' Kane said, leaning his buttocks against the dresser and holding his chin in his hand while gazing down at Jessica. He was comparing the concern on her peach-skinned face to the looks of impertinence and fury he had seen on the day of his arrival home. There was great strength and stubbornness in all her expressions and a sort of primitive wildness. He liked it whichever way she looked.

'Well, she wasn't beaten. She's obviously fled from something and the only marks on her seem to come from that,' Jessica said gravely. 'But whatever it is, she's been literally terrified out of her mind.'

'Jessica,' Clem said soberly, 'do you think she's been… interfered with?'

'I can't tell for sure, but there are no bruises to suggest she was held down or anything.'

Clem kissed the top of her head. 'You need a dish of tea, my cherub. I'll have to go to the well for some more water. Kane, will you look after Jessica please?'

Kane nodded, thinking how perfect Clem's endearing term was for her. 'Even with your bad moods, what a wonderful cherubic face you have,' he whispered to himself.

'What was that?' Jessica asked, eyeing him.

Kane straightened up, his head brushing a bundle of herbs hanging up to dry, and moved over to her. 'Nothing. Are you sure you're all right?'

Jessica made a sudden movement on the settle and knocked her back. Her face became contorted with pain.

Alarmed, Kane crouched at her feet and caught her hands. 'What is it?'

'My… my back…'

Kane put his big hands lightly above her elbows and moved in close until she was leaning against his chest. Jessica closed her eyes and pressed herself into his strength.

Kane quickly undid the laces down the back of her dress and pulled the sides apart. He gasped when he saw the ugly red and purple welt left by the woman's terrified grip. He moved his body so Jessica's

47

head lay on his shoulder and he held her at the waist with one hand while using the other to gently massage round the edges of the angry discoloration on her back.

'Does that help?' he whispered against the tangle of golden curls.

'Mmmm,' Jessica replied and nestled her face in closer to him.

'What the ruddy hell do you think you're doing?' Clem raged as he entered the kitchen and caught sight of his daughter with her back exposed in the young man's arms.

Kane looked up rapidly. 'She's hurt, I wasn't—'

'I'll break your bloody neck if you ever…' Then Clem realised his mistake and set the bucket of water down. 'I'm sorry, Kane, I had no call to jump to wrong conclusions.'

Jessica had lifted her head and Kane let her go. She realised that without the modesty of her tucker she was showing the top of her full bosom and she pulled up her dress to cover herself. Her and Kane's eyes met and melted together. He stepped backwards, then respectfully turned his back.

'I'll make the tea,' he said in a husky voice.

–

That evening the Trenchards gathered round their huge kitchen table to discuss what was to be done with the terrified stranger Jessica had found and brought home. The twins were there and Kenver Trenchard, Clem's disabled brother, who had been resting that afternoon and missed the drama. Also there was Rosie Renfree, Clem and Kenver's sister, who was married to the steward of the Pengarron home farm and horse stud, and Ricketty Jim. He worked regularly on the farm and as an able and intelligent man, his opinion was always asked for and greatly valued. The kitchen door was left open so the cool, refreshing air could filter in and mingle pleasantly with the lingering smell of pigeon pie.

'I nearly came over this afternoon,' Rosie said, glancing around to ascertain the state of the kitchen and pushing aside her one long plait of Trenchard fair hair. 'But the baby's teething and I didn't like to bring her over bawling her little eyes out. I wish I had done now, you could have done with another woman about.'

'We managed,' Clem said, from the head of the table.

'I'll have a look at your back before I go, Jessie,' Rosie said, looking unconvinced.

'Jessica's perfectly all right,' Clem returned impatiently, stretching out a long leg and disturbing his dogs. After they had reshuffled their position at his feet, he continued, 'Don't you think I can cope with anything on my own?'

'No, not really. You need another woman on this farm, haven't I told you often enough?'

'Well, we have another one now,' Clem said tartly.

'Aye, you have, but in no fit state to be of any help and needing plenty herself by the sound of it,' Rosie retorted, ignoring her brother's ill humour. ''Twas a good job Kane Pengarron was here, that's all.'

Clem snatched up his pipe from the table and looked about moodily for his pouch of tobacco. 'But he didn't do anything, not really, did he, Jessica?' his eyes alighting on his unusually quiet daughter.

Jessica became flushed as everyone looked at her. She'd been thinking about the few minutes she'd spent alone with the man in question in this very room. What had happened was too personal to recount, and unsettling every time she thought about it, which was often. 'No… um… not really.'

'But I don't think that's the point Rosie is making,' Kenver said, from the specially adapted chair he always sat in. 'Kane was here if you needed him, Clem, and he could have gone for more help. I couldn't have done much.'

'You were a great help to Kerensa when she was in labour before she gave birth to Kelynen in this house,' Clem said, always eager to bring up that fact.

'You know what Uncle Ken means, Father,' David broke in. 'This is more than just a discussion on what to do with that poor woman asleep in Jessica's bed. It highlights the need for Jessie to have some female help and company on the farm.'

'Aye, I agree, it isn't as if we can't afford to employ some help for her,' Philip added.

'But Jim's been helping her for years, he does most of the drudgery work,' Clem said defensively.

'It's not the same thing. I'm afraid it's time to grasp the nettle firmly, dear brother,' Rosie said.

Clem went quiet and let the others chat among themselves. He knew they were right but in the two years since Alice's death he had resisted all talk of bringing another woman into the house. He knew the extra work was not fair on Jessica but he couldn't bear the thought of another woman trying to take Alice's place in any way, no matter how small.

'What do you think, Jim?' Clem asked the farm's casual helper.

Ricketty Jim, who got his name from his bent legs, gazed at each member of the family from his gentle dark brown eyes. 'Well, I don't mind doing as much work as you like to ease Jessica's work load but I think the maid could do with some company of her own kind.'

'Well, Father,' Jessica challenged him across the table, 'am I to go on being a skivvy by myself much longer?'

—

An hour later Clem was riding alongside Rosie to see her safely home.

'I think everything's been worked out most satisfactorily, don't you?' Rosie said under the darkening sky as they rode with their backs to the setting sun.

'Aye,' Clem said shortly.

'You aren't still sulking?'

'No.'

'Oh, I forget you're a man of many words, Clem Trenchard.'

Clem rose in the saddle to make an unnecessary check that his dogs were running about close by. 'Rosie, 'tis just hard for me to accept another woman into the family.'

'I know that, Clem, and I understand. But no one's suggesting you should replace Alice and I know how possessive you are over Jessica. But Alice wouldn't want all the hard work and responsibility to stand on Jessica's shoulders alone. It's harder for Jessica than it was for me before I married Matthias, when there was Alice and the rest of us. Apart from there being two of us then, Jessica has to work while Miss Cordelia and Miss Olivia can spend much of their time in leisure.'

'She's not the daughter or niece of a wealthy pig-headed baronet!' Clem snapped.

'And that's another thing.'

'Oh, what now?' Clem said in exasperation.

'Jessica being often surrounded by bad-tempered males, you and Philip. And I don't like the way Jessica speaks to you. Matthias and I wouldn't allow one of our girls, or one of the boys for that matter, to speak to us like that and you don't even check her.'

'So what are you saying, that I should punish her every time she's a bit outspoken? Jessica's always been cheeky, she don't mean anything by it. She needs a bit of space, like I do, that's all. Well, 'tis agreed that when that young woman's recovered, we'll offer her work helping Jessica with the household chores.'

'If you ask me, she needs more than that. She needs a woman's hand to help her mature properly.'

'And I suppose the next thing you're going to say is that I should get married again,' Clem muttered.

They had reached the clump of elm trees and Clem reined in and jumped down from his horse.

'What are you looking for?'

'Clues. I want to see if there's anything lying about to give any clue about that young woman.'

'You won't see much in this light.'

'I should have thought of it earlier but I can see well enough. She was lying at the bottom of the middle tree, Jessica said.' Clem lowered himself and ran his hands about the roots of the tree. He peered closely at the ground and up at the branches but there was nothing there to help him. Then he took a scrap of cloth from the woman's dress out of his pocket and held it under the dog's noses, one a black retriever cross, the other two brown and white hunting dogs. They ran off in different directions and sniffed the area thoroughly but came up with the same result as their master.

''Twas a shame Ricketty Jim was helping the twins in the fields this afternoon,' Clem said as they carried on their way, 'or he probably would have seen something from his shack at the top of the valley. I hope that woman is all right, Rosie. Right in the head, I mean. She relies totally on Jessica at the moment. I hope she won't do anything to hurt her.'

'She was all right with me when I went into Jessica's bedroom to see her. But when she caught sight of Philip she went into a panic. I think part of the trouble is that for some reason she's afraid of men, Clem.'

Clem shuddered as they thudded dully up the grassy slope to reach the boundary gate between his and Pengarron property. 'So she was probably raped then?'

'No, you can rest assured she hasn't been abused in that way.'

'How do you know for sure? How can you tell?'

'Oh, Clem, how do you think?' Rosie sighed. 'I had a look.'

'She let you do that?'

'She's very docile when there's only Jessica or me with her.'

'Well, if she decides to stay, I hope she stays docile. To be honest, I hope she gets well again quickly and wants to go back to wherever she came from. I have a feeling she spells trouble.'

'If she does go back to her own home, you'll still have the problem of getting some female company for Jessica,' Rosie said as they passed through the gateway and Clem relatched the gate.

They trotted on for a while, then she added, taking no pains to be casual, 'You've always tried to give Jessica everything she needs. Well, I think she needs a mother's influence and there's only one person can provide her with that, Clem, and that's you.'

Chapter 5

Sebastian Beswetherick led Sir Oliver Pengarron up the stairs to his grandfather's bedchamber. Sebastian was chewing on a handful of liquorice cakes and Oliver declined the roly-poly young man's offer to take one for himself from a small silver salver.

'Grandpaps like to suck on these,' Sebastian said through blackened teeth. 'I'm just taking him up a dishful.'

'Take care to leave some for him,' Oliver said, taking the last of the stairs in one athletic leap. Turning round and putting his hands on the banisters, he bent to face Sebastian as he crammed three more of the little round black cakes into his mouth. 'How is the grand old man today?'

'Crotchety and bad-tempered one minute, full of high spirits the next. Just the same as he's been since he became fully bedridden,' Sebastian answered, his pinkish beady eyes gleaming over the silver tray. He cried out the next moment when Oliver pulled it firmly out of his hands.

'I'll take the liquorice, what's left of it, in to your grandfather. It will save you the last few steps.' Oliver smiled pleasantly but his dark eyes burned disapproval at Sebastian who was puffing loudly at the effort from climbing the stairs.

'Well, um, thank you. I'll go off and see if Luke is at home, although he never seems to find time for me these days now Kane is back.'

'Luke and Kane are together today, at Ker-an-Mor Farm, fully occupied with going over the accounts with my steward. Kane is getting himself familiarised with the running of a busy and prosperous farm again. Then Luke is going to show him over the improvements we've had made to the roads in the parish and then to look over the charity day school we've founded for the parish children. Actually, Matthias Renfree, my farm steward, teaches part time at the school. You're an intelligent fellow, so I've heard, Sebastian. Why don't you ride over to Ker-an-Mor and offer him your services?'

'Oh no!' Sebastian looked most worried. 'I, um, have just remembered I have something very important to do. Must be on my way. I'll bid you a good morning, Sir Oliver.'

Oliver watched the young man waddle his richly dressed, cumbersome body down the stairs, rubbing his sweaty hands together now that he was deprived of his sweetmeats. 'Off somewhere to waste more time, no doubt, probably in a brothel,' Oliver muttered scornfully, knowing of Sebastian's other appetite.

There was a manservant stationed outside Sir Martin's bedchamber. He bowed and asked Oliver formally to wait outside with him.

'Sir Martin is being attended to, m'lord,' the servant explained.

'The doctor is with him?' Oliver asked.

'His nurse and valet, m'lord. Sir Martin is on the chamber pot.'

'I see,' Oliver said, puffing out his cheeks to forestall a laugh. The manservant had spoken as if he was announcing dinner was ready.

'Allow me to relieve you of your tray, m'lord.' Oliver handed over the tray of liquorice and was informed, 'Sir Martin is not allowed to eat these, m'lord.'

Ten minutes passed by and Oliver paced up and down the corridor, stopping to look out of the windows over the landscaped gardens of Tolwithrick House. He could see Kelynen playing on the immaculately mown lawns with Rex, her black retriever, and the four youngest brothers and sisters of Sebastian. On the terrace in front of the lawn was Kerensa, sitting with Sir Martin's daughter-in-law, Lady Rachael, taking refreshment with her and a friend of his, retired sea captain Hezekiah Solomon. Lady Rachael was afraid of dogs and glanced often at where Kelynen was exercising Rex and Oliver hoped his daughter would remember to keep the big energetic dog out of the way.

Occasionally from the bedchamber he was waiting to enter an enormous bellow could be heard accompanied by much shouting and the occasional swear word. The manservant kept a straight face throughout.

The bedchamber door was opened at last and out came a harassed-looking woman wearing what once had been a clean, hygienic apron, carrying a linen-covered chamber pot in outstretched hands which she handed to the footman. Oliver moved further up the corridor to get out of range of the smell of the pot's contents and watched the footman move off towards the servants' staircase with his face still completely deadpan.

The nurse bobbed Oliver a curtsey and hastened away. A few moments later the valet appeared and, seeing Oliver, who was striding towards him with the intention of knocking on the door to find out if he could be admitted, he hastily and humbly apologised.

'I'm very sorry, m'lord. I had no idea you were here. If you'll excuse me, I'll see if Sir Martin will receive you.'

'Are the windows opened?' Oliver demanded to know.

'The… um, windows, sir? Yes, yes, they are. Sir Martin likes to take the air at this time of day.'

'Then I'll go straight in,' Oliver said, moving so the valet had to dodge out of his way. 'I don't need a fanfare to announce my arrival. Good morning, Martin,' Oliver called breezily, going directly to a window and half sticking his dark head out of it.

'Damn me, who's that?' Sir Martin bellowed from the enormous bed he was confined in, propped up by many pillows. 'Oh, it's you, Oliver, is it? Have I kept you waiting? I'm sorry about that, I have a bit of trouble—'

'Yes,' Oliver said, cutting the other baronet off. 'Never mind. How are you today otherwise, Martin?'

'Huh, kept starved and that's a fact! Ruddy medics. Won't let me eat a thing. I ask you, my boy, what else can a man in my condition do to enjoy himself but eat, positively gorge himself! You're a master of the art of smuggling, Oliver. You could smuggle something in for me.'

Oliver believed the strict regime the aged gentleman's doctors kept him to was probably doing him more harm than good. 'What would you like? I'll bring it with me next time.'

'Good, good, you always were a good boy. Some pickled walnuts would be nice,' Sir Martin said excitedly, then he turned grumpy. 'Now come away from that ruddy window! I know why you're over there. I'll have you know this room's as fresh as a spring daisy. That valet of mine, he's a ruddy fool! Only here to keep me a prisoner and see I have no fun! He plonks bowls of scented petals all round the room and lights scented candles when I've done my duty. Now get yourself over here!'

Oliver came forth grinning. He viewed the much-overweight Sir Martin through twinkling eyes, wrapped up as he was in gown, shawls and nightcap, and Oliver saw the future for Sebastian at the grand old age of eighty-four.

'Let me take off some of your wrappings, Martin. They have you done up like a newborn baby.'

'Ruddy fools! They'll kill me. I tell you, my boy, they'll do for me. I didn't want to come here to live, I wanted to stay on at my house at Marazion. But they say I've got to die at Tolwithrick, the family home. My only pleasure in life now is the one and a half pints of port wine I'm prescribed every day for my health. Ah, that's better,' Sir Martin ended gratefully, when he was down to just one shawl. Then he was off again. 'You're a good boy, you always were a good boy. Handsome and tall, a great achiever, grew up to be a man who's done something with his life.'

Oliver sat on the bed, smiling affectionately at the old gentleman who still saw him as a boy even though he had reached middle age. He stayed smiling when the mood of the other suddenly changed again.

'Why didn't you come and see me last week? You were supposed to come and see me last week. I know I'm right so don't you dare say that I'm not. Well, where were you? Too busy, I suppose… everybody's too busy to visit an old, old man like me…'

Oliver took one of Martin's weak, podgy hands gently in his own. 'You know I'll never be too busy to come to see you, Martin. You will always be one of my closest and most respected friends and I look on you with great affection. I sent my apologies to you for last week. Kane had suddenly come home, remember? He's been to see you, do you not recall his visit?'

Sir Martin looked far away and forlorn. 'Kane? Kane? But didn't your little son die?'

'No, that was Joseph, two years ago. Kane is our elder son, our first child. He went away in the army, do you remember now?'

'Oh, Kane… the one you and Kerensa adopted, the one she found ill-treated…'

'Yes, that's Kane. What did you think of him?'

Becoming lucid again, Sir Martin nodded vigorously and Oliver had to straighten his nightcap. 'Ah, he came to see me. A fine figure of a man you have there for a son, Oliver. You and Kerensa must be very proud of him.' Then the aged baronet grinned lecherously and bade Oliver move closer. 'He told me how he got his wound in the stomach, the one that put him out of action for so long. A bit naughty of him, eh? Game for a bit of sport though, like I was in my youth.'

'Well, he was the one trying to rescue another from being naughty, as you put it, and yes, we are proud of him, both Kerensa and I and all the family.'

'Have you been up to the Roscawen mine like I asked you? To see if everything is working in the proper order and the profits are being maintained? I wish I could get out of this bed to see it. It's a new mine, a good mine, should yield as much as the Wheal Ember did in its heyday.'

'I rode up to Lancavel Downs only a few days ago. Everything seemed to be in order. I've had a discreet chat with William and he's confident you'll show a good profit this year. You're doing very well for a mine that's only been in operational order for two years.'

'William! Don't let him pull the wool over your eyes. He may be my eldest son and heir, but he's so soft with Rachael he'll let her spend the family fortune clean away on clothes and fripperies!'

Oliver could hardly upset William Beswetherick by taking too keen an interest in the family's business affairs but he couldn't say so to the old gentleman without upsetting him. He said simply, 'I'm sure you have nothing to worry about, Martin. The Roscawen mine is producing plenty of good-quality tin ore.'

'Well, I'm glad to hear it. Still full of Methodist tinners, I suppose. Pumped full of dissenting rubbish by your farm steward, Renfree, in that meeting house he built for them. You shouldn't have let them put up that building, Oliver. It's more on your land than Lancavel Downs. We'll have to fight to keep the working class in order one of these days, you wait and see. And it'll be the fault of gentlemen like you for allowing them too many liberties. There's been trouble building up for years in the colonies and now they're turning on us. Things are serious in America, the country's young and revolutionary. Wouldn't pay stamp duty in seventeen sixty-five and now shots have been fired against us in a bid for independence.'

'Yes, I know,' Oliver said, amazed how Sir Martin kept up with current affairs despite being bedridden. 'Luke is bitterly disappointed he's not fit enough to go out to help quell the rebellion. But with his frozen arm...'

'Quite, a shame, a pity. How's that new young parson fellow you put in at Perranbarvah? Measuring up all right, is he? You should get your own little family chapel like we have then you wouldn't have to travel to church every week. Mind you, our cleric's an absolute fool. Comes to see me every day but he's no comfort, can't even say a prayer unless he reads it out of a book!'

'The Reverend Timothy Lanyon is rather different to the Reverend Ivey but I'm pleased with him so far. He's honest and good-humoured, two valuable attributes in a parson, and the main thing is he's a believer.'

'Sounds just like your old cleric. Doesn't have anything to do with all this Methodist rubbish, does he?' And Sir Martin was back on one of his favourite subjects.

'He's fairly tolerant of it, Martin. If a thing's not harmful, I believe we should tolerate it.'

'Not harmful!' Sir Martin bellowed and spittle seeped down his worn-out face. 'Good heavens, man, they're a dissenting rabble.

Shouldn't be allowed to go on with it. Their loyalty to the Crown is questionable for a start with them wanting to break away from the established Church, and what's wrong with the Church anyway? And would they fight the French for example? Eh? Eh? We never know when the French are going to sneak up on our coast and endanger our homes and womenfolk. We never had a minute's rest over the French from fifty-six to sixty-three. We never knew then and we never know now when they're going to sneak up and murder us in our beds. Where will all your Methodists be then, eh? In cahoots with their French equivalents over the Channel and refusing to take up arms for King and country!'

'I think you are getting a little over-heated and over-anxious, Martin. Many Methodists still attend church regularly. In fact the ones to be first interested in it were regular attenders and John Wesley chooses his preachers from men who have a love for King and country.'

'You know everything about everything, don't you?' Sir Martin said accusingly, then forgetting Oliver was there he hummed to himself for several moments. He spoke to someone who was not there, at least to someone whom Oliver could not see. 'Yes, Amy' and 'No, Amy,' he said with a boyish smile, and Oliver knew that the old gentleman thought his late wife, Lady Ameline, whom he had always affectionately called Amy, was in the room. Oliver waited patiently to be noticed again.

'Got Kerensa and your little girl with you today?' Sir Martin asked suddenly. 'The little one with the boisterous dog?'

'Yes. Kerensa's out in the gardens taking tea with Rachael and Hezekiah, and Shelley is with your youngest grandchildren. They'll both be up to see you before we leave.'

'She reminds me of your mother Caroline, your little girl does. Did I ever tell you that?'

'No,' Oliver lied and added patiently, 'I'd like to hear about it.' Sir Martin began to drift off to sleep, talking occasionally between little puttering snores. 'A wonderful lady... Caroline... little girl... just like her...'

When he was sleeping deeply, Oliver quietly left the room. He joined those sitting in the shade from a hot sun on the terrace. Finding Rachael's cheek under her wide-brimmed hat he kissed it, then greeted Hezekiah Solomon and kissed Kerensa before sitting down next to her.

'I wager you must be kissed more often by your husband than any other lady in Cornwall,' Rachael purred at Kerensa.

'I wouldn't bet against you, Rachael, I'm happy to say,' Kerensa laughed, holding Oliver's large hand.

'Look at them, Hezekiah, what do you say? They're like newly-weds, aren't they?' Rachael appealed to Hezekiah from her painted face.

'I've always thought Oliver to be the most fortunate of men,' Hezekiah replied, looking at Kerensa from behind his powdered face.

'Why didn't you get married, Hezekiah?' Rachael asked bluntly. 'You have a penchant for the ladies yet we've never seen you with a regular companion adorning your arm.'

Captain Hezekiah Solomon was most secretive and Oliver and Kerensa had learned to respect that in him. They held their breath as his white features, become harsh with age now, hardened into extreme annoyance at the over-dressed matron. He did not reply but brought a bone china teacup to his thin lips in a perfectly manicured hand. His eyes met Kerensa's briefly over the rim and she smiled at him. He smiled back when he lowered the cup, but it was not the angelic smile that once had charmed all who saw it, and the snake-like ice-blue eyes in his macabre white face seemed to be fronting a hidden fury.

Without realising it, Kerensa tightened her fingers round Oliver's hand and he looked at her curiously. She was becoming increasingly uneasy about Hezekiah. He was as well-mannered as he'd always been, he had kept up the standard of flamboyant fashionable dressing that he adhered to, but he was no longer friendly. Not in the warm and humorous sense. She wondered if he was concealing an illness.

She knew he must be well past the age of sixty, and a few months ago he had suddenly sold his ship and bought a house at Penzance close to the Assembly Rooms. To keep up his desire for privacy, he had invited no one there and Kerensa didn't even know if he had servants. He called on Oliver and herself and the Beswethericks occasionally, the only friends he seemed to have made or wanted. He spent most evenings at the Assembly Rooms or the card tables at social outings but no one knew what he did the rest of the time. Kerensa wondered if he was still involved in Oliver's smuggling ventures around the Mount's Bay coastline but she could not picture him carrying contraband up the steep black cliffs.

When Rachael realised Hezekiah was not going to answer her, she giggled shrilly and stood up abruptly. 'Come inside with me, Kerensa, and help me choose what to wear at dear Olivia's twenty-first birthday party. I wish she would allow everyone to wear a costume but I'll probably have something made specially anyway.'

The gentlemen rose to their feet and Kerensa used Oliver's hand to help her rise. She shot him a worried look. Hezekiah was beginning to bring a bad taste to everywhere he went.

'That man is beginning to get on my nerves,' Rachael complained inside the grand house as they mounted the elegant stone stairway. 'He's never rude to you but he certainly is to me!'

Kerensa felt a loyalty to Hezekiah Solomon and replied, 'He likes to keep his privacy, Rachael. He wouldn't have answered me either.'

Rachael had as much difficulty with the ascent as her fat son. Having pushed a strong piece of wood down the stomacher of her gown to stop her belly sticking out, the garment was too tight and uncomfortable. It had the unfortunate effect of thrusting up her bosom which wobbled about in loose wrinkled flesh over the top of her stays. Kerensa wanted to tell Rachael to have a wider piece of lace sewn in there. She herself wore dresses with simple pleating and padding and could take her slender figure up the stairs with youthful poise.

'But don't you think he's rather strange, Kerensa?' Rachael asked, leaning a moment on the stair rail. 'Oh, I admit he's always been a mysterious man and what wouldn't we give to know all about him and his past. But, well, it's never struck me until recently but he's…

oh, I don't know what I'm trying to say, but I was talking to Olivia about him the other day and she told me that he makes her flesh creep.'

Kerensa looked at the struggling matron with scepticism. Lady Rachael Beswetherick was inclined to exaggerate. 'Olivia said that? Why, for goodness' sake? Hezekiah has always been aloof where children are concerned but he's always been kind to her, and generous.'

'But that's the point, Kerensa. Haven't you ever wondered why he's lavished her with so many expensive gifts since she's grown into a woman? Have you ever asked if she cares to receive them? Have you asked Hezekiah if he has any intentions towards her?'

'Hezekiah? Wanting to marry Olivia? You must be imagining things, Rachael. I think he's not taking kindly to growing old, that's all.'

'Kerensa,' Rachael caught her wrist, 'I am deadly serious. I believe there's not just something mysterious about Hezekiah but definitely unhealthy. And I've noticed the way you are beginning to feel uncomfortable in his presence too. I saw the look you gave Oliver outside. If you'll take my advice, you'll keep a careful watch over Olivia when that dandified little man's around.'

–

Oliver and Hezekiah were looking over Rachael's latest proud acquisitions at Tolwithrick, a collection of exotic shrubs in large pots placed in a row on the top step of the terrace. Their distinctive scents were appreciated by Hezekiah.

'I think I shall obtain some of these creations for my garden at Penzance,' he said, the melodic tone of former years now an uneasy rasp on a listener's ear. Time had been no less harsh to his voice than it had been to his looks.

'It's typical of Rachael to overdo it though,' Oliver replied, studying the number of plants and over-decorative pots standing much too close together and spoiling the effect. 'Kane brought home some unusual plants from his travels for Kerensa and me, and I believe she'd kill us to obtain them.'

Hezekiah clasped his hands behind his withered body and moved on to something different. 'I see I am not to be included in the number of those invited to dress in mythological costume at Olivia's birthday party.'

Oliver laughed and touched the rubbery leaf of a plant, releasing its potent fragrance. 'Kerensa and I are also considered too old to be among those included in that part of the celebration, Hezekiah. Rachael is most put out. No doubt she'd come dressed looking like a sea witch and frighten the other guests. We said Olivia could make the arrangements herself. She's been aided and abetted by Cordelia and Jessica Trenchard of Trecath-en Farm. It is their idea to have only the younger people dressed in costume, I'm happy to say.'

'I see,' Hezekiah said.

While Hezekiah had shrivelled in size and lost all manner of attractive appearance, Oliver Pengarron had kept his straight back, proud aristocratic bearing, and great height. His black hair had not dulled and was enhanced by the touches of silver-grey it bore, his striking dark features were distinguished by lines and still turned every woman's head. It was an insult to Hezekiah that this other man, who had Kerensa, the only woman he'd wanted and had never acquired by seduction or force, had kept his looks while even the attribute Hezekiah had been most proud of in himself, his glorious long white hair, had turned a garish yellow and he had to wear a variety of wigs styled on how his hair had once been.

Hezekiah Solomon was a man incapable of any tender feeling. He hated Oliver passionately, because he was the only man he'd been afraid of, and took cruel comfort in the thought that if he couldn't have his wife, there was still the equally beautiful daughter…

'Have you heard any more news about the unfortunate woman who was so brutally murdered in the street where you live, Hezekiah?'

'I find little interest in the killing of a whore, Oliver. She probably deserved it.'

Oliver shot a look at Hezekiah. He'd sounded bored but his expression, as usual, gave nothing away. 'Did you know the woman was Peter Blake's mistress?' he said, to test the other man's mood.

'Yes, I did. It is still the favourite subject of talk at the Assembly Rooms. It is a pity Blake was not dispatched at the same time, don't you think?'

'I don't think I can go as far as to say that about the man, Hezekiah. I'll always despise him for trying to force himself upon Kerensa but it was a long time ago. I know I nearly beat the man to his death then but that was due to the emotion of the moment. I can't forget he helped Luke and Kane when Luke's arm was badly damaged as a child. No, I don't wish him dead.'

Hezekiah gazed heavily at Oliver for a moment, then nodded his head. 'You are more accommodating than I, Oliver.'

'You don't have any reason to wish Peter Blake dead, do you?'

'No, but no reason to wish him well either.'

Oliver suddenly felt cold despite the heat of the day. 'I find these appalling murders blood-chilling. They've been going on for years and the authorities still have no idea who is responsible. I agree with the theory that the culprit is most likely to be a sailor. The murders occur intermittently. Presumably whenever the killer's ship berths in this part of the world, he goes on a murderous binge.'

'And escapes easy detection?'

'Well, that's how most people see it and I agree. I wonder what happened to the maid.'

'What maid?'

'Dinah Tredinnick's maid. Apparently she has disappeared. She was with her mistress earlier in the day because she was seen entering the house following a trip to a dressmaker. It's half expected her body will turn up next, mutilated in a ditch.'

'Some people have too much imagination,' Hezekiah said acidly. 'It was she who probably murdered her mistress and ran off with her jewellery.'

'But Dinah Tredinnick owned little jewellery. She was allergic to precious metals and nothing of value is missing from the house or was disturbed, according to what Peter Blake is said to have told the authorities.'

Hezekiah shrugged his scrawny shoulders. 'Who cares?'

'Did you ever see either of the women, Hezekiah? You live close by.'

'Only one of them,' he answered truthfully.

Kelynen quietly came up behind the two men and tugged on Oliver's coat. 'Papa, is it time to go up and see Great-Uncle Martin now? Rex is getting restless for a good run and it's difficult keeping him quiet for Aunt Rachael's sake.'

Oliver fondly slipped his arm round her shoulders and looked at Hezekiah. 'You've never seen much of Rex, have you, Hezekiah? He's a bundle of energy and I call him Wrecker because of the way he bounds through the house knocking everything over. Strange thing is, he lives up to that name by being an excellent plunderer of a wrecked ship. He dashes in and out of the sea and brings back the most unlikely things in his mouth.' Oliver could see his proud speech had fallen on deaf ears and he was angered at being made to look a fool.

Hezekiah coldly surveyed the tall fair-haired girl attached to Oliver and merely said, 'Really?' and turned away.

'We'll go and find your mother, sweeting,' Oliver said, leading Kelynen away, 'and pay a brief visit to your Great-Uncle Martin.'

Hezekiah glanced up and bowed slightly in farewell and watched the father and daughter walk away.

'Captain Solomon is a strange man. I don't think he likes me,' Kelynen said as she and Oliver strode arm in arm towards the mansion, with Rex walking obediently at her heel.

Oliver hugged her close. 'He's never had time for children but he doesn't seem to have much liking for anyone nowadays, Shelley. He may be ailing and it wouldn't be kind to annoy him. I think it would be best if you keep Rex and yourself well out of his way in the future.'

Oliver did think it was possible that Hezekiah Solomon could be ill. He decided to talk to Kerensa about the possibility and his other concerns over the retired sea captain, unaware that she intended to talk to him about the very same thing and her new concern over what Olivia might mean to Hezekiah.

Chapter 6

On the day of their daughter's birthday party, Oliver crept into the master bedroom of Pengarron Manor and peeking inside the drawn curtains round the massive four-poster bed, grinned a little wickedly at the sight of Kerensa lying there quite still with her arms spread out. She opened one eye, saw him, and smiled widely, then put a finger to her lips.

'What are you doing up here? I've been looking everywhere for you,' he whispered.

'I'm hiding away from everybody, the servants and the children. All over the house people are in a panic. Kelynen let Rex and one of Nathan's gun dogs scurry into the house and they pranced about almost knocking people off their feet. She hates her costume, she says it makes her look like a piskey and she doesn't see why she has to wear it. Luke is being his usual obstructive and sulky self because he isn't the centre of attention today. Olivia is terrified at having decided on a costume party and now wishes she was having a more traditional one instead for her coming-of-age.

'Ruth and Esther King are complaining that the extra help we've employed in the kitchens to help them for tonight are lazy and useless and are only getting in their way. Jack came in groaning about Beatrice upsetting the horses by shouting and screaming in the stables and how fed up he is at having to hide her gin bottles away from her; we'll have to do something about Beatrice, Oliver. Sebastian has arrived early, gorged himself on yesterday's left-overs and has been sick and he's upset Cherry by suggesting – well, you know what his suggestions usually consist of. Only Kane has been quiet, self-controlled and dependable.'

'My poor, dear little love,' Oliver said, kicking off his shoes and getting on the bed. They giggled as they lay in each other's arms hidden behind the curtains. 'Why don't I lock the door and we can stay in here for the rest of the day and all through the night and let the others just get on with it?'

'Oh, I wish we could,' Kerensa murmured, burrowing into his strong arms and nestling against his broad chest. 'Oliver, what are we going to do about Hezekiah?' she asked a moment later, her voice tinged with concern. 'I'm worried about what kind of gift he'll give her tonight. His lavish gifts are the only real indication we have that he has intentions towards her. I know Hezekiah is our friend but,' and Kerensa couldn't help shivering, 'the thought of our daughter married to such a creature is not a pleasant prospect.'

'I think you're worrying over nothing, my love. But why do you call him a creature? Why not a strange little man or a fop?'

'Because he doesn't seem real, just an image he's put up over the years to hide his real self. We hardly know a thing about him. Hezekiah seems to have a strange hint of cruelty about him. I am concerned over Rachael's fixation that he is leading a campaign for Olivia's hand. But on the other hand he's always been a man of elaborate gestures. He probably gives other women expensive jewellery. He gave me that huge sapphire ring, remember, the ugly one I can't bear to wear. He might have given me other jewellery but is afraid of making you jealous.'

'We'll just watch and see what happens,' Oliver said soothingly, lifting her chin and kissing her forehead, then her cheeks, her neck, her lips. 'Now we've managed to snatch a few minutes of peace and quiet alone together, let's talk of something more pleasant. In fact, let's not talk at all...'

―

Olivia collapsed on a chair in the kitchen and gave a satisfied smile to Ruth and Esther King, the tall, plain-faced sisters of Matthew King, the wrestling fisherman, who had been in service at the Manor since her parents' wedding day.

'You've done a wonderful job with Polly and Cherry of decorating the great hall and laying up the tables for tonight, Ruth and Esther,' she said, beaming at the ungainly pair who smiled proudly back. 'Polly and Cherry are on their way down now. Why don't we all share a dish of tea? And I'll call Jack in here. We mustn't forget he did all the climbing about for us.'

Ruth and Esther were quietly pleased and honoured that the 'young miss', as they called her between themselves, wanted to take a rest with them in their domain.

'We're pleased you like our work, Miss Olivia.' Ruth spoke for them both.

'Aye, and it'll be most enjoyable now they others have been sent packing,' Esther remarked rather crossly, referring to the hired help who had got in their way. 'We'll manage much better without them.'

Polly O'Flynn, the Manor's pleasantly mannered and efficient housekeeper, and wife to the estate's gamekeeper and head forester, came into the kitchen blowing out her flushed cheeks and pushing back her greying hair. 'Phew, I think we've finished at last – until the party's ready to get under way, that is.'

Cherry, the Manor's devoted nursemaid, who worked as a lady's maid now there were no young children in the house, followed on her heels.

'We're all having a rest and a dish of tea,' Olivia told them. 'Take a seat and put your feet up.'

'Thank you, Miss Olivia,' Polly said gratefully, glancing all round the kitchen and peering into the ancillary rooms. 'Got rid of they time-wasters, have we? Thank the good Lord for that. My Shaun would be more help than they were and he's only four years old!'

'Shaun's got more sense than all of them put together,' Cherry agreed, stretching out her arms and pushing back on the palms of her pliable hands before sitting on a stool next to the hearth.

'How is the little fellow?' Olivia asked fondly of Polly. 'I haven't seen him all day.'

'With all the preparations going on I thought he would be better kept safely out of the way for the day, so Nathan's taken him over

68

to Ker-an-Mor Farm to play with Rosie Renfree's little ones,' Polly replied.

'He'll enjoy that, it will be good for him to have lots of children to play with,' Olivia said, smiling at the memory of the cheeky little bushy-haired boy who had made his sudden appearance when Polly had already reached the age of forty-five. His parents had sadly believed they'd been doomed to childlessness. Shaun O'Flynn was almost as precious to those who dwelt on the estate as he was to his doting parents.

'You mean where he won't be cosseted and smothered, don't you, Miss Olivia?' Polly said, pouring out cups of tea from the huge china pot Esther had put on the table.

Olivia went pink and glanced guiltily at Ruth, Esther and Cherry.

'Oh, I know what you've all been saying, and you're right,' Polly said, sitting down and sipping from her cup. 'Nathan's been on at me too for being over-protective of Shaun, but when you've been given a little miracle you thought you'd never have after eighteen years of marriage, a mother can't help herself. But I know you're right, you have to learn to let go a little.' It was a bold speech, but Polly still looked anxious.

'Don't worry, Polly. Shaun will be perfectly safe with Rosie,' Cherry said firmly.

'Ais, she'd knaw a thing or two about young'uns. 'Ad three of 'er own,' rasped a hideous old woman who came into the room from outside, leaning heavily on a young man's arm.

'Rosie's had four children, Beatrice,' Polly said patiently. 'Come in and join us, Jack,' she said to the other newcomer.

'Four?' Beatrice screeched. 'When did she 'ave that last one then? Why weren't I told? That maid means a lot to me, 'elps me with me 'erbs 'n' potions. We'm good friends, we are, why weren't I told?'

'You were, but you're getting forgetful,' Ruth called loudly from the larder where she was fetching a biscuit tin, 'and deaf. Rosie had another little maid five months ago. Called her Sarah. She brought her over to show you as soon as she was on her feet again.'

'Did she? Aah…' Beatrice's short-sighted piggy eyes filled with tears and her fat nose trickled something thick and green down over her many chins. 'Fancy that, the little maid being a mother of four. I d'love that maid like she were me own an' I love t'ear of a babe's birth.'

'She's getting sentimental in her old age,' Olivia said to Jack, who found himself pushed up on a bench and was sitting opposite her.

'Aye, Miss Olivia,' he replied shyly, 'her very old age. She must be older than Sir Martin.'

Beatrice sat down on the clumsy old chair kept for her use in the kitchen since before Sir Oliver's birth. She went quiet and hummed like a bee to herself.

'You deserve a break after all your hard work in the house today,' Olivia said to Jack, adding with a smile, 'although I daresay you would prefer to be outside attending to the stables rather than sitting idle in all this female company.'

The Manor's head groom blushed but he felt thoroughly at home. He was used to being fussed over by the Manor's womenfolk, including Kerensa. He had been a twelve-year-old boy when she'd come to the Manor as a bride and she looked on him as 'one of her own'. He was a quiet and reserved young man and lived alone in his little cottage on the Manor's grounds.

Polly poured more tea for the company then looked at the giant kettle singing on the top of the range. 'I should have thought to take her ladyship a tray of tea. I wonder where she is, she's worked as hard as the rest of us today.'

'Ais, don't 'ee be forgettin' the little missus now,' Beatrice rasped, sending a shower of spit towards the table and making those sitting round it duck their heads. 'She must be bleddy parched, dear little soul.' Beatrice doted on her mistress and talked about her as though she was younger than her offspring.

'Um, I suspect Mama is hiding away somewhere with Father, having one of their little quiet times alone,' Olivia said, returning Polly's knowing look. 'Best not to disturb them, I think.'

'I'll wait until she reappears then,' Polly said delicately.

'Where's Miss Cordelia got to?' Esther asked. 'She hasn't had anything to eat since breakfast.'

'She was out in the orchards according to one of the gardeners a little while ago,' Jack supplied. 'Writing a letter he thought she was.'

'And probably still there now, daydreaming,' Olivia said affectionately.

'She made some lovely job of winding all they flowers in and out of the banisters leading up the stairs,' Ruth said.

'She's such a little thing but there's a lot of artistic talent swimming about inside her dear little head,' Polly said.

Olivia nodded in agreement. 'It's a pity she doesn't try her hand at painting, but I've never been able to get her interested.'

'The little maid's 'appy 'nough in 'er own little world, 'tes best to leave things be,' Beatrice snorted, then started up a bout of hacking in Cherry's direction.

Cordelia Drannock had lived at the Manor since her mother died when she was nine years old. The youngest of a family of six children, whom Oliver had set up in various ways when he had discovered he was their uncle by an illegitimate brother, she was the only one still living under his roof. Her two sisters, Naomi and Hannah, had made good marriages and had moved with their husbands out of the county. Her brothers, Jack and Charles, were living in London, and Bartholomew, the eldest of the family, travelled continually overseas and it was never sure where he was at one time. The Pengarron children had taken readily to their poor fisherfolk cousins, even Luke as long as they did his bidding, and Cordelia, small and dainty, was thought of in much the same way as Kelynen.

'Well,' Olivia said, when Beatrice had stopped polluting the air, 'I think I'll take another look at my costume, just to be sure it's all in order – and find out if Mama has surfaced yet.'

'Your mama's where a good woman oughta be, in the arms of 'er lovin' 'usband,' Beatrice rasped loudly, coming out with the sort of comment she could get away with over the rest of the servants. And not content with that, she stabbed a gnarled finger at Olivia and went on, ''Tes' time that you young miss got one of yer own, 'tes time thee got yerself married.'

The others in the kitchen looked eagerly at Olivia for her reply.

'My coming-of-age party is the only social event I intend to have for a very long time!' Olivia snapped and stalked off to her bedroom.

–

A pale blue sky tinged with mauve gave a background to a scattered group of wavy-patterned clouds of glowing orange that evening. Jessica Trenchard had a dress made of the same colours to wear at the birthday party; it was hanging in Olivia's bedroom waiting for her to change into. Olivia had assigned her guests the mythological character that she thought suited them best. Jessica was Artemis, goddess of the wild, mistress of beasts, the virgin hunter, who loved all things and gave succour to those in childbirth. Jessica liked the choice, although she had only helped in the birth of farm animals so far.

She rode over to Pengarron Manor under that cool, restful sky on the back of Tally, her father's mare, sitting in front of her brother David, who was going on to Ker-an-Mor Farm.

'Why don't you stay for the party, David?' she pleaded with him again. 'Philip's coming, you needn't be worried about the stuck-up gentry folk. They don't worry me.'

'I know that, Jessie. You can hold your own in gale-force winds.'

'The young ladies will go out of their way to get a dance with you, what with your blond hair and broad shoulders, not like the sickly-looking gentlemen who'll be there.'

'Well, Philip will be there and as we look very much alike, they won't be missing out on their treat, will they? And there's nothing sickly-looking about either Luke Pengarron or Kane.'

'Don't mention those two to me. I'd enjoy this party far more if they weren't going to be there,' Jessica said haughtily, shaking her mane of curls.

'Well, they're bound to be there, they're Olivia's brothers, you silly little maid,' David said, getting quickly to the point of exasperation his sister often brought her menfolk to. 'I understand why you don't like Luke but Kane's always been a good friend to we Trenchards. You should remember how much he helped you when you came across Kerris that day.'

'Kane this, Kane that! You, Philip and Father think the sun shines out of his ruddy armpits! Why don't we make him a Cornish saint? Name a church after him. Saint Kane the Good, it'll suit him.'

'Oh, don't be so horrible, Jessie. Kane's done you no harm.'

'He's done me no good either! And don't you dare call me a silly little maid again!'

'Well, 'tis how you behave,' David said crossly. 'I'll get Aunty Rosie to speak to you.'

Jessica clamped her lips shut and refused to say another word until they were standing outside the huge, imposing Manor house.

'I'll see you tomorrow, brother dear,' she said coolly. 'I won't be late to get the breakfasts.'

'Now you know Father said you can lie abed here tomorrow and have breakfast with Olivia and Cordelia. He wants you to make an occasion of it for once. Kerris is a good cook, she can do our breakfasts.'

'And you know very well that Kerris will stay hiding in my room until I come home. She's still afraid of you all, all except Uncle Kenver who takes the trouble to speak to her kindly and doesn't tower over her. And I don't want to lie abed, I'm used to rising before dawn. I shall be home.'

'Please yourself, but then you always do. But it's not our fault if we Trenchards are all tall. Kerris is so slight and moves about so quietly we keep falling over her.'

The terrified woman Jessica had found was still staying at Trecathen Farm, and Jessica had decided to call her Kerris since her mind seemed to have closed down completely on her past, including her identity. She chose the name out of fondness for a docile, sickly lamb she had once cared for as she would now have to care for the girl. After two and a half weeks at the farm, Kerris still stayed close to Jessica, often clinging to her bodily, seemingly terrified of the men of the house. She spoke little, and then only in monosyllables in answer to direct questions. When asked anything about her life she became withdrawn and fearful which quickly turned to a blankness. But she was a good worker and willingly helped Jessica with her jobs.

Jessica hadn't wanted to leave Kerris to attend this party. She thought her father would have been glad of the excuse to keep her at home, but although Clem hated her mixing with the Pengarrons, he had spent a lot of money on her costume for the occasion so she would feel proud to go and he knew that she had been eagerly looking forward to it. Clem had pointed out that despite her trauma, Kerris seemed to trust her. Jessica had only to tell her she could stay safe in her room until she returned and there would be no fuss. Clem had added that if Kerris wanted anything, Kenver was prepared to be carried up the stairs to speak to her. And if Jessica wanted to stay the night as she had been invited to do and Kerris was too frightened to get the menfolk's breakfasts, they had no objections to doing it for themselves; it wouldn't hurt Kerris to stay a little longer shut away in the bedroom. Finally Jessica said she would go but insisted she would be back at dawn, knowing that Olivia would arrange for Jack, the Manor's groom, to escort her home.

David pulled one of Jessica's curls and said seriously, 'You will enjoy yourself now, won't you, Jessie?'

'Of course I will and I'll be careful no one slips anything in my drink so I don't end up with company in my bed.'

'Jessie!'

She laughed. 'How's a woman supposed to know how to avoid the wiles of wicked men if she don't trouble herself to find out what they are like? All men aren't as honourable as you, David. Why don't you come in? Just for a little while? The likes of us don't usually get the chance to mix like this with the gentry. Mother would have liked it, it meant a lot to her for us to be friends with the children of her own best friend.'

'Then take on your own reasoning, little sister, and try to be friends with Kane. And I'm still going on to Ker-an-Mor, 'tis more important to me than socialising.'

The Manor door swung open and Oliver's tall figure was framed in the doorway with Kerensa beside him.

'Come on in, Miss Trenchard,' Oliver called out in greeting. 'And you too, young man.'

'I'm going on to Ker-an-Mor Farm, thank you, m'lord,' David said, striding up the stone steps and giving a small bow to the Lord and Lady of the Manor.

'Come inside and take a glass of something before you go, David,' Kerensa said.

'If you don't mind me refusing, m'lady, Matthias Renfree is expecting me very soon,' he explained humbly.

Olivia's head appeared squeezed in between her parents. 'Are you two going to stay out here chatting all night? Hurry up, Jessie, or the other guests will be arriving before you've changed.'

David left and Olivia took Jessica straight to her room.

'Your mother looks beautiful, but then she always does. I hope I look as good as her tonight,' Jessica said, suddenly feeling overawed.

'I don't suppose anyone will ever be as beautiful as Mama,' Olivia said matter-of-factly. 'People say I look like her and of course I do, but my hair will never be quite as glowingly red as hers or my eyes such an exquisite grey-green. Your dress is lovely, Jessie, you'll make a perfect Artemis,' she went on enviously, touching the fine tissue. 'I didn't know you were such a good needlewoman.'

'Kerris made it for me and did all the embroidery, she's some clever that way. She's a great help around the farmhouse and I hope she stays with us for ever.'

'Have you any idea who she is and where she comes from yet?' Olivia asked, tossing all her pairs of dancing slippers out from the bottom of a cupboard so that Jessica, whose small feet were roughly the same size, could select a pair for the night.

'No, and please don't say anything about her to anyone else, will you, Livvy? We'll have everybody in the parish coming over to the farm gawping at the "mystery woman" to see if they know her. She's so frightened all the time, poor soul. I don't want to see her scared witless like she was when I found her ever again. We've decided to wait a month and see if she gets her memory back.'

'She was probably tyrannised by a brutal husband. I hope he never finds her, and don't worry, I won't talk about her. Keep the pair of slippers you decide on, Jessie. It will give you a lasting memory of tonight's events.'

'Thank you, I'll hang them up on my bedroom wall. There won't be much call to wear them around the farm.' Jessica touched an object carved out of wood on Olivia's dressing table. 'What's this? I've never seen anything like it before.'

'It's a birthday gift from Ricketty Jim. It was kind of him, wasn't it? You're holding it the wrong way up. It's a carving of mushrooms and grasses growing against a fallen log.'

'Oh, yes, I can see that now. Didn't know he did things like this.'

'I'll take it down to the display table with the rest of the gifts. He's going to entertain us with some of his colourful stories during the evening.' Olivia tapped Jessica's shoulder. 'Pity you insist on leaving at dawn. You are so stubborn. We could have had such fun in the morning picking over what my guests gave and what they wore, what they said and did.'

'I have to get back for Kerris,' Jessica replied, a little impatiently.

Cordelia came in dressed in her costume as Aphrodite who was famed for her soft feminine beauty. The other two girls admired it and told her she looked lovely. Cordelia was secretly very pleased with her appearance. She knew she was no beauty in the raw sense as Jessica was or the classical sense as Olivia, but she knew she looked specially lovely tonight and nervously hoped to impress some of the gentlemen, one in particular.

'I think your costume is simply wonderful, Jessica,' she said excitedly. 'I can't wait to see you in it and I'm dying to know what the birthday girl here has chosen to wear. Something in green, I bet, to set off her red hair.'

'Yes, what's it like, Livvy?' Jessica asked. 'You can let us in on the secret, we promise not to tell anyone.'

'You can wait and see like the others. Tonight I'm going to copy the outrageous Lady Rachael and make a grand entrance.'

'Well, I'd better get ready myself so I can leave you to dress in secret then,' Jessica said.

'Will you come to my room and help me choose what pieces of jewellery to wear with my dress, please, Olivia?' Cordelia asked. She never had the confidence to decide for herself what to wear. 'Aunt

Kerensa is busy with Cherry trying to coax Kelynen into her costume at the moment.'

'We'll help Jessica first, then I'll come,' Olivia said.

'No, you go now,' Jessica put in quickly. 'I'm quite used to dressing myself.' She wanted the cousins to go and leave her to change her clothes alone, certain that her underclothes would look cheap and shabby compared to what they wore.

'Well, if you're sure,' Olivia said, then sensing Jessica's reasons she caught Cordelia's arm and pulled her along. 'We'll probably be a while, Cordelia will take ages to make up her mind.'

Jessica closed the damask curtain that hung round the bed in the middle of the room and changed quickly behind its privacy. She had to take off her shift to wear the costume and felt really daring as she twirled in the filmy layers of the exotic style Kerris had made for her. Wanting to see what she looked like in Olivia's full-length mirror, she came out from behind the security of the bed hangings. Hearing a step and thinking Olivia had come back, she called out, 'Olivia, do you think—'

At the same moment Luke Pengarron came into the room saying, 'Livvy, will you do—'

They stared at each other in surprise for a moment then Luke, who had swept his dark eyes over Jessica and taken in the brevity of her dress, blurted out, 'You look so beautiful!'

Jessica, who always gave a stinging retort to anything this usually disagreeable young man said to her, was taken aback by his genuine complimentary reaction to her. 'Thank you,' she said.

Luke could not tear his eyes from her. For once his self-confidence and superior sarcasm deserted him. He stammered, embarrassed that he had to admit a weakness. 'W-would you do this brooch up on my shoulder for me, please? I… I can't manage with this s-stiff arm and there's no one else about.'

Jessica stepped up close to him. She felt humbled that he had asked her to do what was a simple task to anyone with two good arms, that he had spoken of his disability.

'The catch looks very fiddly,' she said, to lessen his discomfort as she fastened the large gold brooch.

Luke kept his eyes on her face throughout and when she dropped her arms, he said a simple 'Thank you' and did not move away.

Jessica felt chained to the spot. It was the first time they had ever been civil to each other; it had come unexpectedly and easier than she could have imagined. Luke Pengarron was so good-looking, ruggedly handsome with the intense dark features of his father and their Pengarron forebears. Jessica had been so incensed by his hostile and scathing behaviour towards her and her family, she had not noticed this before. She bit her bottom lip and knew why the husband-hunters among the gentry pursued him so hotly.

She looked from his fine face to his shoulders, both broad and nearly in line despite his disability, then down his arms to his hands which were clenched at his sides. When he stood still, there was nothing to indicate that he had a useless arm – not that it mattered.

Jessica's gaze came back to his face. His expression had not changed. He just kept staring intently at her. Dressed in their mythical costumes, they seemed to be in another world and she felt drawn to him.

Luke put out the hand of his good arm and Jessica lifted hers to place it in his.

'I hope you've finished dressing, Jessie,' Olivia called to her as she ran from Cordelia's room to her own, 'or we'll never be ready on time.'

Jessica swung away from Luke and put her hand guiltily to her side as if she'd let him kiss her fingers and had enjoyed it.

The next moment Olivia was in the room. 'Oh, Luke. You look wonderful, but I hope you don't want me to do anything for you because Mama's finished with Kelynen and is on her way to help me.' Then seeing Jessica, she exclaimed, 'Jessica! You look absolutely beautiful. Doesn't she, Luke?'

'Yes, she does, quite beautiful,' Luke agreed in a soft voice.

Jessica glanced at him to see if his expression had gone back to its habitual bad-temperedness but the look he gave her was almost wistful. He left the room without saying another word.

'He seems to have been absolutely stunned by you. I hope I'll have the same effect on the gentlemen tonight,' Olivia said, unaware that Jessica was feeling just as stunned.

Chapter 7

When she walked down the stairs on Oliver's proud arm that evening, Olivia's appearance had the effect she desired. Her hair and costume was of Circe, the Enchantress, said to have lured men to her island where she gave them a potion that turned them into beasts. She beamed a brilliant smile around the great hall, to deafening applause from her many guests, and over a dozen besotted young men made up their minds to put in an even heavier appeal to their fathers to make a plea to Sir Oliver for his elder daughter's hand.

Olivia and Oliver were followed down the stairs by Kerensa and Cordelia on Kane's arms and Kelynen on Luke's. The family made a scene of rare elegance and beauty.

'Splendid! Splendid!' Lady Rachael Beswetherick trilled at the top of her voice. She had been disappointed at not being allowed to come dressed as Mother Earth but was determined not to be overlooked tonight. She was dressed in a brightly coloured sack-backed gown over wicker panniers so wide they allowed no one a close proximity to her. 'You look absolutely divine, Olivia, deliciously gorgeous! Open your presents at once, my dear. The rest of us will simply die of curiosity if you delay another minute!'

Oliver led his family to the head of a large oval-shaped table where numerous wrapped parcels of every size and shape were sitting under the guard of two burly estate workers. There was a good deal of bustling as people pressed forward to get a good view but Jessica and Philip, with Simon Peter who felt very awkward knowing that Sir Oliver and Lady Pengarron had good reason to despise his father, preferred to stay quietly at the back.

'You look every bit as beautiful as Olivia,' Simon Peter whispered into Jessica's ear as Oliver announced who the presents were from and Olivia opened them and thanked the givers.

'No, I don't,' Jessica returned, wanting this to be entirely Olivia's night. 'See how her eyes are shining; she looks so happy and deserves to be.'

'"Tis time she was thinking of getting married,' Philip remarked. 'Most ladies her age are at least promised to somebody by now. I can see the Harris, Ransoms, Bassets, Arundells, Grenvilles and Rashleighs are here, all eager to be announced as her future husband.'

'Some women are in no hurry to become a man's chattel, Philip,' Jessica hissed, trying to hear what had been given by whom.

'Like you,' Simon Peter said mournfully, pretending to be jostled so he could slip an arm about her waist.

Jessica gave him an impatient look and taking his hand away moved in front of him. It brought her directly into Luke's line of vision and he gazed at her as he'd done earlier. Jessica stared back, expecting his expression to change to one of disdain but it stayed the same. Then she realised someone else was looking at her. Kane was witnessing the joint perusal with some amusement. He grinned and winked at her and Jessica tightened her face and tossed her head. She didn't mind being the object of a Pengarron's disparagement or gentle interest but she would not tolerate being one of amusement.

As the guests were thanked, they moved away from the table and were supplied with more wine before taking the floor to dance. Hezekiah was one of the last to arrive and brought his gift with him. It was inside a long box and he handed it over to Olivia with a flourish of his bejewelled gloved hand. Oliver and Kerensa pointedly glanced at each other.

Olivia took off the lid and cried out, first in wonder then in a revulsion she tried to hide. The box contained two elaborate emerald bracelets that would look right only on the wrists of a gentleman's mistress of gaudy taste.

'Dear Captain Solomon! They're, they're…'

Distasteful and unsuitable – Kerensa and Oliver shared the same thoughts and their daughter's horror. The gift was typical of Hezekiah.

Hezekiah's macabre mask broke into a misshapen smile. 'I'm so pleased you like them, Miss Olivia. I knew your parents were intending to give you the beautiful necklace you are wearing and I thought they would make the ideal complement.' He withdrew with a bow and mingled with the crowd and Olivia turned to her parents in horror.

'He's not expecting me to wear them tonight, is he? They're absolutely awful, they'll ruin my costume.'

'Leave them on the table,' Oliver whispered, feeling uncomfortable as Hezekiah took a glass of wine and looked their way. 'I'll tell him you want them on display.' To Kerensa he said under his breath, 'I've a good mind to tell the men to turn a blind eye if someone tries to steal them.'

The only part of the evening that Philip Trenchard enjoyed was when Ricketty Jim enthralled the gathering by telling folklore and ghost stories, with little Shaun O'Flynn, dressed up proudly by his parents, acting out some of the parts. They received many a generous tip and were asked to perform at other social gatherings. The story-teller firmly declined and Polly and Nathan, who didn't want their son to become an amusement of the gentry, quickly packed him off to bed.

Philip was glad as the celebrations drew to a close and the last of the guests, whom he thought of disparagingly as the 'stiff-nosed and glitter brigade', left. Simon Peter, too, had departed to attend the same meeting on Ker-an-Mor Farm as David. About twenty of the younger people were left, drinking wine in the parlour.

Philip had been bored all night, disgusted at some of the manners of a few of the so-called genteel and the pawing he'd been subjected to from some of their lusty women, and he felt a fool in his ridiculous costume of some sort of messenger. He thought he, not Luke, should have been Zeus, father of the gods and men. He was there only because he wanted to see how the land lay concerning Cordelia

Drannock, and he felt the evening had been worth enduring as he witnessed her gentle spurning of the young blades interested in making a 'good marriage' with a Pengarron niece who would doubtless have a substantial dowry.

Making a beeline for her as she leaned against a table looking dreamily over an empty glass of wine, he offered to replenish it from a bottle he'd found languishing next to a sleeping, drunken Sebastian Beswetherick.

Cordelia's small bird-like face suffused red all over when she realised who had interrupted her daydream. 'No... no, thank you,' she blustered.

Philip looked at Sebastian in disgust. 'I see he's had enough. He made a pig of himself all night, wolfing down food, snaffling drink like it was the last to be found in the world, and slobbering over all you ladies.'

'Yes, it's a good thing he is asleep,' Cordelia said, viewing the fat young gentleman, whose eyes had slid down the dress of every lady there that night, with distaste.

'I notice you don't pay much attention to the men of his class,' Philip said, staring into her face.

'Do I not?' Cordelia edged away and looked across the room at the group of gentlemen presided over by Luke who had suddenly laughed loudly at one of his jokes. 'Luke's enjoying himself,' she said, nervously on account of Philip. She had seen ladies of every age eyeing the muscles of this brawny blond man and dancing attendance on him. She had heard them speculating and giggling about his prowess in other, more intimate matters. It had left her feeling uncomfortable about him. She was sure he was interested in her in a way different to that shown when they'd played together as children, when she'd been introduced into the Pengarron dynasty. A part of her desired that interest, a bigger part of her was afraid of it. And when he was close beside her like this, talking straight at her, her legs turned to jelly and her head felt dizzy.

'Don't move away from me,' Philip said in a hurt voice.

'I'm... I'm sorry, I wasn't aware...'

'You do it every time I get near you. Don't you like me any more?'

'Yes, yes, of course I do. I'm sorry, I didn't mean to seem unfriendly.'

You're as soft as putty, warm and pliable, quite easy for a man to manipulate, Philip thought, as he smiled down on her compact figure with his ready charm. He wanted to manipulate Cordelia Drannock into a marriage bond with him. The wealth of her dowry would bring forward the many plans he had for making Trecath-en Farm the most prosperous small concern in the neighbourhood. It was the biggest and most arable piece of land next to Ker-an-Mor Farm on the Pengarron estate. It had great potential and he was eager to exploit it and make a name for himself other than as a future wrestling champion. He had plans, such as buying and farming more land, and snaring Cordelia Drannock was the first part in them.

'Have you heard from your brothers and sisters of late, Cordelia?' he asked conversationally, knowing she was more relaxed when talking about her family.

'Yes, I have,' she answered more confidently, but still wanting to back away. 'Naomi and Hannah have both delivered a new child this year. Jack and Charles are in London together and Bartholomew has not written for ages, but then he travels about a lot, he could be anywhere.'

'You must miss them,' Philip said kindly.

'I haven't seen any of my brothers for over two years now and my sisters of course are busy about their own families.'

'But you are happy living with this part of your family, are you not?'

'Oh, yes. Aunt Kerensa and Uncle Oliver have taken tits place of my parents to me.'

Philip was just getting satisfied that their conversation was going with ease when Luke saw them and frowned angrily. He called to Cordelia and she excused herself and scuttled away at once.

Philip held Luke's haughty cold stare with one of equal ill feeling but he knew his cause was lost for the night. Luke Pengarron must have suspicions about his cousin's honour where he was concerned.

Philip lifted his glass to Luke in defiance. 'You won't always be around to chaperon your little cousin, Pengarron,' he muttered icily under his breath. Not wanting to stay and risk a pawing from one of the other young ladies and so ruin things further, he decided to leave.

'Has your brother gone?' Kane, who had left the room for a few minutes, said casually to Jessica as he put a small wooden box down on the table behind her.

'Yes, it's not really his form of entertainment,' she answered, as if she wasn't the least bit interested in his observations.

'Pity, I had something to show him,' Kane said, tapping the box.

Jessica knew he wanted her to ask him what was in the box but she would not oblige him. He gave her costume a look of healthy appreciation for a few moments and she wanted him to pay her the same compliment as his brother had, so she could show him again that she wasn't in the least bit interested in anything he had to say... or so she told herself. But his expressive brown eyes looked at her as if she was an amusing child and then he went off to join those huddled around Luke. Jessica was left feeling rather flat.

Oliver popped his head round the door. 'Everything all right in here?' he asked gaily.

'Oh, Father! Haven't you retired yet?' Luke said crossly.

'Your mother and I are just going up,' Oliver replied, as female heads turned and studied him. 'I've just come in to let you know that you have another guest, Olivia.'

'As long as it's not Captain Solomon returning, I don't care who it is,' Olivia whispered to Jessica as she came and stood beside her.

But the newcomer turned out to be every bit as unwelcome, as far as Olivia was concerned. It was the Reverend Timothy Rawlyn Lanyon.

'So sorry to be late,' Timothy said with gusto as he bounded into the room. 'But I had a "last rites" to attend to. Must keep a sense of priority.'

Forcing a wine glass out of Olivia's hand and slapping something small, soft and round in its place, he said heartily, 'Catherine made it for you, hope you like it.' And without even wishing her one 'Happy Birthday', he made straight for the group of men.

'You were a bit sharp with your father then,' Timothy chided Luke with his eyes lowered under a frown. 'Honour thy father and mother, don't you forget.'

'Well, I thought he was going to stay,' Luke replied, and actually had the grace to blush.

'And what if he was?'

'Father is fifty-six years old and hasn't learned to age like a respectable old gentleman,' Luke grumbled. 'He attracts the attentions of every female everywhere he goes and us younger men never get a chance. He's taller than any of us, broader-shouldered...' Luke threw an irritable hand at the cluster of females. 'Did you see the way their heads all turned just then when he looked into the room?'

'I did,' and the Reverend Lanyon gave out a hearty laugh which Olivia found most offensive.

'What did he give you?' Cordelia asked, shaking Olivia's arm and breaking off the harsh stare she was giving the parson.

'Miss Catherine made it,' Olivia said, not wanting the lady's ungracious brother to take any of the credit. She opened a lace-edged square-shaped piece of silk and from a pocket in its centre pulled out three smaller padded pieces of silk. 'They're perfumed clothes sachets,' she said, raising them to her nose. 'They smell lovely, an unusual fragrance. I will have to ask Miss Catherine what it is when I thank her.'

'Why are you all in a huddle?' Timothy asked the men.

'Kane is going to show us what he calls his "never-been-known-to-fail" anti-marriage kit,' Luke said, sniggering loud enough to attract everyone's attention, except for Sebastian who had slid to the floor and been left there.

'And what is that?' Timothy asked eagerly, rubbing his hands together.

'What a position for a parson to take on the matter,' Olivia said haughtily, as if she was an outraged elderly maiden aunt. The young ladies turned to see what entertainment her brother was offering at the end of the party.

Kane moved into the middle of the room and glanced around at his audience. He had their full attention. Fed up with looking like a part of Mount Olympus, he had changed out of his costume and shunned a coat and neckcloth in the heat. He was straight-backed, attractive and confident in brown breeches and open–necked white shirt. Olivia and Cordelia were delighted to have Kane home for this family occasion and watched him closely, and Jessica noticed the other females there were as fascinated with him as they had been with Sir Oliver a little earlier.

Kane had tried to guess what each person's reaction would be to what he was about to say and do and had bets laid with those gentlemen who shared his secret. He looked last at Jessica who glared back and he was sure her reaction would not disappoint him.

'I was taught this trick by a fellow officer out in the Caribbean. He had managed to escape all efforts to snare him in wedlock at the age of fifty–two. He was a brave, handsome man and hotly pursued for his fortune and physical attributes wherever we were stationed. He took no exception to sharing them out but was determined no one would ever tie him down in matrimony. He swore he had the perfect answer to frighten off the most determined husband–hunter. According to him, women are terrified by either the one thing I have secured about me on my person,' there was raucous laughter from the men and tittering from the ladies at this, 'or the thing I have ensconced in that box on the table.' All heads turned to look at the box he pointed at.

'Is it another present for Olivia?' asked a young lady, dressed as a siren, with a weak chin under a long, sharp nose. 'Is it a surprise for her?'

'No, Miss Chynoweth. I promise you it is not for Olivia and I doubt if she'll appreciate it,' Kane replied mysteriously.

Another lady, who was closely scrutinising his body, suddenly shrieked and collapsed in fits of giggles. 'There's something in his pocket! I saw it move, I tell you I saw it!'

'I think it is time for exhibit number one, brother,' called out Luke. 'Before Charlotte kills herself laughing.'

'Yes, you have us all avidly interested,' bawled Timothy.

'Ready, Livvy?' Kane asked Olivia's permission as it was her party.

'Oh, get on with it, Kane,' she retorted rather shortly, vexed that the Reverend Lanyon had spoken.

Kane put his hand into his tight breeches and pulled out a wriggling little brown mouse. 'Exhibit number one. A *micromys minutus* or, if you prefer, a harvest mouse, the smallest of our rodents—'

He was stopped by the screaming of two of the young ladies, one of whom went rushing to the doors. Two more ladies cringed, Cordelia backed away and Luke came forward and put his arm round her protectively. At least three of the gentlemen looked uneasy. Those in on the secret made silly farmyard laughing noises.

Kane seemed satisfied by the response. 'Sorry about that, ladies,' he said, but not at all apologetically. 'But I see some of you were not afraid.'

'Of course some of us aren't!' Jessica snapped scornfully and advanced on Kane. 'And of course some folk are. Just what do you hope to prove by this ridiculous show of yours? I for one don't find it the slightest bit amusing.'

Kane smiled into her flashing blue eyes and held the mouse towards her. 'Would you like to hold him?'

Jessica put out her hands and took the mouse and cradled it close to her body.

Olivia shot a look at the Reverend to see if he was enjoying the floor show and was frustrated to see he was. 'Why don't you go home?' she uttered under her breath.

Kane moved to the table and took Jessica with him by placing a hand on her shoulder and ushering her along.

'My soldier friend's theory was that if a woman is not afraid of mice, then she is afraid of the creature I have in the box – or vice versa, of course.'

The young ladies and gentlemen all crowded round the table. Some leaned on it for a closer look while others stood back a little, warily. Kane suddenly took a tight grip on Jessica's shoulder, pulled her in close to him and held her fast.

She was about to protest strongly when he took the lid off the box. Everyone watched, hushed and mesmerised. Kane put his hand in slowly. Jessica tightened her lips and held her breath. Kane brought his hand back out, turned it over slowly, palm upwards, and opened his fingers.

Jessica froze in terror at what she saw. She didn't realise that most of those gathered round the table had recoiled and moved far away. She heard Kane speaking as though she was in a dream.

'So, if you're not afraid of a mouse, then perhaps you're afraid of a spider.'

'Take… take it away, Kane, please,' Olivia implored. 'It's really huge, it's… it's horrible.'

He still had Jessica held firmly. She tried to move but couldn't and felt trapped. And then she panicked. She dropped the mouse and it scuttled away causing confusion in the room. People jumped up on chairs, screaming, with the ladies holding up their gowns. But no one screamed as loud or as high-pitched as Jessica.

Kane let her go and she ran to the door with her hands held to her head. Then she stopped abruptly. She turned back, her face on fire, her body shaking and her long curls trembling. She glared at Kane as if she wanted him dead and personally hoped to perpetrate the act. He hurriedly put the spider back in the box. Jessica took heavy steps back to Kane who squared up for the confrontation. What he didn't expect was to see that she was crying.

'You are mad,' she got out between bared teeth. 'You are cruel, beastly, insensitive and… and… and…' She turned and ran out of the room.

Oliver and Kerensa, in night clothes, were coming down the stairs and saw Jessica racing off in the direction of the kitchen. Kerensa rushed after her while Oliver strode into the parlour.

He found people standing on or getting down off his furniture. Sebastian was sprawled out on the floor, Olivia and Cordelia were being comforted by Luke, the Reverend Lanyon was putting a lid on a box, and a shamefaced Kane stood deserted in the middle of the room.

Oliver could see it was obviously Kane who was to blame for the sudden scream that had reverberated throughout the Manor house.

He was angry to have the peace of his home disturbed, his daughter's party upset and one of her guests distressed. Some of the servants had come running and Kelynen pushed her head in under Oliver's arm.

'What's going on, Papa?' she asked, squinting in the candlelight.

'That's what I'm about to find out, Shelley,' he said gruffly. 'You go back to bed.'

'Oooh,' muttered Kelynen, disappointed.

Oliver didn't look behind him but knew Cherry would be there. 'Cherry, take Miss Shelley back to bed, please, and make sure she stays there.'

Kelynen's reluctance to be despatched was matched by her former nursemaid's reluctance to despatch her; Cherry, too, was dying to know what had happened.

From the corner of his eye, Oliver saw Ruth and Esther King fidgeting at the doorway's edge, and he could hear Beatrice shuffling up to them. 'The rest of you can retire too,' he ordered. 'I will deal with this.'

When all had gone quiet, his voice reached out towards his elder son. 'I take it I am to look to you for an explanation as to why there was all that screaming. Why Jessica has been rendered distraught and your sister's birthday celebrations have been brought to an unseemly halt.'

Kane hung his head as he told his father what had happened. It sounded stupid and childish told in the cold light of his father's disapproval.

'I'll talk to you in my study, now,' Oliver said coolly. He used the same tone on Timothy. 'I am surprised to find you a party to this childish prank, Reverend Lanyon.'

'Yes, well, I'll take this creature away to a secure place,' Timothy said, as shamefaced as Kane. He lifted the box up carefully. 'Please accept my apologies, Miss Olivia, Sir Oliver,' he added sincerely, and quickly left the room holding the box at arm's length.

Kane apologised to Olivia and the others and, scooping up the mouse which he'd spied by the table leg, he followed the humbled parson.

'Luke, get the party under way again,' Oliver said to the son who for once was not the perpetrator of the trouble. 'And get that,' he pointed angrily at Sebastian who was lying on his back and snoring loudly, 'out of the room.' To the other guests he smiled and said, 'Please enjoy the rest of the evening.'

'I had better go to Jessica, she was in a dreadful state,' Olivia said, and Cordelia made ready to go with her.

'You stay here, your mother is with her. I'm sure Jessica will be back in a little while.' Then Oliver left to give Kane a good dressing-down.

Ten minutes later Kane left his father's study in a dismal mood and made for the kitchens. He was pleased to hear conversation and laughter coming from the parlour; at least the party was back on form again. But what would Jessica say to him?

Jessica, clutching a glass of water, was sitting with Kerensa at the kitchen table.

'And what, may I ask, do you want?' Kerensa said sternly, but she took in the shadow of pain that had come back to lie under his large brown eyes, their startled expression heightened by his concern.

'I've come to apologise to Jessica... Could you leave us alone for a few minutes please, Mama?'

Oliver was outside the door waiting for Kerensa. 'How is she?'

Kerensa shook her head slowly, swirling its glossy red glory over her shoulders. 'She was frightened half to death. I can't understand how Kane could do such a thing. I thought he had more sense than to do something that amounted to little more than a very cruel trick. Most folk are scared of something and hundreds are scared of spiders. How could it have not crossed his mind that at least one person tonight would be terrified in the extreme of what must have been an enormous spider? I told him I won't have it in the house, tomorrow he must get rid of it.'

'He brought it back from the Caribbean. Apparently it's quite harmless. I'm afraid Kane's experiences abroad have clouded his better judgement, my love. I think this has taught him a lesson, but the sooner he gets that farm he wants so badly under way, the better. Then maybe he'll settle down. Is Jessica going back to the party?'

'Oh yes, nothing gets that young lady down for long. I've had a number of chats with her to see if I could influence her into being a little less volatile. But it's probably best to let folk be who they are. I reckon she'll put Kane in his place. She won't spare him.'

'Two lessons in one night,' Oliver laughed as they climbed the stairs arm in arm. 'I'm beginning to feel sorry for our son.'

Kerensa thought back a few minutes to Jessica's distress. Terribly embarrassed, the girl had wanted to go straight home but Kerensa had managed to talk her into staying the rest of the night as planned. She had pointed out that many of the men would have been just as frightened of such a large creature and she had no need to feel ashamed.

At the top of the stairs, as she surrendered to the pleas of Kelynen who had refused to be put back to bed and had waited for her parents to tell her what the commotion had been about, Kerensa was relieved that it hadn't taken long for Jessica's fighting spirit to come back. She didn't like to think about how angry Clem would be if she told him what had happened.

Downstairs, Jessica got up and faced Kane. Her face was pink and a little pinched and Kane wanted to take her in his arms and comfort her as he'd done in Trecath-en farmhouse. But her eyes were shining with hurt and fury.

She flung back her head defiantly. 'I'm all right, I shouldn't have made such a fuss.'

Kane put his hands out in a submissive gesture. 'I am sorry, Jessica. I had no idea that you'd be so scared. I really am sorry, I hope you'll forgive me.'

Jessica shivered at the awful memory of the spider spread out over his big hand. 'Sorry for terrifying me or making me look a stupid little fool?' she asked bitterly.

'For both, of course.'

''Tis a good job Philip went home early or he would have beaten you to a black and blue pulp for what you did,' Jessica said angrily.

'And I would have deserved it, although I believe Philip would know I would never deliberately do anything to harm you. I think you're more angry and upset because you believe I've made you look foolish, but I'm the one who's been made to look a fool. No one will think badly of you, Jessica.'

'Aye, I think that's a right and proper description of you,' she returned sharply.

Kane moved up close and looked down on her. He suddenly wanted to take hold of her head and shake it and make her curls bounce all over the place.

'Why don't you like me any more, Jessica? We were friends during our childhood days. Except for those moments you let me hold you at the farm when Kerris hurt your back, you haven't given me a single kind word since I came home to Cornwall.'

Jessica was unaware that she'd been hurt and felt resentful about Kane's earlier amusement when she'd hoped to receive a compliment from him. She had thought there was something special between them after the way he'd held her in the farmhouse. But she didn't want to be treated like a little girl again.

He wasn't prepared for her sudden wild reaction. 'We're not friends! We've never been friends. I've thought about it since I've grown up. You're a Pengarron, your father is Lord of the Manor and I'm just a working-class maid. And I don't want to hear any rubbish about your mother being born the same as me and coming from Trelynne Cove. She's a real lady deep down, your father's a baronet and you're a gentleman and we Trenchards don't really mean anything to you. And one reason I dislike you as much as your stiff-nosed bullying brother is because you're not your own man, Kane Pengarron, you're Luke's yes-man, his lackey.'

Kane was deeply hurt. 'Well, I haven't noticed you scowling at Luke tonight. And I'll have you know that my real father was a violent sailor and my mother a prostitute, Jessica Trenchard. That means I come from a lower background than you do and don't you dare ever throw that kind of talk at me again! And if I'm obliging to Luke maybe it's because I feel guilty and responsible for the injury to his arm that stopped him having the army career he had his heart set on.' He was quaking with anger now and it was Jessica's turn to feel guilty.

'Kane, I...'

'I hope you enjoy the rest of the party. I'll make my excuses to Olivia so I won't be there to ruin it for you.' His voice had gone quiet and his hand went to his side and gripped it as if he was in pain.

'What is it? Are you hurt there?'

'It's nothing,' Kane said shortly and turned to go, but Jessica grabbed his arm and turned him back. He saw her then for the first time as the other men had seen her tonight. Not as a little tomboyish girl, but as a vibrant young woman, her costume accentuating her fully feminine figure.

There was a feeling of expectancy in the air between them. Kane gave Jessica an intense look. Her blue eyes widened. He seemed to be about to move towards her then he changed his mind.

'I'll take you back to the party,' he said moodily.

'No, thank you,' Jessica said coldly. 'I don't want you near me. I don't trust you not to have another beastly creature about you.'

–

In the small hours, Jessica, Olivia and Cordelia sat on Olivia's bed amidst the finery of their discarded costumes.

'Are you pleased with the night, Livvy?' Cordelia asked, not bothering to stifle a small yawn. 'I think it's the best party I've ever been to.'

Olivia looked out of the window and smiled at the round silver globe she saw high in the sky. 'You might say I'm over the moon about it. I wished the night could have gone on for ever.'

Cordelia tapped Olivia's arm and drew her attention to Jessica's sullen face.

'You're quiet, Jessie. Are you still upset over the spider?' Olivia asked gently.

Jessica glanced up as if her thoughts had been far away. 'I'm fine. It was a wonderful party, Livvy. Thank you for inviting me, I'll never forget it.'

'Kane was truly sorry about the way he frightened you. He seemed to have suffered more than you did in the end, he went very quiet and left shortly afterwards.'

Jessica tightened her features and refused to say anything that intimated she had forgiven Kane. She felt at that moment that she never would. Her heart had turned over at the deep look he had given her in the kitchen. But he hadn't told her she was beautiful like his brother had. Of course he wasn't for her. She had been right. He was reared a gentleman and would look to his own class for a wife. He would never be interested in a country maid, a tomboy he had grown up with as a playmate. Not that she cared. Let Kane Pengarron obtain his piece of land, and no doubt it would be a very large piece; he would never be anything but a gentleman farmer. She wasn't the least bit interested in him!

'I overheard an interesting piece of conversation while I was hovering around the gentlemen tonight,' Cordelia announced, trying to sound mysterious.

'Out with it, little cousin,' Olivia said, laughing and poking her in the side. 'You know you're no good at keeping secrets.'

'They're planning a smuggling run.'

'Who are?' Olivia demanded.

'Luke of course. Kane's going to be in on it and your brother Philip, Jessie.'

'Philip's doing what?' Jessica said stupidly. She hadn't been listening.

'He's planning a smuggling run with Luke and Kane and some of the other young men. Philip's going to contact a sailor he knows who will be able to help them,' Cordelia explained.

'So what? We could do that just as easily as them,' Jessica said haughtily.

'You aren't serious, Jessie?' the other two young women asked together. 'Are you?'

Chapter 8

Catherine Lanyon pulled up her pony at Trecath-en Farm and looked about for a suitable place to dismount. She knew the farmyard wouldn't be too mucky or offensive on a dry summer's day but her concern wasn't for her short riding boots but rather that she wouldn't prove a nuisance to the comings and goings of the Trenchard family. She walked the pony to the barn, slid down gracefully and hitched the reins to a nail.

She wandered about the yard looking for someone to greet, taking pleasure in the sights she saw. Mottled grey ducks bobbing on a pond and others dozing at the edge. White goats munching on anything in their paths, tethered on long ropes to apple trees laden with ripening fruit. A solitary old hawthorn tree where at one end a washing line was tied. Six white pigs sleeping in a sty and fowls hunting for food in the yard. A large hay barn, outbuildings and furze ricks. And Jessica's conical-shaped hen houses. Cow parsley, stinging nettles and pink campion were springing up everywhere and cuckoo spit was dotted on a large variety of wild plants. In a little garden patch on the sunny side of the house were beautiful cabbage roses with purple-pink heads. She was disappointed there were no dogs about to indicate that the owner was at home.

Seeing no one in the yard, Catherine made for the front door of the whitewashed farmhouse and knocked on it in what she hoped would pass for a casual manner. She expected Jessica to come and answer it, or perhaps the woman the Trenchards had taken in. She presumed she had been seen looking around the yard and someone would quickly answer the door but she stood there for several minutes and nothing happened.

'Oh dear,' she murmured, 'it seems I've made a wasted journey.'

She was about to go when she decided to pluck up courage and try the door. The latch lifted easily and she stepped inside into a cool, square hallway. There were four doors leading off it. One to the parlour, one to Kenver Trenchard's little bedroom-cum-workshop, one to a lean-to built on to the side of the farmhouse, the last presumably to the kitchen from where there would be access to the staircase that sloped above her head. Stretching out a hand, Catherine breathed in and gingerly opened the kitchen door.

Her hopes lifted as she heard someone moving about inside.

'Hello,' she called out cautiously. 'Is that you, Jessica? May I come in?'

She moved through the doorway and there he was, the person she had come here really hoping to see. And to her horror and embarrassment Clem was standing in just his breeches, washing his deeply tanned muscular torso over a tin bowl.

'Oh! Mr Trenchard!'

He stood, broad-shouldered, the rest of him lean, his long blond hair hanging loose, looking at her in surprise from those clear blue eyes of his and Catherine thought her heart would stop. His three dogs sprang up from their various positions on the stone-flagged floor and Clem commanded them to lie back down.

'I… I did knock.' Catherine hastily explained her intrusion, getting flustered and retreating behind the door. 'I… I'm sorry to have caught you… at… at…'

Clem said blandly, 'I won't be a moment.'

He carried on with his ablutions, taking his time. Then throwing the water away down the stone sink, he pulled a clean shirt on over his head, slowly tied back his hair and looked calmly at the door where Catherine's white-gloved fingers could be seen gripping the frame.

She cried out when he roughly pulled the door open and she was almost swung against him. Clem had done this on purpose. He was certain she had come chasing after him and he didn't like it. He was going to do nothing at all to make her feel comfortable. But then he heard Kerensa's voice ringing in his head the day they had gone into the Parsonage and he remembered he owed this woman his gratitude for dressing his hand after the dog bite and an apology for not giving it to her there and then.

'Come in,' he said gruffly. He'd been about to move aside and let her step inside the kitchen, but then he remembered her station in life and ushered her into the parlour.

'I hope I'm not intruding…'

He didn't reply. Catherine looked around feeling quite bewildered. This was dreadful. Although hoping to see Clem here today was her main motive, she had also called on an errand of genuine Christian concern, but his manner didn't invite explanations. It seemed he was as sulky as his reputation suggested; his moodiness was said to have seen off many a husband-hunter. Catherine realised that was precisely what she was herself and that it must be obvious to him. She felt sick.

What did she have to offer him that the beautiful Lady Pengarron did not have anyway? How could she possibly have imagined he would ever find her attractive and see her as a replacement for the wife he had also loved. It was all so horrible. She had made a fool of herself at this early stage and she desperately wanted to leave.

'Tea, coffee or a cold drink?' Clem said, over her head.

'I beg your pardon?' She hadn't realised he was so close behind her and she started forward a few paces, then tried to look natural when she turned round to him.

'You must be thirsty after a dusty ride on a hot day. Can I get you some tea, coffee or a cold drink?' he repeated.

Catherine wasn't sure if she should accept or just go and get away quickly. 'Well, I… don't want to put you to any trouble.'

'I've just come in from a hard morning's work clearing a leat, tilling flatpole cabbages and drawing new potatoes. I was about to have a drink of wild mint cordial. You're welcome to join me, 'tis no bother.'

'Yes, that would be very nice. Thank you, Mr Trenchard. I've really come about—'

But he was gone.

Catherine looked about the room. It was very small, no more than eight feet square. There were several touches that could only be a woman's but she couldn't tell whether they were Clem's late wife's, Jessica's, or perhaps one of the earlier Trenchard womenfolk. Little paste figurines stood in a small glass-less cabinet, an embroidered firescreen depicted a floral design, the chairbacks on the sofa and two wooden chairs were crocheted, and lace samplers were scattered over the walls and a little square table.

'Sit down,' Clem instructed her when he came back holding two dripping glasses of green liquid. He wasn't bothering to show any niceties. Catherine wondered if he was doing it deliberately and if he would have served the drinks on a tray if she wasn't the visitor.

When she was seated on the coarse, lumpy sofa, instead of putting the glass down on the table close to her as she'd expected, Clem thrust it into her hand. She thanked him quietly and sipped to cover her discomfiture.

'It's very nice,' she said.

'My sister makes it. Beatrice, the old woman at the Manor house, taught her. Jessica's not interested in learning how to make things with herbs.'

Clem kept on his feet and bolted half the contents of his glass straight down. Catherine felt he wanted to gasp vulgarly and say loudly, 'Ah, that's better!' But he just eyed her in what she thought was unfriendliness. She made up her mind to leave as quickly as she could.

'Where is Jessica, Mr Trenchard?'

'Out walking with Kerris. She's trying to get Kerris used to being away from the farmyard.'

'Actually, it was Kerris, the young woman your daughter stumbled across and in your charity you've given a home to that I came—'

'You'll have to excuse me, Miss Lanyon. I can hear my brother moving about after his nap, he'll need some immediate attention. I won't be gone long.' He turned at the door and added casually, 'Call me Clem.'

Catherine was taken aback and she knew that he knew that she was debating whether to ask him to call her by her first name too.

Instead she asked, 'Is there anything I can do to help?'

'Nothing a lady would like to do,' he replied and looked at her with a deepness that made her blush.

Catherine paced the floor while she was kept waiting again, muttering to herself over and over again, 'This is awful, what on earth made me come here like this?'

She had first thought of riding over to the farm at the beginning of the month. June was the month when hope flourished, when the long-awaited summer had arrived at last, when one could reach out and feel one could climb the highest mountain peak. Catherine had fixed her sights hopefully on the handsome farmer, although it had taken until the last day of the month to pluck up the courage to ride over to his farm. She should have remembered that while the hedges were bursting with greenery, weeds grew in strength and number in June.

'I owe you an apology, Miss Lanyon,' Clem said suddenly from behind her.

She hadn't heard him coining back and lurched forward. 'Must you keep creeping up on me?' she asked despairingly.

'It seems I owe you two then,' he said coolly. 'I forgot to say thank you for treating my hand the day I was bitten by a dog. You have my thanks and full apologies.'

'I accept both,' Catherine said hastily. 'Now I want to get to the reason for my being here today. It's about Kerris. I thought I might be able to do something for her. Jessica is very young, just eighteen years old, I understand. I thought perhaps an older woman might be of some service—'

'There's my sister for that sort of thing.' Clem interrupted her yet again.

Catherine blushed to the roots of her hair. Her offer of help was clearly unwelcome here. Was there no end to the fool she would make of herself today? Apart from that, what was the matter with this family? Didn't they care where Kerris came from, that she might have a family somewhere, a husband, children, who were worried about her? And this man, this tall blond creature she'd thought she'd taken a fancy to, was being more difficult than she understood Sir Oliver Pengarron could be.

'Yes, of course, Mrs Renfree, I quite forgot about her,' Catherine got out, hiding her hurt. 'Well, I really must not take up any more of your time. Good day to you, Mr Trenchard. Thank you for the cordial.'

Clem stood aside to let her pass. Catherine ran to the front door and out into the dusty farmyard, but stopped as she saw a group of people coming towards the house.

David, Philip, Jessica, and a short, slightly built woman who must be the mysterious Kerris, who was trying to keep away from the brawny twins, were coming home for their midday meal. With them was the one-time rover known as Ricketty Jim.

Jessica was indulging in horseplay with her brothers. Philip and David were tossing her between them, her skirts flying up to reveal her long legs. She pulled at their hair and pretended to struggle then Philip lifted her clean above his head with outstretched arms. Jessica laughed until she cried and then she was dumped down on her feet again. It was only then that she and those with her saw the farm's unexpected visitor.

Kerris stared, goggle-eyed, at Catherine for a moment then made a rapid beeline for the kitchen door. Philip and David and Ricketty Jim, who swept off his ancient battered hat, bowed their heads in unison and stood still. Jessica had seen Miss Catherine Lanyon from a distance before and recognised her at once. Stifling a giggle, she went straight towards her.

Clem advanced on Jessica before she could reach Catherine. He had been mortified that this genteel lady should witness his daughter's wild behaviour. Catherine surveyed Jessica with a cool eye.

'This is my daughter Jessica, Miss Lanyon,' Clem said sternly, before Jessica could speak.

There was no 'Pleased to meet you' or 'How do you do, Miss Lanyon' from Jessica. She took in Catherine's fine clothes, then said, 'Did you want to see me?' and Clem realised with a lump in his throat just how unruly and unladylike his daughter was.

'I'm pleased to meet you, Jessica,' Catherine said, and her voice held a deliberate tone to show the difference in their stations. 'Your father will explain why I called. I must be going now. I'll bid you all a good day.'

Clem crossly ordered Jessica into the house, then watched the parson's refined sister ride out of the yard on her thoroughbred pony with his gut in knots. He was ashamed of himself for allowing Jessica to become so out of hand in the two years since Alice had died; Alice would not have approved. Rosie's words came back to haunt him: 'If the girl needs a mother then it's up to you to provide her with one.'

Since Clem had lost Kerensa many years ago, the family he'd had by his subsequent marriage was all he had; he loved them desperately and would do anything for them. If it meant that he had to marry again to provide Jessica with a mother to stop her from disgracing herself and preventing an eventual good marriage, then he would do it. Somehow he had to see Miss Catherine Lanyon again and repair all today's damage.

–

While Catherine was on her fool's errand at Trecath-en Farm, Olivia Pengarron had arrived at the Parsonage. She was shown into the parlour by Nancy Wills and was disappointed to be told that Miss Catherine was abroad on charitable business.

'Do you think she will be away for much longer, Nancy?' Olivia enquired.

'Longer? 'Tis hard to say, Miss Olivia. She didn't say where she was going today and she's been gone a good while, but if she can stay and help the folk she's visiting, she'll do just that. She liaises, that's what she calls it, with your dear mother, Lady Pengarron. They call on as many folk as they can during a week, then they get together to talk over what's happened. I daresay her ladyship could have told you where Miss Catherine is likely to be today.'

'In that case I think I'll take my leave and call on Miss Catherine some other time. You can tell her, Nancy, that the purpose of my visit was to thank her for the lovely birthday gift she made for me.'

'I'll do that, Miss Olivia. She'll be some sorry to have missed you. The Reverend Timothy is in his study. Would you like a word with him before you go? He'd be happy to see you, I know.'

'No, I think I will go now, Nancy.'

The Reverend Lanyon was the last person on earth Olivia wanted to see. But before she could reach the door he barged his way through it. He wore no coat and his shirt was opened at the throat, a state of informal dress that Olivia considered highly improper in a parson. His grey eyes were not on her or even on Nancy; he was looking about the chairs for something.

'Ah, Nancy,' he grunted absentmindedly, 'why didn't you tell me we have a visitor… Oh, it's you, Miss Pengarron.'

'I called to see Miss Catherine but as she is not at home I was just leaving,' Olivia said haughtily, stung by his bad manners.

'Good, good,' Timothy said, rubbing his square chin with his fingers.

Olivia's fury was growing steadily. He had given her no formal greeting and seemed to have forgotten her presence already. It was time this young parson was put in his place.

'I think I will have a word with the Reverend after all, Nancy,' she said in a superior voice. 'It's confidential…'

'Confidential. Well, I'll just go and tend to my linen cupboard then,' Nancy said, withdrawing. It went without speaking that the parson would grant an immediate interview with the daughter of the Lord of the Manor.

'Some spiritual matter, is it?' Timothy asked, still scouring about the room. 'I'm looking for a little black notebook. I left it somewhere. Can't seem to lay my hand on it this morning. It's got one or two important things written down in it.'

'Never mind your notebook! I demand your immediate attention. Now!'

'My dear Miss Pengarron,' and Timothy was suddenly standing to attention, his face full of concern, 'is there something wrong?'

'Yes! With you!' Olivia snapped, putting her hands on her hips in just the way that Oliver did.

'With me?' Timothy pointed to his chest. 'I don't understand.'

Olivia flung up her chin and her eyes blazed. 'You, Timothy Lanyon, are the rudest, most ill-mannered, inconsiderate, bumptious man I have ever had the misfortune to meet! Why my father chose you to take over the parish after the kindly Reverend Joseph Ivey is beyond my comprehension!'

Timothy was stunned. 'What have I done to upset you?'

'Simply by just being you,' Olivia replied, stabbing a finger at him.

'You are a sparky little madam, aren't you?' Timothy said, his humorous eyes twinkling.

'I'm a what? How dare you! Have you no respect for who I am? Who my father is?'

'Yes. Yes. Well, go on, I'm still puzzled over your chagrin with me.'

'Oh, I give up…' Olivia sounded as if she was suddenly out of puff. She stormed to the door, changed her mind, stuck her hands on her hips again and leaned forward. 'Don't you realise that you haven't got even the simplest of manners? That you have no idea how to behave in society, no idea how to address a lady?'

'I treat all people the same,' Timothy said evenly, and in retaliation bent towards her.

'No, you don't. You speak to most men like they're your old friends but you are rude to every woman who has the misfortune to meet you. You've even been disrespectful to my mother on occasions. I don't know how Nancy and Miss Catherine put up with you!'

'I'll have you know that they're perfectly happy with me and I've never been aware of harming your dear mother's sensitivity even once. Sir Oliver was happy to choose me as incumbent for this parish after interviewing me and knowing full well of my character.' Timothy was waving his arms all about. 'I consider myself no better or worse than anybody else, and neither are you, Miss Olivia Pengarron, even though you are a daughter of privilege. You can take me or leave me.'

'Then I'll leave you! And I'll never set foot in this house again while you reside here. In my opinion you have no right to be here, you're nothing like a real parson should be!'

'Oh, am I not?' Timothy sounded much amused and stretching out one long arm he pulled Olivia towards him and before she could exclaim he used the other to twiddle with one of the drop-pearl earrings she was wearing. He let her go and with a scream of rage she slapped his face. The noise resounded around the room.

'I could have you horsewhipped for that!' Olivia hissed. 'How dare you touch me! You're utterly despicable!' Then she angrily wiped at the pearl to remove his tainting.

'I'm an ordinary mortal man, as capable of having my face slapped as any other man,' Timothy said in a stern voice.

'An ordinary man?' Olivia felt she had no energy left and slumped down in a chair. 'There's nothing ordinary about you. I don't understand you at all.'

Timothy sat down too, on the edge of a chair, and leaned over with his arms resting on his knees. He was quiet and thoughtful for a moment, then said, 'Sometimes I don't understand myself. You're correct about me being despicable, Miss Pengarron. I believe no man has the right to force himself in any way upon a woman, and yet it's something I've just done to you… I don't know why I did it. I'm sorry, believe me. I couldn't help myself, you looked so beautiful, all on fire and beautiful.'

He became silent and as Olivia did not want to speak, the only noise for several long moments was the heavy tick-tock from a huge mantelpiece clock.

'Miss Pengarron, if you demand it, I will leave the parish after what I did to you. After all, as you pointed out, you are the daughter of the Lord of the Manor. I couldn't go on here if I lost your father's respect, although he'll probably leap on his horse and ride here at speed to break my neck anyway when you tell him what I have done.'

'I shall not tell my father and you don't have to leave, Reverend Lanyon,' Olivia said, enjoying herself now she had gained the upper hand. 'But you would do well to learn some manners and how to show respect to those to whom it is due. I suggest you ask your sister for advice. She is a perfect lady and would know how to make you something of a gentleman.'

Timothy suddenly grinned. It threw Olivia for a moment and she thought she had lost her ground already. 'What is it?' she demanded.

'I've never had a lady throw her fury at me before. It was rather appealing and you did provoke me.'

'Oh, that's typical of you, Timothy Lanyon. You're a thoroughly bigoted male where women are concerned.' Olivia sprang to her feet. 'I abhor the way you look upon us.'

'Particularly you?' Timothy asked quietly.

'Are you suggesting I'm only angry with you because of the way you treat me?'

Timothy stood up and looked straight into Olivia's green eyes. 'Yes, I am.'

'Oh, you're impossible! I can't stand another moment in your company. Good day to you, Mr Lanyon.'

Olivia left, slamming doors behind her. Nancy Wills came down the stairs carrying an armful of kitchen linen. She eyed her employer carefully as he stood at the parlour window gazing out at Olivia's retreating slender figure.

'Now what have you done?' she asked.

'How do you know it's my fault?' Timothy demanded as Olivia flounced round the corner of the ivy-clad Parsonage to the stables at the rear.

'It's always your fault,' Nancy replied. 'What did you say to upset Miss Olivia?'

'It seems that everything I say upsets the dear young lady.'

'Humph,' snorted Nancy, heading out of the room.

Olivia waited impatiently for the stable hand to get her pony ready. He looked at her flushed, angry face curiously and she turned her back on him. At that moment no man was worth the little piece of ground he stood on. She rode the lanes back to the Manor and swore that if anyone again mentioned she should be seriously thinking of a future husband she would blast them with her tongue to the point where they would never dare to broach the subject again. She would make straight for her painting room at the top of the house, engross herself in her art and never, never think about men, particularly a certain young parson, again.

Kane was enjoying a leisurely ride around the parish with the woman he would never be rude to, the mother whom he adored. They looked over the charity school Oliver and Luke had set up first. It was a small, square granite building on the top of the hill that dipped down into the little fishing village of Perranbarvah. Kane was impressed with it. It was light and well equipped, where pupils aged between seven and eleven attended to learn their elementary lessons and some moral teaching. Anything up to fifty children came each weekday, children from the village and the new Roscawen tin mine, estate workers' and tenants' children. It was part of the parson's duties to hold prayers and teach in it, backed up by the scholarly Matthias Renfree whose help was welcome as long as he steered clear of Methodist ideas. Catherine, Cordelia, Olivia and Luke helped with the supervision in varying degrees.

Kane and Kerensa listened in on one of the classes and Kane played a rough game of leapfrog with the children, which delighted them. Afterwards he and Kerensa went down to the village and walked up and down Perranbarvah's little beach, talking to the fisherfolk and joining Elizabeth King, Matthew's mother, for a dish of tea. From there they rode to the Roscawen mine, whose community bene-fited from regular food and milk supplied by the Blakes, a tradition Peter Blake had started after marrying his bal-maiden wife. Kane was pleased to see so many of the same families there whom he had known since childhood. Finally they rode to the oak plantation that sheltered the Manor house and dismounted in a sunny clearing, sitting on the dry green grass on the bank of the river that ran through the woods.

'Are you glad to be back home, my dear?' Kerensa said, letting a hand drift in the waters of the river.

'I certainly am, as glad as you are to have me back,' Kane grinned.

'I like to have all my family around me.'

Kane was thoughtful for a moment. 'Joseph would be toddling about all over the place now, keeping you happy.'

'Yes, I still miss him so very much. What about you, Kane? Are you really happy?'

'I'm a bit unsettled at the moment but I haven't left a lost love behind me if that's what you're thinking, Mama.'

'But sad memories, I think.'

'You know me better than anyone else,' he smiled. 'Something happened that made me see the sordid side of life. It's nothing for a lady's ears and I want to put it all behind me now.'

'I hope we see no more of your thoughtless pranks,' Kerensa laughed fondly. 'What did you do with that spider, by the way? I've not asked before because I've been dreading the answer.'

'I gave it to an acquaintance of mine who's interested in entomology. He collects specimens of all kinds.'

'Where does he live?'

'Live? At Launceston, why?'

Kerensa laughed with dry humour. 'Just making sure the creature is a long way away. You must have seen some changes at home since you went away.'

Kane rolled over on his back, clasping his hands underneath his neck. 'Well, everyone is two years older to begin with. Only Beatrice seems not to have changed. Do you know, I believe she'll live for ever. She'll be living at the Manor coughing gin-laden breath over the next Pengarron generation and the next.'

'I hope so. Life at home would be strange without her, and Jack. They were the first two people I met when I began my new life as your father's wife.'

'Jack's not changed either. But the Wheal Ember mine has closed down. Luke and I often played around that area when we were boys. And now there's the Roscawen mine set up not too far away. I'm glad of that, it would have been a shame to have seen the mining community broken up and folk going round the county looking for work. I hope they get many years' work out of it. And Adam Renfree finally drank himself to death while I was away and Matthias is our farm steward in his place. It will give him and Rosie a good future.'

'Now you're home, I wonder what the future will bring for us all.'

'Only time will tell.' Kane rolled over on his front and tossed leaves and sticks into the flowing sparkling water. As he watched them being tossed over the stony base of the river and swishing through the clear water, he wondered about his past.

Chapter 9

The start of the day was much the same as any other market day for Philip Trenchard. He took a fattened pig to be sold, left his father's horse at the farrier's to be re-shod, looked over the animal pens and won a wrestling match against a miner from the Roscawen mine. He won two guineas on bets he made on the following match and emptied five tankards of strong ale in a grog shop. Following that he spent a furtive few minutes at the darkened end of an alley with a kitchen maid employed at the Blakes' house, then kept a longer assignation with a woman of higher social standing in the grander surroundings of her large house while her husband was away on business in London. He was paid five guineas for his expertise in that field, and all his earnings would be saved towards the plans he had to improve the farm.

Then, feeling full and satisfied, he made his way to Painted Bessie's clifftop kiddleywink up on Lancavel Downs. He was there to make plans that would enable him to make more money. Before he went inside the ramshackle alehouse, whose main ware consisted of smuggled spirits, he glanced behind and caught sight of a headful of blonde curls. Why was Jessica following his every move this morning?

'What can I get 'ee, boy?' Painted Bessie, an over-made-up hag, hailed him as he looked about the smoke-laden rough interior.

Philip threw some pennies on a scratched table top. 'A clean tankard of ale,' he replied gruffly.

He lit his pipe and his demeanour made clear his wish to remain alone and mind his own business. Philip had been here a few times before but it was a place he disliked. The smell of stale alcohol and unwashed bodies filled every nook of the room and most of the other customers looked unfriendly. He didn't want to sit in this place for long, swilling back the bitter, unpalatable ale. He would give the man he was here to meet no longer than it took him to sup his tankard dry before he left.

The door opened and the miner he'd beaten at wrestling, now the worse for drink, lurched in. He made for Philip's table but a scowl saw him off. Five minutes passed, the pipe had gone out, the tankard was empty and Philip rose to leave.

'Can't I get 'ee anythin' else?' Painted Bessie called to him.

'I'm off,' Philip told her.

'How about a little entertainment then?' and Painted Bessie thumbed at a thin girl still in childhood who smiled wantonly at him.

Philip's answer was to spit on the floor and Painted Bessie's reaction was to cuff the unfortunate girl around the face.

The battered door was opened again and the man Philip had been waiting to see came in. Philip had had enough of the place and muttered, 'We'll talk outside,' to the newcomer.

The other man was a cool-eyed sailor of medium build in his mid-thirties. His clothes were rough but tidy and he smelled clean. He had a friendly air about him but Philip thought there was something hidden in the smile he gave.

'I take it you're Philip Trenchard, been asking about doing a bit of free-trading. I'm Zack Maynard.'

'Can you help me?' Philip said, sounding neither impressed nor particularly interested.

'Aye, perhaps. Got a good landing spot?'

'Aye, got more than one. I'll be working with the sons of the Lord of the Manor hereabouts. It'll be on their land.'

'Glad to hear you've got some organisation under way already. Can't be doing with anyone who doesn't know what he's about. The Lord of the Manor? That'll be Sir Oliver Pengarron. He's been running bootleg for years. How come you and his sons don't want to work with him then?'

Philip looked round the sailor to see if Jessica was anywhere about.

'You expecting someone else?' Zack Maynard asked suspiciously.

'No. We want to make our own money,' Philip replied to the earlier question. 'We're well acquainted with how Sir Oliver's runs are operated. We want the same terms.'

'You're asking too much.'

'We're no fools, Maynard. You don't need to worry about the Revenue men, we'll be bribing the same officials as Sir Oliver.'

'Know about it, will he, Sir Oliver?'

'No, there's no reason for him to. Have we a deal?'

'Mayhap – if you think you're as good at free-trading as you are at wrestling.'

'I was brought up on it, 'tis second nature to farming.'

Zack Maynard gave a small thoughtful nod. 'I'll start you off on a small run. I'll get the details to you in a few days.'

Philip allowed Zack Maynard enough time to leave the cliffs behind before following the same path. He peered all around but there was no sign of his curious sister. What was Jessica up to now? Was she concerned for his moral welfare and had followed him to see if he was meeting another wench? Was she worried he was imbibing too much ale? Philip wished Jessica was like other young women, content to stay dutifully at home to serve her family until a suitable man asked for her in marriage. Clem had mumbled something most odd recently, about getting married again himself for Jessica's sake. Philip had thought it ridiculous at the time but decided now that perhaps it wasn't such a bad idea.

It was mid-afternoon when he arrived home on Clem's newly shod horse. Kerris was out in the yard drawing water from the well. She took one look at him, dropped the pail heavily on the ground and ran inside.

'Jessica's not home yet then,' Philip murmured to himself, knowing that if his errant sister had come home, Kerris would not have been so afraid of him. He dismissed the women of Trecath-en Farm from his thoughts and focused his mind elsewhere. He stabled the mare then moved off to join Clem, David and Ricketty Jim in the fields.

Kerris rushed into the kitchen, stood with her back to the door and pushed her knuckles into her mouth. She was shaking all over and tears were filling her eyes. 'Jessica, where are you?' she moaned.

Jessica had asked Kerris the day before if she was feeling more secure. Not wanting to upset her only comforter and risk being seen as a nuisance, Kerris had said she was and agreed she wouldn't mind being left for longer periods at a time. Jessica had taken Kerris at her word and today she was spending a much longer time selling the butter, eggs, cheese, and her Uncle Kenver's smaller pieces of craftwork at the market.

A rumbling sound was coming towards the kitchen from the hallway and Kerris flew to the table and sat down. Kenver Trenchard was wheeling himself in the special chair he had made towards her and she didn't want him to see her in a panic. She was fairly comfortable in Kenver's presence. He spoke kindly to her and didn't tower over her like the other Trenchard menfolk.

Kenver, however, could easily tell she was in distress again. 'What's the matter, Kerris?' he asked softly when he was through the doorway. 'Are you feeling tired again? Why don't you go and lie down for a little while?'

'I… I'm not tired,' she said, in a voice so small that Kenver inclined his head to listen to her.

It hadn't taken the family long to realise that Kerris had worked before as a servant. She was happier when kept busy. 'Would you mind pouring me a dish of tea, please?' he said kindly.

Kerris poured out black tea from the never-empty giant teapot on the brick oven, glancing over her shoulder every few moments as if she feared Kenver might get up out of his chair and creep up behind her. She put his tea on the table next to him.

Kenver picked it up. 'Jessica not home yet?'

Kerris shook her head.

'She's beginning to put upon you, leaving you to do more and more of the work.'

'I don't mind,' Kerris said quickly.

'I thought I heard you cry out last night.'

'I'm not sleeping all the time now… I'm getting nightmares.'

'That's a shame, but it could mean your mind is beginning to unravel itself,' Kenver said carefully. 'You might remember soon who you really are.'

'No! I don't want to!' Kerris cried out, tears starting from her eyes. 'Oh, God, I'm so frightened. I feel safe here but I'm afraid you might make me leave.'

'Don't be frightened, Kerris. No one's ever going to make you leave. You belong here with the rest of us at Trecath-en now.'

'But what if it's found out I've done something terrible? You'll want me to leave then,' Kerris wailed, her voice rising.

'You're not capable of that, Kerris. 'Tis the other way round. Someone's done something terrible to you. Listen to me, you've no need to be afraid. I think you feel you can trust me a little, so why don't you come over here and talk to me? I promise you I won't move, and anyway I'm more helpless than you are.'

Kerris blinked and tears spilled onto her dress. She held her arms stiffly to her sides with her fists clenched, sniffing and blinking. She felt she could trust this quiet, compassionate man. She took one hesitant step towards him.

'That's it,' he encouraged her. 'Just a little more.'

Her pale grey eyes were huge and shining in her square face when she reached him. Kenver put out a hand then pulled it back to show he was no threat to her. 'We'll always take care of you. I'll always take care of you. You've got nothing to worry about any more.'

'Are you sure?' She wiped more tears away with trembling hands.

'More than that, Kerris, I promise you.'

She knelt down beside him and let Kenver hold her hands.

–

Jessica waited until Zack Maynard was back in Marazion before she attempted to speak to him. She followed him nearly all the way down the one long street and hid behind Matthew King's bulk, whom she met coming the other way, when the sailor stopped at the entrance to a gin shop.

'I hear Philip won a good match against a tinner this forenoon,' Matthew said, full of interest, as Jessica peered round his massive girth. He moved to give her the better view he thought she desired but she ducked back in front of him.

'So I was told,' Jessica replied, standing on tiptoe and trying to see over Matthew's shoulder. 'I missed it. I was busy selling Uncle Kenver's craftwork.' She went a soft pink at the lie. She had guessed that it was while he was in Marazion today that her brother would most likely meet his contact to arrange a smuggling run. She had covertly watched him wrestle so she could follow him afterwards undetected.

'He'll beat me one of these days, your brother, and I'll be pleased 'twill be he and no other. The boy deserves it.'

'Aye,' Jessica said, not listening. She was more interested in the fact that she now spied Matthew's younger brother, Paul, talking to Zack Maynard.

Matthew was puzzled by Jessica's bobbing behaviour. When he turned round, he saw only his brother. Paul King walked quickly towards them. Jessica made a face and Matthew misconstrued her interest. 'Want me to disappear, do 'ee, Jessie?'

'What? Don't be silly, it wasn't Paul I was trying to see!' Jessica replied impatiently, then ran off past Paul without speaking to him.

'What's the matter with her then?' Paul jerked his head backwards.

Matthew rubbed his bristly beard under a giant palm. 'Dunno, boy, but who can catch the wind in their hand?'

Jessica muttered a mild oath. Zack Maynard had disappeared and she had no idea where. She ran up and down the alleys that divided the shops and houses, screamed abuse at a group of scruffy sailors who crudely propositioned her, glanced in all the gin shops and alehouses. Finally she flopped against a water butt outside the back of a house in an alleyway and twisted her face in extreme irritation.

A prickle of fear from out of nowhere crept up her neck. She couldn't hear anyone moving about but she knew someone was there, at the side of the water butt, just behind her. She held her breath and slowly turned her head. Icicles climbed up her spine. She knew it was Zack Maynard and she had a horrible fancy that he was holding a large, sharp knife and would not think twice about plunging it into her heart.

Zack Maynard moved silently and met her full on. There was no sign of a knife and he looked pleased to see her. ''Tisn't every day I get pursued by a lovely young maid. What can I do for you then? Did your brother forget to tell me something? But somehow I don't take you for his messenger.'

Jessica opened her mouth in shock.

'You look so much like Philip Trenchard, who else could you be?' he explained.

Jessica straightened her body and stared at him for a moment defiantly. 'If you knew I was following you, why didn't you speak to me before?'

'If anyone wants to talk to me, I do it on my own terms. What do you want?'

'I want to arrange a smuggling run with you.'

Jessica had expected at first to have to get past his scathing mockery, then probably to be given a blunt refusal to talk further. But Zack Maynard surveyed her calmly from an agreeable countenance.

'What sort of deal are you offering?'

'You don't mind considering working with a woman then?' Jessica asked.

'You're just a girl, Miss Trenchard,' Zack Maynard said, with the first trace of condescension. 'But I do business with anyone who can offer the right conditions to line my pockets.'

'I can't take in as much goods as my brother and I'm interested in smaller, lighter items. My friends aren't up to carrying half-ankers of brandy and rum up the cliffs. But the goods, although different, could be of a higher value and I've got the same landing places as my brother.'

'Own your own pieces of coastline, do you?'

'Of course I don't,' Jessica answered acidly, 'but—'

'But the Pengarron young lady has access to her father's,' Zack said, raising his eyebrows and looking at Jessica with male amusement. He met her stinging glare with the remark, 'I haven't kept several jumps ahead of the law over the years by being stupid, Jessica Trenchard.'

'Know all about me, do you then?'

'When I heard your brother wanted to approach me I made it my business to find out all about him. But I already knew your name. I've watched your brother wrestle. I've seen you watching him. You stand out in the crowd with all that golden hair falling down your back.'

'And you asked someone my name?'

'No, I listened in on others' talk to find out who you were.'

'Why?'

'I like beautiful things. I like to collect beautiful things.'

Jessica instinctively stepped back.

He regarded her with a naked eye. 'I shan't be mixing business with pleasure.'

'Does that mean you will do business with me, Zack Maynard?'

'So you know my name too. I see I'm not the only one who listens in on others. Do you think you and Miss Pengarron will be able to manage all the intrigue of a smuggling run on your own, Jessica?'

Jessica was more than uncomfortable about his familiarity and her fear of him had not left her but she answered bluntly, 'We won't be the only ones. Her cousin will be in on it and we will have a man with us.'

'And who will that be?'

'The head groom at the Manor.'

'And what will be his reward?'

'The same as yours!'

Zack Maynard ran his cool eyes lingeringly down the length of her curls and Jessica felt as if he was actually touching her. She wanted to shout at him to stop but knew she had to allow this blatant intimate scrutiny or he would refuse to do a deal with her. She had spoken out in anger and bravado on the night of the party but now the power of adventure and excitement had taken over and she was eager to take part in a smuggling run.

'Do we have a deal?' she asked urgently, knowing she ought to have been home ages ago for Kerris's sake.

He said a quiet 'Yes.'

Jessica clenched her fists and hoped he didn't want to shake hands on it.

He put his palms loosely together and seemed to look straight into her. 'I'll get in touch with you,' he said.

Jessica felt his eyes still on her as she forced herself to walk out of the alleyway without breaking into a run. She argued with herself all the way home that a smuggling operator could hardly be expected not to be a little frightening.

Zack Maynard made his way back to the gin shop. Inside, he went to a table circled by four men, not as tidily dressed or as clean in the body as himself.

'Where did thee get to?' bawled one of the men. 'Yer were just about to come in when thee went off again.'

'I had someone else to see,' Zack said, sitting in the chair another of the men had vacated for him. Zack Maynard was clearly the leader of the group.

'How did it go with Trenchard?' asked a third man.

'I've got business with not one but two Trenchards.'

'Two? Are they twins putting up separately or somethin'?'

'Not the other twin, the younger sister.'

'What? That pretty little wild thing with the yellow curls?' And a roar of laughter went up.

'That's right. Jessica Trenchard. Spirited and lovely and ripe for plucking in the best way known to man. She believes she can get something going with some friends of hers, two young ladies and a stable groom. Ridiculous, of course, and I've no intention of organising a landing for them. But these two young ladies just happen to be very wealthy, so there's a much better way to make money out of them, and lots of it. Kidnap and ransom.'

'And just who would we be kidnapping?'

'Sir Oliver Pengarron's daughter and niece. They'll make a pretty bundle in the company of the sweet Miss Jessica Trenchard.'

'You'm bloody mazed, clean off yer head! Pengarron will kill us! I wouldn't touch a bloody hen that belonged to him.'

'But this is the clever thing – he'd never suspect us, not with his own sons doing business with us, acting as a perfect cover.'

Zack's henchmen weren't convinced and grumbled among themselves but Zack knew they would come round to his way of thinking. He sat quietly and planned the kidnapping – and the consequences.

'Planning on ransoming the Trenchard girl too, are 'ee?' asked one of his men eventually. 'Don't expect 'er family got no money.'

Zack Maynard smiled. 'I've got other plans for her,' he replied calmly.

–

Four weary men made their way back from the fields of Trecath-en Farm to the farmhouse after dusk. Philip was delighted to see Cordelia was there and would join them for supper. He washed and changed his clothes carefully and managed to seat himself next to her at the table.

'I take it Jack brought you over, Cordelia,' he said. 'How are you getting home?'

'Kane is riding over with the trap for me,' she replied, keeping her head down over her food. 'This is very tasty.' She turned to Jessica. 'Did you make it?'

'No, Kerris did. I was held up in Marazion and she'd already prepared the supper when I got back.' This told Cordelia that Jessica had made the same contact as Philip had; she was dying to find out what had happened so she could relate it to Olivia when she got home, but Kerris had clung close to Jessica from the moment she'd walked into the house and so far Cordelia hadn't been able to speak to Jessica alone.

'I must congratulate Kerris on a lovely meal,' Cordelia said. Kerris didn't eat with the family and quietly withdrew until the meal was over. She would come back later to attend to the dishes.

'She's a good cook,' Philip put in and Cordelia wished he would join in the talk Clem, David, Kenver and Ricketty Jim were holding about the coming harvest.

As soon as the meal was over and the menfolk seemed settled round the hearth with their pipes, Cordelia suggested to Jessica that they take a stroll outside in the cool evening air. They stopped to talk close beside the stall in the barn where Clem kept his horse.

'Well?' Cordelia said at once, grabbing Jessica's hands excitedly. Cordelia was hoping that Luke would be impressed at her taking part in a hazardous smuggling run, that he would see her as something more than his 'dreamy little cousin'. 'Did Philip meet the man you told me and Livvy about? Did you get the chance to speak to him?'

'Aye, he did and I did. His name's Zack Maynard, a sailor. He said he would do business with us.'

'Oh, I can hardly believe it. I can't wait to tell Livvy. Perhaps it will drag her away from her paintings. It's all she wants to do these days. What was he like, this Zack Maynard? Did you have much trouble getting to speak to him?'

'For crying out loud, Cordelia, calm down,' Jessica exhorted her friend, 'or the others will get suspicious. As it is I'm sure Philip saw me following him. I only hope he doesn't ask me about it because I don't know what on earth to tell him. Zack Maynard gave me the slip at one point, then he crept up on me in an alleyway. Nearly frightened the life out of me.'

'What's he like though? Is he good-looking?'

'You and your romantic notions,' Jessica scoffed, but not unkindly. 'He's inside his thirties, clean and tidy and quite ordinary-looking, I suppose, but there was something deep about his eyes. He said he'd get in touch with me again.'

'I won't be able to sleep tonight for thinking about it. You are brave, Jessie. I'd have dropped dead in fright for certain if he'd crept up on me in an alleyway.'

'Well, I'd better go back inside and shoo the men out of the kitchen so Kerris can get on with the dishes,' Jessica said, and added to herself, and keep an eye open for Kane Pengarron so I can make myself scarce. 'You coming?'

'In a little while. I think I'd better calm myself or I'm afraid my face will give away our secret.'

When Jessica was back inside, Cordelia thought to stroll round the perimeter of the yard and then go in to help with the clearing up. She literally jumped off her feet when a male voice surprised her. She backed away towards the stall.

'You looked as if you were about to go for a walk,' Philip said. 'Take my arm and we'll go together.'

'No! No, thank you. I was about to go in and help Jessica.'

'Well, you're going the wrong way for that.'

Cordelia realised she was still taking backward steps and cried out in terror as her slight body touched Tally, Clem's mare. She had been kicked by one of the Pengarron horses when a child, and had been terrified of them ever since.

'There's no need to be afraid,' Philip said, imprisoning her against the mare's flank with his arms as he stroked its back. 'Tally's as gentle as a baby.'

'Please… let me get away,' Cordelia gasped out.

'You don't want to stay scared of horses all of your life, do you, Cordelia?' Philip asked soothingly. 'Don't you know that if you face a fear, you can conquer it?'

'Please…'

A sprinkling of tears appeared along Cordelia's eyelashes. Philip put one hand under her tiny chin and wiped the tears away from an eye with his thumb.

'Just turn round slowly. I'll be here all the time. Just look at Tally, she won't hurt you.'

'No, I want to go!' Cordelia snatched at his hand in panic and moved forward but this only put her in contact with his body.

'It's all right. Just turn round and look at her. If you get over your fear now you'll be glad you did for ever. Save you walking everywhere or having to ask for a carriage every time you want to go out.'

Cordelia's eyes grew huge in her little face and she prayed silently to be taken out of the stall. Philip put his hands on her shoulders and began to turn her round. She fought against him but he was too strong and then she was facing the mare.

Tally had no interest in them and had her head lowered, feeding from a scattering of hay on the ground. Cordelia hurled panicky hands backwards and grasped at Philip's shirt. She stared at Tally in terror. The smell of the mare filled her nostrils and her stricken eyes were stinging with tears.

Philip slid his hand down her arm until it reached her hand. He disentangled her fingers from his shirt and they caught at his rough hand, digging in. Her head was pressed in hard against his breastbone. She wanted to close her eyes, shut out the picture of her terror, but her eyelids were frozen.

When Philip reached out with her hand in his, Cordelia began to blubber, 'No, no… I'll die…'

'You won't die, Cordelia, just trust me. It'll be all over in a minute and then I'll take you away. Touch Tally, just a little, and you'll see there's nothing to fear from a horse.'

Firmly holding her wrist, Philip ran her taut, splayed fingers an inch along Tally's withers. 'There, that's all there is to it. How did it feel?'

'She's warm and smooth,' Cordelia murmured.

After a few moments he said, 'Try again.'

Cordelia let him place her hand on Tally's broad back. He took his hand away and put his arm round her waist and held her close. 'Move your hand, just a little,' he whispered in her ear.

Cordelia's hand shook as she moved it towards Tally's shoulder, then she snatched it away.

'You're doing fine. See, she's completely harmless. Tally's as gentle as a lamb, she wouldn't hurt a fly.'

'She's so big,' Cordelia whispered.

'She wouldn't seem so threatening if you weren't so small.'

Philip lifted Cordelia off her feet until her head was on the same level as his. 'See, Tally don't look so big from up here, do she?'

'N-no.'

'Why don't you touch her one more time, then I'll take you outside.'

Cordelia waited for him to take her hand again but Philip kept his arms round her narrow waist.

'Try on your own,' he urged her.

She put her hand out hesitantly and stroked Tally's back in a rapid movement. Feeling a little less scared, she pushed her head into Philip's chest again and ran her hand all the way down the mare's back to her hindquarters. Tally lifted her head and looked at her. Cordelia gasped and grabbed at Philip's body.

''Tis all right,' he said softly, 'she's only saying hello to you.'

He waited until Tally returned to her feed, then stepped back with Cordelia nestled against him. She turned sharply and threw herself into his arms. He stroked her soft dark hair.

''Tis all over, you're perfectly safe.'

Cordelia felt her legs go and he lifted her up and carried her deeper into the barn. Sitting down on a bale of hay, he cradled her on his lap. She sat subdued but her hands were clenched tight, her arms held stiff.

Philip took her chin and lifted her face to look at him. 'You must feel very proud of yourself,' he said gently.

'I feel terrible.' She shivered.

'You'll stop shaking in a minute. Sorry to have forced you to touch Tally but I saw it as an opportunity not to be missed. You'll feel much easier around horses from now on. I'll help you, if you like.'

'Will you let me go, Philip?' Cordelia asked, struggling to free herself, thinking how unseemly it must look for her to be sitting on his lap.

Philip complied. He didn't want her to become terrified of him and have his plans to romance her spoiled but he kept his hands on her arms so she couldn't flee from him.

'Are you steady?' he asked kindly, smiling with all his charm.

'My legs still feel weak,' she admitted.

'You're welcome to lean on me as long as you like,' he said huskily.

Cordelia looked up at him and gulped. She had never been this close to a man outside her family before, and this man, so sought after, often ruthlessly, by many of the local females, had held her as close as a man could get.

'Cordelia, you know I have a great regard for you.'

'Have you? I mean, let me go, Philip… Please, I must go…'

Philip stood up and gathered her in. Holding the back of her head, he brought his lips to meet hers. Cordelia had no strength to fight against him and coped with the kiss by shutting her eyes tightly and trying to think of something else.

'It'll be good when you get used to it,' Philip said, preparing for a second helping.

'No! I'll never like it!' Cordelia cried. 'Let go of me!'

'I don't think you understand. I'm not amusing myself with you, my dear Cordelia. I think very highly of you. I think perhaps that I love you. I think we would be good together.'

'What on earth do you mean by that?' Cordelia said angrily. 'Good together for what? If you mean—'

'No, no, Cordelia. You're getting me all wrong. I'm not asking you to lie with me. I'm asking you to marry me.'

'You're what? How dare you! I couldn't trust a man like you. You care only for yourself and what could you possibly offer me in a marriage?'

Philip was shocked at Cordelia's outrage. He had expected her to be flattered, even grateful.

'Well, I can offer you a lot,' he replied, frowning but trying to keep his voice soft and kind. 'I'll have the tenancy of Trecath-en Farm one day. David's not interested in it. My father doesn't know it yet but David's planning on going off later in the year, with Simon Peter Blake, to be a preacher. You've seen for yourself what my father has done for the farm and if we get married, Sir Oliver would probably give it to us. I've got more ambition than my father. I've got bigger plans for the farm, Cordelia. I've got money put by earned by betting on wrestling matches and from other means.' Philip couldn't conceal his pride but Cordelia knocked him off the pedestal of his own making.

'And plans for the money from my dowry, no doubt,' she said sharply. 'You don't fool me, Philip Trenchard. You have no regard for me, or any woman, for that matter. Any woman who does find herself unfortunate enough to become your wife will have to look for you in several other beds. I despise you.'

Philip was mortified. 'You little bitch! I was doing you a favour offering you marriage. No gentleman is going to be interested in you except for the amount your uncle will settle on you. Everyone knows you're no lady, you're just the feeble daughter of a common fisherman.

You're not pretty, you have no figure, you are nothing. Who do you think will possibly love you?'

'My grandfather was a titled gentleman and my uncle is one, so that makes me a much better person than you are! And as for who loves me, well, the Pengarrons are my family and they love me and I love them. They are all I need. So you see, Philip Trenchard, you offered me precisely nothing.'

Philip raised his hand as if to strike her. Cordelia flinched but remained still. He scowled and spat at her feet. 'Make your own way back past the ruddy horse,' he said and stormed out of the barn.

Knowing she had won the battle, Cordelia kept her head held high for several moments then sank down on the bale of hay and wept.

Kane found her staring into space with red-rimmed eyes. She threw herself into his arms.

'What's the matter, sweeting? What are you doing in here like this?'

Cordelia didn't tell him about Philip; she did not want a scene. 'I found myself inside the barn and then I was too scared to leave past the horse,' she murmured.

Kane cuddled her for a moment then raised her to her feet. 'Come on, I'll take you straight home,' he said. 'You've had a bad fright and when I popped my head round the kitchen door just now I found half of the Trenchards were in a foul mood.'

Kane had been home for six weeks and he had not found it easy to settle down. He had changed. After the behaviour of his fellow officer abroad, he did not trust folk as readily as he once had. Where before he had taken for granted Luke's superior attitude and demands to be the centre of attention, now he found them petty and distracting. Other people had changed too. Olivia had become sulky. Clem hardly spoke, as though he had some big problem on his mind. And Jessica was downright hostile.

Kane felt unsettled. He had not been able to make progress on choosing the right piece of land for his farm. And as he drove home with Cordelia, the other member of the Pengarron dynasty who some people felt didn't quite belong in it, he knew why. There was something he had to do before he could find the peace to go forward with his life. It might bring discontent and cause great trouble, but it had to be risked.

Chapter 10

The next day Kane was in the east side of Marazion. He had business there and that business was in a brothel. The brothel was a large building which was gradually being turned into a high-class establishment. It was beginning to attract customers of better means than those of its usual clientele from a working-class background. The improvements had started in the spring with fresh paintwork on the outside doors and walls. When the front door was opened to Kane, however, the interior smelled of a sickly combination of sweat, stale alcohol and tobacco, and too much cheap perfume.

Kane waved a hand in front of his face as he stepped inside but there was a definite improvement when he was shown by a clean and smartly dressed maidservant into a darkened room she proudly called the parlour.

With an excited squeak she hurried from the room, 'T'fetch Missus Nansmere at once fer 'ee, sur,' taking the smell of harsh soap with her.

Mrs Nansmere arrived in a flurry of flimsy floating silks. 'My dear sir,' she said in a low, sultry voice, 'please allow me to offer you my apologies.' She tut-tutted and flung back the heavy green velvet curtains at the windows to let in the strong sunlight. 'Mary should have drawn these for you.'

Kane saw that it was on this well-furnished room that most of the money earned in the establishment was being spent. It was styled on one of the rooms he had dined in of a powerful aristocratic Cornish family and he gathered that Mrs Nansmere had at one time been well connected.

'We don't usually get a gentleman calling on us this early,' the madam said, whirling back to him in a provocative movement.

'It is just after midday, Mrs Nansmere,' Kane pointed out, employing his husky voice in an agreeable tone.

Mrs Nansmere had immediately recognised who her unexpected caller was. She hugged a filmy scarf round her wide shoulders and walked over to him with her voluptuous body swaying. She was a young woman, beautiful in a common way, her figure shapely. Kane wondered what she was doing in this establishment. She let the scarf fall to reveal an almost naked bosom.

'We tend to keep late hours in this business, Captain Pengarron. I'm afraid none of my girls will be ready to receive you. But then a gentleman such as yourself deserves only the best.' She floated closer. 'It will be an honour to see to you myself.'

'You are too kind,' Kane drawled, and for the benefit of his expedition here he gazed down on her flesh.

'You like?'

'I like very much.'

'Where would you prefer? Here or upstairs?'

'Here will serve me well.'

'And I shall serve you well. I reserve myself for only the cream of my clientele. My name is Frances,' Mrs Nansmere said, reaching out with long-nailed fingers and leading Kane to a sofa.

Kane pulled off his frockcoat and allowed it to be placed over a chairback. He sat on the sofa and put his big hands protectively on his lap, but not wanting to give out the wrong signals he lifted his arms and spread them along the sofa's back.

'Frances – a lovely name,' he said, turning on the charm.

'Thank you, kind sir,' Frances said with a curtsey that risked the little modesty she retained. 'Can I get you some wine?'

'A little too early in the day for me.'

'Tea perhaps? I shall see to it myself, make it in front of your eyes in this room. You can be assured of clean china.'

Kane was pleased. He only wanted conversation with this woman and he could keep her talking while she made the tea. 'I would find a dish of tea most welcome, Frances. Have you been here long?' he asked, taking in the interior of the room, eyeing a replica painting of a certain gentleman's spaniel dog. The gentleman had died recently and Frances must have been done out of a lucrative living.

'Oh no, this is a come-down for me, Captain Pengarron. But I bought this place cheaply and intend to make alterations and obtain more personable girls. The ones I have at present are all clean, I can assure anyone of that; they just need to adjust their level of drinking, and I have to say that occasionally it's a gentleman who disgraces himself here.'

Kane frowned. He wanted to talk to someone who had worked here twenty-four years ago. Had Frances Nansmere got rid of all the 'staff' of that period?

'Something is wrong?' Frances purred.

'No, not at all.' Kane flashed a smile.

'Why, I do declare, Captain Pengarron. When you smile like that you are even better looking than your father. I have seen him abroad, it is an honour for a woman to pass him on the street.'

Kane couldn't help smiling for its own sake. He liked Frances Nansmere and her flowery language. He patted the sofa seat. 'Come and sit. And please call me Kane.'

'You do me an honour, sir... Kane.'

Frances sat close, placing a hand on his leg in a feathery movement. Kane took her hand in his and raised it to his face. It smelled fresh and delicately perfumed and he placed a light kiss on her pale skin.

'I'll get straight to the point, Frances. There is a particular reason why I have come here today.'

'Oh dear, don't tell me you have come here only to talk?' She made a disappointed face and put her bosom on his arm and ran a fingertip along his chin. Kane met her sparkling eyes; they had nearly the same shade and depth as Jessica Trenchard's. Frances ran her tongue along her lower lip and Kane blinked, telling himself to keep control.

'I like being in your company, Frances,' Kane said in answer.

'Well, why don't we get the talking out of the way first over that dish of tea?'

Kane was impressed by the china Frances produced from a locked cupboard.

'A present from a titled gentleman. He provided for me very well. Unfortunately he died recently and I have had to move on. I could have provided excellent service for several gentlemen, I had plenty of offers, but I fancied being my own mistress for a change. Now, enough about me, my dear Kane. You want to talk and in your case I'm most interested to hear what you have to say.'

Kane smiled. 'I have no affair of the heart I want to lament about. I need information.'

'Ah, in my profession it is not unusual for a gentleman to take a liking to one of the girls and wish to set her up for his own exclusive convenience. I take it you are enquiring about one before my time?'

'That is correct but it is not for the reasons you are thinking. I shall come straight to the point again, Frances, for I feel you will be discreet and understanding. The lady I am interested in worked her about twenty-four years ago. She died, unfortunately, of one of the illnesses that is occasionally acquired by a lady of your profession. The lady was my mother – my real mother.'

Frances gaped at him for a moment. 'I knew, of course, that you were not the natural son of Sir Oliver and the beautiful Lady Pengarron. You have reason to believe your real mother worked here?'

'I know for certain she did. I knew from an early age that I was adopted. It was common knowledge, and my parents, knowing the truth could not be withheld from me, wisely told me the moment I could understand. When I reached manhood I asked my father for the details. He told me that my real father was a sailor, a rather horrible individual from all accounts, and that my real mother used to work here. I will have you know, Frances, that I consider myself a Pengarron and am content with that aspect of my life. But, for various reasons, I am curious about my origins. I believe that if I can find out something about my mother then I might learn something of my father also. This establishment was not as you have it now, it was utterly degrading. I do not expect to find out anything that will be a comfort to me, but...'

'But you have to know.' Frances patted Kane's hand, clenched on his thigh. 'You have just left your regiment, have you not? About to start a new life. It is a good idea to put the past behind you before starting a new one.'

'I knew you would understand. I have plans for the future but feel at this moment I cannot proceed with them.'

'My dear Kane, leave it with me. I can probably find out what you want to know quicker than if you asked for yourself. Some of the girls have been here a long time and may know where to find those who worked here in your mother's time. I shall ask the necessary questions.' She took his teacup and put it down, adding before making for his lips, 'I will tell you what I've learned when you come again.'

—

Clem Trenchard also had something pressing to do. The harvesting would soon begin in earnest and he had to get this out of the way first before he got too busy in the fields. He spruced himself up in his Sunday-best clothes, which he hated wearing, took some time combing and tying back his hair and even made sure his nails were clean. Then, leaving his dogs behind, he rode over to Perranbarvah's Parsonage to court the parson's sister.

He didn't want to. He'd argued with himself that it wasn't really necessary to give Jessica a stepmother, but since the Pengarron girl's birthday party, her behaviour had become even more unruly. She was barely civil to Kane when he called, and Kerensa had sent a note to inform him that she had been most rude to Oliver and if it occurred again she could be told not to visit the Manor house. Clem's first reaction had been to say 'Good!' but he didn't want Jessica to lose her self-esteem and her friendship with Olivia and Cordelia. Come to that, Clem thought, she must have offended Cordelia too because she hadn't come over to Trecath-en Farm for some time.

Clem had wanted to ask Kerensa if she would mind if he married again. Not that she had any real cause to object. True, she had been forced to marry Sir Oliver Pengarron twenty-two years ago, leaving Clem distraught and bitter, but she had later fallen in love with her husband. She was hardly likely to mind. But he had never stopped loving her and her opinion meant a lot to him. He knew that she would wish to see him happy, and because he did not intend to ask Catherine Lanyon to marry him for love, he was afraid Kerensa would talk him out of it. He did not want that. A stepmother for Jessica seemed the only way to ensure that the girl did not become totally unmanageable.

Clem didn't have a lot to offer Miss Catherine Lanyon. But she was past the age of being choosy about her marriage prospects and she had shown more than a passing interest in him.

Clem had sounded out the Reverend Timothy Lanyon on his feelings about his paying court to his sister. The young parson must have shared Clem's thoughts on his sister's eligibility, because after coming to terms with the shock and after much humming and hawing he said he had only one big objection. While he tolerated the Methodist movement, he would not see his sister married to a dissenter. Clem said he was willing to come back fully to the Church; he would rather risk David's and Matthias Renfree's disappointment by the change than Jessica's reputation if she was not soon tamed. Timothy then intimated that if his sister found the marriage proposal agreeable, he would not stand in their way.

Clem had chosen today to make his first approach because he knew that Timothy had been called away to a meeting with the Archdeacon of Cornwall.

Nancy Wills answered the door to him and didn't bother to hide her shock as he swept off his plain tricorn hat. 'What on earth are you doing here all dressed up, Clem? There isn't no wedding in the church.'

Kenver, who was artistic and learned, had prepared a calling card. Clem kept a serious face as he passed it to Nancy. 'Please present this to your mistress.'

'Mistress... Please step inside, Mr Trenchard,' Nancy said, awed. 'I'll see if Miss Catherine is receiving visitors. She has someone with her at present.'

'Oh!'

Nancy's face was flushed with the prospect of what she hoped was Clem's reason for this sudden call and she gave him a confidential look. ''Tis a child, her sister's boy, Miss Catherine's little nephew. Lives at Falmouth. He's spending the day and night here while his parents are up-along at Lanhydrock House,' she informed him before heading for the parlour.

Catherine stared in disbelief at the card she'd taken off the silver tray. 'Clem Trenchard! What is he doing here? Are you sure he doesn't want to see Timothy?'

'Timothy. No. "Please present this to your mistress," he said as bold as brass. 'Tis you he's come to see and he's all dressed up and looking some handsome, enough to melt a maiden's heart.'

'I cannot possibly see him,' Catherine said haughtily. 'Besides, I'm busy entertaining Thomas.'

Nancy glanced fondly at a curly-headed child who was sleeping peacefully on a sofa. 'Young Thomas'll be asleep a while longer yet and anyway he's no trouble when he's up playing. I'll show Clem in then.'

Catherine's humiliation at Trecath-en Farm was still fresh in her mind. 'No! Don't you dare! I… I… I don't want to see him. Send him away, tell him I already have a visitor and, if he asks, tell him I'll be tied up with charity work into the distant future.'

'What's the matter with you? I thought you liked him. He looks a real treat, you'd have to be mazed not to—'

'Nancy, do as you're told!'

'Very well, if that's the way you want it,' Nancy muttered, shaking her head as she left the room. 'But you'll regret it.'

Clem wasn't going to be put off. He hadn't preened himself up only to be sent packing at the first hurdle. Nancy told him that the child would wake soon from a nap and a suggestion would be made to her mistress that he might like to play outside in the gardens.

Nancy Wills was true to her word. Twenty minutes later Catherine appeared in a wide straw sunhat accompanied by a robust boy of about four years who ran ahead of her tossing a patchwork ball. The ball hit the solitary apple tree in the middle of the lawn, landed heavily on the grass and rolled in Clem's direction. Clem stepped out from an overhang of foliage on the Parsonage wall and swept up the ball.

He smiled widely at Catherine, ignoring her flush of anger. To the boy who ran up for his ball he said, 'One of my favourite games is playing ball.'

'We must go back inside, Thomas,' Catherine said stiffly. 'I'm afraid the sun is too fierce to stay out any longer.'

'But we've only just left the house, Aunt Catherine,' Thomas protested.

Clem lowered himself down and spoke to the boy. 'I have a daughter who has fair curls just like yours, Master Thomas.'

'Is she the same age as me?' Thomas asked, and Catherine was horrified when he allowed Clem to lift him into his arms.

'Oh, she's a little older than you are but she's still a little girl to me. Her name is Jessica.' Clem turned to Catherine. 'I like children.'

'Put my nephew down this instant, Mr Trenchard, and take your leave,' Catherine demanded, shaking in anger.

Thomas pulled on Clem's neckcloth which thankfully loosened the restriction on his windpipe. Catherine marched up to them and pulled Thomas into her own arms.

'Miss Catherine, I—'

Catherine whirled round and stalked away with Thomas who looked curiously at Clem over her shoulder.

'I will not give up,' Clem said loudly.

Catherine kept walking.

Nancy appeared, holding her arms out to the boy. 'You come with me, my handsome. I've got a nice ginger biscuit and glass of milk waiting for you in the kitchen.'

Catherine tried to restrain Thomas but he wriggled free and Nancy ushered him round the side of the house. Catherine stood rigid, her face trembling, her feelings hurt and buffeted. She refused to look Clem in the eye when he came up and faced her.

'Thank you for allowing me to speak to you,' he said softly.

'You are taking liberties and I find them offensive,' Catherine retorted.

'You have my humble apologies and I have had so many to give you of late. I was extremely rude to you the day you rode over to the farm and you had come on an errand of mercy. I am a foolish, stubborn man, Miss Catherine. I resented what I saw as interference. I wish only to make it up to you now. If you can find it in your heart to forgive me, I would like to invite you to come over to the farm to dine with me and my family.'

'You are asking me…?' Catherine was astonished.

'Will you at least consider it?'

'Well, I… I…' She spread her hands.

'On Sunday, after the service. The Reverend Lanyon has told me he is dining with Mr Ralph Harrt, the local coroner. I understand you don't care for his or his wife's company and have declined their invitation.'

'You know a lot about my plans, Mr Trenchard,' Catherine said, disapprovingly. She walked to the edge of a rose tree plot where he could not gain the advantage of gazing down on her face. Her heart beat so fast she thought it must be apparent to him, there was a catch in her throat and her palms had become damp.

Not very long ago she had made an utter fool of herself at his farm, his home territory. He had seen her off quite ruthlessly then, but now here he was, making it plain he had spoken to her brother and had gone to the trouble of ascertaining her future movements. Her mind was in turmoil. Why had he suddenly changed his mind about the way he felt about her? What precisely were his intentions towards her? Did she want to go and eat a meal at his farmhouse?

'I hope I have not offended you further, Miss Lanyon,' Clem said earnestly. 'I admit I have been underhanded but I really want to repair the rift I've caused between us and I would like you to see my family as they really are. Will you come? Please. You could meet Kerris, it would be useful to have your opinion about her plight. You might even know her.'

Catherine was so distressed she thought she would faint. If this man had from the start shown her the respect due to her from his lower class, and this invitation had been a natural progress in the relationship she had been hoping to form, she would have been delighted, nervous but delighted. But he had cruelly abused her tentative approaches and now had sprung himself on her like a thoughtless, selfish rake. How dare he? He was a working-class farmer, rough and ready, who worked the earth with his bare hands and his shirt off. He made a poor income compared to the small allowance she had for her own use. But… he was tall and handsome, he possessed those wonderful, soulful, summer-blue eyes and a moody spirit that was both arresting and challenging.

Did she want to go to his wretched little farm and dine with him and his family?

'I… I suppose it is possible I might know Kerris…'

'The family will be as delighted as I am,' Clem said with finality.

–

That night Oliver was stealthily occupied in Trelynne Cove taking in goods at the end of a smuggling run. One of the men he employed in the operation was Matthew King. The following night, unknown to Oliver, Matthew King's younger brother Paul was in the same place, doing the same thing with Oliver's two sons.

Luke, Kane and Paul had all had experience of smuggling before and the operation, a small trial run at Zack Maynard's behest, was completed quickly and without trouble. Twenty workmen were employed to help. Luke, who had felt useful at making the contacts to hide and buy the goods, felt emasculated at not being able to carry the heavier goods up the cliffs due to his useless arm. He felt Philip Trenchard was mocking him as he put his muscles to work almost effortlessly. Luke sulked and put his spite on display by bullying the hired men. Much later in the night he hid his feelings of inadequacy by becoming rapidly drunk.

He and Kane, together with Philip, Paul King, Sebastian Beswetherick and Zack Maynard, had gathered in Painted Bessie's kiddley-wink and were watched suspiciously by the woman from behind her thick mask of powder and rouge.

Kane, who was an expert at figures, estimated that the landers' end of the run would make in excess of two hundred pounds on this trial run. 'I think we can all agree the night has been a great success,' he remarked, lifting his glass to Painted Bessie and receiving a raddled smile back.

'I think we'll be able to have a long and prosperous partnership, gentlemen,' Zack Maynard said, saluting them all with his tankard. 'When would you like to be doing the next run? I'm easy to get hold of. My ship is only a small local concern, delivering cargo around the county's ports. It's regularly tied up at St Michael's Mount.'

'It will have to be after the harvesting,' Kane replied vaguely.

Luke guffawed and Kane put out a hand to stop him falling off his chair. Luke pushed it moodily aside. 'Just because you don't mind getting your hands dirtied like a peasant in the fields, brother, it doesn't mean the rest of us can't slip in and out of the coves and creeks at any time we choose.'

'I'm afraid I won't have a minute to spare for at least a month or so after this weekend,' Philip said.

'I'm not particularly interested in your plans, Trenchard!' Luke blasted.

'Have a care, Luke,' Kane cautioned. 'We need Philip's broad back and if the pilchards come in in plenty, we won't have the likes of Paul either. We must also plan carefully so as not to clash in the same place on the same night as Father's next operation.'

'Aye, I hope to be kept busy at harvesting time. 'Tes been a good summer for fleas so should be a good summer for fish,' Paul King said. 'And I always help out on Trecath-en Farm if I can for the harvesting.'

'What wages do you get for working on a harvest, Trenchard?' Zack asked Philip, who Kane had noticed was as moody as Luke these days. 'P'raps I'll turn up on your father's farm looking to earn an extra crust.'

'A few shillings at the most. Won't be worth the boot leather for you to walk over compared to what can be earned free-trading,' Philip answered.

'A pity,' Zack said. A pity, he thought. It would have been a good opportunity to get close to your delicious little sister.

Zack was impatient to put his kidnap plan into action but first he had to build up a good working relationship with these young men in order to provide a cover. The ransom for the Pengarron and Drannock women would ensure him a quick fortune and a new life elsewhere. And during the time they were held prisoner, kept completely unharmed to lessen Sir Oliver Pengarron's wrath, sweet Jessica Trenchard would be his...

Kane, too, was thinking of Jessica. When he was a boy and his father had been out of the country, Kerensa and Alice Trenchard had agreed that their children should be allowed to mix and play together and he had enjoyed the time spent on Trecath-en Farm. He got on well with the twins and Clem had already been his friend. Jessica had been a cherubic-looking child with a wild spirit and he had liked her joining in with their games, not seeing her as a nuisance as her brothers did. She had been his friend too. Now he could not understand her continuing hostility towards him.

He had apologised for his cruel trick with the spider. Surely she need not be so unforgiving. When Kerris had hurt Jessica's back, she had leaned yieldingly into his arms, seeking comfort. She had felt good. No longer a little girl but a woman. A woman innocent of man had a different quality about her than one who cheapened herself, and he had enjoyed holding her. Kane fancied she kept herself respectable to remain fiercely in control of her own life. How would the man feel who could get Jessica Trenchard to yield? If she would ever yield. That man would have to be someone special, someone who would allow her a good measure of freedom.

Kane's eyes met Zack's and Zack gave him his lazy smile but shuffled in his seat. At that moment Kane knew the smuggling sailor could not be trusted.

Chapter 11

There were several people lingering about Perranbarvah's church-yard after the Sunday service, and despite the Reverend Lanyon's much-praised sermon on the theme of 'Love thy neighbour', many individuals who had attended were set on ignoring others.

Timothy himself was in a subdued mood and had not waved his arms about during the service. He gave Olivia a friendly 'Good morning' afterwards as he received his congregation at the door, but she returned only a cool reply.

Olivia, feeling disturbed, hurried away to her infant brother's grave. Cordelia, intent on avoiding Philip who had scorned her in the church as though she was suffering from some biblical plague, followed on her heels. They stood together, holding hands, gazing gloomily down at Joseph Pengarron's small headstone. Jessica had slipped away from Simon Peter Blake and he had immediately left the churchyard in low spirits to await his mother in their carriage.

Kane, who was fed up with Jessica's attitude, had urged Luke away as soon as the last word of prayer had been said. And although Clem had greeted Kerensa with a nod, she'd found him somehow defensive. He'd then hurried away to the Parsonage stable to see if Catherine's pony was being saddled for the journey to Trecath-en Farm, and to avoid Oliver.

'Everybody seems miserable and uncommunicative this morning, Reverend Lanyon,' Matthias Renfree remarked, watching the retreating backs.

'Yes,' Timothy said quietly, shaking Matthias's stocky hand, knowing that he was one of those labelled as miserable. 'I'm wondering how well my sermon went down.'

He had mentioned forgiveness in his sermon, hoping Olivia would forgive him for offending her. He could hardly believe he had taken that liberty with her. Was it because he was a member of a large family with many female relatives? It wasn't an important family; he had three elder brothers with first claim on the small family fortune, and they had not been reared in a sensitive household. Not until the encounter with Olivia had he realised how he had taken women for granted. She had been right about the way he treated women. How could he have slipped into being so unfeeling towards them?

'Your sermon was excellent, Reverend Lanyon,' said a middle-aged man in an old-fashioned periwig at Matthias's side. 'I understand that you preach straight from the Bible and on spiritual matters.'

'Allow me to introduce Mr John Whitehead to you, Reverend,' Matthias said, smiling broadly. 'He's an itinerant preacher and is to preach in the open air at Gunwalloe this evening.'

'Is he indeed?' Timothy said, putting out his hand. 'I suppose I should feel it an honour to have him attend my church.'

'I expect all the Methodists I meet on the circuit to be devout in church and sacrament,' John Whitehead said stoutly.

'Some of your people stay in what I call the uncommitted circle, Whitehead. They play at being Methodists and misuse the parish church,' Timothy said coolly.

'We don't approve of folk like that either,' Matthias said, and taking John Whitehead by the arm he steered him away.

'I thought you said he was an agreeable fellow, Matthias,' John Whitehead remarked as they crunched down the new covering of gravel chippings Oliver had had laid. 'He was almost hostile and he certainly showed none of the hospitality I received from the Reverend Ivey when he was parson here.'

'He doesn't approve of folk round here calling me preacher. He doesn't approve of the Movement in the way the old Reverend did. He thinks that all monies the Movement receives belong more properly to the Church and I suppose I can sympathise with that from his point of view.'

'All wealth belongs to God,' John Whitehead said forcefully.

'Yes, of course,' Matthias replied. 'Did I tell you about the time I spoke to Mr John Wesley at Gwenap?' he said, changing the subject just as forcefully. Matthias was not going to offend the young parson by allowing the other man to preach in the churchyard.

Rosina Blake, at least, was eager to seek out someone for an amicable conversation. She considered herself a Methodist but, like Matthias, she felt it proper to take Communion in a church and this Sunday she had returned to her old parish church to do so. She shook hands with Timothy Lanyon and then limped up to Jessica Trenchard who was complaining to her Aunt Rosie. Rosina kept a discreet distance, waiting for their conversation to end.

'I don't know why Father had to drag us along here today. I prefer to go to the Bible classes. The service was most boring,' Jessica sulked.

'It wouldn't have been if you'd paid some attention,' Rosie Renfree said sharply, smoothing her baby daughter's wispy hair from her hot face. 'You have to put something into life to get something out. Don't let your uncle hear you going on, you know he finds your attitude bewildering at times.'

'But what are we all doing here so suddenly? David comes here occasionally but Father hasn't gone to church for years and Philip usually refuses to go anywhere.'

'Haven't you realised yet?' Rosie said incredulously. 'It's something to do with the person your father has invited to dinner today.'

'So that's what this is all about. Who's he invited then? He refused to tell me anything.'

'He's asked me to tell you that. It's Miss Catherine.'

'What? But why her? We've never had someone like her to dinner at the farm before.'

Rosie thought it better not to tell Jessica the full reason for the invitation. Jessica was jealous of anyone taking her father's attention and would probably go out of her way to make Miss Catherine Lanyon feel uncomfortable. Clem's courtship could be brought to an abrupt end. It would be better to let the girl realise it slowly for herself.

'He thought he was rather rude and offhand to Miss Catherine the other day and wants to make it up to her. I hope you will be mindful of your manners and show her the respect a lady deserves.'

Jessica put a gentle finger on her baby cousin's button nose, then looked suspiciously at her aunt. 'No wonder we've got a whole hindquarter of lamb roasting on the spit. Sounds all very mysterious to me. What's going on?'

Rosie caught sight of Rosina and dropped a curtsey. 'Mistress Blake. Good day to you. Are you wanting a word with me?'

'Well, actually I'd like to talk to Jessica, if I may,' Rosina replied softly. 'But don't let me bring your conversation to an early end.' Rosina didn't want to intrude. She had never taken her position as a gentleman's wife for granted and saw herself as no better than the kind of folk she had shared her previous fife with.

'It's all right,' Rosie smiled warmly. Like all who knew Rosina Blake, she liked and respected her. Rosie looked at her baby. 'Sarah looks as if she's about to demand a feed. If you'll excuse me, I'd better make for our cart.'

Rosie left and was joined by Matthias and John Whitehead who had mustered the other Renfree children.

'But what's going on, Aunty Rosie?' Jessica called after her. With three noisy children all about her and her baby crying in her arms, Rosie didn't hear Jessica. 'Damn!' she muttered crossly.

'Jessica.' Rosina tapped her arm, seeing she was about to lurch after her aunt.

'Oh, sorry. Sorry, Mistress Blake. I said a bad word, didn't I? And outside a church too. I wanted to speak to my Aunty Rosie. Something's going on, you see. Father's having a whole hindquarter of lamb roasted today and now I've heard who's coming to dinner.'

'Would you like to run after Mrs Renfree and find out more about it?' Rosina said, looking anxiously at the lychgate in case Simon Peter appeared.

'No, I s'pose I'll find out soon enough. Is there something wrong? You look worried all of a sudden.'

'Well, I want to talk to you about Simon Peter and I don't want him to see us together.'

Jessica started walking back into the churchyard. 'Why not? Is there something wrong with Simon then?'

'Jessica, did you know that Simon Peter is going away?'

'No! What for? Where's he going?' Jessica was genuinely upset and was sorry that she had so recently snubbed him.

'He's going on the Methodist circuit. Mr Blake and I knew he'd always planned to. We had hoped he'd join either the Cornwall east circuit around the St Austell area or the Cornwall west circuit around Redruth and St Ives, then he wouldn't have been too far away from us. But he has asked to be taken out of the county. Mr Blake and I, of course, don't want him to go.

'Jessica, I know it is a liberty to ask you, but won't you reconsider your feelings towards Simon Peter? He loves you so very much and I believe it's because you won't accept his proposal of marriage that he wants to go so far away. What I want to say to you may make you feel differently. Mr Blake has no objections to you as Simon Peter's choice. I know that Mr Blake is not… well thought of in Mount's Bay, or in the county even, but you wouldn't have to live in our house. My husband will set you and Simon Peter up in your own house, anywhere you like, and he will settle a generous amount on you both, in both your names. Then you will never have to feel dependent on Simon Peter, or us, and if you were to be left a widow you would still have your own means. What do you say, Jessica?'

Jessica had listened with a heavy heart. 'How wonderful you are, Mistress Blake, how kind and caring. I know it must have been difficult for you to say all that. It's a very generous offer, it would be very tempting to another girl.'

'But not to you?' Rosina sighed.

'Mistress Blake, of all the folk I know, except for Aunty Rosie and Uncle Matthias, you and Mr Blake are the only ones who married for love. I want that sort of love for myself or I don't want to marry at all. I know love can grow, my father's did for my mother despite the fact he'll always have a care for Lady Pengarron. And although Lady Pengarron and Sir Oliver love each other deeply and openly now, their marriage began as a business deal over a scrap of land, which broke my father's heart. I want to love my husband, if I have one, like you did, from the very first day. I am very fond of Simon Peter but I don't love him and my wild and reckless ways would only bring him misery. I hope you take that as my answer, Mistress Blake, and will not press me.'

Rosina had listened quietly. She smiled submissively, took Jessica's hand and kissed her cheek. 'Then that is the way things will be. Simon Peter must go away and one day, Jessica, I am sure you will meet a man who will love you for just the way you are, and that you can love too.'

—

'I didn't know you were interested in salvation, Trenchard, or in the parson's horses.'

Clem had Catherine's pony by the reins and was waiting for her to appear after changing into a riding habit. 'Are you talking to me?' he asked Oliver icily.

'Well, I suppose I would rather talk to one of your dogs,' Oliver replied mockingly. He could not resist the chance to jibe at his old enemy. 'I would certainly receive better manners in return.'

'Do you want something… sir?' Clem said sarcastically.

'You can move aside. My family's horses are stabled here and you are in the way.'

'And you don't want me to be here when Kerensa and Kelynen come for their mounts?' Clem said in challenge.

'I object to them sharing the same air you breathe, Trenchard. Be careful with what you are doing with Miss Lanyon's pony, it's a good piece of horseflesh.'

They were too absorbed in their snipes to notice Kelynen had crept up on them and she promptly gave them reason to feel ashamed. 'Love thy neighbour,' she murmured and walked up to the pale brown pony Clem was holding and smoothed its white blaze.

But neither man felt any shame. There were too many years of hate and distrust between them for that.

'Get on your pony, Shelley,' Oliver said tightly. He hated it when his daughter was close to Clem Trenchard. 'You can wait for your mother and me at the end of the carriageway.'

'Good day to you, Kelynen,' Clem said, glancing defiantly at Oliver.

'Good day to you, Clem,' Kelynen replied brightly, then she hugged her father and went off to do his bidding.

When she was out of earshot, Oliver said angrily, 'If you must speak to my daughter, then you will use the prefix Miss, Trenchard!'

'What's going on here?' Kerensa asked, coming up to the two men and feeling the tension in the air.

'Despite what some people might think,' Oliver replied, looking as if he would like to twist a knife in Clem's heart, 'absolutely nothing.'

Kerensa gave Clem a swift 'must you always annoy each other' look. She took Oliver's arm to prise him away but he had seen a lady in a discreet hat and riding clothes coming out of the Parsonage's back door and he refused to be pulled away.

The lady hesitated, but realising she had been seen, came forward reluctantly. Oliver was curious now as to the reason why Clem Trenchard was holding Miss Catherine Lanyon's pony. Surely they weren't intending to ride somewhere together? And why had Trenchard brought himself and his family to church today anyway?

Catherine wished anyone other than the beautiful Lady Pengarron was here to witness her intended ride to Trecath-en Farm with Clem. But then, why shouldn't Clem Trenchard take an interest in another woman? Kerensa Pengarron didn't own him. Even if Clem did still love her, Kerensa was married to another man, and a woman couldn't set her sights higher than the wealthy and powerful Lord of the Manor.

Catherine smiled at Clem but propriety demanded she speak first to the baronet and his wife. 'Sir Oliver, m'lady, I hope you enjoyed the service.'

Oliver answered pleasantly, looking as if he intended to stay and converse. 'We did, Miss Lanyon, thank you.'

Catherine glanced at Kerensa, then said, 'Are you ready to go, Clem?'

Kerensa looked from face to face. Oliver looked as if he couldn't believe his eyes – so they *were* going riding together! Clem was blushing and Miss Catherine was looking fierce.

'I'll help you up,' Clem said awkwardly, moving so his back was to the Pengarrons.

Oliver was smirking now. 'Have you been invited out to luncheon, Miss Lanyon?'

Kerensa pinched Oliver's arm. She was worried he would cause some unpleasantness.

'Mr Trenchard has invited me to eat with his family,' Catherine replied sweetly.

Oliver looked at Clem then shook his head. 'Has he indeed? In that case I wish you well, Miss Lanyon.'

Catherine ignored the jibe at Clem.

Kerensa tugged on Oliver's arm and this time she was determined to make him move.

'What kind of a remark was that to make?' she hissed when she had got him beside their horses which the stable hand was holding ready for them.

'I only wished the lady well, beloved,' Oliver replied, grinning boyishly at her.

'You were trying to make trouble for Clem and you could have embarrassed Miss Catherine. You had no right to ask her where she was going, it's none of our business. Help me onto my pony. I want us to go now so they can leave in peace.'

'I love it when you're angry with me,' Oliver laughed. He made to kiss Kerensa but she moved away. 'As for Trenchard, he makes his own trouble. What's he doing anyway, giving out invitations to a lady? I find it hard to believe that he's romantically interested in her.'

'Nancy Wills muttered something just now about Jessica getting a new stepmother.'

'Oh, so that's the reason, is it? Jessica Trenchard is a delightful girl but without a doubt she needs a woman's influence.'

Oliver mounted and they trotted up to Kelynen then let her ride on ahead.

'How do you feel about it?' Oliver suddenly asked.

'Catherine might be good for Jessica,' Kerensa replied, brushing away persistent insects from her face.

'That's not what I meant.'

'I know.'

'Well?'

'I'm not jealous of her, if that's what you mean. I love only you in that way. It would be good for Clem to find happiness again like he had with Alice, but…'

'But Catherine Lanyon is hardly his type of woman?'

'No, she isn't. But I suppose if anything does come of it, it could work out. She is obviously interested in him.'

'For his good looks presumably.'

'I didn't expect you ever to pay Clem a compliment, Oliver.'

'Well, it can't be for his disposition,' Oliver said dryly. 'But a farmer needs a wife like Alice was, or Rosie Renfree is, not a refined lady.'

'Perhaps Miss Catherine has qualities we don't know about.'

'Well, if she does end up as Jessica Trenchard's stepmother, I hope for her sake that she has. It's quite a risk to take, marrying the moodiest man in Mount's Bay just to end the shame of being an unmarried woman.'

–

Clem had seated Jessica and Catherine in the parlour. He poured out glasses of gooseberry wine and sat with them in the thankfully cool room.

'It is pleasant in here,' Catherine said, 'after a hot dusty ride.' She had placed her purse and fan on a little table put in the middle of the room.

Jessica eyed the fan. 'Would you like me to pass you your fan, Miss Catherine?'

'No, thank you, I'm quite comfortable. The cooking smells coming from the kitchen are delicious.'

''Tis a whole hindquarter of lamb,' Jessica told her casually, as if they roasted one every Sunday. She had an inkling now what her father was up to. He had brought this fine lady here to show her some good manners. He had been moaning at her a lot lately over her wild behaviour. Jessica decided to play the lady of the house and put on a high-faluting voice which she knew would irritate Clem.

'Kerris is a very good cook. I'm afraid I'm not terribly good at it but we do have excellent meals these days. I hope you like sauces, Miss Catherine. Kerris makes an excellent variety of sauces.'

Clem looked at Jessica in annoyance. Was she trying to make a fool of herself, or perhaps of him? Catherine didn't seem disturbed, but was it her lady's training not to show it?

'I'm looking forward to the meal, Jessica.'

Jessica met Clem's look. 'My father did not tell me he'd invited you here today, Miss Catherine, but it is nice to have some female company.'

'I'm pleased to hear it, Jessica, though you have Kerris here now. How is she? Have you any notion of who she really is yet?'

'No, we've learned nothing at all about her, but we're not that concerned really, we're happy to have her here with us for ever. She's settled down quite well but is still fearful of my father and brothers although she seems quite at ease with my Uncle Kenver. You haven't been introduced to him yet, have you? He's helping Kerris in the kitchen.'

'I'd be fascinated to meet your uncle. I have seen some of his craftwork and was impressed with its quality and workmanship. In fact my brother bought a set of carved wooden animals for our nephew Thomas's birthday gift.'

'A lovely little boy, your nephew, Miss Catherine,' Clem said, thinking it was about time he made a contribution to the conversation. Despite Jessica's silly voice, he was pleased that things seemed to be going well.

'To bring the conversation back to Kerris for a moment,' Catherine said. 'I have a theory about her.'

'Oh? I'd be most interested to hear it,' Clem said.

'Well, it's quite a chilling idea of mine actually. I haven't even mentioned it to my brother in case he accused me of being fanciful. A few weeks ago a woman was brutally murdered in Penzance. Her maid disappeared and everyone expected her body to be found a few days later, as has happened before, but nothing like that so far has occurred.'

'You think Kerris is, or rather was, that woman's maid?' Jessica interrupted, gasping.

'It's a possibility, don't you think? She's obviously been in service, and I've noticed that she stares at me which could be because of my clothes and bearing. The murdered woman was not one of virtue but she was of high breeding.'

Clem put his glass down and said thoughtfully, 'If you are right, Miss Catherine, then that would explain the terrible state Kerris was in when Jessica found her. The murderer is almost certainly a man because of the... of the brute strength used in his horrible crimes and that could account for Kerris's fear of men. She feels safe with Kenver because he's stuck in a chair and seems no threat to her.'

'Dear Lord,' Jessica breathed, shuddering and no longer feeling like play-acting. 'It's horrible... poor Kerris. What you say suggests she saw the murder.'

'At least she's safe here with us,' Clem said grimly.

'I'm glad you don't think me fanciful,' Catherine said, repressing a shudder herself. 'I shall make enquiries at Penzance to ascertain the maid's name and age and what she looked like.'

'No,' Clem said firmly, 'I would rather you did not. It could be dangerous. Let me see to it, please.'

'Very well, if you think that would be best.' Despite the horrific reason, Catherine was pleased; it gave them a mutual interest.

Kerris's predicament was forgotten when David popped his head round the door to inform them the meal was ready to be served.

Clem carved the lamb, and Kerris, who stared at Catherine after dropping a perfect curtsey, was helped by Jessica to serve the vegetables. Instead of the usual wooden platters, the meal was served on Alice Trenchard's china plates which had come from the Manor, given to her by Kerensa. Clem had usually objected to using Pengarron plates, but Alice had been proud to produce them on special occasions. They were not all of the same size and pattern but with flowers and good linen they made up a fine table.

Philip Trenchard was the happiest one of the family to have Catherine there. He'd been as surprised as the others that his moody, secretive father had insisted they all go to church and that he had invited someone back for lunch. He'd been shocked to hear it was Miss Catherine Lanyon, but the moment he'd realised what his father's intentions were, he'd been delighted. If his father could pull off this marriage, Catherine Lanyon would bring a dowry with her, probably too small for a gentleman to be interested in but a sizeable one for simple farming folk. His plans for the farm, which had fallen flat on their face when Cordelia Drannock had spurned him, could be brought wonderfully to fruition. And he wouldn't have to get married at all himself now; he could use women as much as he wanted and never be shackled to one of them.

'The vegetables are from our own garden, Miss Catherine,' he said gallantly, passing her the gravy.

'They look succulent,' Catherine replied, smiling shyly at the strapping young man from her position at the foot of the table where Clem had placed her. She felt ill at ease now. Her confidence had been slipping away since she'd left home and it was nerve-racking to sit round the table of a whole family and have no one with her herself. Philip kept her spirits up with bright conversation. She asked him about his wrestling and he vainly filled her in on all the details.

She used the time while the meal was being served to look around the room. There was an impressive oak dresser, its china display now on the table, and lots of cupboards nailed with haphazard butterfly hinges, including a little one for spice near the hearth. The flagstone floor was clean, the walls were uneven but looked sound, the settle and the rest of the furniture were gleamingly polished. Catherine decided she liked this large room; it was cosy and productive, and made a perfect woman's domain.

Clem was seated at the head of the table. He was quite nervous himself, hoping that Catherine would not think it too common to eat round a kitchen table. He hoped none of his family would let themselves down with their table manners and that Jessica would not suddenly revert to kind and start giggling and fooling about with her brothers. Thankfully she had behaved well enough so far but he knew she wasn't really pleased to have Catherine Lanyon here.

'Kenver will be glad to show you some of his work later on,' Clem said to her.

'That's right, Miss Catherine,' Kenver nodded, eating from a tray across his special wheeled chair. 'I will be honoured.'

Good man, Kenver, Clem thought. She could see his brother was not rough and common and she must be impressed by Rosie's position, married to the Pengarron farm steward. Clem was a bit concerned about the parson's quietness this morning. He hoped Timothy hadn't changed his mind, but he hadn't stopped Catherine coming here today.

Catherine felt calmer when the meat course, which she would have found delicious if she hadn't felt so self-conscious and which she ate at a slower pace than the others, was cleared away. The redcurrant tart, custard and scalded cream were to her taste and she delighted Kerris, who had kept mainly out of the way on a three-legged stool, by accepting a second helping.

I must remember you have a sweet tooth, Clem thought.

'Thank you for a most delicious meal,' Catherine said sincerely as Clem helped her from her chair. She repeated it to Kerris who smiled for the first time since Jessica had found her.

Clem escorted Catherine back to the parlour, with the twins following and Kenver wheeling through after them, confident the dinner had been a success. Jessica brought in coffee and after a short period of small talk, Clem asked Catherine if she would care to go for a stroll and see around the farm. Catherine accepted gratefully; there were too many Trenchards packed about her in this little room.

The other menfolk looked forward to changing out of their best clothes and going about their usual Sunday afternoon activities. Jessica said that if Miss Catherine wouldn't mind, after she had helped Kerris with the dishes she would go over to the Manor to see the Misses Olivia and Cordelia. Catherine said she did not mind at all and Clem was glad to get rid of his family so he could go about the serious business of courting.

Chapter 12

Catherine had seen over the yard before, on the day she had taken the initiative and ridden over to the farm. As Clem's three dogs followed them quietly about, she saw that all the weeds and stinging nettles had been pulled up and there was nothing lying about. Even the animals, which she was more interested in, seemed to have been put in their rightful places and were content to stay there. The yard echoed a perfect restful Sunday afternoon.

She stopped to sniff the glorious warm aroma of fat rosy apples laid out and drying in the sun.

'I'll get you a basketful to take home with you,' Clem said.

He suggested they stroll further and he ran back inside to fetch one of Jessica's sunhats. It was battered but afforded better protection from the sun than Catherine's discreet hat.

They left the yard and Catherine exclaimed at the beauty of the clusters of white flowers on an elderberry tree. Clem remarked that she must take home a bottle of Ricketty Jim's elderberry wine. They would pick some fresh flowers on their way back and after the walk Kerris would brew a delicious dish of honey-flavoured tea to refresh her. Clem offered his arm and soon they were strolling along by the tinkling river at the bottom of Trecath-en valley. Catherine pointed to the adjoining field and asked what was growing in it.

'Wheat. 'Tis pale now but will soon mellow to bronze when ready for reaping,' he explained. 'We have oats in the next field. They're in their first year of a four-year rotation. Next year we'll plant rye, vetches and kale for winter feed, and the next it will be the turn of the turnips and we'll hurdle the sheep over 'em to manure the ground for the following year's barley. We have fields in each stage of the rotation.'

'How interesting.'

'You really think so?'

'Yes, I do. It sounds most efficient and very hard work.'

'Aye, it is, specially at harvest time which is coming up.'

'But at least you have two strapping sons and the man, Ricketty Jim, to help you work the land.'

'Aye, and I can afford to hire more hands,' Clem said proudly.

Catherine watched a colourful butterfly flitting close to the bank of the fast-moving river. 'It's so peaceful here,' she murmured.

Clem stopped at a spot on the river's bank where some huge granite boulders formed a cosy place to sit. He thought Catherine would seat herself sedately on a boulder but she floated gracefully down to sit on the grass. One of the dogs promptly laid its head on her lap.

'Gracie, come here,' Clem called, patting his leg to bring the dog back.

'No, don't call her away. I like dogs.'

Gracie was half up, looking hopefully at Clem from large dark eyes. Clem nodded to her and the dog sank back into Catherine's soft skirts.

Clem sat with his back against a boulder and the other two dogs lay either side of him. He thought he would be feeling so nervous at this point he would blurt out his marriage proposal, but Catherine made him feel relaxed. She was an agreeable woman, her liking for animals was genuine. She was kind and feminine and he could see why folk spoke highly of her. Even Kerensa had recommended her in the way she'd spoken of her that time in the Parsonage. Clem was comfortable in the company of the third woman he was to ask to marry him.

'Are you comfortable, Miss Catherine?'

'Yes, thank you.'

Clem had his eyes on Catherine's face which was partly hidden by the hat's brim as she stroked Gracie's head.

'What are your other dogs called, Mr Trenchard?' she asked looking up, and when she saw that he was looking at her she smiled in her shy way.

Smiling back, Clem said, 'This is Gawen,' he stroked the dog at his right leg, 'and the other one is Halwyn.'

'You have given them good names.' She glanced at each dog. 'They suit them well.'

'You might as well call me Clem now, if you'd like to… and may I call you Catherine?'

'Yes, of course, please do,' Catherine said happily. And she was happy. It was wonderful to be quite alone in the company of such an attractive man. She was sure many a lady of her station in life would be flattered to be in her position.

'I think I will get a dog, Clem. Perhaps you could tell me where you acquired these beautiful creatures.'

This was a good moment to begin the proposal. 'You, um, don't have to acquire one for the Parsonage, Catherine. You could,' and Clem grew steadily red, 'share these dogs, if you like.'

Catherine's heart began to dance. 'What do you mean, Clem?'

Clem moved Halwyn aside and crouched before her. 'You could share the dogs with me, on the farm. Share my family, share my life… I mean, please don't be offended… you aren't used to men of my worth asking you such a thing.'

'You are asking me to marry you?' and Catherine's amber eyes shone with hope in her child-like face which was framed by a less severe hairstyle today.

'Yes. 'Tis for Jessica's sake. You've seen her, how unruly she can be, how unladylike she is. I'm worried about her. She needs a woman to show her the finer things in life, to groom her for an eventual good marriage.'

Catherine was elated and at the same time terribly disappointed. Since Clem's invitation to dinner she had dreamed it was with the intention of asking her to be his wife. She hadn't been sure what his reason would be and she knew it wouldn't be because he loved her. But she wished he'd pretended, or at least had not come up with his real reason so soon.

'You're very quiet,' Clem said, reaching for her hand. 'Have I angered you, have I offended you?'

Catherine looked down at her small lace-gloved hand engulfed in his. 'No, no, you've taken me by surprise and I...'

'You want to think about it? Look, I know it's a liberty but I've spoken to your brother. Of course I wouldn't have asked you here today if I hadn't done that first, and he said he will offer no objection as long as I come back to the Church, and I am happy to do that. I can assure you that you will always be treated like a lady, Catherine, and you wouldn't have to do any heavy work. We have Kerris now, and Ricketty Jim to help out, and I can afford to employ more help if you want it. It's a small farm but my sons and I work it hard and it's yielding well and I have a little money put by from other sources. Any money that you have I want to remain entirely in your name for your own comforts. You'll be free to come and go as you like and have folk call on you, not the Pengarrons, of course, but that would be because of me not you, but I'm sure they would still receive you at the Manor. Jessica needs you, Catherine. I hope you will at least consider...'

'Your proposal,' Catherine finished for him.

She could make him wait for his answer. She could play at being coy. She could insist on making the point that he was of lower birth than herself and it was a matter of great consideration. But was he a patient man? He didn't seem the kind to appreciate games. He might ask another woman to become his daughter's stepmother and she would deny herself what was probably her one chance of becoming his wife. She wondered if it had occurred to Clem that Jessica, with her lovely fair looks and sparkling spirit, was probably not far off from marriage herself. Would he feel stuck with her then? Catherine knew Clem could be sulky, that he liked his privacy and was inclined to wander off for hours alone with his dogs. Would he welcome her having visitors then? She was thirty-one years old, she had no dowry to speak of. Her only alternatives were spinsterhood or marriage to a dreary impoverished gentleman who would deem he had done her a favour.

She knew she had already made up her mind. She would risk it. This man was worth it. And although she had not known him for long, although he had once cruelly dismissed her in humiliation from the farm he was asking her to become mistress of, she had fallen in love with him.

'Catherine…' Clem prompted, gripping her hand tighter.

She lifted her face to look into his eyes, the same colour as the clear sky behind his head. 'I don't need to think about it, Clem. My answer is yes.'

Clem stared at her for an age. 'Did you say yes?'

She nodded and he shook his head as if he didn't quite believe his ears. What a good woman she was. She had offered none of the indignation or prattle he'd expected.

He peeled off one of her gloves and pressed his lips to her milk-white skin. It was soft and warm and fragrant.

Catherine's eyelashes flickered and her heart raced. His touch was exquisite and she wanted him to take her into his strong arms.

Clem was about to retreat but suddenly couldn't resist kissing her lips to seal the moment. It was only the briefest touch yet it made him realise how long he had been comfortless. He sat close beside her and kept hold of her hand. He worked his thumb up and down her palm and it did alarming things to Catherine's most inner feelings.

'We'll tell the family when we get back,' he said.

'Do you think they'll approve, Clem?'

'Aye, and without any gripes. 'Tis always been said we need another woman about the farm. David is very easy-going, Philip looked besotted with you at the dinner table and Kenver thinks you are most charming. I'm sure Kerris will be glad to have you around, she'll feel more secure with a lady telling her what to do, she's quite incapable of making any decisions for herself. And Ricketty Jim won't mind, he doesn't mind anything.'

Catherine was heartened to hear all this but she frowned. 'You haven't mentioned the most important person to be involved – Jessica. How will she react to my becoming her stepmother? She might hate me for trying to take her mother's place.'

'Jessica's wild but she has no hate in her. She might balk at first but when she realises she won't have to bear all the responsibility of the house alone she'll come round.'

'Are you sure of that, Clem?' Catherine asked, feeling niggles of panic. 'If she resents me she won't be shy in showing it.' Inside she was thinking, she might get you to change your mind about me, make a promise to behave more ladylike so you don't marry me.

'You aren't afraid of Jessica, are you?'

'No… yes. I think I am a little…'

Clem gripped her hand firmly and raised it against the side of his cheek. 'She might put up a protest but it'll only be a token one. She'll soon grow to like you, in fact I think she does like you.'

'So you'll tell her as soon as she comes home?'

'Aye.'

'I'll probably have left the farm by then. Will you please tell me what she says or send word to me?'

'I'll come over straightaway and we'll talk to your brother then about the wedding arrangements.'

'Clem, I don't want a rushed wedding, that would be too unseemly.'

'Well, I'll be busy with the harvest for the next couple of months anyway. I suppose it wouldn't be very good for you to try to settle in with your new family with the whole place busy and chaotic. Shall we say at the beginning of September then?'

'Could we say at the end of October? I would like people to see me being… courted.'

Clem was feeling confident. He kissed her hand again. 'As you please, my dear.'

Finding some boldness Catherine took off the sunhat and rested her head on his arm. She was mindful of the intangible hold that the Lady of the Manor had on Clem and wanted to lay claim to him. She glanced up at him to see what he thought of it. He settled himself more comfortably with a smile on his fair features, but she could not tell what his thoughts were behind them.

Jessica had not gone to the Manor house; she went to see Simon Peter Blake at his home.

Peter and Rosina Blake welcomed her enthusiastically, convinced she had had second thoughts about what she had told Rosina in Perranbarvah's churchyard. She was ushered into a quiet little room and Simon Peter, who was upstairs packing, was sent for.

As she waited under Peter Blake's encouraging smiles, she thought it ironic that if this gentleman wasn't so hated by the gentry he would think her fit only to work in his kitchens or share his extra-marital bed and not as a bride for his son.

Simon Peter clattered down the stairs and rushed into the room. His parents withdrew, making a show of closing the door behind them. Jessica had refused to sit down and he went straight to where she stood, stiff-backed, and took her hands. His cornflower-blue eyes were bright with hope.

'Does this mean…?'

'No, Simon,' she replied, pulling her hands away, and hating herself as his face fell. 'I simply had to come to say goodbye to you. I couldn't let you go away without saying sorry for being unkind to you.'

'Oh.' Simon Peter turned away.

'I'm sorry.'

'Well, I can't make you love me.'

'Simon…'

He turned back. 'Yes, Jessica?'

'I don't know what else to say.' There were tears in his eyes and Jessica pressed her lips together and creased her features in a bid to stop her own. 'I'll miss you.'

'I'll miss you all of my life, Jessica. Can I kiss you goodbye?'

She nodded and he came forward. Putting his soft hands either side of her face, he kissed her lips. It felt gentle and warm and she responded in the same way. Then Simon Peter held her tightly and they cried.

When she left the grand house at Trevenner, she couldn't face seeing Olivia and Cordelia. They would want to know all the details and it would make her weep. She didn't want to go home with Miss Catherine Lanyon there and have to be on her best behaviour. So instead she went to Trelynne Cove.

All the way there, Jessica sobbed. She had known Simon Peter Blake all her life and had thought of him as a brother. Spurned by peers of his own class, he had been glad to make friends with her and the twins who saw no reason to hate him because of his father's sins. Simon Peter had had only them, and Olivia and Cordelia who had become his friends too. Kane was cordial but Luke scorned him. Jessica concluded that although Simon Peter had wealth, he didn't have much of a life and falling in love with her had only made it worse. She hoped he would find solace in his faith and the new life he was embarking on.

Jessica knew Trelynne Cove well from going there with Olivia and Cordelia. There was a little hidey-hole up in the rocks. Olivia had told her that her great-grandfather, Old Tom Trelynne, the rascally old man who had sold her mother and the cove to Sir Oliver, had used it to hide contraband in, and since Jessica had emerged as the leader of the girls' adventurous plan, she had decided that was where they would hide their smuggled goods too.

Jessica couldn't wait to do the first run and was getting exasperated with Zack Maynard. He kept saying he was taking his time in planning their first smuggling run, that he needed to be more careful when working with a group of women and was waiting for the right opportunity. Perhaps if she studied the cove and worked out the details in her mind, Zack Maynard would be impressed enough to arrange a date.

Jessica climbed up the rocks and stared at the triangular-shaped opening, which was closed over with a rock, and pictured herself and the other two girls and Jack passing contraband into it. The next day they would load the goods onto Olivia's and Jack's horses and quite openly take it to the wayside cottage halfway to Marazion where Jessica had arranged a buyer. No one would suspect the daughter and niece of the Lord of the Manor of free-trading. It would be easy and wonderfully exciting and Jessica intended to save the money she made to keep her independence.

Turning to gaze across the sea to picture a rowing boat mounting the waves and coming ashore with her contraband in it, she was stunned to see she wasn't the only person in Trelynne Cove. On a tall outcrop of black granite on the shoreline sat a young man and she could tell by the long black hair and broad stiff-shouldered outline that it was Luke Pengarron.

She thought at first to leave but there was something dejected about Luke's figure and she remembered the way he had looked at her on the night of Olivia's birthday. She knew him as a cruel-tongued, arrogant womaniser but the look on his face that night had been purely complimentary, and seemingly innocent.

She climbed up beside him and he stared coolly at her.

'What are you doing here?'

'Can I sit down?'

'Typical peasant! Answer a question with another one. Where are your manners, girl?'

Jessica was stung into a fury. 'I don't know why I could ever think you could be anything but spiteful and conceited. Excuse me, Mr Luke Pengarron! I'll take my low-class presence from yours this instant.' She would have gone too but he was massaging his stiff right arm with a pained look on his face. 'What's the matter, does your arm hurt?'

'It always hurts,' he said through gritted teeth.

All anger forgotten, Jessica said sympathetically, 'Shall I rub it for you? It might help.'

Luke looked at her suspiciously as the wind took her mane of curls and swept it towards the sea. 'Are you mocking me?'

'No. You shouldn't be so bad-tempered when someone offers to help you. Do you insist I go?'

'Do what you like,' he said sullenly.

Jessica sat facing him. 'I'd like to kick you, that's what I'd like to do. 'Tis what you deserve.' She raised herself and touched his shoulder light-handedly but he winced and sucked in his breath. 'Sorry.'

Jessica could feel his muscles knotted tightly under his shirt. He watched her face as she worked, very slowly and gently, moving both hands all round his shoulder and up and down the top of his arm, then increasing the speed and pressure as his flesh began to relax.

'Oh, that feels like heaven,' he said after a few minutes. His eyes were closed and the expression on his dark face matched his words.

'You should get Beatrice to give you one of her herbal liniments to rub in,' Jessica said. 'If you had it rubbed in like this every day it would help you a lot. Olivia told me you get a lot of pain. It's probably one of the things what makes you so grumpy.'

His eyes snapped open. 'Feel sorry for me, do you?'

'No.'

'I'm pleased to hear that. I don't want your pity.'

'You bring your troubles on yourself, Luke Pengarron.' Jessica let her hands fall away.

'Don't stop,' he said, looking deep into her eyes.

'That will have to do,' she said stubbornly.

Luke moved his arm back and forth and up and down. 'It feels much better, less painful now. Thank you.'

'Is that why you came here?' Jessica asked, swivelling round so she faced the sea as he did. 'Because the pain was getting you down?'

'Partly.'

'But you don't want to tell me any more.'

'I get frustrated because I can't do all the things other men do, because of this useless arm!' he said passionately, thinking of the night he'd not been able to carry heavy contraband into this cove.

Jessica looked at his flushed, angry face. It was so like the proud profile of his handsome father. She said boldly, 'From what I hear of it, you can do most things other men do.'

Luke swung round to meet her mischievous eyes. 'That almost sounds like a compliment on certain abilities, Jessica Trenchard.'

'Well, I wouldn't know about that.'

'You don't have to remain in ignorance.'

'I shouldn't have started this,' Jessica snapped.

'You're always ready with a sharp tongue where I am concerned. I wonder what you really think of me.'

'You really want to know? I think you have all the bad points your father had years ago and none of his good ones.'

Luke laughed out loud. 'I agree, that's a very good description of me and you do me an honour with it.' Leaning closer to her he went on, 'What sort of bad points do you suppose my father had?'

'He broke my father's heart. Took your mother away from him over this place we're sitting in.'

'Your father deserved it.' Then Luke said teasingly, 'Wouldn't it be strange if one of my mother's children fell in love with one of your father's?'

'That will never happen,' she retorted.

Luke's face was so close, Jessica could feel his breath on her cheek. Her eyes, as blue as the summer sky, sank into his, as black as the granite they sat on. He was in no mood for further battle and brought his good left hand round and tugged on one of her curls. 'Could I have one of your curls, Jessica?' he asked in a husky voice.

'What?'

'Just one. I'm thinking of having a special doll made for Cordelia's collection. I'd like its hair to be the same colour as yours.'

Jessica looked doubtful.

'Please. For Cordelia?'

'Well, all right. But don't leave my hair in a mess.'

He lifted a handful of hair at the back of her head and chose a curl where its absence would not be noticed. He asked her to hold it out while he cut it off with his pocket knife. Taking a handkerchief from his breeches pocket, he wrapped the curl in it reverently and put it away. He eyed Jessica and thought about the wager he had made with Sebastian Beswetherick.

'Thank you, Jessica,' he said pleasantly. 'I suppose you have to hurry home to your work on the farm now.'

'Not yet awhile, my father has company and I want to keep out of the way.'

Luke grinned to himself. 'Good. You can entertain me for a little while longer.'

Someone else was out from home that Sunday afternoon. Kane Pengarron was calling again on Frances Nansmere.

'You do me an honour, Captain Pengarron,' Frances said cosily. She looked warm and flushed, having risen from an afternoon nap to receive her important caller.

'Forgive me for intruding on your Sunday afternoon, Frances. I have given you several days to make enquiries for me and was wondering if you have any news yet. I was suddenly overwhelmed with the desire to know, and here I am.'

'You are welcome here at any time, my dear Kane,' she said, leading him to the sofa in her parlour and pressing her body into his. 'Perhaps when we have talked you would care to join me in my boudoir… free of charge.'

'You are too kind.' Kane moved away but it was futile. The madam had taken a fancy to him and he could see she would match his every move with a closer one of her own, so he capitulated to her caresses. 'You have learned something for me?' he asked eagerly.

'I have indeed.'

He took hold of her hands and held them tightly despite her efforts to touch him. She used her chin in their place, nuzzling his arm. 'My news, Frances?'

'I could tell you later,' she whispered in his ear.

'Now, if you please,' he said, getting impatient.

'Oh, don't be vexed with me.' To his relief Frances moved away and looked serious. 'Very well, your news *first*. From what I found out from the girls that work here now, I went myself to look up those who used to work here in your mother's day. Of course some have moved away and are untraceable, some are dead and others are quite old. I have managed to track down four altogether. The trouble is that all of them were most reluctant to talk to me. A little money managed to loosen their tongues.'

'I will reimburse you,' Kane said.

'Thank you,' Frances said, returning a hand to his chest. 'Anyway, I'm afraid it seems there is some sort of mystery surrounding your mother's death.'

'A mystery?'

'Yes. As I mentioned, all four women didn't want to talk about it. One muttered something like, "I don't want to get into any trouble." The most information I got was from an old woman called Meg, the only name I could get out of her. She said your poor mother took a fall down the stairs, broke her neck and died instantly. I'm sorry, Kane, sorry for the way your mother apparently died and sorry because that was all I could find out for you.'

Kane removed Frances's hand from wandering in on his bare skin and leaned away from her in thought. 'But when my mother, Lady Pengarron that is, rescued me from my father, the evil sailor, he told her she had died of the pox.'

'Would you like me to ask more questions for you? You don't want to cause any trouble about the past, do you? I'm sure I can find a way to wring out the truth from one of the women if I can assure them of that.'

'I don't want any of the past brought out into the open. As far as I'm concerned Sir Oliver and Lady Pengarron are my parents. I just want to know my true origins. I'll go to see the old woman myself, you only have to give me her address.'

'I hope that doesn't mean our association will come to an abrupt end,' Frances said, sounding disappointed. She made an assault on his body but he grasped her hands and pushed her away. Frances wasn't disturbed. She stood up and viewed him with a critical eye. 'You're in love with someone, aren't you?'

'I am not!' Kane denied hotly.

'You are and it seems you don't even realise it yet. I am an expert on these matters. What other reason is there for you to deny yourself the pleasures of my body, now and the last time you were here? You're not too shy or too chaste.'

'Just give me that address,' he growled, displeased at being under her scrutinising eye and amused smiles. He made to go but then stopped and apologised. 'I'm finding it harder to adjust to my new life than I thought, that's all.'

'Well, if you want to continue to fool yourself, that's up to you. Now, let me tell you where you can find the old woman Meg.'

–

Rosina Blake had something on her mind which she could no longer keep silent about. After Jessica had left and Simon Peter had returned disconsolately to his packing, her husband had followed him upstairs and tried for a whole hour to talk him out of going away. Peter Blake came back downstairs and shook his head miserably.

'He won't change his mind, my beloved. He's set on going. That Trenchard girl coming here has made him more stubborn than ever.' He flopped down in an armchair by the parlour hearthside and put his head between his soft white hands.

Rosina went to him and cradled his head against her bosom. 'Peter, I want to talk to you.'

'About Simon Peter?'

'No. Our son has made his decision. It's something he has to do, and as hard as it is and no matter how much I long to have him close by me, I've accepted it. I want to talk about you, my love.'

'You're afraid I won't be able to cope with Simon leaving?'

'You'll find it very hard, I know, but we will face it together and hope he'll come back to Cornwall one day. No, it's something else,' and her cheeks flushed to a deep redness even though he couldn't see her face. 'It's about someone you know. Or rather someone you knew. Dinah Tredinnick.'

'What?' he breathed in shock, his head snapping backwards to look at her.

Rosina took a deep breath. 'I want you to understand, dearest, that I know all about her. It's dreadful what happened to her and I feel sorry for you. I can see what her death is doing to you. You won't eat, you can't sleep, you've lost weight and you're beginning to go gaunt and pale. I'm worried about you, Peter. I want to see you happy again, laughing, enjoying yourself. You've had me believe it's Simon Peter going away that's made you so miserable but I know your other reason and I want to help you.'

Blake couldn't bring himself to speak. He sobbed wretchedly in Rosina's arms and she held him like a baby, smoothing his soft dark hair. At last he said in a muffled voice, 'I'm sorry, so sorry…'

'It's all right, Peter, I do try to understand,' she murmured soothingly.

'That I've been unfaithful to you for many years? That I've kept another woman?' he sobbed into her bosom.

'I try not to think of your reasons, only that you had a need and Dinah Tredinnick filled it. I'm sorry about the way she met her horrific death, no one deserves to die that way. It's eating away inside you and I want you to come to terms with it for your own sake.'

'How can I do that?' he appealed to her. 'And what I've done to you too?'

'But you cared for Dinah, didn't you? Please say you did. I couldn't bear it if you went with her without some semblance of love or finer feelings for her.'

'Oh Rosina! This must be torturing you. How could I have believed I could be unfaithful all those years and you would never know? I'm sorry. But I did have a fondness for Dinah, and her maid who's disappeared. What can I do to rid my mind of this wretchedness and make a fresh start with you?'

'You can stop feeling sorry for yourself, Peter. You can eat a good meal today and come back to loving me tonight. Then tomorrow you can make the first moves in finding out who killed Dinah Tredinnick and what happened to her maid.'

Chapter 13

Although some hay had been mown before, the harvesting began in earnest at the beginning of August. Clem thought Kerris's identity could keep until after this busy period was over, and having ridden over to the Parsonage to arrange the wedding date with the Lanyons, he thought he could forget about that, too, while he laboured in the fields. And even though Jessica objected to his forthcoming marriage, scornfully shouting that he must be mad and it would never work, he was determined to go through with it, seeing by her reaction that it was the best thing that he could do where she was concerned, and hoping the prospect itself would calm her down. It worked to some extent because she became quietly and moodily abusive as opposed to being her usual noisy, boisterous self. He hadn't told Catherine of Jessica's objections, only that she had misgivings over their plans.

Kerensa had mixed feelings about Clem getting married again. Even after her long and mainly happy marriage to Oliver, the love she kept in her heart for Clem made her a little jealous of Catherine Lanyon. And she couldn't see how the genteel lady would make a suitable wife for a working-class farmer who was one of nature's loners and inclined to moodiness. Kerensa had overheard Jessica lamenting about it to Olivia and Cordelia and she felt there was trouble ahead. Clem was in danger of making himself very unhappy.

Oliver treated the subject with scorn. He made Kerensa wince with his sarcastic remarks. 'Is the oaf trying to better himself by marrying a lady?' he sneered. 'If he ever sees that the logical answer to the problem of his unruly daughter is to marry her off to a suitable young man straight away he'll back out of this marriage and make an even bigger fool of himself.' She almost felt Oliver was trying to hurt her in some way. She knew he was still jealous of the fact that she had once been betrothed to Clem and was suspicious that she still loved him. He was probably afraid even now that there was some risk that Clem could take her heart away from him. She was careful not to discuss the Trenchards with Oliver now.

But while Oliver could dismiss the matter as a source of scornful amusement and apply himself to the hard work of harvesting the fields of Ker-an-Mor Farm, Clem found he could not. As a happy bride-to-be Catherine Lanyon was eager to show off her new position and insisted on riding to Trecath-en Farm every day to help prepare the food for the harvesters.

Surprisingly, Jessica did not object to this. With Kerris content to be left in Catherine's company, it meant she could leave the farmhouse kitchen this year and do what she liked best – work with the other women in the fields.

She had her own hook, inherited from her great-grandmother, and joined the long row of women, bent nearly double, as they made their way down the length of a field, not stopping until they had reached its end. Then they walked back to the starting side and began the journey again. They worked under the baking sun in light clothes and long bonnets from early morning until ten o'clock when Kerris and Catherine arrived promptly each day with the 'fuggan', the traditional raisin cake, freshly baked and delicious.

After a brief rest the harvesters went back to work and the two other women retreated back to the kitchen, leaving food and ale for the dinnertime crib. They returned with the late-afternoon provisions and sometimes stayed, keeping out of the way, until it was too dark to work and the daily toil ended.

Like the other women, Jessica couldn't help being impressed by Catherine's behaviour. She walked across the fields alongside Kerris instead of riding her pony and was careful not to get in anyone's way. As she poured out cider, which the Trenchards brought along in the early morning in heavy jugs, she spoke to everyone without airs or graces. Most noticeably of all, she gave Clem plenty of space. Except for giving him a longer, brighter smile, she doled out his food and drink in the same way as she did the other men's. The labourers were impressed that a lady should spend time among them when they were work-dusty and sweating. The children liked her because she brought sweetmeats and biscuits for them every day and had a ready supply of cloths and ointments to tend their blisters and sunburn.

Clem employed a small army of men, women and children who came from all over the district, most of whom who were happy to work for their food, cider and ale and the companionship they shared. The harvesting was a time of reunion, of meeting old friends, of fondly remembering those who had died since the last harvest.

While Jessica worked in one field in the formation of women going before the men who bound, tossed and pitched the sheaves, Clem and the twins and Ricketty Jim worked in another, reaping with specially made hooks of extended length. This was skilled labour and they worked with Matthew and Paul King who spent their time here when not fishing each year, for the chance of earning some extra shillings. They swung their scythes in each hand alternately, swathing down the com, urging the accumulating burden forward until they had enough for a sheaf. These were then bound up by women, some of them fishwives and bal-maidens who came straight from their shift at the mines. Behind both work forces came the children, garnering the remains of the corn into 'riskans' – little bundles – and the old men who set up the sheaves expertly in the proper position for the 'shocks'.

Kane came to help during the third week, feeling he had put in enough loyal work on Ker-an-Mor Farm for a while. Luke had not wanted him to work on the land at all, but he was furious at him helping the Trenchards and would hardly speak to him now. Kane knew Luke's reasons and he was sympathetic. He could cut up to two acres a day but Luke couldn't even swing a scythe owing to his useless arm. But he wasn't going to allow his younger brother to bully him.

He stood at the top of Trecath-en's valley and looked across the patchwork of barley bleached grey by the sun, yellow oats and tanned wheat, with roughly half cut and sheaved. The remainder swayed in the warm winds, bending and rolling not unlike the sea and sighing like a distant tide.

It was easy to pick out Jessica, her waist-length mane of golden curls bright against the pale landscape. She worked first in the line of women, as befitted her position as the farmer's daughter, and Kane was captivated by the grace and ease with which she moved despite the back-breaking work. He could tell even from this distance that she shared in the cheerful pride and satisfaction of the harvesters. But he doubted if she would have a cheerful word for him.

Jessica reached the end of the field and instinct made her look up. She saw Kane striding towards them leading his horse and she stared at his commanding figure as she walked back to the starting side of the field. He was tall and upright and his bearing was so much like Sir Oliver's he could be his natural son. Perhaps he was, Jessica mused. The Lord of the Manor had been a notorious womaniser before his marriage. She made up her mind not to look into Kane Pengarron's eyes. It was not easy to keep up the barrier she had erected against him when she looked into those startlingly gorgeous brown eyes.

It was the afternoon crib time and after arranging with Clem to work in his field, Kane sat down beside Ricketty Jim under the baking sun, leaving the women to the shade of the hedge and a solitary elm tree.

Ricketty Jim broke off a piece of treacle toffee he'd been keeping cool under a large slab of granite and passed it to Kane. 'In return for this excellent wine you're sharing with me, sir,' he said, swigging from a bottle. 'You were always fond of a piece of toffee as a young'un, as I do remember.'

'Yes,' Kane laughed. 'The other children and I used to pester you as much for your toffee as for your stories.'

'Aye, 'tis hard to believe you've all grown up now. But I've another brood taking your place. Rosie and Matthias Renfree's children come over to see me in my little shack, and sometimes Miss Kelynen with her dog. How's the harvesting going on Ker-an-Mor?'

'Very well. Father and Matthias are pleased. It's cooler working there where the fields reach down to the cliff edge and the sea breezes blow in than it is here.' Kane glanced around Trecath-en's fields. 'I should think Clem will finish his harvesting at about the same time.'

'Let's hope we don't get no rain to speak of. We had a few drops last week and for a while it looked like the clouds were building up. I've seen too many crops flattened and ruined by a sudden heavy shower.'

Kane was looking at Catherine Lanyon who was occupied with the children. 'What do you think about Clem planning to marry the parson's sister?'

'Well, 'tisn't for me to say whether he should marry her or no. But, to speak as I find, she's a grand lady, is Miss Catherine. Ready to pitch in where she's needed and doesn't interfere where she's not.'

Kane grinned. 'Sounds like the ideal woman.'

'Could be, but I don't know much about them,' Ricketty Jim said, looking at Kane from his shrewd brown eyes. 'Are you by any chance…?'

'Looking for an ideal woman?' Kane chewed thoughtfully on his toffee. 'My first priority is setting up my own farm.'

'If you don't mind the presumption, sir, I thought p'raps you would be taking over Ker-an-Mor Farm as your own one day.'

'It's been suggested, even by my brother who will inherit all rights to the Pengarron properties, that my father gives me Ker-an-Mor Farm, including the stud. But I want to set out on my own, build up my own life. I don't mind taking risks.' He picked up a stone and turned it over in his hand. 'What do you reckon Jessica thinks about Catherine Lanyon becoming her stepmother, Jim?' he asked. 'It's all round the parish that it's in hope of taming her wild behaviour that Clem is taking a lady as his second wife, that he's taking another wife at all.' Kane tried not to but his eyes sought Jessica often. Ricketty Jim noticed this. His eyes took on a shrewder look and seemed to bore into Kane's.

'Course, if the maid married herself then Clem wouldn't have to get married again.'

Kane had been absently tossing the stone in the palm of his hand. Now he struck the ground with it hard, making dust rise. 'I asked you a question.'

'Aye, so you did,' Jim replied mildly, picking up the stone and weighing it in his own hand. 'Who can say what goes on in that particular mind?'

Jessica was sitting with a group of woman who were discussing the physical attributes of the male harvesters. She had not been taking in what they said until a certain gentleman's name was mentioned.

'I thought 'twas a toss-up between Philip and his father, well developed as they are, as to who cut the best figure here,' one woman said amid much stifled laughter. 'But when I saw Cap'n Pengarron walking down this way, well!'

Another woman prodded Jessica with her tankard of ale. 'What do you think, Jessie?'

She went bright red at the sudden question and the gathering roared with laughter.

'Well, you d'knaw Cap'n Pengarron better than we, don't 'ee, Jessie?' a girl of her own age giggled. 'Played as a young'un with un back-along, probably been lookin' un over since he's been back, eh?'

Jessica felt almost panicky and couldn't understand why. She thought desperately for the right thing to say to ward off the interest of those now staring at her in amused anticipation. A small child saved her further embarrassment by falling on a sharp stone and setting up a loud wail. Jessica sprang up and reached the child the same time as Catherine.

'Is he all right?' she asked Catherine in a shaken voice.

Catherine picked the little boy up and gently pulled his hand away from his leg. 'It's only a small cut but he fell very hard. I've brought the Reverend Timothy's medicine box with me. If you would like to hold him, Jessica, I'll clean the cut and apply some ointment.'

Catherine motioned for the boy's concerned mother to sit and enjoy her rest and Jessica followed Catherine to the medicine box.

'I've brought some fresh tuckers with me if you'd like to replace the one you're wearing, Jessica,' Catherine said kindly as she cleaned the child's cut.

'You're very thoughtful,' Jessica replied, rather brightly owing to her recent escape, and Catherine thought they were becoming friends at last.

Clem, who couldn't bear to see children hurt, came up to them. 'What happened?' he asked.

'He fell over,' Catherine explained, smiling up at her fiancé. 'It isn't serious though, he'll forget all about it in a few minutes.'

Clem lifted the little boy up and took him to his mother, bouncing him up and down on the way until the child squealed with laughter.

'Your father told me he likes children,' Catherine said, watching proudly.

'Aye, he does. Me and the twins are the most important things in his life,' Jessica said pointedly as she changed her tucker and cast the sweat-stained one carelessly on the ground.

Catherine picked it up and put it in a linen bag, her lips taut at the rebuff. Then Jessica touched her arm. 'Thank you, you've been a great help bringing these little comforts for all of us.'

'As long as I'm not getting in the way.'

'No, you're not doing that here.'

Jessica walked away and found Kane on her heels. She refused to turn round and show the respect he was due as a gentleman. He spoke over her shoulder. 'Was the little fellow badly hurt?'

Angrily aware that the other women were watching them intently, Jessica whirled on him. 'We don't need your help in tending the young'uns!'

Kane brought his lips together and lifted his chin. He gazed angrily at her then moved off to his horse to fetch his scythe.

Clem had overheard her stinging retort. Taking her by the arm he marched her out of earshot of the others. She struggled to run away but he held her firmly.

'I've had just about enough of your rudeness to my friends, Jessica! You're getting spiteful now and I won't have it, do you hear? One more remark like that and I'll confine you to the farmhouse with your uncle. Why are you so nasty to Kane anyway?'

He shook her when she didn't answer and was surprised to see tears streaming down her face. He let her go and she ran off. He stared after her until he realised that Catherine had come to stand beside him. He shook his head. 'I just don't understand her any more. She was actually crying. Have you any idea what that could be about?'

'It could be because of me,' Catherine replied quietly.

'I don't think it was that.'

Catherine offered no more suggestions but her mind was busy thinking. Since his proposal of marriage, Clem had not even held her hand and she wanted so much for him to hold her. Could his daughter be wanting someone to hold her too?

Clem passed Kane the sharpening stone for his scythe. 'I'm sorry about Jessica just now. I'll get her to apologise properly to you.'

'There's no need for that,' Kane said, glancing at Clem then attacking the stone.

'I'd rather she did. I don't want her to go on behaving like an ill-bred waif and stray, thinking she can do and say what she likes to who she likes.'

Kane passed the stone to another reaper and waited until he'd moved away. 'There'd be no point if she did not mean it.'

'You think she wouldn't?'

Kane shrugged, looking at the field he was about to begin work in. 'It doesn't really matter.'

Kane toiled behind David, who worked behind Philip, with Clem in front. David became concerned at Kane's rapid, furious strokes at the wheat. Afraid of getting his ankles sliced through, he suggested they change places. Philip's arms were stronger than his and he moved faster, so he was safe from Kane's pace.

Kane had not yet gone to see the old woman called Meg who might be able to give him information about his real mother. He wasn't sure why not. He'd asked himself if he was afraid of what he might stir up. It was obvious by the way he had been kept starved and ill-treated as an infant that his real mother had not loved him; probably the reverse. But he wanted to know something about her. What her name was, how old she had been when she died, that sort of thing. Frances had said there was a mystery of some sort surrounding her death. Instead of simply learning about his past, something gruesome might come to light and the episode could escalate and he didn't want to upset his parents. Kane also considered that if Meg couldn't or wouldn't help him, it would mean another visit to Frances Nansmere for the names of the other harlots who had known his real mother.

Did he want to step into the madam's parlour again? He liked her but he wished she wasn't quite so persistent in her amorous advances. And he certainly didn't want to listen to any more of her nonsense about his being in love!

A stab of pain in his side made him straighten up and gasp. David stayed his scythe and signalled to the other men to halt.

'You all right, Kane?' he asked. 'Can I get you a drink of water?'

'No, no, thank you,' Kane replied, smiling to make light of the sudden interest he'd caused. Philip and Clem had come to his side. 'It's just my old wound playing up. Catches me out now and again.'

Kane was embarrassed. Clem was staring at him as if he was a nuisance and he knew the wheat would be cut faster without unnecessary hold-ups caused by the Lord of the Manor's son. He also felt responsible for the dampening of spirits caused by the spite he'd received from Jessica. If he hadn't turned up, the work would have been progressing satisfactorily. He had a sudden urge to shake Jessica Trenchard. He wanted to bruise her emotions as she had his. She had quite spoiled his homecoming when it had been important to him to return to the way things had been before he'd joined his regiment.

'Let's get back to work,' he growled. 'I promise I won't stop again.'

He wouldn't stop now if his stomach burned and threatened to spill out of his flesh. He swore under his breath in the foulest oath he knew. Damn that incident in the Caribbean! Not that it mattered in itself. But all those months he had lain recovering his life and strength he had suffered the recurrence of his childhood nightmares. They obviously derived from the days he'd spent in that brothel. He dreamed of shadowy figures rushing about, shouting and screaming at him. Of being hurled away from all he sought comfort from. Of wild laughter, leering faces and voices. Of a terrible hunger and fighting to get food. And beatings. Always he was beaten. Kicked in the legs, whipped across his back and punched in the face. Worst of all, when he cried for his mother, a hundred voices screamed back at him, hissing, 'What mother?'

After that Sunday afternoon visit to Frances Nansmere, he'd gone home and drifted off to sleep in a chair and one of those awful nightmares had returned. Kerensa had woken him and he had clung to her in fear for a few moments. It was more likely that this was the reason he had not gone to see the old harlot Meg. It was better to be working on the land again, filling his lungs with dust, smelling the earth, stretching his back.

The day's work came to an end without further incident and Kane stalked off and made straight for his horse. Clem had to run to catch him before he mounted.

'You're in a hurry. Didn't even give me a chance to thank you.'

'I promised my mother I'd get back in time for a family supper on Ker-an-Mor Farm.'

'I see. How is she?'

'She's very well. Happier now she has all her children home.'

'Yes, of course. Thanks for your help today, Kane. If the weather stays kind we should have all the fields done in another week or so.'

Kane knew that Clem was wishing he could ask to have his regards given to his mother. He doubted the wisdom of Clem's getting married again. As far as he could see nothing would change Jessica Trenchard's character.

'You coming tomorrow?' Clem asked, feeling shy at asking. Kane Pengarron had the title of captain now. He was no longer a little boy playing with his own sons but a gentleman he should touch his forelock to.

'I thought to help out at Orchard Hill Farm tomorrow,' Kane replied lightly.

'Well, you've been a grand help here today.'

'I'm glad to hear it.' Kane swung into the saddle and was about to say goodbye when he saw Jessica standing quietly alone in front of his horse.

When Clem noticed her, he said, 'I'll see you, then,' and moved away. He hoped that Jessica would put things right. It wasn't good to have bad feelings building up between Kane and Jessica. Clem liked Kane but even though Jessica was entirely in the wrong he would have to side with her in the end and on top of everything else that would cause uneasy feelings between him and Kerensa.

'I'd like to talk to you for a minute, please,' Jessica said to Kane in a rigid voice. Her face was flushed and dust-streaked from her day's labour and she held her bonnet loosely in her fingers, allowing her long golden hair to sweep down over her shoulders. Kane was mesmerised for a moment then got off his horse and started to walk in the direction of Ker-an-Mor Farm. Jessica fell in step beside him.

'I was very rude to you earlier on. I owe you an apology,' she said, looking down at the ground.

Kane looked at her closely to see what kind of mood she was in. He could only think that she looked as cherubic as she had as a little girl, and that didn't help.

'Did your father tell you to talk to me?'

'No, I don't need anyone to tell me what's a right and proper thing to do!' she snapped.

'Well, if you can't even make an apology without being rude then I'm not in the least bit interested to hear it.' Kane mounted and rode off, leaving Jessica wide-eyed and biting her lip.

'I didn't mean it to come out like that,' she lamented to herself. 'Oh, what is it about that man that makes me…' And she knew she had hurt herself this time more than she had him.

Chapter 14

Knowing that Oliver and Kerensa would stay at Ker-an-Mor Farm for the harvest period, Hezekiah Solomon took the liberty of calling at the Manor in the hope of seeing Olivia alone. This could be the ideal opportunity to work on the plans he had to seduce her. He knew Luke would be busy in the farm's office, that Cordelia found the farm an ideal place to daydream, and Kelynen, whom he hated, would never be far from her parents' side. Olivia, who had her own painting studio in the Manor house, was most likely to be at home.

Polly O'Flynn told him firmly that there was no one to receive him, but having made a point of checking that Olivia's pony was in the stables, Hezekiah insisted on paying her his respects – 'Now that I am here,' he hissed.

Olivia was furious at being dragged away from her painting, especially by this horrid little man. She hated his debauched face, his ornate clothes and his overpowering colognes and she hated the very thought that he might be considering her as a wife. Whatever his reason for calling on her, she would not see him alone. She brought Shaun O'Flynn, who had been sitting for her, into the parlour with her and kept Polly in close attendance.

'It is a pity you have had a wasted journey, Captain Solomon,' Olivia said coolly, reluctantly giving her hand to be bent over and kissed, still wearing her painting smock over her dress. She did not ask him to sit down or offer any refreshment.

'But it is always a pleasure to spend even a few moments in your delightful company, Miss Olivia.' Hezekiah looked unperturbed but inside he felt venomous that he should be treated so discourteously and that she should bring a loathsome child into the room with her.

'It is a most busy time of the year for the family,' Olivia said, looking at the door.

Hezekiah kept up his smiles which Olivia found ugly. 'I know and it is for that reason that I felt I could not call at Ker-an-Mor Farm and ask after the health of your dear parents. I do miss their company.'

'They are well,' she said curtly.

Shaun had been fiddling with a book on a table and sent it thumping onto the floor. Hezekiah jumped back and looked at the boy as though he'd like to kill him. Polly gathered up the book and Shaun ran to clutch her skirts. They shared the same feelings of fear that gripped Olivia every time the strange retired sea captain was about.

'Ah, an endearing little boy,' Hezekiah smiled, but his teeth were clenched tightly. 'How old is he now?'

'He's… he's four, nearly five,' Olivia blurted out.

Hezekiah took a shilling from a pocket. 'Here you are, little boy.'

Shaun refused to take it. He moved behind Polly's back and hid his face away.

'Oh dear,' Hezekiah said, the words rolling off his darting tongue like acid. 'He's a little shy.'

Olivia knew she had no choice but to take the money for the boy herself. Swallowing a hard lump in her throat, she moved towards the hateful little man. He pulled his hand towards his chest so she would have to come closer.

'Thank you, Captain Solomon. I'll see that Shaun gets it later.'

Hezekiah had removed his gloves and Olivia could feel his warm clammy flesh when he took her hand and slowly placed the coin in her palm. His serpent eyes claimed her fearful attention as he retained her hand for a moment.

He'd known he wouldn't be able to stay for long, but Olivia's cool behaviour meant it was time to go already. His plan was not working out at all. Damn these Pengarron women! What made them so unseducible? Why did they ignore or spurn his subtle attempts at bedding them? Kerensa Pengarron cared only for her husband and this girl was probably 'saving herself' for her future partner, all properly legal and churched. He swore at that moment that he would not let Olivia Pengarron slip through his fingers as he had her mother. And when that time came he would not spare her. There would be no gentleness, no light touches, just delicious lingering pain.

As if she read his thoughts, Olivia snatched her hand away and the shilling hit the floor and rolled away. Hezekiah kept his eyes on her as he retrieved it and put it on a table.

'I must bid you good day, Miss Olivia,' he said in an amiable tone. 'I have other friends I wish to see before the afternoon is over.'

'Thank you for calling, Captain Solomon. I'll tell my parents that you enquired after them.'

Hezekiah knew he was being given a rebuff but he also knew she was shaken. He would use the tactic of staying away from her for a little while – and then he would pounce!

When he had gone, Olivia sank down on the nearest chair. Polly came back from the main doors after seeing him out of the house, with her son still clutching her.

'Are you all right, Polly?' Olivia gasped, waving a hand in front of her face.

'I was going to ask you that, Miss Olivia,' the housekeeper answered, shaken through and through. 'I don't care what excuse I have to make in future, I shan't let that awful man into the house again unless his lordship's home.'

'Open all the windows in the room, will you, please? I shall feel we haven't truly rid ourselves of that dreadful little fop's presence until his perfumes have been erased.'

With the help of a plateful of sweetmeats, Olivia had just persuaded Shaun to adopt the position she required for the sitting again when there was a tap on her painting-room door. Shaun sprang up and rushed to cling to her and they watched the door wide-eyed in fear that Hezekiah Solomon had come back.

The Reverend Timothy Lanyon was shocked by the expressions on their faces when he put his head round the door. 'Good Lord! Surely I have not startled you so much?'

'No, no! We thought you were someone else,' Olivia cried out.

Coming fully into the well-lit room, Timothy went straight to them. 'You have both been frightened out of your wits. What has happened, Miss Pengarron? Who did you think I was?'

Shaun stared up at the parson who grinned down on him. When the boy grinned back, Olivia began to feel rather foolish.

'Captain Solomon was here a short time ago, Reverend Lanyon. I find him rather discomfiting.'

'Did he frighten you?' Timothy persisted.

'Yes, I admit he did, a little. I was most annoyed that he had called. I was trying to paint.'

'And now you have me disturbing you,' Timothy said uncertainly. 'Polly sent me up, she didn't think you'd mind for a moment or two. I'll say goodbye and leave you to get on.'

After Hezekiah Solomon's frightening presence Timothy Lanyon's was utterly desirable. 'I shall not mind if you stay, Reverend Lanyon,' Olivia said, and the parson's delight was evident.

Shaun went back to his seat and plate of sweetmeats and Timothy looked cautiously at the sketching on the easel. He didn't want to risk stirring up her artistic temperament. The expression under his dark brows was full of admiration. 'This is excellent, Miss Olivia. You have made a good likeness of young Shaun and captured the very essence of his spirit.'

Olivia was embarrassed and suspicious of his sincerity. 'I don't like my work being seen until it is finished,' she said sharply. The afternoon was not working out at all well. It had taken a lot of cajoling to get Polly to agree to Shaun sitting for her in the first place.

Timothy ignored her outburst and moved tactfully to the other side of the easel but swept his grey eyes over some of her finished work propped up or hanging on the walls. She watched him from the corner of her eye, wondering what he was thinking. If he criticised her work, she would order him to leave.

'I see you have painted many of the servants. They are very good. I believe there is one of your earlier works in the Parsonage. It is signed o. E. M. Pengarron. They are not Sir Oliver's initials, I understand.'

'You are correct, Reverend Lanyon.' He wasn't like the brash man she had quarrelled with at the Parsonage a few weeks ago and since then she had noticed he had been politeness itself to her and the other ladies after the Sunday morning services. She put her paintbrushes down and moved across the room to him. 'Do you really like my work?'

Before he could answer, Shaun wailed, 'Can I go now, Miss Livvy? My head's aching and I want to go outside to play.'

'Very well, you may run along, Shaun,' she replied indulgently. 'We will carry on with your picture another day.'

'His mother is not far away,' Timothy said, explaining that he had taken no liberties by entering her private domain at the top of the house.

'His mother is never far away,' Olivia whispered confidentially and made Timothy smile in conspiracy.

When Shaun had rushed off, noisily clattering along the corridor and down the stairs, with Polly calling after him to be more careful, Olivia swept a hand through her auburn-red hair then took off her smock. 'I also have had enough of being in this stuffy room for one day. I think I will take a walk outside.'

'Would you care for me to accompany you?' Timothy asked carefully. 'I've really called to see Beatrice but I daresay she can wait a little longer.'

Olivia made a quick comparison between this young man and the shrivelled-up elderly fop who had recently left. 'Yes, I think I would, thank you. I'll get Polly to serve cold drinks in the summerhouse.'

They took a long walk around the gardens, straying into the parklands, hardly speaking. When they were seated in the cool summerhouse, Timothy said, 'You have a good studio at the top of the house, Miss Olivia.'

'My father had the room adapted for me. I would not have thought you'd approve of ladies taking up the occupation of painting, Reverend Lanyon.' Olivia was suddenly eager that he would thoroughly approve, that someone other than her indulgent family should be genuinely interested in her work.

'Oh, I don't think that you ladies should always be retained solely for household and childbed duties,' he smiled back, brushing at the wispy bits of hair that fell about his strong face.

Olivia smiled too. 'You are a surprising man.'

'Am I? In what way?'

After hating being in the company of one man who had called at the Manor this afternoon, she was enjoying being hostess to this other. She began to wonder why she had been so outraged with Timothy Lanyon before. 'Oh, I don't know,' she said, 'you just are.'

His grey eyes looked humorously at her over his glass. 'I trust you meant that kindly.'

'Yes, I did.'

'Well, I am not surprised that you are such a talented young lady. I hear you are having an exhibition of your work.'

'Yes, I'm quite excited about it. It's nothing grand, just a chance to show off my skills and hope that other people will be in agreement with you. Will you come to view it?'

'Indeed I will. Oh!' Timothy suddenly jumped up and splashed his drink down his frockcoat. Then he was worried she thought he was being ill-mannered again. 'Forgive me, Miss Olivia.'

She was alarmed. 'What is it?' and without thinking, she added, 'Timothy?'

He blinked and looked delighted while being flummoxed at the same time. 'I... I... have just remembered that I have an appointment in Marazion at four of the clock this afternoon and I haven't yet seen Beatrice. I'm afraid I'm not at all organised with my sister spending so much of her time at Trecath-en Farm.' It was somehow endearing to see him flapping about in his natural manner.

'I know the reason that a parson calls on a parishioner is confidential but I am curious as to why you are calling on Beatrice. I've never known her to ask for you, or the Reverend Ivey before you, until now.'

'She hasn't asked to see me. I was told she was very ill. I feel I have a duty to his lordship's servants to offer comfort to them when they are ailing.'

Olivia laughed gaily. 'There is no need for concern, Reverend Lanyon. Beatrice has not been ill. I'm afraid the truth is that she's been very drunk again. If you go now, you will not be late for your appointment.' She held out her hand and he took it, kissing it lightly while looking into her eyes.

'May I venture to ask whether, if I have reason to call here again, my presence will be more welcome than a certain retired sea captain's?'

'I can assure you that I could never think of you in the same way that I do that man,' Olivia answered softly. 'The door will always be open to you.'

She clasped her hands together after he had gone. She knew she had been rather brazen, having no right to offer such an invitation to a young man, even the parish parson, without her father's consent or at least her mother's presence. Sitting back to relax in the summerhouse, she didn't care all that much.

–

With the able-bodied Trenchard menfolk in the fields from dawn to dusk, Kerris was enjoying the quietness at the farm with only Catherine and Kenver around her. She kept the house spotlessly clean, did the laundry, fed the fowls, attended to the dairy and vegetable patch and Jessica's flower garden. While she worked she made up stories about who she was, sometimes pretending that she was mistress of the house. When she made the daily walk to the fields with Miss Catherine, she kept well away from the harvesters and was always happy to get back to the peace of the farm again.

Catherine, who had unsuccessfully argued with Clem that Kerris's identity was too important to be left until after the harvesting, plied her with questions. But Kerris warded them off by asking questions of her own about the wedding and what changes Catherine was proposing to make once she was installed as mistress here, or by humming to herself and looking blank. Catherine soon realised she was getting nowhere with her enquiries and gave them up.

Kerris was getting less and less shy of Kenver and often when they were alone in the afternoon, with one or more of Clem's dogs who remained as guards, they would sit in the sun outside the kitchen door or inside in the cool, and chat. They spoke of the forthcoming marriage, the weather, about Kenver's crafts, the chores Kerris had done, how much she'd come to love the dogs and Kenver's favourite subject, something that he was amazed about – the way the wild cats that abounded on the farm allowed her to touch them and pick them up.

Kerris knew these idyllic days were drawing to an end. The day before, Clem had told Catherine that the reaping of the crops would take just another day or two. Kerris felt apprehensive about having the other Trenchard menfolk round about the farm again, even of having Jessica back. She was still kind to her but she was bad tempered these days. And Kerris was still unsure of her position, despite Kenver's promise that she would never be put off the farm. She felt more secure knowing that Clem was to marry Catherine. It meant that even if Jessica married and left, Catherine would still be here and would need her to do the heavier work. She felt safe with the kind, attractive lady.

After she went home, Catherine sometimes forgot some of her possessions and Kerris would find them lying carelessly about the farmhouse – a fan, her purse, her hat if she'd been wearing one of Jessica's sunhats. It didn't occur to Kerris that they might have been left deliberately to mark the lady's territory and keep her in Clem's mind. But the thing Kerris came across in the parlour that day was nearly her undoing. A tiny bottle of perfume had been left on the table. She picked it up, the glass cool in her rough palm, and gently touched the stopper at the top. Then, as if the thing had come to life on its own, the stopper fell off and the scent spilled over onto her hands and dropped on her apron. It was a soft, subtle fragrance but with so much of it released in the warm muggy air, it was very strong and terrible memories of an earlier time this year, when she had smelled another overpowering fragrance, flooded her mind in warped, fast-moving pictures. She didn't want those memories. She panicked. Dropping the bottle, she ran screaming from the room.

Kenver, who was resting in his bedroom–cum–workshop next door, hauled himself up on his bed to a sitting position and shouted to her, 'Kerris! Kerris! What is it? Come here to me!'

His words didn't break through her hysteria but she was running to him anyway. She flew through the door and flung herself onto the bed. She'd stopped screaming now and had gone white and rigid. Kenver eased her body closer until she was lying down beside him. She burrowed herself into his arms like a mouse in a nest and he held her tight, saying soothing words.

Kerris stayed rigid until she noticed the beat of Kenver's heart in her ear. The steady rhythm helped to calm her and she slowly allowed herself to relax. She moved away to loosen her tight muscles then snuggled back in and put her arm round his waist.

'What happened, Kerris? What made you panic?' he asked softly.

'I'm sorry,' she whispered.

'There's no need to be sorry. I'm only interested in why you were so frightened and whether I can help you.'

'You are so kind to me,' she said into his shirt.

'Well, I like you.'

'Do you mean it? I must be a worry to your family, coming from nowhere and not knowing anything about me.'

'I've got no reason to lie to you, Kerris. Do you trust me?'

'Yes.'

'You're perfectly safe here with me. Nothing can hurt you. Now, my dear, tell me what happened.'

Kerris gripped his shirt with both hands and put her face against his warm chest. 'I... I... picked up a bottle of perfume belonging to Miss Catherine. The stopper came out the top and suddenly there was perfume all over me. The smell was so strong and it terrified me for some reason... I... don't want to think about it, Kenver. Please don't make me remember.'

Kenver pulled one of her hands away and sniffed it. 'You smell lovely. Is it frightening you now?'

'No, not when I'm with you. I hope Miss Catherine won't be angry with me.'

'I'm sure Miss Catherine won't mind at all. She seems a very reasonable person.'

'Do you think so? So do I. I think it'll be good having her around the house. I didn't mean to spill her perfume. I'm afraid I dropped the bottle on the parlour floor. I'd better go and pick it up.'

'It can wait for a minute, can't it?' They were chatting in the way they usually did on a quiet afternoon but with the big difference that she was lying in his arms. Kenver didn't want to let her go yet. If he was comforting her, it was having a similar effect on him.

'I s'pose not,' she whispered back shyly, and snuggled down again.

After several peaceful minutes he said, 'I've never held a woman in my arms before. I'm thirty-eight years old and this is the first time I've been close to someone like this. It's wonderful. I had no idea someone could feel so soft and warm and alive.'

Kerris thought about this, then said softly, 'Nor did I.'

Kenver gently pulled off her cap and caressed her hair. He was reluctant to spoil the moment, but he had to ask, 'How do you know, Kerris? How can you know for sure that you haven't lain in a man's arms before? You might be married, have had children.'

She shivered and moved in closer. 'I like children. I've been quite happy playing with the little ones belonging to they working in the fields. I've thought about that and I'm sure if I had any children I would never forget them. I don't think I've been married either.' She looked him in the face and smiled shyly. 'This feels like a new experience for me too.'

'Does it?' Kenver said, much pleased. 'One you're liking?'

'Yes, very much,' she said at once.

He hugged her tight then laid his head on the pillow, smiling at her. 'I don't care who you are. I'm glad that it was someone from my family who found you and brought you here.'

Her pale grey eyes lit up and gave roundness to her square face. 'Your brother is chased after by lots of women, did you know that. It's not surprising the beautiful lady I've heard about, Cap'n Pengarron's mother, was in love with him. She probably still is. And that Miss Catherine wanted him before he asked her to marry him. But did you know that you are as good-looking as he is? I reckon if you left the farm, a woman like me would get killed in the rush.'

'What do you mean, a woman like you? You're beautiful.'

Kerris made a face. 'I said you were a kind man.'

'I mean it!' Kenver protested.

She smiled and lifted the long white-blond hair, so soft and silky, that he never tied back. He gathered her in tight and bringing his face close, gave her a tentative kiss on the lips. 'Do you mind?' he murmured.

'No,' she replied huskily, tears of emotion sprinkling her eyelids.

They kissed tenderly and there was no indication that she was experienced in this either.

–

Clem found them asleep in each other's arms. He frowned heavily. What had been going on between these two while they'd been spending so much time alone? He thought it possible that the initial reason for them lying together like this was Kerris seeking comfort. He'd noticed Catherine's perfume bottle lying on the parlour floor. But what had happened after that? The look on Kenver's face was one of pure contentment. Was he falling in love with this mysterious little woman he was cuddling so tightly? It would be wonderful if his disabled brother could find romance, love and happiness. But what did Kerris feel for Kenver? With her unknown circumstances, Clem was nervous of Kenver getting hurt.

He walked silently from the room and closed the door on them. He didn't want to embarrass them and was glad he had come back from the fields before the others who had stayed to watch a friendly wrestling match between Philip and the Barvah Giant. But before he got married in just over six weeks' time, with everything hopefully settling down for Jessica's sake, he vowed he would find out just exactly who the mysterious Kerris was.

–

Luke Pengarron eased his aching left arm and leaned back heavily from the oak desk in Ker-an-Mor's farmhouse parlour. He hated harvest time, when Matthias Renfree got to work outside all the time and he was expected to pore over the accounts and paperwork in this dingy small room. He had little time to see Sebastian Beswetherick and enjoy their usual gambling and carnal pursuits. This year was even worse. Luke had looked forward to spending some good times with Kane but all he wanted to do was work like a common labourer in the fields. He had added insult to injury by going over to Trecath-en Farm. Well, he'd better not have any ideas about the comely Jessica Trenchard! She would be his in the fullness of time – but then his elder brother had not returned to Trecath-en Farm the following day. Luke grinned. Had Kane tried his luck and been sent away with a flea in his ear by the wild young minx?

A small boy toddled into the room followed by his mother carrying a tray of tea. 'Here you are, Master Luke. Have a nice cup of tea. You've been busy at those papers all afternoon,' Rosie Renfree said in her motherly fashion.

'You are good to me, Rosie,' Luke replied, turning and stretching out his long legs. He watched her set the tray down and pour him a cup from a china teapot. She was thirty-four years old and looked much younger. Being a wife and mother suited her and she exuded contentment and health. He liked her golden hair, the same colour as Jessica's. What is it about you Trenchard women? he thought. You know how to stir a man's loins without realising it, yet are expert at keeping him at arm's length. He moved over to the tea tray rubbing his stiff arm.

'Thank you, Rosie,' he said, then bending down to her son, 'and how are you today, young man?' He looked enquiringly at Rosie. 'James, isn't it?'

'That's right, sir,' she answered proudly, but going red in the face. 'Our next to youngest, the one who's most like his father.'

Luke looked at the child's face closely. 'Yes, he is rather like Matthias, isn't he?' Luke suddenly had an idea how to make the tediousness of the harvest time a lot more interesting for himself. He made a face and rubbed vigorously at his right arm and let out a small grunt of pain, then returned to the subject of children. 'You are to be congratulated on a fine healthy family, Rosie.'

'Thank you, sir,' Rosie said, rearranging the things on the tea tray so she wouldn't have to see his dark face. She didn't like the way Luke Pengarron looked at her at times.

'I don't know much about children,' Luke said, touching James cautiously, who didn't seem to mind and was intent on watching the tall man's pocket-watch chain glinting on his waistcoat.

'You aren't expected to, sir,' his mother replied shyly, clearing her throat, wanting to go. 'You're a gentleman.'

Luke made a show of rubbing his bad arm again. 'But I've noticed Matthias playing with your older children and I remember my own father giving my brother and sisters and me lots of attention. He and Miss Kelynen are practically inseparable.'

'Be different when you have your own children, I expect, sir,' Rosie said.

'I suppose it will.' He stepped closer to Rosie and, as he expected, she moved away. He grasped his arm and made a face.

'Are you in pain, sir?' she asked, alarmed.

'Agony would be a better description. I suppose I ought to ask Beatrice for a liniment to ease the tight muscles. You make up her concoctions, do you not? Do you have something here I could use? The pain is almost unbearable.'

It sent Rosie into a fluster. He fastened his eyes on her burning face and knew she could not easily deny the master's son. 'I… I'll see what I can find, sir.' She held out her hand to her son. 'Come along, James.'

'No, he's all right with me. I'll watch over him while you look for the liniment.'

Rosie stared a moment at the young gentleman, the heir to the property on which her husband worked. If it had been Master Kane who had made the request, she wouldn't have thought twice about it. But she didn't trust the motives of his spoiled younger brother who could be spiteful and vengeful if he didn't get his own way. She felt as though he was keeping her son a prisoner. She had a good idea why and her heart sank but her anger was rising.

'I shall be back shortly, sir,' she said curtly, bobbing a curtsey and looking uncertainly at James as if he might be in danger.

Rosie would have made up a coriander seed poultice to ease Master Luke's painful joints but she wasn't in the mood to provide him with comfort. She rushed out to the stables and returned with a bottle of horse liniment to find James sitting on Luke's lap, holding a biscuit in his fist and trying to clutch at the watch chain.

'I'm afraid it doesn't smell very nice, sir,' she said coldly, putting the bottle down on the table. 'Come along, James, you'll get Master Luke's clothes covered in crumbs.' She reached for her son but Luke held him.

'Crumbs won't hurt,' Luke said softly, glancing at James and receiving a sunny smile in return. 'See, he likes me. How is the liniment used?'

'Just rub it into your arm and shoulder, sir, wherever it hurts.'

Luke eyed her in a way that dared her to challenge him. 'You do it for me.'

Rosie looked about helplessly. 'I'd rather not, sir. I have work to do.'

He raised a black brow into a dangerous arch. 'More important than relieving me from my agonising pain?'

'It wouldn't be seemly.'

'What could anyone possibly construe but the innocent truth, with us in the office and with me holding your child on my lap?'

There was harshness in his voice now and he was taunting her. Then it occurred to him that if he upset this woman and she told her husband and her brother, there would be an unpleasant scene, especially from the uncouth farmer who cared so much for his wretched womenfolk, and then his desire to seduce Jessica Trenchard would never bear fruit. He wanted her, and he wanted her willing and eager, not spitting fury. He changed tack. The aunt could wait till a later date.

Forcing a look of contrition, he said quietly, 'I'm sorry, Rosie. Forgive me. I wasn't thinking clearly about how it would seem from your point of view. I hope I haven't offended you. Take James with you, I'll see to my arm myself.'

He released the hold he had on James and made a show of looking humbly at the floor as she lifted the child away from him. He glanced up and repeated that he was sorry.

Rosie hurried out feeling relieved but not fooled for one minute. If he couldn't have got round her by his charms, he would have had no conscience about trying to 'blackmail' her into an affair by threatening to say that things had gone further than her rubbing liniment into his arm with his shirt off. Luke Pengarron was a ruthless swine! She would tell Matthias what had happened and they would ensure a dairy maid would always be about the farm in future when Master Luke was likely to be there. And Rosie would have to look out for the dairy maid's virtue and safety too. It worried her why he had suddenly changed his mind about what he had obviously been set on. It wouldn't have been because he was afraid of Matthias. Luke Pengarron had faced angry cuckolded husbands before without blinking an eyelid. Could it be fear of his father? Sir Oliver would be furious if Matthias upped and left the farm steward position. Renfrees had worked for Pengarrons going back centuries. Rosie prayed that her narrow escape didn't mean trouble for some other poor maid.

Chapter 15

On the last day of the harvesting, Jessica was up before the dawn. She left Kerris to get the men's breakfasts and taking Gracie with her set off to walk the riverside at the bottom of the valley. A fine fairy-tale mist hung low and chilled her bones and she wished she'd brought her shawl. She hoped the coldness of the early hour and the loneliness would help to clear her mind.

Until a few months ago everything in her life had been steady and predictable. She'd known whom she liked and whom she despised. She'd despised Luke Pengarron. But now she had seen another side of him in Trelynne Cove. When he wasn't being superior and demanding his own way, he seemed kind enough and she felt sympathy for the continual pain he suffered. She had been flattered by his appreciation of her looks; he'd said she was a 'most beautiful creature' and had the 'loveliest hair in the world'. He had asked her if she would like to see the doll he was having made for Cordelia and give her opinion of it before he presented it to his cousin. Jessica had felt honoured and said so. When the pain from his useless arm had eased, he had smiled lazily at her in a way that made her heart give a wild somersault. She would never trust Luke Pengarron but now she didn't know if she could still despise him; she wanted to, it was easier not to have futile maidenly dreams about a handsome man not of your class if you hated him.

Other things had happened this year that had unsettled her greatly. Simon Peter had gone away preaching and David was secretly planning to join him. Cordelia was refusing to come to the farm because of something Philip had done to upset her. Kane Pengarron had left the army and come home to the parish for good and for some reason she found this unsettling. Worst of all, her father was planning to marry again.

Jessica knew the sole reason for Clem's matrimonial plan was her own behaviour. Of course it wasn't improbable that he might want to marry again one day. He was still young and handsome and probably missed the comforts only a wife could provide him with. There were many women who would have made a good choice as a wife for him, widows and daughters reared on a farm, used to long hours and hard work, someone of their own class. But to ask a lady, someone he barely knew, was ridiculous. Clem thought it would take a lady to teach her the much-needed manners and refined ways he thought she should have. It was only a little while ago that her behaviour wouldn't have been seen as unladylike and unacceptable.

It wasn't that Jessica disliked Catherine Lanyon. But even with the efforts she had made during the harvest period and her unassuming manner, Jessica couldn't see how Catherine could possibly be happy living on a farm. She would soon find the farmhouse too small, the yard dirty and muddy, the long hours frustratingly lonely when Clem worked or went off on his own, their way of life rough and common. Philip would drop his gentlemanly behaviour and start swearing again and walk into the house without his shirt on. If David didn't leave he would upset her with his ardent Methodist talk. And Jessica didn't think she could ever change that much, not even to suit the father she adored, and the marriage would be all for nothing.

Last night she had begged her father to put an end to his marriage plans. She'd promised she'd try hard not to let him down, that she'd dress and behave more ladylike without a genteel stepmother to show her how to do it. But for the first time in her life he had refused to give in to her pleadings, saying the last straw had come in her direct rudeness to Kane Pengarron in front of everybody in the fields. That man again! Why did he have to come home and make things so much worse for her?

She sat down on the granite slab where her father had proposed to his bride-to-be. Gracie stood beside her, looking at her sorrowfully from huge dark eyes.

'Why did he have to come back, Gracie? Why is everything so complicated now? If I must have a stepmother why couldn't it be someone I could talk to and ask about how I feel?'

Her feelings about Kane were so confusing. She had been very fond of him as a little girl. He had been kind to her and let her join in the games when Luke and the twins wanted her and the other two girls left out. It had annoyed her that he allowed Luke to get away with so many bad tempers and tantrums and spoil their games. When she'd got older she saw it as a sign of weakness and resented him for it. It had not occurred to her until his outburst after the spider incident at Olivia's birthday party that it was because he felt guilty about Luke's disability. She had then felt angry with him for making her feel guilty at being insensitive. And she was oddly resentful that he hadn't complimented her in the way Luke had.

She tried not to admit that while she found Luke attractive, it was Kane who, ever since the time he had held her close against him in the farmhouse kitchen, made her feel weak-kneed in a silly female way merely by his presence. She hated feeling this vulnerable and she was afraid of inadvertently revealing her emotions to him. It was all round the parish how much female interest he was arousing. There was no talk of his reciprocating the interest in either a romantic or a carnal way. But he would never be interested in her; she may have been a childhood friend but she was only the daughter of one of the estate's farm tenants.

She wished, though, she had put things right with him that day in the field. She told her father she had, to stop him from insisting she go over to the Manor and apologise again. She couldn't eat that much humble pie. He hadn't come again to help at Trecath-en and she was very disappointed. She could have seized the opportunity to put things right then but now it looked as if she'd have to do it at some stage at the Manor and she dreaded that.

'Oh Gracie, everything seems to be in a mess and most of it seems to be my fault,' she said mournfully, winding her arms round the dog's strong neck.

But at least she had the excitement of a smuggling run to look forward to. The minute she could leave the farm she would seek out

Zack Maynard or, as it seemed, allow him to find her, and press him for a definite date.

–

Timothy Lanyon had only seen his intended brother-in-law at church since his betrothal to his sister and he chose today to arrive at the farm for a friendly visit. Clem, the twins and Ricketty Jim were about to leave the yard when he rode up.

'I've not come to stop your work, Clem,' he called out gaily. He was back to his usual animated self now that he was on good terms with Olivia. 'I'll stable my horse and come with you. I've got old clothes on and I'm not afraid to put my back into a bit of hard work. It will give me an excellent opportunity to meet many of my parishioners. Catherine will be over later to help with the food for the feast you've got planned for tonight. She says you're reaping the last field today. I'll lead a prayer of thanks after the last handful has been cut.'

'We'll be glad to have you with us,' Clem said truthfully. Like most people in the parish, he had taken to the young parson.

The harvesters were in high spirits all day. They sang as they worked and watched excitedly as the last field was gradually reduced to nothing but stubble, with the last few handfuls of corn standing in the middle. Towards evening the harvesters gathered there and divided into three bands. Clem severed the last swathe and held it high above his head.

The first group of people cried out in one noisy voice, 'We 'ave it! We 'ave it!'

The second group demanded joyfully, 'What 'ave 'ee? What 'ave 'ee?'

The third replied, 'A neck! A neck! A neck!'

Then the whole gathering, holding on to each other, shouted, 'Hip! Hip! Hip! Hurrah for the neck! Hurrah for Farmer Trenchard!'

Clem hugged Jessica and Philip and David. Timothy came up, hot, dusty and sweaty but looking very content, and slapped Clem on the back. 'Well done, man! You must have worked hard this year to yield such a crop.'

'You can load up your tithe and take it with you, Reverend,' Clem grinned.

'Well, I don't know if I can take it if you're going to be one of my family and my sister one of yours!' he laughed. 'There must be other good yields in the parish. It's a sight I like to see and "crying the neck" is a sound I like to hear. It's a pity Catherine's not here to have witnessed it. You must insist on it next year, man!'

He hugged Jessica just as heartily and shook the hand of every harvester, patted the head of every child. All went silent as he said a prayer of thanks and then at last the jugs of cider were lifted and parched throats were satisfied.

Jessica and the younger women took the neck of corn from Clem. They plaited it and dressed it with cornflowers and poppies and ran off laughing to the farmhouse to install it in its place of honour over the kitchen chimneypiece. Catherine, who had taken the trouble to find out about the harvest customs, delighted the maidens by curtseying to the 'neck' and escorting it to its appointed place. It would stay there until the following year when the 'corn spirit' would be dug into the earth to ensure a bountiful harvest next year.

After washing at the well in the yard, the young women disappeared into the barn to change into their best dresses for the celebration. Later they would help set up bales of hay round the yard to provide seating and extra tables to hold the food and drink. When Jessica had changed in her tiny room, she returned to the kitchen and joined Catherine and Kerris.

'I expect you could do with a strong cup of tea,' Catherine said, studying her to see if the ancient ceremony of cutting the neck had left the girl in the same happy mood as her friends. 'Will the others be here soon?'

'Father and the men will be a little while yet. They'll set up as many shocks as they can till evening draws in. The older women and those with young'uns will start drifting in though.'

Jessica sipped her tea and gazed at the table. There wasn't a speck of wooden table, white-scrubbed with age, to be seen under the plates stacked high with food. 'You've done us proud,' she said, nodding at Catherine and Kerris. 'You must've worked for hours.'

Kerris just smiled shyly but seemed to gain height when Miss Catherine put her arm round her shoulders. 'We've done roasted beef, broiled pork and potatoes, oat and ginger biscuits, apple pies and scalded cream, custards, and there's fresh bread and cheese and lots of fuggan cake of course. We planned it all on the first day of the harvesting. Kenver helped us to prepare the food, in fact he has every day. Everyone has worked so hard, you deserve a feast fit for a king.'

'Well, it's certainly going to be that. You've both been a good help this year.'

Catherine blushed and glanced at her feet. Jessica knew her efforts were out of kindness as much as trying to make her bridegroom see she was indispensable. She wondered if her father would ever notice that she was also a rather attractive woman.

'Your friends are coming over to join us this evening, Jessica,' Catherine said, making herself busy at the table. 'Miss Olivia and Miss Cordelia have sent word from the Manor. You'll be glad to see them again, I daresay.'

'It seems ages since I've seen them!' Jessica exclaimed. 'It's even longer since Cordelia was over here. I think Philip proposed to her and she took exception to it.'

'Really?' Catherine asked, hoping she could keep Jessica engaged in this sort of 'mother and daughter' chat. It would please Clem; she was fearful that if Jessica seemed unable to get along with her he might cancel the wedding. She had thoroughly enjoyed these last six weeks. They had brought her closer to Clem emotionally and she loved him deeply now. It would break her heart if she lost him.

'You think Miss Cordelia has been too embarrassed to come over?' she asked delicately.

'No, not embarrassed. She's always been a little afraid of Philip, and he don't like it when he can't get his own way. I reckon he was horrible to her.'

'That's a shame. Philip has always been very nice to me.' Catherine took a china teapot, which she had brought over from the Parsonage, to Jessica and refilled her cup. She looked straight into Jessica's deep blue eyes and asked in a forthright manner, 'Do you think he might resent me living here as his stepmother?'

'You have no need to worry about Philip, he thoroughly approves of you. So does David.'

'David's very gentle. As is your Uncle Kenver.'

'Aye, p'raps if it was David who was interested in Cordelia things might have been different. But then…'

'Yes?'

'Cordelia loves living at the Manor. If she married she'd want her husband to live there with her, not her with his family. Funny though, if she married one of the twins, there'd be two ladies living under this roof.'

'How would you feel about that, Jessica?'

'One's enough to be going on with!'

Catherine flinched; it was just the merest change in her serene features but Jessica knew she was hurt deep inside.

'I'm sorry, I didn't mean that unkindly. I'm just all mixed up in my own mind about the way I feel, without a…'

Catherine put the teapot down. 'A mother?'

Jessica raised her eyebrows and sighed. 'Yes, without having a mother to confide in I don't know how to sort out my mixed-up feelings.'

'We both know that I can never replace your mother totally, Jessica. But if I can be of any help, if you ever want someone to talk to confidentially, I shall be happy to listen.'

Jessica got up and made for the door. 'I'd better help they outside, mustn't get lazy.' Then she stopped to say, 'I don't think it's the right thing for you and my father to marry but only because I don't think you're right for one another. I made up my mind to be horrible to you. But when a person gets to know you, that's quite impossible. Whatever happens, I wish you well, and I'll never let anyone else be horrible to you.'

Catherine would have liked to have gained Jessica's wholehearted support but she felt she had won a great victory. She smiled happily. 'It's made me very glad to hear you say that.'

'Catherine. It's all right if I call you Catherine, is it?'

'Yes, certainly it is, my dear.'

'Do you happen to know if anyone else is coming over with Olivia and Cordelia?'

'I understand it's just them. Were you expecting someone else?'

'No,' Jessica sighed, 'no one.'

–

The food was carried outside, looked over with amazed eyes and awaited eagerly by hungry bellies, blessed by Timothy, and rapidly demolished. Two fiddlers and a drummer provided music for the dancing and Philip, Matthew King and some other men provided entertainment by wrestling. So that no one's day would be spoilt by going home with an empty pocket, Clem banned all betting and many men queued up to take part in the friendly matches despite their hard day's work.

Timothy wanted to wrestle but was afraid Olivia would think it unseemly for a man of his station and refuse to speak to him again. He wanted to ask her to dance with him but thought that a lady who had honoured a humble farmer's yard with her presence might balk at dancing in it. He was frustrated at not being able to snatch a few minutes' private conversation with her, but her cousin stayed close and there seemed to be a secretive conversation going on between them and Jessica. He supposed it was what young ladies did, especially if they were close friends and hadn't seen much of each other of late. Olivia would be going home soon, he noticed miserably. Her escort, Jack, and the stable boy who'd driven Miss Cordelia over had already gone to get their horses ready.

He'd been disappointed at not seeing Olivia again before now. He'd called at the Manor on some pretext but Polly had told him that the episode with Captain Solomon had unnerved Miss Olivia so much she was staying at Ker-an-Mor Farm until Sir Oliver and Lady Pengarron came home. Timothy had dashed straight off to the farm but Olivia had gone out with Cordelia to paint a harvest scene.

Kerensa had been there with Kelynen and he had spent a pleasant half-hour talking to them. He had suggested it must be a bit of a squeeze, all the family staying at the farm with the Renfrees. But Kerensa had happily stated that Luke and Kane weren't sleeping there and the three young ladies didn't mind sharing a room. He hadn't been able to go back to Ker-an-Mor Farm because there had been a fatal accident at the Roscawen mine involving several miners and he'd had to spend a lot of time burying the dead and comforting the bereaved.

He'd just have to call at the Manor again and see how things would progress, see if there was any prospect of laying a claim on Olivia Pengarron's heart. But this would be under Sir Oliver's watchful paternal eye, Timothy thought with a sinking heart. The baronet might approve of him as parson but he was probably looking much higher up for a son-in-law.

Timothy shuddered as he thought of something Peter Blake had told him today. There had been another vicious murder at Penzance, with the victim being cruelly hacked to death. There was a chilling similarity between the victim and Olivia, a young woman of the same height and build, with red hair. It made Timothy fear for Olivia's safety. He wanted to warn her to take extra care although he was sure that Sir Oliver had heard the news and had warned all his family accordingly. Peter Blake had also said an acquaintance of his had been one of the killer's victims and he was making enquiries about all the deceased to see if there was a link. He was putting up a substantial reward for information but so far there had been none. It convinced Blake that the killer was no ordinary man; he was intelligent and terrifyingly cunning. I hope you learn something to catch him soon, Timothy said to Blake's image in his mind, then looked at Olivia again.

'You're being stared at,' Jessica whispered into Olivia's ear as they sat side by side on bales of straw.

'I know,' Olivia replied airily.

'Don't you mind?'

'Why should I?' Olivia asked. She was in fact very pleased about it.

Jessica reached round Olivia's back and touched Cordelia's arm. 'What's been going on? She's obviously changed her mind about the good-looking parson and you haven't as much as hinted to me.'

Cordelia made an impatient face. 'She's been keeping secrets from me too, Jessie. As far as I knew she still hated him.'

'Out with it,' Jessica demanded. 'Cordelia and I want to know what's happened to bring about this sudden change of attitude.'

'There's nothing to tell you. The Reverend Timothy Lanyon is not quite as ill-mannered as I first thought, that's all.'

'That's all! I'm having none of that, Livvy Pengarron. I bet you've been passing him furtive looks all evening. Are you meeting him secretly?' Jessica twisted her friend's face round to hers.

'I have not and I am not,' Olivia said brightly, gently pushing Jessica's hand away.

Now Cordelia pulled her round by the chin to face her. 'Something has obviously happened and we won't stop hounding you until you tell us all about it. You've been going to church alone while the rest of us have been preoccupied with the harvesting. Did he say something you particularly liked in one of his sermons or something?'

'He happened to come over to the Manor—'

'Without Uncle Oliver and Aunt Kerensa there? What on earth did he want?'

'It was all quite proper. He was told that Beatrice was very ill and came to give her succour.'

'And?' Jessica prompted impatiently.

'I didn't know Beatrice had been ill,' Cordelia said. 'What was the matter with her? She's fully recovered now, thank God.'

'I was able to tell the Reverend Lanyon that she was not very ill but very drunk. That was all there was to it,' Olivia answered, as if she was talking to two stupid children.

Jessica eyed her suspiciously. 'And you want us simply to believe that you found him not as bad-mannered as you thought?'

'Yes.' And that was all Olivia would say on the matter. She had wondered since the day the grey-eyed parson had called at the Manor whether she had seen him in a better light than he really was owing to the fright the vile Hezekiah Solomon had given her. Would he have been so kind and thoughtful, and flattering, if he had not found her and little Shaun O'Flynn in a state of fear? She didn't object to the way he was stealing glances at her now and she'd noticed he was restraining his usual exuberant manner. Was that for her benefit? Or because he didn't want her to give her father a bad report of him? She'd heard he liked to wrestle. She'd like to see him join in with the other men. She thought he'd cut a fine figure in wrestling garb.

'Keep an eye on them,' Jessica said to Cordelia. And the subject was closed as she brought up the matter of the smuggling run. 'Are either of you having second thoughts?'

'No,' Olivia answered. 'If my brothers and your brother can do it, I don't see why we cannot. We all know the coast well and have made all the right contacts. The only problem is Jack. He thinks our plans could be dangerous and he's flatly refused to help us.'

'We need at least one man, Jessie,' Cordelia said, 'and we don't think we can trust the stable boys or any of the gardeners in the way we do Jack.'

'Well, you'll just have to get Jack to change his mind, won't you.?' Jessica challenged them tartly.

–

As it grew dark, people started to leave. Those remaining sat quietly and pleasantly tired outside in the cool fresh air, and Catherine finally managed to get Clem alone. He'd publicly thanked her for her help and privately congratulated her. She told him how much she had enjoyed the last few weeks, had waved a fan coyly in front of her face and said she felt like taking a little walk. Suddenly reminded of his duty as a lover, he offered his arm and they slipped away, Clem holding a lantern to light their path now the sky was growing dark, the three dogs bounding on before them.

He didn't speak, so Catherine took the initiative. 'Your poor hands,' she said.

'Eh? I mean, what about them?' He turned them over and over under the lantern's light, looking puzzled.

'They look sore and blistered.'

'They don't hurt a bit,' he said. 'I'm proud of these hands, takes years to toughen them up like this.'

Catherine smiled and looked away.

'What? What have I said?'

'Nothing wrong. You say such unexpected things, that's all. I like to hear them.'

Clem waved gnats away from their faces. 'I don't suppose I do have the conversation of a gentleman.' He suddenly came over in a panic and stopped walking. 'I... I've been neglecting you, haven't I? You wanted to be courted before we got married. You haven't changed your mind, have you?'

She almost collapsed with relief that he shared the same worry as she did. 'Not one little bit,' she reassured him. 'These last few weeks have been the happiest of my life. And I like everything about you and your family and Trecath-en Farm, Clem.'

He held the lantern up, staring at her face as if he hadn't seen it before. He stepped closer to her. She couldn't tear her eyes away and thought she would die soon if she didn't find out what he was thinking.

'Do... do you like me?'

'Yes, I rather think I do.'

She smiled and blushed, glanced away and looked back at him. She blushed furiously because he was looking her up and down.

'You've blossomed like a field of golden corn,' he said huskily. Then he laughed, 'I'm not usually given to romantic talk.'

'I hope I hear more of it.'

'Don't count on it every day but something might just slip out occasionally.'

Catherine wanted to ask him what he'd seen about her that had made him blurt out the compliment but she was nervous it would embarrass him and he'd clam up for good. It wasn't important. He hadn't changed his mind about marrying her and that was all that mattered. She had asked him if he liked her, he had thought about it and admitted he did, and at last he had taken some notice of her.

He was a man who had lived without the physical benefits of having a wife for over two years. She was a little nervous that now they were quite alone under a darkening sky and their wedding day not far away he might try to anticipate the wedding night. Yet he didn't seem a man forward in that way and had no reputation as a rake. He'd asked her to become Jessica's stepmother; perhaps he hadn't given any thought to the fact that marriage meant a nuptial bed too. He might not want one. If only he would kiss her and give her some indication of how he was feeling in that respect.

She looked at his wide sensuous mouth and longed to be kissed by him. He put the lantern down, raised her hands and lightly kissed them both. She became hopeful. Then he looked all around as if he was making sure they were unobserved. He did kiss her lips, tenderly and for just a little while, and she didn't know what reason he had for holding himself back.

—

The harvesting on Ker-an-Mor Farm had been finished the day before and Kerensa was glad to be back home in the Manor. She had laughed as Olivia had joyfully run upstairs straight to her painting room, imploring her mother to find Shaun O'Flynn and arrange for him to sit for her immediately. Kerensa had been vexed that Hezekiah's behaviour had forced Olivia to abandon her favourite pastime for so long. But it had given her something to think about to witness her daughter's deep disappointment at Ker-an-Mor Farm when she had learned that her painting expedition in the cornfields meant she had missed the Reverend Timothy Lanyon's visit to the farm.

Oliver was very pleased with the harvesting. His yields were up thirty per cent on last year's and the whole estate had fared well generally. This was one good year to give hope and optimism against the bad times. He had given the workers and Matthias Renfree a generous bonus and left the Renfrees to the peace of the farmhouse. Matthias had been in a rather stern mood, continually checking on the morals of the harvesters during the latter part of their labours. Oliver supposed he was wanting time alone with Rosie, and perhaps didn't want others to be getting what he apparently was not, with so many of the Pengarron family packed into the farmhouse this year. Oliver and Kerensa would have been shocked to know that their normally passive steward badly wanted to put his gentle hands round their younger son's throat and choke the life out of him for trying to seduce his wife.

The Manor was quiet. Olivia and Cordelia were at Trecath-en, Luke and Kane were out socialising, and Kelynen had gone to bed early. Kerensa stood outside, enjoying the cool evening air. Oliver came to her and slipped his strong arms about her slender waist and Kerensa shivered delightfully when he made the tender skin behind her ears burn with his demanding lips. Passion for him unfolded inside her like a flower to the heat and light at his touch and she leaned back against him for more.

'We've got some time to ourselves at last, my love,' he whispered provocatively.

His breath on her skin came quickly and she knew his desire for her was building, but she wanted to tease him… just for a little while. 'Shall we take a stroll round the gardens then?' she said. He turned her round to look into his formidable black eyes. Then without a word he lifted her up into his arms and swept her upstairs.

A long time later, when their almost savage fervour had been finally quenched, they lay in a close embrace, his fingertips caressing the marble smoothness of her skin.

'It's been a wonderful summer,' Kerensa whispered through the warm silvery darkness.

Oliver kissed her hot, damp forehead. 'Kane will probably be harvesting the crops of his own farm next year,' he said proudly.

'Oh, I hope he doesn't go too far away. Speak to him, Oliver, and forbid him to go too far. I like my family around me.'

'I don't think you'll have much to worry about, my love. Kane's been casting an eye on a property round the bay and I think he's quite interested in it. But you can't keep the children here for ever, you know. You'll have to accept that one day. One by one they'll probably leave the nest.'

Kerensa leaned over him, feeling somewhat annoyed. But Oliver's eyes looked dreamy in the dim light and she came instantly under his spell again. She kissed him passionately, unfolding his lips to hers once more. Her voice was low and sultry but lashed out like a storm hitting the coast. 'Then you had better give me more babies, hadn't you?'

Chapter 16

'You could have called on me at least once,' Sir Martin muttered peevishly. 'I don't care how busy you were. How would you like to be left lying in a stuffy bedchamber, half starved to death, with no friends bothering to give you even a few minutes of their time? You've got labourers to work in your fields. I don't see why you have to insist on getting your hands dirty! It isn't the way of a gentleman, and your son, the one with the reddish hair, is going the same way. No one cares about you when you're old. Just wait till you grow old, see if anyone wants you then!'

For about the twentieth time in the fifteen minutes since he'd arrived Oliver explained patiently to the other baronet that he had called on him twice during the past six weeks and that both times he had been fast asleep. That despite his servants' insistence that he was not to be disturbed, Oliver had entered his bedchamber and stayed at least twenty minutes each time, but 'You did not stir, Martin, not even when I called you loudly by name.'

'Then why wasn't I told? Damn me, what's William and that noisy Rachael thinking of, not telling me when I've had a visitor. I should cut them out of my will. I should dismiss all the ruddy servants. They're all trying to kill me as it is!'

Oliver was too tactful to suggest to his elderly friend that he probably was told of his visits and had subsequently forgotten. He took something from out of his coat. 'Here's a jar of pickled walnuts for you. I brought them on my last two visits but took them away again in case you weren't allowed to have them. Shall I open the jar for you?'

'Yes, indeed. Brilliant. I shall munch away while I have the opportunity, no one will dare to enter this room with you here keeping me company.'

When Sir Martin was cheerfully munching his pickled walnuts, with the aid of a fine set of new false teeth, Oliver asked, 'Would you like me to arrange for you to be taken downstairs and outside in the fresh air, Martin? William's not here to argue with me and no one else will defy me if I insist upon it, not even Rachael. It's a hot September day out there.' He cast a hand at the windows. They were open and not a breath of wind disturbed the curtains. 'There is no question of you catching a chill.'

'Yes, yes.' Sir Martin clapped his hands gleefully and his wrinkled face perked up like a child promised a treat. Then his hands flopped down at his sides from the effort. 'In a little while. I'll take tea outside with Kerensa. She's downstairs, I remember you saying so. Brought no offspring with you today then?'

'No. Luke and Kane are at the school today with the Reverend Lanyon, checking on how it's running. Olivia has taken a sudden interest in it too and insisted on dragging Shelley along with her.'

'The poor aren't short of a good teacher then, with all your brood making them chant the alphabet, though I can't see Luke having that much patience. That Renfree fellow teaches there too, doesn't he? Don't know why you want to teach girls as well as boys. It's a waste of time! All they're interested in is finding a husband as soon as they're old enough to procreate.'

'All people should be given the chance to learn to read and write, Martin.'

'Huh! Utter poppycock!' Sir Martin splurted out bits of walnut and followed it with a tight cough. 'The next thing you'll be saying is… is, oh, I don't know. Sometimes I think you are a strange man, Oliver Pengarron.'

Oliver grinned. 'There's many who would agree with you and many more who would call me something quite different.'

Sir Martin coughed again and thumped his chest to clear it. It made a hollow sound which seemed to echo back. Spittle dribbled down from the corners of his mouth which he wiped away with a trembling hand.

Oliver frowned and, taking away the jar of walnuts, passed him a handkerchief from a clean pile on the bedside table. 'Can I get you something to ease that?'

The elderly gentleman waved an impatient hand at a tray of medicines situated over by the windows and out of his reach. 'See what's over there. Damned medics keep calling and leaving all manner of stuff. Nothing helps. My chest is so tight and my heart thumps like a hammer.'

Oliver went to the tray and glanced at the labels on the many bottles and phials standing there, together with a long list of instructions as to their usage. He continued to chat to Sir Martin as he read the list.

'How are your other children and grandchildren faring nowadays, Martin? Have you heard any interesting news? How about the one hoping to stand for Parliament in the next elections? And young Martin in the Thirty-second Foot? Kane hasn't heard of him since they were in the Caribbean together.'

Sir Martin started rambling, seemingly speaking to his late wife again, saying feebly, 'Yes, Amy. Of course, my dear.'

Oliver glanced round and saw the old gentleman gazing into space. He turned back to the medicines and went on talking. 'My sons are tending to be in poor temper these days. I shall have to speak to them. Kane hasn't settled down since he's been back in Cornwall and he and Luke both think I'm stupid. They've been bringing in smuggled goods, in Trelynne Cove and elsewhere, and think I don't know about it. Kerensa and I are still concerned that Hezekiah is showing an unhealthy interest in Olivia. He called at the Manor while we were staying at Ker-an-Mor Farm. It made her feel most uncomfortable and she came over to the farm and stayed until the harvesting was over. Apart from that she seems much happier of late. Kerensa thinks she's falling in love. Goodness knows who with. I hope not, not yet. I don't want to lose any of my children in a love match or for any other reason for a long time. It's good having all the family around us again, even if they are moody. At least Shelley is too young for high emotional feelings.' Oliver looked closer at a bottle and was about to remark on its contents when instinct made him swing round. 'Martin…'

He put the bottle down and walked quickly to the bed. Sir Martin was lying with his hands clasped over his fat stomach on the outside of the sheet. He was gazing, without seeing, up at the ceiling. His jaw hung down and there was a hint of a satisfied smile on his raddled face.

Oliver shook his arm but there was no response. Tears pricked his eyes. 'Oh, Martin,' he whispered.

He closed the old baronet's eyelids and stayed with him a few moments in silence, sitting on the bed, his mind turning over the lifetime of good memories that he had shared with Sir Martin Beswetherick.

–

Kerensa was in the dining room with Lady Rachael who was proudly showing her the new dinner service she had had commissioned, with the family crest painted in gold upon it. Sebastian was lounging on a chair cramming liquorice cakes into his mouth.

'You simply must get a set, Kerensa, with the Pengarron crest, of course. Isn't it divine? I'm going to invite the sheriff and all the top gentry in the county to a supper party. I can't wait to use them.'

'They're lovely,' Kerensa said, admiring the gold design on a plate, not daring to touch it. She glanced disapprovingly at Sebastian who was making wet chomping noises. 'Sebastian is very fond of liquorice, isn't he?'

'Oh yes,' Rachael said indulgently. Sebastian was the favourite of her fourteen offspring. 'I have them sent straight from the manufacturers for him. Don't eat too many, dear heart,' she cooed at her flabby son who only looked up with a grunt. 'Or you won't eat your lunch. It's your favourite, roasted lobster.'

Kerensa suppressed a shudder at the disgusting exhibition and looked back at the table of fine china. 'Your dinner service is perfect, Rachael. It would grace even the King's table.'

'Oh, do you really think so? I wonder if their Majesties would come if I invited them to dine.' She laughed shrilly. 'Can you imagine Queen Charlotte sitting just there? We have a lot in common, we both have a large family.'

A strange watery gagging noise made Kerensa turn round. Sebastian had risen from his chair and was clutching his throat. 'What's the matter, Sebastian?' An instant later, she was crying, 'Dear God, he's choking!'

Rachael shrieked and clasped her hands to her breast. Kerensa rushed to the young gentleman and pummelled his back in an effort to dislodge a gooey mass of liquorice caught in his throat. Sebastian waved his arms about frantically. His face was turning blue and his mother was screaming and shouting for the servants. Kerensa quickly moved round to face Sebastian. She pushed his scrabbling hands away and tried to force her fingers into his mouth. He thrashed his head from side to side, his piggy red eyes bulging with fear.

'Keep still!' Kerensa shouted. Grabbing his wet, blackened chin she pushed her hand inside his mouth, getting it bitten as she tried to reach the obstruction.

Oliver had left Sir Martin's bedchamber to inform the family of his death and had reached the top of the stairway when the screaming and panic from downstairs reached his ears.

He was down the stairs in a flash. Young Beswethericks and servants were tearing about the hall, shrieking and crying, and Oliver caught hold of a footman by the collar and shook him until he blurted out the cause of the panic.

Oliver dived into the dining room, pushing aside Rachael who was wringing her hands in a frenzy. Kerensa was still trying desperately to dislodge the liquorice from Sebastian's throat. He was now purple-faced, with his eyes rolling back in his head. Blackish dribble ran down his chin onto his coat front and Kerensa's dress. Oliver pulled her away from the fat youth and bent him double at the waist and thumped his back hard. Horrible choking and gagging noises came from Sebastian's throat and his arms flailed wildly.

Kerensa attempted to restrain Rachael as she tried to wrest her son away from Oliver. 'It's not working! It's not working!' she screamed. Hurling Kerensa aside, she attacked Oliver like a wild animal, scratching his face and kicking him in the shins until one of her other adult sons and a footman managed to force her, shrieking, out of the room.

Oliver stopped thumping Sebastian's back and yanked back his head. He thrust his fingers into his mouth and tried to reach the big wedge of liquorice in the same way his wife had done. But it was too late. The grandson who most closely resembled Sir Martin Beswetherick had joined him in death.

'There's nothing more you can do, Sir Oliver,' one of Sebastian's brothers said. 'He's dead, Sebastian's dead.'

Kerensa stood shaking and ashen-faced. Oliver looked at her in despair then with the brother's help he laid Sebastian's limp body on the floor. With trembling hands he tore a handkerchief out of his pocket. 'Clean him up,' he ordered Sebastian's brother. 'Don't let your mother see him like this.'

Kerensa rushed into Oliver's arms. She stayed there a moment until Rachael's wails and protests broke through her horror. 'We'd better tell her, Oliver,' she whispered with tears streaming down her face.

'I'm afraid this is not all, Kerensa,' Oliver whispered sombrely to her. 'I was leaving Martin's bedchamber anyway when I heard all the commotion. He passed away peacefully a few minutes ago.'

Kerensa collapsed against him and sobbed wretchedly. But Oliver only allowed her to express her grief for a minute or two. Taking her by the shoulders, he held her away from him. 'You'll have to calm yourself, beloved. You must be strong for Rachael's sake.'

For the rest of the day Rachael was inconsolable and Kerensa and Oliver stayed at Tolwithrick to give help and comfort. The night turned unexpectedly cold which facilitated the lying-in-state of Sir Martin. Sebastian's face was so horribly contorted that his father, William, ordered his coffin lid to be nailed down. Rachael would not leave her son and Kerensa sat up through the night with her, shivering in the cold. A feeling of foreboding hung heavily in the air. Kerensa knew there was a storm brewing and had a wretched feeling there would be something more than that.

That evening Timothy Lanyon called at the Manor. He was shown into the parlour where he found Kane, Luke, Olivia and Cordelia sitting about dolefully, dressed in black.

'What's happened?' Timothy asked in alarm. His eyes flitted from one to another, lingered on Olivia and reluctantly settled on Kane in search of an answer.

'There's been a double tragedy,' Kane said, and he explained how two of the Beswethericks had just died, one naturally, one horribly.

'That's dreadful,' Timothy gasped. 'I'm glad I called. You will need spiritual comfort.'

'Have you come to see Father?' Luke asked irritably. He was angry that such a thing as respect for the dead required him and Kane to stay at home to attend his sister and cousin, making them miss their first smuggling run after the harvesting. He needed the excitement to dispel the long weeks of boredom cooped up on Ker-an-Mor Farm, and he didn't trust Philip Trenchard not to slip some booty away to line his own pockets.

Timothy had been looking at Olivia who was gazing steadily back at him. He hesitated before answering. 'I… just a little parish business… Nothing important.'

'Can we offer you some refreshment, Reverend Lanyon?' Olivia asked kindly. She didn't want him to leave immediately.

'I would appreciate a glass of port wine, Miss Olivia,' he replied, smiling and giving a polite bow.

Irritated by their making eyes at each other Luke let out a loud, impatient sigh, then suddenly saw a way of turning things to his advantage. 'Kane and I were hoping to attend to a little business ourselves tonight, Reverend,' he said, getting to his feet. 'I was wondering… could we presume on your kindness and ask you to sit with the Misses Olivia and Cordelia?'

Without hesitation Timothy replied, 'I'd be glad to.'

'Do you mind, Livvy? Cordelia?' Kane asked, delighted to have the opportunity to escape and take part in the planned smuggling run.

Cordelia looked at Luke with disappointment on her face but did not argue when Olivia replied firmly, 'Of course not, after the terrible way that Sebastian died it will be a comfort to have the Reverend stay with us.'

When her brothers had gone Olivia poured Timothy a glass of port wine. She handed it to him and was about to ask Cordelia if she would like a drink but her cousin had gone off into one of her daydreams. Olivia and the Reverend were effectively alone.

'It was kind of you to stay, Timothy,' she said, using his Christian name as if it was the natural thing to do.

A welcome gleam entered Timothy's grey eyes. 'I shall always be glad to do anything I can for you, at any time, Olivia.'

She raised her chin perkily. 'Are you still of a mind to view my exhibition?'

'I wouldn't miss it for the world. When and where is it to be?'

'I shall decide on a date after the funerals. It will be here in the house. My father's going to arrange a little gathering of knowledgeable people from around the county.'

'I'm sure they will be as enchanted by your paintings as I am.' Timothy glanced at Cordelia. 'Your cousin looks a little lost, Olivia.'

'Cordelia always does when Luke's not around,' Olivia sighed.

Having ascertained that Cordelia was still in a world of her own Timothy moved closer to Olivia. 'I'm glad your brothers had business elsewhere. I could not have wished to have been left in charge of more charming company.'

Knowing what errand Kane and Luke were on, Olivia smiled into Timothy's eyes. 'They will be gone for hours I fear. I hope you will not mind having to wait for so long.'

Timothy looked perfectly comfortable. 'The night can go on forever as far as I'm concerned, Olivia.'

—

The next day was hot and airless. After Jessica had finished her morning chores, she walked to the Manor, arriving tired and breathless. Stopping to take a drink of water from the pump in the stable yard, she saw Jack eyeing her stony-faced from where he was grooming a pony. She was about to go over and speak to him when Luke rode up.

'Are you coming or going, Jessica?' he asked kindly as he passed the reins of his fine bay horse to a stable boy.

'I've just got here,' she replied, pushing back damp curls from her face. 'Do you know where I can find Olivia and Cordelia? They're not expecting me today and I'm hoping they're not abroad somewhere.'

'I think they're up in Livvy's studio. Cordelia's sitting for her. I'll take you up but first I'll provide you with better refreshment than pump water.'

'I wouldn't mind a dish of tea,' she admitted, waving a hand in front of her face. 'I'm parched. I hate this clammy weather, I can't breathe in it.'

'Come inside and I'll get Polly to arrange some tea for us both.'

A few minutes later they were sitting in the great hall sipping tea. The huge stone fireplace looked strangely empty with no fire blazing in it. Jessica kept glancing anxiously up the wide oak stairway.

Luke, who had been gazing at her all the time, said, 'Don't worry, they won't slip away without us noticing. Once Olivia gets a paint-brush in her hands she'll keep her unfortunate sitter chained down in the position she desires for hours.'

Jessica smiled wanly. 'I don't want to miss them.'

'Something important, is it?' and he raised an enquiring eyebrow in a most endearing gesture and looked at her intently.

Her reaction was to have a sudden attack of butterflies in the stomach and fear that he could read her mind. She gulped. ''Tis nothing really. But I don't want to miss them now I'm here. Livvy must have painted nearly all your family by now,' she said, looking in awe at the portraits of the Pengarron forebears she could see ascending the stairs.

'She ought to paint you, Jessica. It would be a beautiful picture although I doubt if she could capture your vivacity on canvas.'

Jessica was flattered but changed the subject. 'I was sorry to hear about Sir Martin Beswetherick and his grandson. Ricketty Jim told me about it. You must feel very sad, Mr Sebastian was your friend.'

'Yes, very sad,' Luke returned, but he sounded almost bored.

'I didn't like Mr Sebastian but he didn't deserve to die like that.' She shuddered, and stared at her cup.

'No, most undignified. How are your father's wedding arrangements coming along?'

'Why do you ask?'

'Just being conversational.'

'Are you?' she asked suspiciously. 'It's only going to be a quiet wedding. Just us and one of Miss Catherine's sisters and the Parsonage housekeeper will be there. Apparently there is to be something formal happening in the Parsonage afterwards.'

'You don't sound terribly interested. You don't approve of this marriage, I understand. I must admit it's a strange alliance, a parson's sister and a common farmer.'

'No one asked or cares about your opinion on it. It's none of your business.'

'Loyal to the bitter end,' Luke laughed. 'I like that about you. You will benefit from this marriage of course. I understand Miss Catherine is worth one thousand a year. A piffling amount to a gentleman such as I am when selecting a bride but a fortune to your family. You should manage to obtain a few new dresses out of it.'

Jessica was open-mouthed. 'I hadn't thought about it. I assumed Miss Catherine was supported entirely by the Reverend Lanyon. I'm sure my father has not thought of it either.'

'No, I don't imagine he has,' Luke said unexpectedly. She knew he despised her father and had expected a sneering response. 'He loves you so much, all he wants is to do his best for you. I think he genuinely believes he should provide you with a lady for a new mother. I find him a curious man. He can be sullen but he loves the women in his life deeply enough to sacrifice himself for them. He loved my mother passionately, probably still does, and yet he loved your mother too. Miss Catherine Lanyon may be coming down in the world in one way, agreeing to marry a poor farmer, but for an old maid she will fare very well.'

Jessica looked at him in amazement. 'I didn't know you were such a thoughtful man. It would never have crossed my mind that you knew, or, at least, thought you knew, my father so well.'

Luke rubbed his stiff arm. 'When your physical activity is restricted, you tend to spend more time thinking.'

Jessica looked about for Polly. She couldn't wander about the Manor house on her own and although she liked being in this surprising man's company she was eager to see her friends.

'I said I'd take you up,' Luke said, guessing her thoughts.

He rose and held out his good arm. Jessica ignored it and mounted the stairs one step behind him. When they reached the top, instead of going up the next flight, he started down the corridor. Jessica stayed where she was, frowning.

'Follow me,' Luke called to her.

'Why?' she asked suspiciously.

He came back to her. 'I want to show you the doll I had made for Cordelia, the one with hair that matches the colour of the curl I asked you for. I'd like you to see it before I give it to her.'

'I'm not going to your bedchamber,' Jessica said stoutly, folding her arms and glaring at him.

'I'm not intending to do anything untoward to you, Jessie,' he laughed.

He may have been kinder to her of late but she still didn't trust the gleam behind his dark eyes and stayed her ground.

'You have my word as a gentleman I won't lay a finger on you.'

Pursing her lips she tilted her head and sighed impatiently.

'What have I got to do to convince you I only want to show you the ruddy doll?'

'You can bring it here.'

Luke looked at her and nodded his head as if he was summing her up. 'Very well. I have no objection to that – as long as we're vigilant that Cordelia doesn't come down the stairs and see it.'

'I've got good hearing,' Jessica retorted.

He breathed in heavily through his nose and moved off down the corridor. Jessica moved to a window where she could be clearly seen from both flights of stairs. She looked down at the gardeners working on the flower beds bordering a wide expanse of lawn and murmured to herself, 'Does he think I'm stupid or something?'

Luke returned with a parcel about twelve inches long, rounded in shape and wrapped in silver tissue. He glanced up and down the stairs then carefully unwrapped it. For several moments Jessica studied the doll's delicate porcelain face which was surrounded by a wealth of real hair almost the same colour as her own. The doll's dress was a replica of the costume Cordelia had worn at her cousin's birthday party.

'It's beautiful,' Jessica announced, gingerly touching the filmy material of its dress. 'Cordelia will be thrilled to receive it.'

'I could have one made for you, if you like,' Luke said, wrapping the gift securely again. 'I shall always remember the costume you wore in perfect detail.'

'No, thank you,' she replied, making to go upstairs.

'Oh, but I insist.'

'And I shall insist on not receiving it,' she said, just as firmly.

Luke smiled in surrender. 'What a strong-willed creature you are, stubborn but very, very beautiful.' He raised his cousin's gift. 'I must return this. I won't be long.'

Jessica waited for him halfway up the next flight of stairs. He smiled resignedly again then walked up in front of her. At the top of this flight he pulled her into the second-floor corridor and held her against a wall.

Before she could protest, he blurted out, 'You're driving me out of my mind, Jessica Trenchard! Don't you realise that I've fallen hopelessly in love with you? I don't think I can bear to live another moment if you don't say I mean something to you too. I adore you. I think of you every moment of every day. Give me some hope, anything, just some small token that will stop this torture you're giving to my heart and mind.'

She eyed him for a moment. 'Utter rubbish,' she said.

Luke let her go and bowed. 'You should learn to fence swords, my dear,' he laughed in genuine amusement. 'You'd master the art in a trice. You're absolutely remarkable and I really do think I could fall in love with you.'

'Can I see Olivia and Cordelia now?' she said as if he were a trying child.

'Of course. I would not dream of detaining you against your will. You would beat me off furiously and I would be sure to suffer greatly. But…'

'But?'

'Just one kiss? For friendship's sake?'

'No one could trust you, Luke Pengarron, even as a friend. If I ever kiss you it will be because I want to.'

'And you don't want to now?'

She looked at his wide mouth. It held a cruel line most of the time but always it was sensuous and inviting. 'One day I just might, but right now I'm only interested in seeing my friends.'

'I'll look forward to that day,' he whispered, gazing at her lips.

Further along the corridor someone closed a door and walked towards them. They both looked to see who it was and Luke moved in closer to her. Jessica's heart fell when she saw it was Kane. He grunted their names with a grim look on his face as he passed them, then ran down the stairs.

'He's going over to Tolwithrick to offer his condolences,' Luke said blandly, and Jessica got the impression he wanted to yawn.

Jessica began the ascent of the short set of stairs to the servant's quarters and Olivia's studio. Luke came behind her. 'Are you going over to Tolwithrick?' she challenged him, hopping away from him on the landing and wishing Kane had not seen them together.

'Eventually.'

'You don't sound very concerned,' Jessica said.

'Why should I be? Sir Martin was eighty-four. It's about time he made his way into the next world. And Sebastian was bound to gorge or drink or whore himself to death. It's just a pity for him that it wasn't the latter.'

'Well, really! I don't like that sort of talk.'

'Which part in particular?'

'Everything you said. You can be so beastly at times, Luke Pengarron!'

He stopped at the studio door and leaned towards her. 'Did you think I had changed, Jessica?'

'No!'

He pulled one other curls which she immediately swiped out of his fingers. 'I think you're lying. I think you're beginning to like me a little bit. I'm not all bad, my dear. Here in my breast there beats a heart of love and kindness. You should let me show it to you sometime.'

'Oh, just get out of my way!'

He moved aside and knocked on the studio door. 'I love it when you're angry with me,' he laughed and walked away.

'Come in!' Olivia called from the studio but Jessica stayed to stare at Luke's back. The door opened. 'Oh, it's you, Jessie,' Olivia said. 'Why didn't you come in when I called to you?'

'I didn't hear you,' Jessica replied moodily, and swept through the door to greet Cordelia who was standing holding a flower across her skirt.

Olivia glanced down the corridor before coming back into the room. 'You were too busy quarrelling with Luke again.'

'What were you quarrelling about this time?' Cordelia asked, trying not to fidget as Olivia looked at her warningly.

'Oh, something and nothing. We'll never agree for more than five minutes at a time.'

'No, I don't suppose you will,' Cordelia said, and she went off into her own thoughts.

'Don't leave us now,' Jessica said, waving a hand in front of her face. 'I've got some news for you both.'

'About Zack Maynard?' Olivia whispered, then said sternly, 'Don't you dare move, Cordelia. Just a few more minutes and I'll have your outline perfectly.'

'Thank the Lord for that,' her cousin replied with feeling. 'You have a date for us, Jessie?'

Jessica hesitated before answering as a distant rumbling sound was heard. Olivia glanced anxiously out of the window. The sky was pink and soupy. 'Aye, I have,' Jessica replied. 'I met Zack Maynard in Marazion yesterday, that is to say I was selling eggs and he came up and bought some and told me he would meet me on the road on the way home. He must have known I'd walked over by myself. The man seems to know my movements better than I do myself.'

'I don't like the sound of that,' Olivia remarked, frowning heavily at Cordelia's right shoulder then measuring the piece of canvas she was working on with the head of her paintbrush. 'Are you sure it's safe to work with him? Perhaps we should call the whole thing off.'

'We will not! True, the man makes me feel uneasy and it wouldn't take much encouragement for him to turn our meetings onto another footing but I want the run to go ahead. Even if we do it only once, it will be exciting enough to always remember, something to tell our grandchildren about.'

'What did he say?' Cordelia asked, alert now, her eyes shining.

'He suddenly appeared after I passed through the toll gate. There was no one about and he carried my baskets for me. Said to say he was enquiring after Philip's wrestling if anyone saw us and got curious. He said the run is planned for this time next week.'

'Next week!' Cordelia hissed excitedly. She couldn't help moving and Olivia was too excited herself to care. The three young women got in a huddle in the centre of the room.

'We're to go to Trelynne Cove and wait there until well after dark. He's going to row into the cove himself first, carrying no contraband. He'll meet up with us and check for himself that there's no Revenue men about. He'll then signal to the smuggling ship and another rowing boat will bring in tea, coffee, spices, all broken down in small containers. There won't be much because it's a trial ran. If it's successful, we can receive more the next time. He said it's up to us to make contacts for the "hides" but he can help us with buyers if need be. I didn't tell him about your great-grandfather's hidey-hole, Livvy. I thought it would be better to keep that to ourselves. It might come in handy for us to hide in if anything went wrong.'

'You did the right thing. I don't trust this Zack Maynard and I expect his gang are just as bad,' Cordelia commented.

'We'll have no problems with hiding the goods. Jack is in charge of the stables and we can put some things in there. The rest can go in the corner of the wine cellar. No Revenue men will dare to ask to look around the Manor, and if Father finds out, he might be very angry but we'll just have to promise we won't do it again. But we still have the problem with Jack. He absolutely refuses to come with us.'

'Surely you can talk him round,' Jessica said impatiently. 'He's always adored you, should be easy enough.'

Olivia shook her head. 'I don't know. I haven't succeeded so far. And if he won't go then Cordelia won't be able to ride and we can't have her walking across the cliffs. Apart from the time it will take, it wouldn't be any good if we have to make a quick getaway. She's got just about enough courage to ride behind Jack.'

'You don't have to worry about me,' Cordelia said brightly. 'Your brother Philip helped me to get over the worst of my fears about horses, Jessie, and Luke has been helping me to rid myself of the rest of them. Uncle Oliver says I can choose a pony from the stud and I shall have my own mount by next week.'

'Bravo!' cried Olivia.

'So Philip did you some good as well as offending you,' Jessica said, looking pleased. She hated it when someone had something against one of her family. 'It's just up to you now, Olivia, to work on Jack.'

The rumbling noise came again, the unmistakable voice of thunder.

'You can't breathe in this air,' Jessica said irritably, pulling at her tucker.

'I hope it doesn't come to anything,' Olivia muttered, shooting an anxious look at Cordelia.

Chapter 17

When Kane got back from Tolwithrick he found Olivia and Cordelia in the parlour looking anxiously out of the windows. They asked after the Beswethericks and when Kerensa and Oliver were coming home, then returned to their stations, apparently scanning the heavy skies.

'What's the matter with you two?' Kane asked grumpily, flopping down in a chair. 'Don't you like the idea of Mama and Father staying away for a few days? Is the failing light hampering your precious painting too much?'

'We're not in the least bit concerned with that,' Olivia replied tartly, feeling in no mood for her brother's bad humour.

'There's going to be a storm,' Cordelia said, without turning round.

'That much is obvious. The air has been getting heavier and the thunder closer all afternoon,' Kane said, drumming his fingers restlessly on the arm of the chair.

'I'm going after her,' Olivia said to Cordelia. 'She'll never arrive at the farm in time before the thunder gets really loud and if there's lightning as well I hate to think what she'll do. We should have insisted she stay here until the storm had passed over.'

'I'd come with you but I'm not that confident on a horse yet. If the thunder makes it jumpy I might panic and then you'll have two terrified females on your hands. Why don't you take Jack with you in case she gets the hysterics?'

Kane was all ears at this. 'Where are you going? Who are you talking about?'

'Never you mind, Mr Crosspatch,' Olivia said, flouncing past him.

He sprang up and took her arm. 'What's going on? With Father and Mama staying at Tolwithrick, I am in charge.'

'It's Jessica,' Cordelia said, from behind him. 'She left to go home a short time ago and she's terrified of thunder and lightning. We're afraid she won't get home in time.'

'Jessica is that frightened of storms?'

'She won't admit it,' Olivia said, 'but her Aunt Rosie told us about her fear. She made it sound as though her terror at that huge spider you brought back from the Caribbean was very small compared to the way she's frightened of a storm.'

'I'll go,' Kane said, and he would have none of his sister's protests. 'I'm dressed for riding and Jack won't have unsaddled my horse yet.'

-

Jessica ran over the ground of Ker-an-Mor Farm telling herself the reason she was running was because she had stayed too long at the Manor and was late getting home, that it had nothing to do with the rumbles of thunder which were growing louder and more frequent. She kept her head down, eyes fixed to the ground rushing under her feet. If she saw just one streak of lightning dash across the sky, she knew she would panic. The sound of her heart thudded in her ears as she ran through the fields and she didn't slow down until she reached the top of Ker-an-Mor valley. She could see the gate that divided Pengarron and Trenchard land and kept her eyes rooted on it. If she could just get through the gate and on to her side of the valley, it would take only a few minutes more to reach the safety of home.

Rain started to fall and quickly picked up momentum. With no wind, it came down straight and heavy and before she'd run another hundred yards she was soaked through to the skin. She wished she'd brought her shawl with her now, then she could put it over her head and narrow her field of vision, hide away in it.

There had been no rumbles for several moments and she was hopeful the storm was passing away. Then a sudden and deafening clap of thunder, which seemed to be right at her back, made her jerk rigidly to a standstill. Her heart leapt painfully and every nerve in her body was tense: she whirled round in fright and backed away, staring wide-eyed as if some horrible monster was there and about to devour her. She turned again and tried to run on but her feet skidded out from under her and she fell down on the wet, slippery ground. Then through the torrential rain she saw the sky light up in a long, jagged streak of lightning.

Without realising it she was screaming. She leapt to her feet and ran on wildly towards the gate, holding her hands to her ears. She lost her footing again and fell heavily forward, slipping on her hands and knees. She scrambled to regain her feet. Another clap of thunder reduced her senses to those of a desperate trapped animal. She shrieked and pounded the ground with her fists. A brilliant flash of lightning made her scream hysterically and somehow she was on her feet but instead of running for home and safety she danced round in a frenzied circle.

Kane saw her hysteria. Leaping off his horse he ran towards her, calling her name. She didn't hear or see him and began to run again, her arms thrashing in the air, her long wet curls sticking to her face and back. Kane kept calling to her; even with his long legs he was having trouble catching up with her at the speed she was running. Then she fell. She hit the muddy ground with a sickening thump. Her frantic movements caused her to slide and she began to roll over and over down the valley. Hurtling after her at breakneck speed, he managed to reach her. He made a grab at her shoulder and gained a handful of her dress. Not realising help was at hand, she fought him off like someone demented.

'Jessie! Jessie! Keep still! It's me, Kane! I've come to help you!'

His shouts could not penetrate the terror engulfing her brain and he lost his footing too and slid with her further down the valley. He fought their crazy slide and managed to get his buttocks on the ground and dig his boots in hard to bring them to a halt. Then forcing her flailing arms behind her back and pinning them down, he put his free arm under her knees. With a struggle he got to his feet with the terrified girl in his arms. He held her tight until she went still, her eyes clamped shut. The rain poured down their faces and dripped off their clothes.

'Jessica, can you hear me? Open your eyes and look at me. It's Kane. I've got hold of you and you're quite safe now.'

She was whimpering, her face screwed up in fear.

'Jessica, look at me,' Kane said loudly, glancing around, desperate to get her away somewhere before the next round of thunder and lightning reverberated through the valley. 'We can't stay here like this.'

She opened one eye, then the other. When she looked into those large soulful brown eyes of his she gave a cry and buried her face in his neck. There was a flash of lightning and a roll of thunder. She cried and went rigid in his arms and cried out again.

'You're safe now,' he said into her ear. 'The nearest place is Ricketty Jim's. I'm going to take you there until the storm's over.'

He carried her up the valley, walking with care so as not to slip and precipitate another downward plunge. He pushed through the gate bordering the farmlands without bothering to shut it after him, talking to her all the while to calm her fears.

'We'll soon be warm and dry. Jim's usually got a cheerful fire going and his shack is cosy and watertight. He'll make us a nice mug of hot tea. You'll be safe there. I'll find my horse or walk to Trecath-en and tell them you'll be home when it's all quiet again. Don't worry, Jessica, I won't let anything harm you.'

Still carrying Jessica, Kane pushed his way through Ricketty Jim's door and found that although there was a cosy fire burning under his makeshift chimney, there was no sign of the farm hand. It was smoky inside the little shack and it made them both cough. Kane stood Jessica in front of the fire but still held her, afraid she was too weak to stand. She kept her head pressed to his chest and gripped his shirt at the back with taut fingers.

'Jessica.'

'Mmmm?'

'Ricketty Jim isn't here.'

Her head shot up to look at him in fresh panic. 'You're not going to leave me here alone?'

'No, I promise I won't leave you.' He rubbed her arms gently in reassurance. 'We're soaked through to the skin. We'd better get out of some of these wet clothes, then I'll make us some tea. Jim won't mind, I'm sure, and I'll replace the tea.'

It was dark in the shack and the lightning couldn't be seen. Another clap of thunder came. Its sound was muffled in the small but thick-walled shack, as was the rain pounding down on the roof. Jessica felt safer but still shuddered in Kane's arms.

She became aware of her wet and muddy condition and shivered. She moved away from Kane and looked down at her dress and shoes. 'I didn't realise I'd got into such a mess. Look at you, you're just as wet and muddy. I'm sorry, Kane. I fought against you and you were trying to help me.'

'That doesn't matter. You fell very heavily down the valley. Are you hurt?'

'I feel a bit skinned and bruised,' she managed a small smile, 'all over.'

He swept a shabby blanket off Ricketty Jim's low bed. 'Here, put this round you.'

He began to pull his clinging shirt out from his breeches and she turned away. Putting the blanket over her shoulders, she eased all her wet clothes, except for her shift, down to her feet and stepped out of them. She felt a tug on them and allowed Kane to take them from her. He hung her dress, tucker and petticoat over the line strung up close to the fire next to his shirt. Jessica stared at him as he stood back from the fire in his breeches and boots, noting the scars on his torso, and the scratches and bruises from their fall.

'Just a few war wounds,' he smiled, noticing her scrutiny.

'Well, you certainly have been through the wars, so to speak,' she replied. She sat on Ricketty Jim's bed. 'I don't want any tea, 'tis better not to touch Jim's things. He likes them just so.'

'As you please, Jessie. Are you hurt much?'

'I don't think so,' she said, peeping inside the blanket at the areas where her flesh was tender. There was thunder again and she shook, murmuring, 'I wish it would go away.'

He sat beside her and took her hand. 'Listen for the next clap of thunder. You'll notice they're getting fewer and lower. The storm's passing over. I wouldn't be surprised if Clem or one of the twins appears up here looking for you.'

Jessica made a rueful face. 'They'll probably think I had the sense to stay at the Manor until it's all over. It was obvious there was going to be a storm. Cordelia and Olivia begged me to stay but I was too stubborn as usual. Did they send you after me?'

'Olivia was going to come. I said I would.'

'I'm glad you found me. I would have gone mad out there.' She thought about how she must have looked to him. 'I feel a bit of a fool now.'

'There's no need to feel like that, and at least I've made up for frightening you with the spider. You're a strange mixture, Jessica Trenchard. So fearless one minute, you're afraid of no man seemingly, and yet you can be so frightened of some things.' She glanced at him, looking very vulnerable. 'Would you like me to hold you?' he asked softly.

'Yes, please,' she replied, shivering. 'If you're cold you can share this blanket. I'm sure my honour is quite safe with you, 'tisn't as if you're your brother.'

Kane took the blanket from her and swept it round them both and held her in his arms. She placed her face against his bare chest, liking the feel of it there, and put her arms round him.

'Is that what he was doing earlier today when I saw you together? Propositioning you?' he asked with a note of anger in his voice.

'He told me he loved me.'

'I'll break his neck!'

'Why?' She looked at him in surprise. 'I can handle Luke, he doesn't bother me. In fact we get on quite well these days, in our own way.'

'Do you now?' he asked rather bitterly.

'Look, I really am sorry about being rude to you since you've got back home. My apology came out all wrong in the fields. I'm sorry for upsetting you. Say you'll forgive me.' She put on an appealing face.

'Oh, very well, Miss Curlylocks,' he said, moving a mass of her wet hair from his skin. 'So, what is it you like about Luke? I'd be most curious to know.'

'Well, I know what his reasons are behind him being nice to me but he pays me some lovely compliments.'

He tilted her chin and looked into her eyes, then studied her lips. 'You like flattery, do you?'

'A maid has no objections to being told she's beautiful.'

'Would you be flattered if I said you've got lips like rose petals?'

'Don't make fun of me!'

But he was looking at her steadily and his eyes glowed with a raw strength that seemed to come from deep within him. She felt she could be drawn into their very depths and wanted to make that journey there to its end, and then to draw back the same from him and enshrine it in her soul.

Bending his head, he briefly kissed her trembling lips, then asked huskily, 'And what if I said your lips taste like ripe strawberries, Jessica?' He was no longer teasing her.

And Jessica was just as serious as she replied in the softest whisper, 'I'd say do it again.'

They kissed with an intense longing, wrapping their arms round each other tighter and tighter, giving more and more of themselves until they were lost in a tide of passion. Then when they were quite out of breath, they drew apart and sat still, listening to the rain.

Kane looked around Ricketty Jim's shack. He was feeling wonderfully alive, yet quiet inside at the way Jessica had yielded and taken from him. He had never felt like that before with any other women he had held in his arms. 'Who would have thought when we were children playing around Jim's makeshift home that we would end up one day sitting and kissing inside it?' he said, brushing his lips over her closed eyelids.

'I wish I had known,' she said dreamily. 'I would have had all those years to look forward to it.'

She was running her hand slowly down his back, finding the narrow scar that ran all the way down from his neck. He shivered and knew she didn't realise all the feelings she was sending coursing through his body, and when she brought her hand round and touched the deeper, wider scar on his stomach, he took it away and held it.

'I know how you got the scar down your back,' Jessica said softly. 'It comes from the beatings you received in your childhood.' She looked again at the scar on his stomach which showed above his breeches. 'But how did this happen, Kane? It's like a pit.'

'It happened when I was overseas,' he explained, touching it gingerly. 'I was thrust into by a sword which was twisted round inside me. I very nearly died. The surgeon removed part of my insides; he said some of the bits didn't matter anyway. It still hurts at times.'

'That's terrible! Oh, you poor thing. All the suffering you've had to put up with in your life and I've been so horrible to you.' She touched a bruise on his shoulder. 'And now you're bruised and battered all over again because of my fear of thunderstorms.'

'It's not that bad.' He grinned at her intensity.

She kissed the bruised area on his shoulder and it made him shiver again.

'Well, perhaps it is quite serious,' he said with a twinkle in his eye. 'All my injuries are serious.'

She raised herself up and kissed him possessively. 'I don't think I will be afraid of thunder and lightning storms from now on. I know I'm *very* grateful to this one.'

'So am I,' he said, kissing her soundly then listening for noises outside. 'The rain has nearly stopped. I'm afraid I'll have to take you home soon.'

'I don't want to go,' she said vehemently, snuggling even closer to him.

'And I don't want to take you yet, my beloved. Just think though, if your father or one of your brothers found us like this, I'd be skinned alive.' He became very serious. 'Jessica, I want to see you again, to spend lots of time with you, just the two of us. If our families learn how we feel about each other they'll not give us a moment's peace. Clem might even try to stop us meeting. I shall be kept busy for the next week or so. Will it be all right if I ride over to Trecath-en after that to arrange something quietly? When I've thought of somewhere we can go where we won't be disturbed? In fact by then I might have the very place. What do you say, my love?'

'I say yes, Kane,' she replied, smiling into his entrancing eyes. 'I'll eagerly look forward to it.'

He pulled her close. 'Then let's not waste the time we have left now.'

—

Hezekiah Solomon did not allow the storm that shook Mount's Bay to put him off calling on the Reverend Lanyon. He had written requesting an interview and Timothy had written back straightaway suggesting this afternoon. He was most curious as to why the dandified gentleman wanted to see him and waited in anticipation in his lantern-lit study for his arrival. Hezekiah arrived promptly in a fine carriage, the newest one in Cornwall, which was causing quite a stir in the county. It was drawn by four grey horses, all of the same age, height, build and length of mane and tail. Timothy saw the spectacle from his study window and wondered if Captain Solomon had chosen the horses himself in his usual fastidious manner.

Hezekiah bowed low as Nancy Wills announced him and after enquiring if refreshment was required, which was declined, hastened back to Catherine to work on the wedding clothes.

'A dismal afternoon, Captain Solomon,' Timothy said amiably as Hezekiah fussed with his wig in front of a small square mirror near the door. 'Please be seated. If you do not want a dish of tea, may I offer you a glass of Madeira?'

'That would be most agreeable, thank you, Mr Lanyon. It is very good of you to see me at such short notice. You must be wondering why I have asked to see you, with me living in the parish of St Mary's, Madron, at Penzance. And I understand there is to be a wedding in your family in a few weeks' time. You must be very busy.' Hezekiah sat down with flowing movements and crossed his ankles neatly.

'The Parsonage has been full of dressmakers and materials, Captain Solomon. My sisters and my housekeeper chatter about nothing else. I think at times I am quite forgotten but, I might add, that is not always a bad thing.'

'Yes, indeed.' Hezekiah smiled, then sipped his Madeira. 'I shall try to be brief, Mr Lanyon. I know I should be talking to the vicar of my own parish but I do not know him, or the curate who is sometimes to be found at the chapel down the street where I live. I know that Sir Oliver and Lady Pengarron set great store by you, Mr Lanyon. The thing is, I've spent all my life as a non-believer but now that I have retired from the sea and have had time to think and… well, you see, I'm beginning to think it is time to give serious consideration to the possibility of there being a God, a creator. To try to understand what the Gospel is all about. I found myself listening to an open-air Methodist preacher recently in Penzance. He spoke of things that I'd never thought of before. That if we don't believe, we will die in our sins. It brought me up sharply. Of course I could not bring myself to speak to such a fellow and the next obvious step was to speak to an ordained clergyman. I hope you don't mind me choosing you. We have met briefly at Pengarron Manor and I thought of you. Perhaps, apart from the Holy Scriptures, you can recommend some suitable books for me to read. I would like to do some deep studying before putting my questions to someone.'

'I do not mind in the least, Captain Solomon. I would not like to see a single soul lost. I should be able to find something to fit your requirements. Please excuse me a minute.'

Timothy went to his packed bookshelves, keeping an eye on his visitor. He doubted if the other man was being truthful.

Hezekiah's eyes darted over the desk, preying on a letter the parson had been writing.

Timothy covered up the letter when he brought back two thick clothbound books. They were brown with age. 'These should be of help to begin with, Captain Solomon, and I recommend that you read all the Gospels, paying particular attention to St John, and then the Acts of the Apostles. Take your time in reading, there is no hurry to return the books. I will be most interested to know what you think at the end of it. I would also recommend that you try to pray.'

'Thank you, Mr Lanyon. You have been most kind and considerate. Could I encroach on a little more of your time and ask you to write down your recommendations? Which Gospel was it in particular and the Acts of whom? I can see I have a lot to learn and I fear I will forget what you have so kindly told me.' Timothy thought this a most odd request. This little man, he knew, had a perfect eye and ear for minute detail. He obliged him as Hezekiah finished his Madeira. When he left, Timothy opened the windows wide to rid his study of the other's effeminate smell.

In his carriage, Hezekiah opened the front covers of both theological books then tossed them carelessly onto the seat opposite. He kept hold of the instructions Timothy had written down and as he was driven back to Marazion he studied the strong, open handwriting. Hezekiah chuckled. Clerics were rarely known to scribble; it would be easy to copy his lettering and the signature he'd found in one of the books.

Hezekiah had been irked at first when it became apparent that the Reverend Lanyon was interested in Olivia Pengarron and she, it seemed, in him. It had not gone beyond the pair passing lingering looks and participating in the occasional quiet conversation, which her parents did not seem to have noticed. Hezekiah didn't think anything would come out of a dalliance between the Lord of the Manor's daughter and the young parson. Timothy Lanyon might have youth and good looks but he did not have the wealth or position to be considered as a suitable husband. Nevertheless, there was a romance brewing and Hezekiah had decided to use it to his advantage.

He had given up showing an interest in the young lady himself. Much to his chagrin, it was obvious that Oliver would never accept him as a suitor for his daughter. He was too old and Oliver knew of his baser appetites, which was fine for a prostitute but not for Olivia. There were many others interested in her, young gentlemen from the top county families, and Hezekiah would stand no chance against any one of them. But what angered Hezekiah the most was the fact that Olivia obviously loathed him and took no pains to hide it.

So he was trying a different tactic. He would stay away from the Manor and meet Oliver only at the gaming tables or on social occasions. He had recently taken up with a young rich widow who shared his carnal perversions. It kept him satisfied for the most part and he hoped it would put Miss Olivia Pengarron off her guard. Because he meant to have her.

Chapter 18

After his crops were ricked, or threshed and sent to the miller, Clem had found time to ride over to Penzance in a bid to establish Kerris's true identity. He began his investigations by paying a visit to a popular local inn and listening in on the gossip there. It wasn't long before the horrific murders were mentioned and a rather hushed discussion was started.

A grim-faced sailor asked him, 'Know what we're talking about, do 'ee?'

'Aye,' Clem said, as if he was only half interested, as all faces turned to him. 'I come from further round the bay, two miles from Marazion. There's been some awful murders round there too over the past twenty-odd years. You must have heard about them.'

'Aye, we have,' the serving girl interjected, raising her shoulders as if her heavy bosom was too cumbersome to be carried comfortably. 'From what some folk do say, 'tes not only round the bay but up-along too.'

Clem gave an involuntary shudder. It made the business he was here on uncomfortably close to home. 'Makes you nervous for your kin, though 'tis only the immoral and low life being killed.'

'Not the last one!' exclaimed the landlord, slamming down tankards of frothing ale on the bar. He glared at Clem with hostility. There was bad feeling between Penzance and Marazion folk, ever since the former had ousted the latter as the principal market of the region. 'She were a good, decent little maid. Well brought up, she was, a Methodist. Her father's a silversmith. They got a nice little house up Causehead.'

Clem ignored the frostiness of the landlord. 'There's many theories going round to who the killer is. Some say he could be a sailor, begging your pardon,' he added to the first man who had spoken to him. 'They happen sporadically so it could be when a ship moors up here or at the Mount.'

'Aye, Penzanns is a seafront town, 'tes what most folk think 'ere too,' someone else said.

'Didn't one of the victims have a maidservant go missing? One who was never found?' Clem queried, glancing round at the men and the well-built serving girl who gave him a come-on eye.

'Why do 'ee ask?' the landlord spat, and Clem was suddenly surrounded by suspicious faces.

'No reason, forget I asked.' He scowled at them. 'Just being conversational.' He drank up and left, the landlord putting a restraining hand on the serving girl. Clem didn't think she had any information to pass on; more than likely she just wanted to proposition him. He couldn't tell anyone he suspected the missing maid was living on his farm. If he spoke to the killer or someone who knew the killer, he would put Kerris's life, and possibly his family's, in terrible danger.

He wandered about Penzance, listening to talk among traders and customers around the Market House at the top of Market Jew Street and round the corner at Greenmarket. He browsed in some of the shops, buying a length of ribbon and some lace for Jessica in a haberdasher's. He hoped to hear some gossip from the women in there but he had the opposite effect on them. They stopped talking and stared at him as he paid for his purchases and put them in his pocket. He had no luck that day and returned again the following week. He walked up the side streets and alleyways then made his way slowly down Chapel Street where most of the coinage town's gentry lived, and slipped down a path leading to the Customs House. There were Revenue men and soldiers standing about but they didn't look as if they would gladly talk to him. Stopping to light his pipe he made to retrace his steps and came face to face with three painted and bewigged harlots who had come down that way looking for trade. Clem quickly debated with himself whether to try for information from this quarter and decided against it. He made to walk round them.

'Now don't 'ee be goin' off, me 'an'some,' one of the women said with a cackly laugh, swinging her hips. 'If you come with me I can promise thee a good time.'

Clem made an impatient face and the women surrounded him. Another of them said in a sultry voice, 'Mmmm, aren't you some good-looking with such a moody face. We could all give you a good time together, if you like. What do you say, girls?'

The last one said loudly, which made the Revenue men and soldiers roar with laughter, 'I say let's take him back to my place and his wife will never see him again!'

Clem pushed himself roughly through the women and walked off to an accompaniment of cheers and catcalls from them and the uniformed men. When he was about to turn up the little side path again he turned back and bowed ceremoniously to the prostitutes and gave them his best smile. They fell about laughing and called after him to change his mind.

Back in Chapel Street he made his way just a little further along, crossed the street and stopped by St Mary's Chapel, where a legless beggar hailed him. 'Got a penny for an old soldier, sir?'

Clem tossed the beggar, who may have been an old soldier but was not an old man, and unusually clean-looking for one of his trade, a shilling and crouched down to talk to him. 'Have you done well today?'

'Not too bad, thank 'ee, sir. A fine-lookin' gentleman just gived me a two-shillin' piece. My son and I will eat bread and meat tonight.'

'Where's your son now?'

'Oh, he's off lookin' fer any labourin' job he can do. He'll be back to pick me up on our cart, which is our home, hopin' I haven't fell foul of one of the constables and been locked up fer vagrancy.' The beggar pointed to the space where his legs should have been and grinned widely. 'I don't get too much trouble from 'em, 'tisn't as if they can put me in the stocks!'

'What's your name?' Clem asked.

'Jacob Penberthy and me son's called Ben. Got work fer him by any chance, have 'ee, sir? Ben's got a strong, broad back and I can turn me hands to anything, nothing wrong with them.' Jacob Penberthy held up two large calloused hands as proof of his statement.

'My name's Clem Trenchard and I'm the tenant farmer of Trecathen Farm on the Pengarron estate, which is round the bay, past Marazion. I'm sure I can find something for you both for a few days and you're welcome to sleep in my barn. Tell me, Jacob, do you use this spot often?'

'Well, 'tes a rich man's street. If they'm in a generous mood I do quite well and the curate in there,' he thumbed towards the Anglican chapel behind him, 'I don't think he likes me being here but he rarely tells me to clear off. I do the rounds of the bay, been coming here fer years. Why yer asking?'

'Well, you must know about the gruesome murder of a woman in this very street recently.'

'Aye, Miss Tredinnick. She was some good to me, 'twas a terrible shame about she.'

'Do you remember Miss Tredinnick's maid? She disappeared on the night of the murder.'

'No.' Jacob Penberthy crushed Clem's hopes as soon as they were raised. 'They lived further up the street and I can't see folk coming and going up that far. I never did see Miss Tredinnick with anyone.'

'So you've no idea what the maid looked like or what she was called? From folk talking about it perhaps?'

'Weren't round here back in the spring when the murder happened and folk are reluctant to talk about such a terrible thing openly in case it brings 'em bad luck. But...'

'But what, Jacob? Think hard.'

'Well, once or twice Miss Tredinnick mentioned the name Amy. That could be the maid, I s'pose.' Jacob looked keenly at Clem, glanced up and down the street and cautiously behind them. 'Think you know where she is, do 'ee?'

'I might, but 'tis better I don't say any more. The name might be useful though. I thank you, Jacob.'

Jacob eyed Clem and touched his arm. 'The gentleman who gave me the two shillings today asked me a few questions about Miss Tredinnick and her missing maid too.'

Clem felt real panic over this. 'Do you know who he was?'

'I don't think it's anything for you to worry about, sir. He's called Mr Blake. Do you know who he is?'

Clem breathed a sigh of relief. It wasn't strange for a man who had set Dinah Tredinnick up in a house in this street to be asking questions about her. He searched about in his pockets and gave Jacob a few more pennies. 'I have to be going now, Jacob. Find your way over to the farm sometime. I'll be glad to see you again.'

''Twill be an honour, sir.' Jacob saluted him.

'Not sir, call me Clem.'

He made off down the steep hill that ran to the seafront, leaving behind the chapel with its sharply pointed whitewashed spire that acted as a ship's landmark. The smells of pitch, salt and fish filled his nostrils.

He heard his name called and turned. Peter Blake was standing a few paces from him.

'Get out of my sight, Blake, or I'll push you out of it.' Clem hated him for the same reason that Sir Oliver Pengarron did, that he had once tried to force himself upon Kerensa.

Blake looked uncertain but did not move. 'I wish to speak to you, Trenchard. It's come to my notice that you've been asking questions about Dinah Tredinnick's maid.'

'What if I am?'

'I don't know your reasons but I'm most anxious to trace the maid myself. She was a kind and loyal servant and Miss Tredinnick and I greatly valued her. If her whereabouts can be ascertained then this evil murderer might trace her too and she could be in terrible danger. I've been putting two and two together. I know you have a woman staying at your farm who has lost her memory. Do you think she could be Miss Tredinnick's maid? Is this why you are in Penzance asking questions?'

At least the man was being honest about his relationship with Dinah Tredinnick, Clem thought grudgingly. He asked cautiously, 'What was the maid's name and what did she look like?'

An expression of hope passed across Peter Blake's finely featured face. 'She's called Amy Venton. She is short and dark with a sort of square face.'

'I think you'd better come back to the farm with me,' Clem said grimly.

–

Kerris was in the kitchen with Jessica when Clem arrived back. Because Clem had been sharp with Kerris before he'd left earlier that morning, she moved uneasily to Jessica's side. He had been questioning her, trying to get her to remember something to help him with his enquiries but she had panicked, imploring him to leave her alone.

Clem had grabbed her wrists as she'd made to run from the kitchen. 'You must have some idea who you are, for goodness' sake! You've been here over four months, you must remember something,' he'd said impatiently.

She'd struggled to get free. 'I don't, I don't! Let me go! Kenver!'

'That's right, call for Kenver. You always use him to run to, to hide behind. Why's that, Kerris? What are you trying to hide? Don't you want to know who you are?'

'Clem!' shouted Kenver from the doorway, his face white with anger. 'Let her go or I swear, cripple or not, I'll find a way to break your back!'

Clem abruptly let Kerris go.

'I'll have you know,' Kenver said coldly, as she ran to him, 'that Kerris turns to me for help because I take the trouble to be gentle and patient with her, not because she has anything to hide. We've grown very close over the weeks she's been here; in fact we love one another and we want to get married. Kerris is as keen as you evidently are to find out who she is, to know if the way is clear for us.'

Clem had apologised, ashamed to have frightened Kerris. He felt sorry for her now as he watched her hovering fearfully close to Jessica. He was certain she was Dinah Tredinnick's lost maid and if Peter

Blake, who was waiting outside to see her, jogged her memory back to its fullness, it was likely to be a distressing experience for her.

'Will you go and fetch Kenver, please, Jessica,' Clem said. 'There's someone waiting outside who thinks he knows Kerris, and Kenver ought to be here.'

When Kenver had wheeled himself through and Kerris was standing between his chair and Jessica for support, clutching their hands, Clem called Peter Blake inside.

Blake entered the doorway and his face exclaimed instant recognition. 'Amy!' he gasped softly. 'Amy, it's me, Mr Blake. Thank God you're safe.' And his eyes brimmed over with tears.

Kerris stared at him, wide-eyed and open-mouthed, tightening her grip on Jessica and Kenver's hands. She blinked rapidly and her mouth was working but no words came out.

'Do you remember Mr Blake, Amy?' Kenver said gently, using her real name to help her memory.

'Mr Blake says he knows you, Amy,' Clem said softly, from the other side of the kitchen. 'He thinks you used to live in a house in Penzance that he used to visit regularly.'

Kerris's eyes bulged. Her hands went limp and she pulled them away from the others.

Blake took a step towards her and stretched out a hand. 'It's so good to see you, Amy.'

'Is that you, Mr Blake?' she asked in a faint voice.

'Yes, it's me, Amy. I've been looking for you for months and there seemed to be no trace of you, and you were here all the time.'

Kerris became confused. 'Wh… what am I doing here?'

'You worked for Miss Dinah Tredinnick in Chapel Street at Penzance, do you remember, my dear? I used to call there.' Blake produced something from his waistcoat pocket, a small, round, enamelled brooch with a floral picture on it and held it out in his hand, moving closer to Kerris. 'I gave you this for your twenty-fourth birthday. That was back in February of this year. You left it behind… when you ran away.'

Kerris moved forward, as if in slow motion, and took the brooch from his hand. She held it closely to her eyes and a glimmer of a smile passed her lips.

Blake took one of her hands and supported her above the elbow. He shot Clem a worried look. 'You ran away from Miss Tredinnick's house, Amy. Why was that? What happened there?'

Kerris was twisting the brooch round and round and staring at it from all angles. 'You gave one something like this to Miss Dinah, sir. It had red and white roses on it and she wore it often. It was one of her favourite pieces because she couldn't wear much jewellery. She had it on the night... the night...'

'The night?' Blake prompted gently.

'The night he came...'

Jessica put her hand on Kenver's shoulder and he reached up and held it. Clem swallowed hard. Blake steeled himself to ask, 'Who was it, Amy? Who came to Miss Tredinnick's house?'

The woman whom the Trenchards knew as Kerris went rigid and her eyes glazed over. Kenver was behind her and strained to see her face. Jessica stepped back so he could wheel his chair closer to her.

'He came when it was dark...' Kerris began to shake and Blake put his arms about her. 'Miss Dinah let him in, she said for me to stay in my room and not to come out. She said she had something to see to and it needn't concern me.'

Kerris said nothing for several moments and Blake, whose presence was the only one she seemed to realise was there now, prompted, 'What did she have to see to, Amy?'

'I don't know!' and her voice became panicky. 'She didn't look happy about it, whatever it was. I... I think she was frightened, sir. Oh sir!'

'It's all right, Amy. You're perfectly safe here with me and the Trenchards. Try to remember everything and then it will be all over.'

In her mind Kerris was utterly alone, in another house, another time. 'There was a scream, it was a terrible noise! A strange noise like an animal would make. It was the mistress and she made no other noises, not loud ones anyway. I knew he was hurting her and I was

243

too scared to help her. I was so scared I sank down to the floor and stayed behind the door. There was strange noises coming from the sitting room… like an animal grunting and snuffling. It was him! It was him, oh God help me! I crawled across the room and hid in an alcove behind the curtains. I was so scared I couldn't shout for help. I should have shouted for help and saved the mistress! …After what seemed like ages, it went quiet. My bedroom door was opened and he looked in but he must have thought the mistress had sent me out because he went away. I stayed there nearly all night, in the dark, until the sky began to get lighter… Then I went to the mistress. I waited for her to call me but she didn't… then I went to her.' Kerris's body shook violently. 'She was all cut and slashed! She only screamed once because he had gagged her!' Kerris swayed on her feet and then collapsed in a faint across Kenver's lap.

Jessica, who'd had her hands to her face in horror, rushed to get some brandy from the parlour. Clem followed her and with shaking hands they set out glasses together, tactfully leaving Kenver and Blake to look after Kerris for a few moments. Clem held Jessica to stop her trembling.

'That's the worst thing I've ever heard,' she said, shuddering. 'Aye, the poor soul. No wonder her mind shut itself off. It had to come out one day though, my love. But she's got Kenver to help her to get over it now.'

'You know how they feel about each other then?'

Clem nodded. 'Kenver told me earlier today.'

A splash of cold water over her face and a few drops of brandy on her lips and Kerris began to come round. She groaned, her head lolling heavily on Kenver's chest. Jessica knelt and forced her to drink some water. When she was fully conscious Kenver lifted her chin and looked worriedly into her eyes. He blinked away tears of relief to see there was no glazing over her eyes; they were clear and grey, and looking steadily at him.

'It's all over, my love,' he said tenderly.

She stroked his face and whispered, 'I know who I am, Ken. And I know now that I'm not married.'

He kissed her gently and they clung to each other.

Peter Blake was staring at them, almost as shocked by this as by the details of Dinah Tredinnick's death. Clem handed him a glass of brandy and he bolted it down. 'They mean something to each other?' He motioned to them with his glass.

'Aye,' Clem replied. 'Looks like she'll be changing her last name as well as her first.'

'I was going to offer her a place at my house at Trevenner but I see that won't be necessary.' Clem was looking at him curiously and he added, 'My wife is very understanding... and of course Amy – Kerris – will be better off with you than with me until this maniac is caught.'

'We had better not make any more enquiries,' Clem said, moving Blake away so Kerris could not hear their conversation. 'There is the risk that we could put the murderer on to us.'

'It's been a terrible burden,' Blake agreed. 'While I was making enquiries about Amy I had to keep that in mind. I'd offered a generous sum of money to loosen tongues but I was always afraid I'd end up talking to the murderer himself. Whoever he is he's a very intelligent man. I believe he made sure no one saw him going to Miss Tredinnick's house. He must have approached her before, she seemed to have been expecting him. It was a mercy that she kept Amy out of the way, it saved her life. But we still have no clue who he was.'

'Mr Blake...'

Blake turned to see Kerris now sitting on the settle with Jessica's arms round her and Kenver holding her hands. She was still shivering and he could see it would take time for her to get over the full shock of her mistress's death and regaining her memory. 'You're feeling better, my dear?' he asked kindly.

'I just want to say it's good to see you again, and thank you for coming,' she replied shyly.

'I'm glad that you'll be in good company,' he said with a smile which included Kenver. 'There is one other thing,' he ventured.

'Oh?' Kerris said nervously.

'I'm shutting up Miss Tredinnick's house tomorrow. Would you like to come with me to collect your things? I know it's a lot to ask, but if you can bear to go into the house again, something might jog your memory into remembering something about this man. Until he's caught he's a threat to everyone. It might also help you to recover more quickly if you face the situation again...'

Kerris looked uncertainly at Kenver and Jessica.

'I'll come with you,' Jessica offered.

'If only Kenver could come,' Kerris said with a small wail.

'I'll send my carriage over,' Blake said at once. 'Perhaps Clem will come as well. You'll be perfectly safe with all of us, my dear.'

It was agreed, and as it was family business Clem suggested he send a message over to Catherine to ask her if she would like to come too. He thought the younger women might be glad of her calm presence. And Blake, who felt he owed it to his wife not to exclude her from the final chapter of the tale of his unfortunate mistress, said Rosina would probably wish to go also.

Chapter 19

While Clem had been in Penzance seeking information, Kane was riding to the home of the prostitute called Meg on the same errand. He found her house quite easily, according to Frances Nansmere's instructions. It was little more than a hovel on the outskirts of the town near the swamps and looked less comfortable than Ricketty Jim's shack. It was one of a few similar buildings, thrown up out of any available material that could be found, housing the outcasts and the poorest of the locality. Meg's stood out because it was the only one with a pointed roof, making it look like a giant chicken coop.

A woman was sitting outside on the doorstep, dressed in ragged clothes and smoking lazily on a dirty clay pipe with a broken stem. She was stroking a pure white cat curled up in the well of the faded purple skirt that hung between her parted legs. She watched Kane through hostile, searching eyes as he rode up, dismounted and walked purposefully towards her.

Before he could speak she snarled at him, 'So thee've come at last, 'ave 'ee? I don't want no trouble. Known too much of it in my lifetime!' She spat on a pile of sticks beside the door.

Kane surveyed her calmly. He could see why Frances had called her old but he put her at perhaps no more than forty-five. Her appearance made it impossible for her to work in a brothel now; no man would want this woman, even free of charge. Her skin was as wrinkled as a pickled walnut, her hair grey and frizzy. She had had a full bosom once but now her breasts sagged. She met his steady gaze with more hostility but Kane could see she was also frightened.

'Are you Meg?' he asked in a quiet voice.

'What if I am?'

247

'Do you know who I am?'

'Course I do! Everybody round these 'ere parts knows who you are! A tall good-looking man with reddish hair and a soldier's bearing and the assured manner of a man brought up amongst the gentry. Cap'n Kane Pengarron, the took-in son of the mighty Sir Oliver Pengarron and his beautiful working-class wife.'

Kane ignored the contempt in her scratchy voice. 'Has a woman called Frances Nansmere come here to see you in recent weeks?'

'A woman? Another prostitute you mean! She's no better'n me. Just because she's dressed up in they fine clo'es, got money to spend on powder and paint and owns the place I used to work in, she's no better'n me, the bitch!'

'I have not come to cause you any trouble, Meg. If you don't want to be seen talking to me I'll lead my horse to somewhere more discreet and we could go inside your house.'

Meg sniggered. 'P'raps you shouldn't be seen talkin' to me, Cap'n Pengarron. Folk might think you've come fer services rendered! I 'ave t'make a livin' some'ow and there's always someone desprit enough.' She cackled horribly, and Kane tried not to grimace when she lifted her breasts, pushed her tongue out of her thin, cracked lips and said, 'You sure I can't int'rest thee in my beautiful body! I might be past my best in looks but I 'aven't lost my touch. I still know how to satisfy a gentleman and you look like you can afford to pay me a pretty penny or two.'

'I will pay you well for some information,' Kane said, pulling a fat leather pouch from his coat pocket. 'If I consider it to be honest and truthful, I'll give you enough to find somewhere better to live, to buy a pretty new dress and something to put the colour back into your cheeks. Make up your mind quickly, Meg. You know what I want, and there are three other women I can ask. I'm sure I can loosen one of their tongues. Be thankful you have been given the first opportunity.'

Meg's eyes darted from side to side, following the movement of the pouch as he swung it from the tips of his fingers. 'Do 'ee promise thee won't cause any trouble, no matter what I tell 'ee?'

'You have my word as a Pengarron, a name I'm proud to bear.'

Meg pointed at the money pouch with her pipe. 'All right. Your father's word's always bin known as steadfast and true so I'll tell you what you want to know, young sir. Money first.'

She made a snatch at the pouch but Kane whipped it out of her reach. 'How much you receive depends on what and how much you tell me.' She scowled and spat again. 'I can be very generous,' he added coaxingly.

She glanced around. There were a few people about and they had stopped to look at them. A cart was travelling along the pitted track that ran several yards away from Meg's hovel and the occupants stared at them curiously. She glared at them all, shouting at them, 'Bugger off!' The people complied, some shouting back abuse in more profane language.

Meg tossed her frizzled head. 'Let's git inside. 'Tes nothin' grand like you'm used to, sir. You'll just 'ave to put up with the smells.'

The smells in question came from a variety of animals – two dogs, a pig, a goat, numerous cats, fowls, rabbits and a hare. Kane had a rapport with animals and found he could just about tolerate the mixed odours of these.

'They'm my family,' Meg explained affectionately, patting the heads of both dogs. 'All I've got in the world. Gotta be careful somebody don't steal 'em, that's why they'm in here. Folk are always hungry or mean enough.'

'You have a lovely family, Meg,' Kane said sincerely. The animals and fowls were well cared for and their smells came from being shut up in the stuffy room where there was only one small opening to serve as a window. He picked up one of the rabbits, a young grey creature with very long ears. He stroked it as he sat down on an old ale crate, part of the hovel's sparse furniture. Within moments, two of the cats had slunk up to him; one crept up his chest beside the rabbit while the other sat on his shoulder and rubbed its black furry cheek against his ear, purring in ecstasy.

Meg sat on a lump of wood by the place where she burned a fire. A cat jumped up onto her lap and mewed, its eyes on Kane.

'This one likes you too,' Meg said, breaking into a reluctant smile that took a few years off her premature ageing.

'I've always liked animals,' Kane said.

'So I see. I've 'eard about your family over the years. You all like creatures, don't 'ee?'

'Yes,' he answered. 'My younger sister has a dog called Rex, a very boisterous black retriever,' he said conversationally. 'I had a dog myself when I was younger. He died from old age last year. I was upset to be away from home at the time.'

'And now you're back,' Meg said, looking him straight in the eye. 'And for some reason wanting to know about yer past. I think the past should be left in the past. With the fine home and parents that you've got, don't 'ee think you should be grateful fer that and leave things lie?'

Kane stroked the rabbit and the cat on his chest simultaneously. 'I shall always be grateful to my parents but I want to know something of my past before I settle down and make a future for myself.'

'I've feared fer years that Sir Oliver would come an' ask questions about you. Mayhap 'e don't want to know anythin'.'

'Perhaps Sir Oliver thought the decision should be left to me whether to ask about my past or not.' Kane smiled.

Meg nodded to that. 'You'm wearin' black. Laid someone to rest, 'ave 'ee?' she asked, softening the scratch in her voice.

'I've been to a double funeral, of a grandfather and his grandson aged twenty-two years. It makes you realise that we're all mortal, that we can die at any time. It impressed upon me the need to get on and find out what I can about my origins, no matter how distasteful or distressing they are.'

Meg relit her dirty pipe and blew smoke in the doorway's direction. 'What do you know already?'

'My parents have told me that my real mother worked in the brothel that Frances Nansmere now owns and my father, who seems to have hated her, was a sailor. My mother died, of the pox according to the sailor. The other women in the brothel refused to look after me any longer so the sailor decided to sell me in the marketplace. That's when my adoptive mother, Lady Pengarron, saw us and bought me from him – in exchange for a guinea and her pony's saddle. She took me home to the Manor house and Sir Oliver agreed to bring me up as their own.'

'Ais, 'tes what everyone's thinks to be true.'

'And is it not?' Kane leaned forward, disturbing the animals and the black cat jumped down.

'No, yer mother was no 'arlot an' yer father was no sailor, you'll be pleased to 'ear.'

'Then who were they?'

A moment of fear crossed Meg's wrinkled face. 'Yer promised to cause no trouble, mind. I'm takin' a risk trustin' thee an' if thee talks it could cost me my life.'

'I gave you my word, Meg, and I meant it,' Kane said, rearranging the position of the remaining cat and the rabbit.

'The woman who the sailor said wus yer mother wus really yer aunt, yer mother's sister. Yer mother wus called Peggy Wearne. Like I said, she wus no 'arlot, never gave 'erself to any man save who got 'er with child. She said 'e wus a rover an' never knew 'e fathered a child, went off on 'is travels an' left the poor maid in trouble. She could 'ave bin no more than sixteen at the time. She came to the brothel beggin' 'er sister to 'elp 'er. She were a right bitch, that one! An evil woman, 'ad ways with men like, well, I went say an animal, more like a savage. Anyway, she got the sister a job as a maid-of-all-works at the brothel. Cookin', cleanin', fetchin' an' carryin' fer the rest of us, an' the poor little soul 'ad t'work right up to the time of 'er labour. She had a long an' difficult time an' you were born.'

'So she didn't have much of a life,' Kane said mournfully.

'No, but how she loved you. You wus such a good little baby, 'ardly 'eard thee cry. She wanted t'spend every minute of the day with you but 'ad to work 'ard to keep the both of you.'

'What did she look like, Peggy Wearne, my mother?' Kane asked, a film of mist covering his eyes.

Meg studied him a minute. 'You'm a lot like 'er, tall, strong-bodied, same colour hair… but not the eyes. You'm got yer father's eyes.'

'How do you know that?'

'Cus she talked about yer father all the time. Said he was a fine-looking man with large brown eyes, as beautiful as velvet. She was convinced 'e'd come back t'Marazion on 'is travels an' when 'e knew 'e 'ad a little small baby 'e'd marry 'er an' they'd settle down together.'

'Did she say what his name was? Did she say anything else about him?'

'No, I'm sorry, sir. I asked 'erself more 'n' once what the father was called but she just smiled an' said that wus 'er secret.'

'Meg, what was the name my mother gave me? Is my real name Kane?'

'Ais. Dunno why she called you that either. Said she just liked the sound of it.'

'So something in my life is really mine,' he said softly. He concentrated on stroking the cat and rabbit and the prostitute stayed silent until he was ready to speak again. 'How did she die?'

''Er ruddy sister, damn 'er!' Meg shook her fist and got heated. 'Wus always on to the maid about joinin' the rest of us, said she would make more money that way. Rest of us b'lieved the sister was jealous of yer mother, she wus pretty and clean and pleasant t'talk to. Used to bathe us when we got beaten up, see to us when we got drunk. Trouble wus, the customers took a fancy to 'er and the richer ones pestered our madam to let them, as they'd say "break 'er in". They took bets on who'd be the first among 'em, offered the madam good money, an' the poor little soul was under some pressure. But she always refused, nursin' this romantic notion that 'er baby's father would come back fer 'er an' they'd go off an' live 'appily like they do in fairy tales. One night, though, the sister was determined to change the maid's mind. A certain gentleman, a depraved sod 'e wus, wanted her in particular, and they worked up a scheme with the madam to make her give in.'

Kane's face darkened. 'What did they do?'

'She, yer aunt, damn 'er rotten soul, took you from Peggy's room and said she couldn't 'ave you back until she favoured the gentleman. Told Peggy she'd be all right when she'd done it once, after all she weren't pure no more, said she'd be grateful when she wus earnin' well an' could buy nice things fer 'er little boy. Peggy panicked an' fought to grab thee back an'… an' the gentleman gave 'er a mighty push an' she wus sent 'eadlong down the stairs. She broke 'er neck, died at once. We all saw it, come to see what all the shoutin' wus about. Yer aunt gave you to me, you wus frightened an' cryin' some loud. The gentleman cuffed you cross the face. You 'ave a scar down yer back, 'aven't thee? Startin' from the neck, goin' right down?'

Kane nodded grimly.

'The gentleman – we wus all terrified of' im – 'e grabbed thee from my arms an' slammed yer little body 'gainst the wall an' let you slide down. There wus a nail on the wall, it dug into yer back all the way down.' Meg was crying now, rocking back and forth, cradling the cat in her arms as though she was holding a baby. 'Oh, 'ow you did cry! 'E picked you up an' threw you into a cupboard an' forbade us to go to you. 'E said 'e would fix it with the coroner to say Peggy died of the pox an' if any one of us talked about what 'appened 'e would come an' kill us. We 'ad no choice but to do what 'e said. 'E wus a wealthy an' powerful man an' if 'e could treat a child in the way 'e did you… We wus all so scared, sir.'

'Is he still alive, Meg?' Kane hissed, his face white with shock and bitter memories of what he'd suffered. 'The man who did that to my mother and me?'

Meg looked up, terrified. 'No, sir, but 'is sons are an' they aren't much better. They would kill us to protect 'is memory and their family's name. Please don't do anythin', sir. You promised…'

Kane put a hand on her scrawny shoulder. 'I won't do anything, I won't go back on my promise to you. Would I know this family? Would I be likely to socialise with them?'

'Not round 'ere, sir. 'E wasn't local, 'e come a long way to spend 'is lust. One of the girls 'ad a speciality that suited 'im. I'm glad to say 'e never wanted me.'

'And this aunt of mine, Peggy's sister. Why did she say she was my mother?'

'To please the gentleman, sir, an' to spite the sailor. Not that they were married. They used to live together an' she came to the brothel just before 'er sister did. With Peggy's death 'ushed up, folk 'ad no reason to b'lieve the sister wusn't yer mother.'

'My poor mother,' Kane said to himself. He wiped tears from his eyes and felt an aching for her, for the wretched life she had lived and the terrible death she'd suffered. And painful memories were flooding his mind and filling him with horror. 'After Peggy's death, why was I so badly treated, Meg? It sounds as though you cared about me.'

'I did, an' so did most of the girls. We may be sluts but we aren't all cruel. The madam kept you in the cellar, told us she and yer aunt would look after you down there and take you out in the daytime. But then yer aunt died suddenly, justice saw to that, got an infection from the pox. The madam said she had given you away to some family who wanted a son but the wife wus barren. 'Ad no idea you were still kept in the cellar, never 'eard you cry, until the sailor turned up askin' fer 'is mate. The madam kept you there hopin' she could get money off the sailor fer what she called yer keep. Some of us cried when we saw the state you were in when she brought you up. Filthy dirty and in rags and yer large brown eyes lookin' so deep an' startled.' Meg looked at him intently for a moment. 'Some 'an'some you are now, Cap'n Pengarron, an' that's a wonder to me. But yer eyes still show what you went through. I was some pleased when I 'eard that the young Lady Pengarron 'ad got thee off that swine of a sailor an' you were given a good home. It's eased my conscience over the years.'

'Is that the whole story?' Kane whispered.

'Ais, I promise thee, sir. I don't know anythin' else.'

'There are a few minor details and I might as well know them all. What was my aunt called? And the sailor?'

Meg pushed a hand across her face to wipe away her tears. 'That bitch was called Agnes, Agnes Wearne. The sailor I only know as Jake.'

'So the man who was thought of as my father was called Jake and all you know about the real one is that he was a rover with large brown eyes.' Kane suddenly paled. Meg sprang up and went to him.

'Cap'n Pengarron! Are 'ee all right?'

'Yes, yes, Meg,' he gasped, clutching her hand. 'It's made me think of something, that's all.'

'Don't tell me you've an idea who your father might be?'

'I know of one possibility,' he said, shaking and gently pushing away the black cat who was trying to get back onto his shoulder.

'I'll get 'ee a drop o' brandy. Always keep some about the place.'

Kane accepted the spirit gratefully, drinking it straight from the bottle.

''Tes bin a lot fer 'ee to take in,' Meg said understandingly. She stood behind him and stroked his hair and Kane knew it was done with maternal feeling. He handed her the money pouch.

'There's fifty guineas in there, Meg,' he said, looking round at her pets. 'You've earned it. It should be enough to help you make a fresh start for yourself and your family. And thank you for being good to Peggy and me when I was an infant.'

'Thank you, sir,' she said, in a gentle voice. 'Will you be able to make a new start? The one you must want so badly?'

'I'm getting there, Meg. After what you've told me I've made a big leap forward but now I will have to take time to think carefully before I decide what to do next.'

'Don't live in the past, sir,' Meg said, coming round to face him. 'I've done it all me life an' look at the state of me. Tired, worn out, friendless, bitter. I 'ad a few bad knocks early on an' instead of learnin' a lesson an' lettin' it make somethin' of me, I let it turn me into this. Look at me, Cap'n. Yer life shows in yer face. Compare mine to yer beautiful mother's. Things 'appened years ago an' she wus forced to marry Sir Oliver. But she didn't brood, become spiteful an' plot revenge. She had goodness in 'er an' accepted it and rose above it, makin' 'er strong. Then she an' Sir Oliver fell in love an' 'ad a lovely family. Even that young farmer who lost yer mother didn't live a life of bitterness fer ever. He found a strength from somewhere to live with it. 'Ow I do envy the strong and good in character.'

'You are a good woman, Meg,' Kane said, placing a gentle hand on her shoulder.

She laughed, not the cackle he had heard outside. 'You'll be sayin' next I ought to be listenin' to they Methodist preachers.'

'Well…' Kane smiled. 'One life's better than another. I hope the money will help.'

'It will, Cap'n, an' you won't see us when you ride this way again.'

'Where will you go? I'd like to keep in touch.'

'I'd rather not. Now you know the truth, keep the past in the past, sir.'

'I'll respect your right to your privacy, Meg, but I've still got something more to sort out and it could complicate things,' Kane said quietly.

'I bet it's a maid,' Meg said, grinning all over her ravaged face. 'Someone you know who 'as large brown eyes, and a maid.'

–

Kerensa lay nestled in Oliver's arms late that night as they talked over the day's events.

'It's been an awful day,' she said. 'I'm glad William decided to take Rachael up to London to spend time with some of their other children. I don't think I could've faced much more of her mourning.'

'I thought Martin's funeral would have been a dignified, poignant occasion. A good turn-out at the little chapel at Tolwithrick, a solemn burial, then a few drinks while the mourners mulled over their affectionate memories of him. He was quite a character. I shall miss him very much.'

'Yes, so will I.'

'I didn't expect to see Sebastian buried beside him and have Rachael wailing throughout for her son,' Oliver sighed irritably.

Kerensa shuddered and he held her closer. 'I shall never forget how Sebastian died,' she murmured.

'Try to put that out of your mind, beloved,' he said, kissing her brow then both cheeks. 'I don't like thinking about that myself – the difference in their deaths.'

'No wonder Kane left the wake soon afterwards. I wonder where he went,' Kerensa mused. 'He was very quiet when he came home for supper.'

'A woman probably,' Oliver said, grinning.

'Do you think so? Who could it be? He's been rather secretive since he left the regiment. He used to tell me everything.'

'Now don't get jealous, my love. If Kane had been with a woman, he would hardly tell his mother about it.'

'It's not amusing, Oliver.'

'I'm not suggesting it is amusing, but you've got to let him grow up sometime, my love.'

'Do you think I want to keep the children as babies?' she asked seriously.

'Well,' and Oliver dragged out the word. 'Because Jack was a boy when we married, you've always mothered him. He's now a man of thirty-four and I heard you yesterday telling him to make sure he puts on his coat now the evenings are getting chilly.'

'I didn't! Did I?'

'You did, so that will give you some idea how you treat our children at times.'

'Well, I don't want them growing up and leaving home. Kelynen's nearly fifteen and because she's tall she looks older.'

Oliver kissed Kerensa's lips tenderly then gazed at her steadily.

'What?'

'You don't know yourself, do you, my precious one? It never ceases to amaze me.'

He rolled over onto his back, grinning in the amused way he had when he knew a secret that she should know herself. Kerensa leaned across his chest and put her arms on his broad shoulders. 'Tell me at once or I'll do something terrible to you.'

Pulling her down to him, he said huskily, 'You do something terrible to me and then I'll tell you.'

'Oliver!'

'All right, calm down. You become so absorbed with other people you never keep a check on yourself. This time it's been Kane and Rachael's grief that has kept you preoccupied.'

'What do you mean?'

'I mean, my sweeting, that you don't have to worry too much about the children growing up and leaving home because next year there will a new addition to the nursery.'

'You mean… ?'

'I do. You ordered me to give you more babies and apparently I'd already done it,' he said, rather proudly.

Kerensa lay down on her side of the bed and made calculations in her head while Oliver made them out loud. 'We were together this week, last week, and the week before and before that… I didn't need Beatrice to tell me this time because I've been home for several weeks.'

Kerensa lay quietly in her thoughts. Then she was overwhelmed with joy, and the next moment crying. Oliver held her tightly in his arms. 'Is it Joseph?' he whispered.

'Yes, it still hurts so much. But it's wonderful news, Oliver, isn't it?'

'Yes, my love,' he replied softly into her hair, 'wonderful.'

A little later when they had cried out their joy and grief, Oliver said, 'I have business in Penzance with the mayor tomorrow, my love. Why don't you come with me? You can do some shopping and we'll have a quiet luncheon together.'

Chapter 20

Olivia woke up early the next morning. She waited for her parents to ride off before she got out of bed, unaware that they were heading for her own intended destination a short time later in the day. She was pleased that Cordelia wanted to spend the day with Luke, supporting him in his business duties, and she sat up in bed rereading over and over again a secret note that she had been given last night.

There were only three days left before the smuggling enterprise and she had been out in the tack room trying to persuade Jack to come with them. 'We can't do it without you, Jack,' she'd pleaded. 'We need to be as quick as possible and some of the things might be too heavy for us to carry up the cliff. You must come, there is no one else we trust as we do you.'

Jack had kept on with his work. 'I'm sorry, Miss Olivia, but I've told you before and I'll tell you again. I'm not going and that's that. His lordship and her ladyship would never forgive me if it went wrong and something happened to you or Miss Cordelia, or Jessica Trenchard, come to that. 'Tis a foolhardy thing you've got planned and I beg you to drop it before one of you gets hurt.'

'Don't be like that, Jack. It's not dangerous. We've got the whole operation planned to the finest detail. Nothing can possibly go wrong. Other women smuggle in goods, it's going on all the time. We're not bringing in very much this time, it's only a trial run. Say yes, Jack. Just this once, please.'

Jack moved the saddles into a neater line then inspected other items of tack to see if the stable boys were doing their jobs properly. Olivia trotted behind him, passing him things, but he refused to look at her. Finally, in a quiet, no-nonsense voice, he said, 'You know I'd do anything for you, Miss Olivia, but not this. There was a time a few years ago, just before Miss Kelynen was born, when I should have stopped her ladyship from doing something foolhardy. I didn't and it almost cost us our lives.'

Olivia pouted and picked at a splinter of wood on a post. 'I won't take no for an answer, Jack. This is different to what Mama wanted you to do. Think about it. I'll talk to you again.'

She'd flounced out of the tack room before Jack could reply and nearly walked into one of the stable boys.

'I'm sorry, miss!' he exclaimed and hastily pulled something out of his coat pocket. 'I wus asked to give this to 'ee, miss.'

It was a letter but it had no seal on it. Olivia took it and turned it over curiously. 'Who gave this to you, Conan?'

''Twas the parson's stable boy, Miss Olivia. Said he wus paid well to keep quiet. I went say anything, miss.'

Olivia was cross with herself for flushing. 'Thank you, Conan. I'll, um, give you something for the same consideration.'

'Eh?'

'If you will keep quiet too,' she explained impatiently.

'Oh, I'll do that, miss, never fear.'

She raced away to her room to read the letter, ignoring the call for supper, praying as she ran that it was from Timothy. He called more regularly at the Manor and was very gracious to her. She was sure he was romantically interested in her and had the feeling he was trying to get her father to see him as other than the parish parson before he made any direct approach to her. He spoke to her as often and as long as he could without breaching propriety.

She pulled open the letter with trembling fingers. It was in Timothy's handwriting which she had seen many times on documents on her father's desk.

My Dear Miss Olivia,
     Forgive me taking this Liberty but I would like to see You Alone. It may be a Presumption but I Feel that you Share the same Feelings for Me as I Have for You.

I would like to Speak to Sir Oliver, but first I want to ask you for your Permission. I shall be in Penzance tomorrow. There is an empty house, in good repair, that I have rented for a short time. Please, I Beg You, My Dearest,

Meet me there at the Address below at Eleven of the clock Tomorrow.

Your Faithful Servant,

Timothy Lanyon

Olivia had no qualms about meeting the young parson alone. She didn't doubt for a moment that he would behave honourably towards her at all times. Timothy was in her thoughts constantly. He was always at the Manor. Oliver had raised his eyebrows at the sudden amount of 'parish business' Timothy had found to discuss. Kerensa invited him to stay for meals during which he talked a lot about the forthcoming painting exhibition and Olivia knew she could count on his support. Twice Timothy managed to persuade Olivia to walk round the gardens with him, just the two of them. On the last occasion he'd held her hand for much longer than her father would have approved of. Timothy had made her quite forget her assertions earlier this year that she was not interested in getting married. She could hardly wait for the time to pass when she could set out for the short ride around the bay to Penzance.

–

Kane left the Manor before Olivia did, riding over to Ker-an-Mor Farm in the company of Luke and Cordelia who had become a confident rider. He then rode on to Trecath-en Farm and was amazed to find no one there but Ricketty Jim.

'Where's everybody gone, Jim?' he asked, looking around the yard as if he believed the absentees would materialise.

'They'm all gone over to Penzanns, sir, 'cept for Philip and David who're out cutting furze,' Ricketty Jim said. 'Surprised the life out of me, all of 'em going off like that in Mr Blake's coach with his lovely wife in it.'

'Peter and Rosina Blake? What on earth for? What's going on?'

'Dunno, sir, 'cept it's something to do with Kerris. Jessie told me her real name's Amy so they must've found out who she is at last. The maid said Kerris wouldn't go without she and Kenver, and even Miss Catherine's going.'

'But what's Peter Blake got to do with Kerris?'

'Dunno that either. But he wus here yesterday an' from all accounts she was some glad to see him.'

Kane thought hard for a few minutes and then the truth hit him. 'Peter Blake's mistress was murdered back in the spring and her maid-servant went missing. That's who Kerris must be, the maidservant, and her real name is Amy.'

'Thought it might be something like that,' Jim said, shaking his head.

Kane grinned. 'You could have said so at the beginning, Jim. If they're going over to Penzance, they must be taking Kerris back to her old surroundings for some reason. Perhaps she doesn't remember everything about herself yet.'

'Or who killed her mistress.'

'I don't like the sound of that. It could spell danger for her and Jessica. Dear God!'

'Getting partial to young Jessie, are 'ee?'

'I might be,' Kane said offhandedly, but his eyes were shining and Jim knew he was right. 'I might ride over to Penzance later. I know it's really none of my business...'

''Tis if you're partial to the little maid, and Clem wouldn't mind. He would be if 'twas your brother but he's got a fondness for you. Be some proud if something happened between you two I do reckon.' Ricketty Jim put his head on one side like an attentive sparrow. He'd noticed Kane had been looking closely at him since they'd been talking. 'I'm just as curious as to why you're staring at me as to why they've gone off to Penzanns,' he said.

262

'I didn't come over to see Clem today, or even Jessica – well, not yet. I wanted to speak to you first and when you weren't to be found at your shack, I rode down here.'

'Want me to tell a few stories at a party, do 'ee?'

'No, I want to tell you about my childhood.'

Ricketty Jim lifted his thick brows. 'Well, I'm a good listener, come inside.' He led the way into the farmhouse. He'd promised to make the weekly bread and he set to work kneading the dough he'd had proving next to the brick oven. Kane watched his strong-handed movements, leaning against the dresser.

'Go on,' Jim said, as he threw a handful of flour lightly on the oven, which burned with a blaze of sparks, informing him it had reached the required heat. Next he sprinkled flour on a well-used marble slab that had been in the Trenchard family for generations. He broke off a lump of dough and thumped it down on the cold marble. 'I've always got a ready ear for listening though most folk do think I'm only wanting to talk.'

Kane cleared his throat and began. This wasn't going to be easy. 'You know that Sir Oliver and Lady Pengarron are not my real parents?'

'Aye.'

'When I left the army this year, I decided to find out about my past.'

'Understandable,' Jim said, stretching the dough and thumping the ends back to the centre.

'I started life in a local brothel. It was thought my mother was a prostitute working there and my father a rather unsavoury sailor. I found out yesterday that my mother was in fact the prostitute's sister, not a prostitute herself, and the man who fathered me was not the sailor and he was the only man she'd known in that way.'

'That must be a comfort to you, though 'tis a sad tale whichever way you look at it. Would 'ee mind passing me they tin trays there beside 'ee, sir? This is nearly ready and the oven's nice and hot, the stones have changed to the proper red colour. I'll make some round loaves next, I make a nice tasty bit of bread, if I do say so myself. A man's hand is stronger for the kneading, you see.'

Kane passed the trays and held them still as Jim tossed smaller lumps of dough on them.

'Go on,' Jim said again, pushing the bread with his knuckles until he'd got the desired shapes. 'Your mother was this prostitute's sister. What happened to her then?'

'She died… in an accident.'

'That was a shame.'

Kane went silent and Jim looked up at him. 'Next bit hard to say, is it?'

'Yes, especially to you, Jim.'

'To me? How's that then?'

'I've been told that my mother used to say that my father, the only information I have about him, was a rover with large brown eyes.'

Ricketty Jim dropped a bread tray on the table with a clatter. 'A rover with… Upon my soul, young Kane, you don't think it was me? That I'm your father?'

Kane raised his dark brows over his wonderfully sad, large brown eyes. 'You fit the description. Your eyes are the same colour as mine and it hasn't been many years since you've settled down.'

'Oh, Kane.' Jim staggered back to the three-legged stool that Kerris liked to sit on and fell down on it. 'It's not possible!'

'Why not? Don't you think you could have ever met my mother? She was a sixteen-year-old girl when she became with child, she had red hair like mine and was called Peggy Wearne. Isn't it possible you could have met her and fathered me without knowing it? She was sure my father would come back to these parts one day, and… here you are, Jim.'

'It is true that I was a rover, that over many years I wandered in and out of Mount's Bay, but it is impossible for me to be your father.'

Kane didn't look convinced.

'I'd be honoured to think I was your father,' Ricketty Jim said slowly, 'but, you see, I've never known a woman in my life, not ever. I've never felt the need and have been content to keep myself to myself all my life.'

Kane felt a choking feeling creeping up his chest, which came out in an embarrassed cough. 'I'm sorry, Jim. I feel such a fool.'

'There's no need for that, 'twas only natural for you to ask. Tis a pity it wasn't me... or is that not what you wanted?'

'I suppose a part of me did hope it wasn't you,' Kane admitted. 'I would have known for sure without any more searching but I admit I have mixed feelings about the man who fathered me. He must have seduced Peggy and then gone off on his travels again without a backward thought. It's a terrible way to treat any girl. Yet I want to know him, to know that basically he's a good and decent man, and you're certainly that, Jim. If you had turned out to be my father though, it would have made things very difficult for Sir Oliver, with you living so close. At least that's one thing I don't have to worry about.'

'And at least you won't inherit my bowed legs,' Jim smiled. 'You're a tall, well-built man, any man anywhere would be proud to think he was your father. Sometimes 'tis something I regret, not getting married and raising a family.'

'It's not too late.'

'Tush! Some things aren't meant to be and that's the way of it. I couldn't have changed in my younger days, I had to get the wanderlust out of my system. And who knows if I won't suddenly take off again some day. That's why I like my little shack, 'tis sort of semi-permanent. Will you go on searching for your real father, sir?'

Kane thought about it. 'Call me Kane, all of the time, Jim. It never feels right when you call me sir. As for your question, I don't know. I'll sleep on it, perhaps for several years, though it will probably be too late by then. Maybe I'm never meant to know who my real father was.' Kane smiled softly. 'Sir Oliver is such a powerful character, he is more than enough as my father and he's always treated me like his own son.' He gazed at the settle where he'd held Jessica in her pain and remembered Kerensa's usual concern over him at breakfast that day. 'And it will take a very special woman to take my mother's place as the most important woman in my heart.'

'Well, I reckon you already know her.' Jim put his first batch of bread into the oven and sealed it down, then said, 'I know 'tis a woman's drink but would you like to take a dish of tea with me? I know I could do with one. Won't take a minute.'

'Just one quickly. I've a notion to ride over to Penzance.'

'Kane,' Jim said, as he poured boiling water on the leaves, 'have you told Sir Oliver and her ladyship what you've found out?'

'Not yet. I will if I feel the time is right.'

''Tis best to keep our conversation to ourselves then, don't you think?'

'Yes, I do.' Kane looked at the settle again. 'I've got other things to keep my mind occupied now.'

—

Jessica felt excited to be riding in a carriage for the first time in her life, travelling over the gravel chippings that the Pengarrons had had put down, making the roads much easier to ride over. It wasn't as big or as grand as any of the Pengarron conveyances but it was a real gentleman's coach and one of the few in Cornwall; it was Peter Blake's proudest acquisition. She would have put her head out of the window to announce her presence in it to passers-by but the name of Peter Blake bore too much shame for that. She wondered what Kane would think of her being here. He probably wouldn't approve, but it was her father's doing. She had hoped Kane would turn up at the farm last night so she could tell him of this excursion. She hadn't seen him since they'd sheltered in Ricketty Jim's shack and she was looking forward to the time he would ride over to the farm and tell her where they could meet quietly. That would be any day now by his reckoning and she was getting impatient.

She sat next to Rosina Blake who, despite being slight of figure, was jammed in between her and Catherine. The two older women were politely conversing about the forthcoming wedding.

'You must be getting very excited about it, Jessica,' Rosina said, turning to her as they lurched over the rougher roads.

Catherine glanced round Rosina, anxious as to what Jessica's answer would be. Jessica knew Catherine's smile was one of relief when she said, quite truthfully now that she was getting used to the idea, 'Aye, specially as it's going to be a double wedding with Uncle Kenver marrying Kerris.'

Rosina and Catherine looked at the couple sitting close together opposite. They were holding hands and Kerris looked down at their entwined fingers, blushing shyly.

'Oh really? Congratulations to you both,' Rosina said, smiling serenely at them.

'Thank you, Mistress Blake,' Kenver said, looking proudly at his bride-to-be. 'Trecath-en Farm's never seen so many happy changes in one year.'

'I hope you won't find the experience of going home too harrowing, Kerris,' Rosina said.

No one called Kerris by her rightful name of Amy. It had been decided the day before that she would leave her old life behind and from now on be known as Kerris Trenchard. Now the greater part of her memory had come back, she no longer looked haunted or was quite as easily scared. Her true nature was to say, very carefully, what was on her mind.

'I'll be glad when it's over, Mistress Blake,' she said now. 'But it can't be easy for you either. You probably haven't known about me for very long and didn't want to meet me.'

'My husband is most distressed over Dinah Tredinnick's death and I feel a sympathy for her for the dreadful way she died. I wish only to see Mr Blake returned to his usual contented self, and I should be pleased if you too can settle down to a new and happy life.'

'You are the most charitable of ladies,' Kenver said.

Rosina bowed her head and Catherine thought it prudent to change the subject. She spoke to her future brother-in-law. 'I understand this is the very first time you have left the farm, Kenver?'

'Aye, it is, Catherine. I'm enjoying the sights I can see out of the window.'

'There will be plenty to see at Penzance.'

'Have you heard from Simon Peter?' Jessica asked Rosina.

'Yes, I have,' she answered, her face brightening.

As Rosina told Jessica about her son's life as an itinerant preacher in Yorkshire, Catherine looked out at Clem's back as he rode ahead in front of the coach. She had been thrilled when David had arrived at the Parsonage last night with a note from Clem. He had not bothered to learn to write well when Matthias Renfree had taught the family years ago and David explained the scrappy writing in more detail. It had warmed her heart that Clem wanted her along on this family excursion and she felt nothing could now prevent their marriage from taking place. She felt like a married woman already, that she had first claim on the blond-haired man she spied from the erratically moving coach. Catherine hoped she would get the opportunity to parade about Penzance on his arm and receive envious looks from other woman at her handsome, masculine escort – her man. She had his letter in her purse. It was headed 'Dear Catherine' and signed simply in spidery handwriting 'Clem', but to her it was the most intimate love letter ever sent and received.

'So you're confident Simon Peter is enjoying his work on the Yorkshire circuit,' Jessica was saying.

'Well, he seems to have settled down but Mr Blake and I won't be truly happy until he's back in Cornwall. We're hoping he might come home for a few days soon.'

'It will be lovely to see him again,' Jessica agreed.

It took nearly two hours to complete the journey from the time the coach left Trecath-en Farm, collected Catherine at the Parsonage, journeyed through Marazion then Long Rock, to reach the outskirts of Penzance. They had started out at a sedate pace but were held up by a fracas in the street in Marazion and an overturned cart on the road after leaving Long Rock. Peter Blake was impatient to carry on with the journey but Clem insisted on helping the carter right his conveyance and reload the tin ore he was taking to Penzance to be stamped.

As they travelled alongside Eastern Green, Rosina, who was feeling as nervous as Kerris was, said, 'We're almost there.'

Kerris gripped Kenver's strong hand painfully tight, her square face paled and she let out a frightened gulp. Jessica leaned forward and pressed a comforting hand on her knee. 'You'll be all right, Kerris. We're here to help you.'

'And to protect you no matter what,' Kenver promised, his face set hard and grim.

Oliver had finished his business with the mayor of Penzance sooner than he'd anticipated and he joined Kerensa on her third shopping port of call, the same haberdasher's that Clem had been in the week before. They were strolling arm in arm now up Market Jew Street, talking about their expected baby as excitedly as if it was their first.

'I thought Beatrice would have said something by now, she's usually the first to know,' Oliver laughed, moving aside to allow two elderly ladies in wide-hooped gowns an easy passage. He gave them his striking smile and bowed graciously, and they went on their way greatly flattered and tittering behind their fans.

'They'll make me jealous,' Kerensa laughed gaily. 'You can smile at me like that now.'

He gladly obeyed and she stood on tiptoe to receive a gentle kiss on her cheek. They bought a few things at the Market House then made for Chapel Street to dine at a friend's house. Oliver was the first to see the Blake/Trenchard entourage coming towards them and he stopped and stared.

'What is it?' Kerensa asked, following his amazed dark eyes.

'What on earth is Clem Trenchard doing alongside Peter Blake? He's certainly keeping surprising company these days. And that's Blake's coach coming after them.' Oliver pulled Kerensa into a doorway where they watched Blake and Clem dismount next to a group of exclusive houses and apartments. They were even more shocked when the coach stopped and the door was opened and a footman handed out Jessica. Then Clem signalled the footman away and helped Catherine Lanyon and a small woman neither Kerensa nor Oliver had seen before down onto the dusty ground. Oliver propelled Kerensa along quickly until they were standing in front of the unexpected gathering. Clem had given Catherine his arm, and Jessica was holding the small woman who was shrinking back, when Clem saw his arch-enemy and the woman he had always loved.

No one spoke, all faces were stunned. All but Oliver's showed signs of being uncomfortable. He spoke first, bowing his head to Catherine.

'Good morning to you, Miss Catherine. This is a most unexpected meeting.'

She could only squeak, with a small curtsey, 'Sir Oliver.' And seeing Kerensa's eyes on Clem, she clung to him possessively.

'Is something wrong?' Kerensa asked. No one replied. 'Jessica? Clem?'

There was still no answer and Oliver demanded in icy tones, 'Her ladyship has asked you a question. I hope one of you will have the decency and respect to answer!'

A serene voice from within the coach broke through the tension. 'We have come here for Kerris's sake, Sir Oliver,' Rosina answered, peeping out of the coach door. 'Kerris is the woman with Jessica. She was the maid of the unfortunate Miss Dinah Tredinnick and up until yesterday, when my husband confronted her on Trecath-en Farm, she had lost her memory of the terrible night she was forced to run away from here. She's here now to collect her belongings and, hopefully, painful though it may be, to see if she has any recollection of who might have been responsible for her mistress's death.'

Oliver went up to the coach and was surprised to see Kenver ensconced in it, a blanket covering his useless legs. 'I can see this is serious business,' he said, amazement clearly written on his face.

'And it is none of yours,' Clem said coldly at Oliver's back.

Oliver swung round and looked as if he was going to swipe Clem across the face. Kerensa hastily moved between them. 'Please, Oliver, I don't want any trouble. It's not our concern. Let's go.'

He pulled her gently out of the way. 'It is everybody's business to find out who has been perpetrating these vicious murders. The family of the last murdered girl was known to me.' He turned on the man he despised. 'Well, Blake? Have you nothing to say? I'm aware that this was your mistress's house.'

Rosina gasped from within the coach and Catherine made a noise that indicated her outrage at what the baronet had said. Jessica glared at him and Clem's face went dark with anger. 'There was no need for that!' he snarled.

'Why don't you just go to hell, Pengarron,' Blake uttered, 'where you belong!'

Kerensa's face paled and she tugged on Oliver's arm but he was not prepared to go yet. He stared at Kerris. She shrank back behind Jessica and began to whimper.

'Please, Sir Oliver,' Jessica begged, 'I know you have the right to speak but you're making things worse for Kerris. I'll come over to the Manor later and explain everything to you and her ladyship if you like.'

'That won't be necessary, Jessica,' Oliver said icily. 'Her ladyship asked you all if anything was the matter. We both would have offered any assistance to you but your father and others see fit to throw only contempt upon us.' Without another word, he took Kerensa's arm.

–

The house Olivia went to was in a quiet area of Penzance known as Back Lane where the houses backed onto fields. There were tidily kept flower beds in front of it and iron latticework supporting climbing plants reached up the walls.

She knocked quietly but there was no response. She tried the front door and finding it unlocked stepped into a dark hallway. Venturing further into the house, she found all the downstairs rooms had their curtains drawn. She peeped out of every window in each room, looking for signs of the active figure of Timothy Lanyon. In the parlour she stopped in front of a mirror and through the gloom patted her red hair back in place after the ride. She had left her pony in a hostelry, hoping no one would recognise it.

A few minutes ticked by and her excitement grew at secretly meeting a man she was more than attracted to. Every nerve in her body was on end. A clock on the mantelpiece struck eleven o'clock, the appointed hour for the meeting. When the last chime died away, she jumped at the sound of the outside door being opened and closed quietly. Light footsteps moved through the hall, went up the stairs and entered a room overhead.

Olivia waited a short time longer, then assuming Timothy had gone to an upstairs room to watch for her own approach, she went back to the hallway and called his name.

'Timothy? I'm down here.'

There was no answer. There were no more sounds. Eventually, believing that perhaps she had imagined an entrance in her eager anticipation, she tentatively climbed the stairs, pausing on each step, listening.

Up on the landing she saw there were four doors, two leading into rooms at the front of the house, two at the back. All were open wide. Olivia thought it would do no harm to peek into each room. If there was still no sign of Timothy, she would leave. She wasn't going to hang about waiting for any man, not even the good-looking parson.

She looked in the two back rooms first. They were both spotlessly clean and, apart from a few basic items of furniture, empty and cheerless. She could detect a slight whiff of perfume and wondered if other ladies had come here to meet a secret lover – but surely not Timothy. The first front bedroom she entered was much the same as the other two. She went to the windows. People were about in the locality but no one could be seen approaching the house. That was it then, she decided, a quick glance in the last bedroom and she would go. And Timothy Lanyon could go to purgatory for all she cared!

The furnishings in the last room were in complete contrast to the others. They were packed in close together and lavish drapes hung from the window and round a huge four-poster bed. Fresh flowers were arranged in crystal vases. A full china tea service set for two people sat on a lace cloth on a walnut table at the side of the room. A sparkling silver kettle hanging from a shiny hook was simmering over a tiny fire.

There was a ghostly atmosphere about this room but despite horrid little prickles of fear tormenting her spine, she stepped further inside. Surely all this could have nothing to do with Timothy. He was a man of the cloth. That didn't necessarily mean complete obedience to his calling but if he had designs on her person it would be nothing like this. It was as if a scene for a grand seduction had been set... and left deserted.

Then she smelled a strong wave of perfume, sickly, sweet, over-powering. And before she could turn round in terror, she knew she had walked into a trap.

Chapter 21

'Good morning, Olivia. It was good of you to accept my invitation.'

'Captain Solomon!'

'Won't you sit down and make yourself comfortable, my dear?'

Hezekiah was behind the door, reclining in a plush upholstered chair. His clothes today were discreetly elegant, his pure white wig not overdone in style. Olivia knew she was in danger, she knew what it was that he wanted from her. Her mind raced and she quickly deduced there was only one way out of this situation. She would have to play along with the hateful dandy until she could find a means of escape. She forced a beaming smile to her lips.

Hezekiah knew she feared him and raised a rounded eyebrow, the only expression that revealed his surprise at her not showing terror and pleading with him to let her go, and Olivia knew she had bought a little time.

She put her purse down on the table beside the tea things. 'I knew it was you,' she said, summoning up all her courage and employing what she hoped passed for a sultry voice.

'Oh? Not the handsome Reverend Timothy Lanyon?'

'I hardly think the parson's style is to write a billet-doux to procure a secret meeting with a lady. From what I know of Timothy Lanyon, he is rather gauche and bashful.' She hated to lie like this about Timothy who was the direct opposite of manhood to Hezekiah Solomon. 'And I saw little inflections in the letter's handwriting that I knew could only be yours.'

'But I thought you cared for him, Olivia,' Hezekiah said, utterly relaxed and in control, his words flowing easily from his cruel lips.

She narrowed her eyes then dropped them, raising them the next instant with pouting lips. 'Not when there are other gentlemen around taking a deeper interest in me.'

'Gentleman such as I?'

She hoped he did not see her gulp. 'Such as a gentleman who is a seasoned lover, has his own means and lavishes a lady with exquisite jewellery.'

'You wear my gifts?' he challenged her.

'Quite often,' she lied. 'In public, and in private when I think only of you.'

Hezekiah's serpent eyes swept intimately over her slender body. 'I thought you had no care for me.'

'A lady does not like to give in to the chase too quickly, Hezekiah,' she got out, trying to sound flirtatious, though the words grazed her throat. 'I have not seen you of late. You have not been to the Manor to see the interest I have in you.'

'It delights me to hear you say so, my dear.' Hezekiah rose and glided towards her and she knew it was to claim a kiss as proof of her assertions.

She closed her eyes tightly; she would not be able to go through with it if she looked at him up close. He put his effeminate soft white hands on her shoulders. His lips were silky smooth, not clammy and cold as she feared, and he moved them so delicately, so lingeringly, so persuasively over hers she couldn't help but respond to him a little. If it helped to fool him, it also increased her terror that he had breached a small, sacred part of her.

'Relieve yourself of your hat and cloak, my dear, and we will take tea together,' he said cordially.

Olivia faced the window, noting the bottom half was very slightly raised, as she slowly removed her hat and cloak. If she couldn't rush past her captor and down the stairs and out of the house, perhaps she could thrust open the window and somehow climb down the trellis outside. She would rather throw herself to her death than let this vile man do what he intended to her.

When she returned her attention to Hezekiah he was coming back from the door which he had closed. He was putting the key in his waistcoat pocket.

He showed her to a chair at the table. She sat trying not to shake, forcing a smile which she feared was rigid. He placed a small silver teapot on the table.

'Would you care to pour, Olivia, my dear heart?' he said with a graciousness she found sickening.

'Of course,' she replied, but couldn't stop her hands from trembling.

'You are nervous,' he remarked, sitting opposite her, his chair nearest the door.

'Well, it is my... I haven't done...'

'Of course, I understand. But have no worries. As you have said, I am a seasoned lover. You are not regretting your decision to come, are you?'

'No,' she said with a long, nervous laugh.

She was turning the consequences of this entrapment over in her mind. There was no doubt Hezekiah Solomon intended to ravish her, but how did he think he could get away with it? Was he really willing to risk her telling her father? Hezekiah couldn't rely on saying that she had agreed to meet, lie with him, and was crying out in shame. For all he knew, she might have left the supposed letter from Timothy Lanyon at home which proved she thought she had been embarking on an innocent romantic meeting with the young parson. Would Hezekiah have his way then kill her, perhaps make her look like a victim of the horrific murders perpetrated around the bay? A thought occurred to her so terrifying that it almost made her gag. She put her teacup to her face to hide her despair. Might Hezekiah Solomon be the murderer who was known to torture and cut up his victims?

'This is a splendid room,' she said, making the next sentence a bid for her life. 'We could meet here often.'

'You would like me to lavish more gifts and attention on you, Olivia?'

'Very much,' she replied, sipping tea without realising she'd done it.

Hezekiah put a thumbnail to his lips and pondered on the lovely young woman across the table. Was she telling him the truth? She was very nervous. But then any woman about to lose her virginity would be. She was proud and haughty and intelligent. Had she really thought she was meeting that foolish parson? Had she worked out the truth of the situation and was attempting to dupe him? As far as he could tell, she had spurned his many expensive gifts. She had been openly hostile to his face. But it didn't matter now. She was here and she would be his, on his terms.

She drank a second cup of tea and the pot was empty. There was nothing more she could do to spin out the time.

He smiled, and the ravages of time fell from his face; he had his prize at last, and his smile was angelic, recognisable from his younger days. It chilled Olivia to the marrow. He made a flowing turn with his hands. 'Shall we proceed, my dear?'

She couldn't speak. She would never consent. She allowed him to pull back her chair and aid her to her feet.

'Are you frightened?' he said softly in her ear.

'Yes,' she admitted.

'That is good. I am suspicious of a lady's previous virtue if she doesn't admit to being frightened.'

Olivia swiftly moved away from him and a dark look crossed his face. 'I need a little space, Hezekiah,' she explained with a forced smile.

She was watching and praying for the least chance of escape. If she stood close to him and tried to slip the door key out of his pocket he would be sure to notice. She didn't want to make him angry if she could avoid it. She didn't doubt that behind his effeminate appearance he was not only cruel but very strong.

She took off her fichu, revealing the creamy skin above her bosom which he looked at appreciatively. Olivia thought the window her only possible means of escape, but she couldn't climb out easily in her skirts. Perhaps she could turn this terrible situation to her advantage. Hope gave her bravado and she began to undress with a sort of eagerness, which she hoped would deflect any suspicions he had regarding her compliance.

He looked satisfied and removed his dresscoat, folding it with meticulous care over the back of the chair behind the door. She noted this; perhaps she could use his fastidiousness. Her dress was off and she stood vulnerable in her shift and stays – a lover wouldn't expect a girl to disrobe completely her first time. Now all she had to do was to watch him. She moved towards him and he looked pleased, unbuttoning his waistcoat and turning slightly to give it the same treatment as his dresscoat. This was her opportunity, possibly the only one she would have.

She grabbed the chair he sat on at the table and lunged at him, bringing it viciously down on his shoulders. He howled like a wild animal, spitting and swearing at the pain and her deception. Praying the sashes would move easily, she flung up the bottom window, bruising her hands as she did so. She screamed as she heard him throw off the chair and get to his feet.

She saw the flash of a sharp blade in his hand and threw herself over the wide windowsill. Her feet scrabbled for the trellis and she felt a sting across the back of one hand clinging to the sill and knew he'd cut her deeply. Snatching both hands away she threw herself on the mercy of the trellis. She couldn't gain a firm purchase and slipped, only saving herself from a plunge by clutching at ironwork on the way down. Her arms were wrenched in their sockets, her fingers scraped of skin, but she didn't feel a thing. She hit the flowerbeds a second later in a crumpled heap and heard Hezekiah shouting profanities and pounding down the stairs. She had to get away.

She'd got to her feet when he rounded the side of the house. His wig had fallen off and his thin yellowing hair lay plastered to his scalp. His withered face was contorted with hate and fury and madness. He held a long-bladed knife in one hand.

Olivia backed away from him, unsure whether her legs would carry her weight after the fall. They hurt badly. A desperate scream tore from her throat and she turned and ran back the way she had come earlier this morning, which now seemed like an eternity ago.

Hezekiah ran after her, assaulting her ears with the things he would do to her when he caught her. 'You bitch! You deserve this! You've been asking for it for years!'

A shout in front of her broke through her terror. Forcing her eyes to focus, she saw Kane.

He had seen her pony in the hostelry and had been scouring the town for sight of her or the Trenchards and Blakes. He had heard her screams through the bustle of the Greenmarket and had torn along Back Lane to be confronted by the horrifying sight of his sister running half naked down the lane pursued by Hezekiah Solomon.

Kane thrust Olivia aside and pulled out his sword.

Hezekiah surveyed him with a hideous smugness. 'Scum,' he hissed. 'Prostitute's spawn. Just like that bitch there, you deserve to die!'

'Put that knife down, Solomon,' Kane warned. 'You can't win against a sword and my youth and strength.'

'No, I probably can't,' the sea captain said conversationally. He threw back his hand and with tremendous force sent the knife towards Kane's belly. Kane cried out and dodged. The knife skimmed the side of his stomach. Olivia, huddled on the ground where she had collapsed, screamed and screamed again as Hezekiah advanced on her and kicked her viciously in the body. He hadn't killed Kane Pengarron but the assault on his sister would ensure she received his attention while he made his escape.

While Kane attended to Olivia, Hezekiah ran on until he came to more houses, then slowed down to a quick walk so as not to arouse curiosity. As it was, people would wonder why the dapper Captain Hezekiah Solomon was abroad improperly dressed. He smoothed his scrappy hair and straightened his shirt, making quickly for the house he lived in to pick up some of his personal belongings, some clothes, his money and jewellery. He had to get away before Kane Pengarron caught up with him and raised the alarm. Hezekiah was not unduly worried though. He'd known Sir Oliver Pengarron would not rest until he tracked down the murderer of his pathetic offspring and he had a berth on a ship bought and paid for, ready to make his escape to

France. Kane Pengarron might search all of Penzance, but the captain would be bribed to keep his silence.

Hezekiah grinned evilly as he rounded the house where he had brutally murdered Dinah Tredinnick. He could amuse himself with plenty of entertaining memories of the time he'd spent around Mount's Bay. The next moment he was brought up short in surprise at the gathering of familiar faces standing outside the Tredinnick woman's house.

Oliver Pengarron was escorting Kerensa away from the main body. 'Hezekiah!' he exclaimed when he saw him. 'What's happened to you? Have you been robbed?'

Kerensa's concern was lost under a shrill scream and anguished cries from Kerris. She stabbed an agitated finger at Hezekiah. 'That's him! That's the man who murdered my mistress! I remember now, I smelled his perfume, it's him!'

'Stop him, Father!' Kane called out frantically behind Hezekiah. He had gathered Olivia up and was half carrying her wrapped in his cloak, part of which was covered in blood from the cut on her hand. 'He tried to kill Olivia.'

'*What?*' Oliver could hardly believe his ears. He felt as though he was moving in slow motion as he pushed Kerensa behind him out of harm's way. This ridiculous-looking, ageing little fop, a gentleman he had always found an enigma but numbered among his friends, had tried to kill his daughter? Had murdered Dinah Tredinnick, and the silversmith's daughter, most likely making him the foul murderer of Mount's Bay for over twenty years?

Oliver reached for his sword, unaware of Kerris's hysteria, of others trying to comfort her, of Kerensa calling his name, pleading with him to be careful. Hezekiah stood before him, staring icily at him out of his snake's eyes. 'Why did I never guess it was you?' Oliver said incredulously.

'Because you're a fool, Pengarron. Interested only in your land, your estate and your family. I hate you. I've always hated you more than any other man on this infernal earth.'

Oliver paced forward and put the tip of his sword at Hezekiah's throat. 'Why? I thought we were friends.'

'Friends! Aah! You and your fine dark looks, your great height, having every woman admire and dance attendance on you whenever you enter a room. And you had the one thing I always wanted and could never have. Something I could not steal, something I could not seduce away from you.'

'And what was that?' Oliver asked icily, his heart pounding with shock and fury.

Hezekiah's eyes rolled until they rested on Kerensa. 'Her. Kerensa.'

Kerensa gasped and clutched her throat as if he was strangling her. Olivia moaned in Kane's arms. Clem released Catherine's arm and skirting round Hezekiah and Oliver went to Kerensa and put his hands firmly on her shoulders. Kerensa knew she should make Clem remove them but she was afraid she would faint. Hezekiah saw it and jeered.

'See. Look behind you, Pengarron. The handsome young farmer has his arms about your dear wife and still thinks he has a hold over her. He's a fool and you're a bigger one! Trenchard was never a real threat to you, or that bastard Peter Blake even though he tried to rape her. But I was! For many years I thought of ways to get her away from you and, like you, because she trusted my honour, she did not realise it. If I could not have the woman I desired so much, then I'd have the daughter. Your daughter, Pengarron. I was going to take her and make her suffer more than any of the useless scum I've killed in the past.'

'I should put this sword straight through your throat now!' Oliver snarled, his dark eyes blazing, his heart heavy with the pain and shame of being tricked for so long.

'Oliver, don't,' Kerensa gasped.

'You should have come to me, Kerensa,' Hezekiah said to her, taunting her. 'I would never have hurt you and I wouldn't have gone after your daughter.'

'Shut up!' Oliver warned. 'I don't want to hear one more word out of your filthy, disgusting mouth. I should have known it was you. I would have been able to put a stop to these killings, stopped the suffering.'

Peter Blake had handed Kerris back into the carriage to be comforted by Kenver and Rosina. He tried to get Jessica and

Catherine into it too but they held each other's hands, refusing to budge. He came up beside Clem and Kerensa and said coolly, 'Kill him, Pengarron. If you don't then I will, for what he did to Dinah Tredinnick.'

Hezekiah laughed horribly. 'He can't, Blake. He's a fool and a coward!'

'Don't, Father!' Kane shouted. 'Let him be brought to trial and hang for his crimes. He won't be able to dress like a gentleman and be so fussy in gaol. Let him go there and rot until he swings on the gallows.'

Oliver's hand wavered. He shifted his stance but kept his eyes on the evil little man and his sword taut at his throat.

'What do you say, Trenchard?' Hezekiah sniggered. 'We might as well have your opinion on what to do with me. As well as the comfort you're giving his wife, I'm sure Sir Oliver would value your opinion.'

'I say kill him,' Clem said without hesitation. 'The last girl he killed was a respectable Methodist.'

'Kill him!' Blake shouted, unsheathing his own sword. 'What are you waiting for, Pengarron? A confession to cleanse his soul? He has no soul!'

'You could be right about that, Blake,' Hezekiah said, with a high laugh. He suddenly spat in Oliver's face. Oliver blinked and grimaced. 'What are you going to do, Pengarron? I can't get away. I've got your sword at my throat, Blake's at my side and the prostitute's spawn is at my back. And I dare say your pouting daughter would like to plunge a weapon of some kind into my body. Who's it going to be, Pengarron? For I've no intention of giving myself over meekly to the law.'

'Why, you… you aren't human,' Oliver rasped.

'Maybe I'm not but I won't give you the satisfaction of seeing me die like some animal!' Hezekiah cried.

He made one sharp movement forward; Oliver's sword ran through his throat and out the back of his neck. He died with a horrible choking noise. Oliver let go of the sword and jumped back, and Hezekiah's body fell like a stone to the ground. Kerensa screamed. Oliver pushed Clem away from her and took her into his arms. Shaken through and through, he could say nothing, he could only stare at the body of the man he had thought of as his friend.

Jessica and Catherine were whimpering in fright and horror and allowed Blake to bundle them back into the coach where they clutched each other. Jessica whispered, 'He is dead, Kerris,' and the other woman cried with relief and shock in Kenver and Rosina's arms.

Kane carried Olivia to the coach and put her in beside Jessica, saying grimly, 'Look after her, Jessie.'

Catherine stared blankly at the coach's interior, the sight of Clem holding Kerensa filtering through and replacing the memory of the horror she had witnessed.

A crowd was gathering. Oliver took off his cloak to cover the hideous body and ordered a bystander to run and fetch the constables.

'Are you all right, Kerensa?' Clem asked her gently.

'Get away from us!' Oliver shouted ferociously. 'Or I'll put my sword through you too!'

Kerensa nodded to Clem then buried her face in Oliver's chest as he came back to comfort her possessively. Clem shot Oliver a look of hatred then stalked off to stand beside the coach.

Blake was next at the Pengarrons' side. 'Will Lady Pengarron be all right?' he asked in concern even though he was fearful of the baronet's temper. 'She seems very distressed. Shall I open Miss Tredinnick's house for her to rest in?'

'I don't want to go in there,' Kerensa cried in horror. 'Not after...'

'I'll get my son to take her ladyship home while I explain to the authorities what has happened here,' Oliver said grimly. 'Will you be good enough to take my daughter home to the Manor, Blake?'

'Of course, Sir Oliver. I shall leave without delay. My own wife must be equally distressed.'

'And Blake,' Oliver said, still feeling wrath at Clem Trenchard's insolence, 'make sure the Trenchard girl does not remain on my property after you leave.'

When Hezekiah Solomon's body had been removed from the street and Oliver had explained to the authorities how he had met his death, he moved off to Hezekiah's home address, just a few houses down across the street. Shadows were falling to herald the evening and it was cold and inhospitable inside Hezekiah's house. Oliver lit lanterns and lots of candles to dispel the chill that crept over him. Outside he could hear people shouting and celebrating and he knew they were revelling in the unmasking and death of the murderer who had made them live in such fear for so long.

In the sitting room he found Hezekiah's things all packed up. With icy finality he knew he had meant to rape and kill Olivia before fleeing the country. Oliver didn't really know why he was here. It was a gruesome place to be, a gruesome thing to do to root about in the dead man's things. But he had to try to find out something about the mysterious sea captain. There had been too many long years when he had kept his secrets to himself.

In a chest were his clothes. His toilet boxes were full of perfumes and cosmetics. There was nothing of interest until Oliver opened a box and came across a collection of diaries and two theological books, the ones Timothy had lent him and which were now badly slashed.

Oliver put the books carefully aside and sat down to read the diaries. He soon recoiled at their contents. Every murder, rape, and act of torture was clearly documented. It was only now that Oliver learned what had happened many years ago to a missing miner called Colly Pearce, who had been Rosina Blake's bullying, drunken brother. Pearce's throat had been cut and he had been thrown off the cliffs near Painted Bessie's kiddley. He was shocked and horrified to learn of the rape of Miss Ameline Beswetherick, Sir Martin's granddaughter, under his very roof, when she had stayed at Pengarron Manor. No wonder Ameline had married and moved out of the county and had refused to come back to attend her grandfather's and brother's funerals. And as well as insulting Kane by calling him 'prostitute's spawn', in reference to the woman who was thought to have been his real mother, Hezekiah had also butchered his father, the disgusting sailor from whom Kerensa had bought Kane as an infant. Oliver had had no idea that the sailor had turned up in Marazion again, but the delicate flowing handwriting recorded that Hezekiah had murdered the sailor as a service to Kerensa. Oliver had seen that body and he shuddered violently at the memory, glad that Kerensa knew nothing about it.

He read about the way Hezekiah had tried to woo Dinah Tredinnick, with the intention of eventually killing her. Dinah had spurned his every advance, and so he had blackmailed her by saying he would inform Peter Blake that she had been unfaithful to him if she did not admit him to her house. She had tragically met her gruesome death anyway.

It cut Oliver to the bone to read the accounts of the times Hezekiah had plotted Kerensa's seduction, his most hopeful attempt when Oliver was out of the country. But Kerensa's pregnancy with Kelynen had put paid to that. Hezekiah had had a horror of women in that condition and had always refused to come to the Manor when Kerensa had been with child. Worst of all was to read of the plot to trap, rape and kill Olivia and to know that he had nearly succeeded just a few hours ago. Hezekiah wrote with gusto how he had duped the Reverend Timothy Lanyon into lending him two religious books and writing a note so he could forge his handwriting. How Olivia, 'the infinitely silly creature', would no doubt agree to a secret liaison with the 'ridiculous young puppy who believed in a heaven'. What Hezekiah believed was 'heaven', Oliver couldn't bear to read.

He lit a fire in the grate and burned the diaries along with the remains of Timothy's books. It would be better that no one ever saw them; he alone would carry the burden of their contents. Now he must go home. His family needed him. Kerensa was with child and must be in shock, and Olivia would need him. When the opportunity was right, he would ask Kane how he felt about the insult Hezekiah Solomon had hurled at him. He shook his dark head. How was it he had never known Hezekiah was the Mount's Bay murderer? How many lives and how much suffering could he have prevented over the years? But Hezekiah had been a secretive man and Oliver had allowed him what he'd thought was the dignity to keep his life private. It was a great pity he hadn't been more curious and perceptive.

Oliver glared at the fire with its curling paper ashes. He wanted to raze this revolting perfumed house to the ground! And it wasn't the only reason hate and fury were bubbling over inside him. While Hezekiah Solomon had kept his secret life to himself, there were other individuals who chose not to keep their feelings to themselves, even when they had a fiancée present. He hoped Catherine Lanyon would see sense and finish her association with Clem Trenchard.

Chapter 22

For all those involved in Captain Hezekiah Solomon's death, the next day was spent in trying to come to terms with what had happened.

At Trevenner, the Blakes were making an effort to put the incident, and the whole Dinah Tredinnick affair, behind them. Rosina resolved never to mention it again and Blake that he would never stop making it up to her. He did not go about his business today but planned to take Rosina for a ride over the moors on Lancavel Downs, to let their beauty and starkness purge their souls of any last morbid feelings.

Catherine was in a state of despondency. She had allowed Clem to escort her to the Parsonage door when they'd got back to Perranbarvah. She had been in a restrained mood then, her face long, her deportment stiff. Clem had left her in Nancy Wills's care, saying they had endured a harrowing experience and her mistress would need to talk to the Reverend at length for comfort. Clem did not know his bride-to-be was harbouring hurt feelings against him for the way he had gone to comfort Kerensa in Penzance and taken the liberty of putting his hands on her, even in Sir Oliver's presence. Catherine's fears that he still loved the other lady so deeply he would run to her at the drop of a glove had been confirmed in a way that had humiliated her.

She had refused to speak much that night when Timothy had come home. After a restless night, in which she had hardly slept, she had finally told him all the terrible details of the evil sea captain's death. Timothy was horrified. He stayed with Catherine to comfort and pray with her, but said that he would have to leave her soon to go to the Manor. He was about to leave when Jack arrived with a summons for him to attend at the Manor at once.

Clem had been angered at Sir Oliver's fury with him, outraged that he had been spoken to like a mongrel dog. After he told Philip and David and Ricketty Jim what had happened at Penzance, he had gone off all night with his dogs, and today he was keeping out of everyone's way.

Jessica was horrified at the suffering Olivia had been subjected to and was able to give her friend her first thoughts, now that Kerris could be left totally in Kenver's care. She wanted to go over to the Manor and offer Olivia comfort, but yesterday, as they had pulled up at the doors, Peter Blake had made it clear she was not welcome there and Olivia had been in no fit state to notice or reason why. Now, like her father, Jessica mooched about the farm keeping herself to herself and hoping that Kane would ride over to see her.

Kerris, though somewhat distressed at regaining her full memory, was utterly relieved her mistress's murderer had been apprehended and was now dead. She had nothing to fear from the past and a happy, settled future to look forward to. She hadn't been able to bear going into Dinah Tredinnick's house and after the terrible event on the street outside, it hadn't been necessary. Peter Blake had said he would arrange for her few personal possessions to be sent over to her on the farm. She spent all her time with Kenver who was having a difficult time coming to terms with yesterday's events himself. He had found his first excursion away from the farm exciting and enlightening but had been frustrated to be confined to the carriage while the womenfolk witnessed the distressing scene outside. And now after spending his entire life in other people's care, he had a new future to look forward to and the responsibility of taking a wife. He was both fearful and exhilarated at the prospect.

Olivia, who was the most distraught, had refused to come out of her room since she'd got home. She just wanted to be in her own chamber with her own familiar things around her. She allowed Kerensa, who had refused to lie abed, reassuring Oliver that the shock had not harmed her or their unborn child, to sit with her. Olivia could hardly bear to speak of what had happened to her but occasionally managed to answer a question so her mother could fit together all the details of why she had been in Penzance and what she was doing in the house Hezekiah Solomon had rented for his murderous purposes.

'What I don't understand, Mama,' Olivia said miserably, shuddering in horror and clutching Kerensa's hands for comfort, 'is why he said I'd been asking for it for years. Was it because I'd been so cool towards him and he was seeking revenge or was it because somehow he thought I was giving him encouragement?'

'I think it was because he'd always wanted me,' Kerensa replied, retying the bandage on Olivia's cut hand so her daughter would not see her recoil at the thought. 'If only we'd realised how he felt, we would have stopped receiving him years ago.'

'It wouldn't have stopped him. He would have come after you or me somehow. He was obsessed with us.' Olivia went quiet, picturing how she'd had to undress. 'I… I feel so ashamed. I had to pretend to go along with him to give me time to think of a way to escape…'

Kerensa gently smoothed Olivia's hair away from her brow. The gleaming red length was tangled because her daughter had not bothered to brush it since yesterday, although she had torn off all her clothing and ordered it to be burnt. Kerensa fetched a brush and began removing the tangles, knowing that if Olivia looked better she would feel better too.

'It wasn't your fault, not any of it, Olivia,' she said calmly. 'You must never feel that way. The man was insane. I thank the Lord he's dead and can harm no one else. If he hadn't killed himself on your father's sword, I'd be too afraid to sleep at night.' She heard a horse trotting up the carriageway and glanced out of the window. 'Well, well, the man you thought you were going to meet has just turned up.'

'Do you think Papa will be angry with me for going to meet the Reverend Lanyon alone?' Olivia asked, suddenly anxious that her hair should be restored to its former glory. If she saw Timothy today she didn't want to look a mess. She jerked her chair round to face her dressing table mirrors, but she could not bring herself to look out on the man who'd just arrived. Timothy must know all about yesterday; what did he think of her going off to see a man alone, even though she'd thought it was him? If he despised her, she would want to die.

'Well, your father is not pleased,' Kerensa answered her, glad she was perking up. 'You cannot expect him to be, Olivia. He knows why you went to Penzance but will not tell me how he knows.'

'And you, Mama?'

Kerensa smiled softly at her daughter's reflection in the mirror. 'I've seen the way you look at one another. I understand your reasons.'

'Will Timothy, I wonder,' Olivia moaned wretchedly.

'We'll just have to wait and see. Your father will talk to him first.'

Timothy was shown into Sir Oliver's study. He found the baronet sitting at his desk, fingers clasped, staring at the wall in front of him. It took Oliver a few moments to register Timothy's presence there after Polly had announced him. He blinked and pointed to a chair.

'I would have come at once, my lord,' Timothy said in reverential tones. He was feeling very nervous. Catherine had told him that in the coach Olivia had kept muttering 'I thought it was Timothy', over and over again. Apparently Olivia had thought she was going to meet him. What in heaven's name would Sir Oliver think was going on between him and his daughter?

Oliver did not speak, so to avoid an uncomfortable silence, Timothy went on quickly, 'You see, Sir Oliver, it was only a short while ago that I obtained the full story from my sister. Yesterday she was too distressed to tell me everything that had happened. All I could get out of her then was that someone had been killed on Penzance streets. I thought the expedition with… um, Clem Trenchard and Jessica to Penzance was to purchase some items for her new home. I had no idea they had gone in the Blakes' coach and with the woman Kerris. I regret my neglect of duty in that respect. I should have made enquiries about Kerris, Amy Venton, instead of leaving it to Catherine and… and Clem Trenchard. But how are you, Sir Oliver? And her ladyship, and Master Kane and, of course, Miss Olivia? I'd like to speak to her if I may.'

'I am utterly and completely stunned, Timothy,' Oliver said, his tone so constrained that Timothy was fearful as to what Olivia's full ordeal had been. 'I never guessed for one moment the murderer was Hezekiah Solomon. I thought of him as a friend, albeit a fop. But all the time he hated me. I should have known. I could have saved so many lives, so much suffering. Olivia wouldn't have gone through her ordeal. I cannot bear to think what would have happened to her if Kane hadn't turned up in Penzance.'

'Nor I,' Timothy said at once.

'Kane was insulted by that… that vile little creature,' Oliver said angrily. 'And my dear wife, her ladyship, hearing and seeing it all, and – please keep this to yourself – she is with child.'

'The poor dear lady. Is she quite well?'

'Yes, thank God. She is confident she and the child have suffered no harm. Solomon, he wanted to… be with her ever since he saw her, on the day we were married. I read it in his repulsive diaries.'

Timothy let his breath out through pursed lips. 'I can see I shall need to give spiritual comfort to you all. A brush with that much evil will lie heavily on the soul.' He was fearful of the baronet's reaction to what he was going to say next, but plunged on. 'But what of Miss Olivia? It is she I am most concerned about. May I see her?'

'I think not,' Oliver said slowly, eyeing the young parson sternly. 'She does not want to see anyone at the moment. She refuses to see Kane because he was involved in yesterday's ordeal and will not see Luke and Cordelia because they were not. I thank God that at least some of my family did not suffer tarnishment at that man's hands. Apparently Olivia was at Penzance yesterday in the belief she was seeing you, Timothy Lanyon. In one of Solomon's diaries I found an account of how he obtained samples of your handwriting and wrote her a letter, asking her to meet you at a certain house, one he had in fact rented to do his murderous deeds in. That is how she came to be in his company.'

'My sister told me she thought Miss Olivia had believed it was me she was meeting,' Timothy said contritely. Then suddenly he didn't care what the baronet had construed about him and Olivia. He blurted out, under Oliver's heavy eyes, 'I must see her, Sir Oliver! Please, may I see her, just for a little while? I promise I won't distress her.'

Oliver kept his eyes on Timothy's stricken face while he absent-mindedly toyed with a paperknife. At last he replied, 'Very well, I suppose a few moments won't hurt.'

–

There was a little rap on the bedchamber door and Olivia, who was pacing the room, jumped and clutched at the bedpost. Oliver opened the door a crack and said softly, 'I have the Reverend Lanyon with me. Is it all right if he comes in for a little while?'

Olivia gave a small cry. Kerensa looked alarmed but Olivia nodded her head emphatically. She had to know what Timothy thought of her.

The two men entered tentatively, Oliver first. He was stunned by his daughter's reaction to the young parson. She stared at him through wide grey-green eyes, her hands gripping the bedpost as though it supported her very life.

'I thought it was you, Timothy!' she gasped. 'I thought you had sent me the letter.'

'Did you want it to be, Olivia?' he asked earnestly, pushing past Oliver and going right up to her with outstretched arms.

'Oh yes, yes!'

The next instant they were in each other's arms, Olivia clinging to him, Timothy hugging her close, both oblivious of her parents.

'It would be better if we left them alone,' Kerensa said, taking Oliver's arm.

'I'll be damned if I…'

But Kerensa was pushing him towards the door. 'We will keep the door open to satisfy your sense of propriety, but leave them we will.'

Oliver insisted on having the last word. 'Take the Reverend Lanyon up to your studio, Olivia. I will not have you staying with him in your bedchamber!'

Kerensa pulled him from the room.

'Have you gone mad?' Oliver asked her, the instant they were on the other side of the door. 'I know you are deeply distressed by yesterday's events but it seems you have lost your reasoning.'

'I am completely in my right mind,' Kerensa replied firmly, dragging him along the corridor and making for the stairs.

'To leave our daughter in the arms of the parson. I hardly call that spiritual comfort!' he protested.

'That is another matter, Oliver. They are embracing because they are in love.'

'Don't be silly, Kerensa. They hardly know each other. Did you know this had been going on?'

Kerensa got them down the stairs and pulled Oliver into her sitting room. 'It's just like you to say that I am too interested in others to realise when I'm with child, Oliver, when you don't even notice when our grown-up children are in love. And nothing's been going on, as you put it. They haven't long realised themselves how much they mean to each other. Now stop playing the outraged father and ring for some tea, it'll do us good.'

'I don't want any tea,' he said grumpily, pacing up and down the room under Kerensa's amused eyes.

'Is Kane in love?' he demanded to know.

'I believe he is, yes,' she said lightly. 'You said once that you thought he was seeing a woman.'

'Is Luke?'

'No, I don't think Luke is, but of course one never knows.'

Oliver snorted. 'What about Cordelia?'

'Yes, I rather think Cordelia is in love too.'

'Who are they in love with?'

'Perhaps it would be better if I keep that to myself for the time being.'

'I don't believe anyone except possibly Olivia is in love. Time will tell I'm right, you'll see.' He rang for Polly to fetch a tray of tea and something to tempt her mistress to eat, then sat down. 'So, who are they in love with?' he asked again.

'Well, I know for certain that Olivia and Timothy are in love. It's obvious from the way they've been looking at each other over the last few weeks. I believe Timothy has made no approaches because he thinks we would not approve of him as Olivia's suitor. You don't mind, do you, Oliver? We haven't really discussed who we would want our children to marry. Of course, with my background, I'd probably see things differently to you.'

Oliver had relaxed a little and had been thinking. 'Kerensa, my dear, when I think of who was interested in our daughter and what he very nearly did to her, if she is in love and happy with the Reverend Timothy, then I will be happy too.'

'I was hoping you would say that. It looks like we'll be having a double celebration in the family, a new baby to look forward to and a wedding – at least one wedding.'

'We'll make the parish of Perranbarvah dance for a week with the celebrations. Timothy will be kept busy preparing to marry Olivia, and incidentally if he doesn't come down those stairs and ask for her hand I'll break his neck for the liberty he's taken. He'll also have to perform the marriage of his stupid sister to that idiot farmer!'

Kerensa went red. She regretted not pushing Clem's hands off her the day before and felt Oliver had a right to be angry. 'I'm sorry about what Clem did yesterday.'

'How dare that swine touch you! If he ever does it again I'll horsewhip him.'

'I know you're angry, Oliver, and I understand that, specially with all the dreadful events of yesterday, but I wish you wouldn't speak like that.'

He took her hands in his. 'I'm sorry, my love. I just can't bear that man coming near you.'

'I know, but Clem was only concerned for me. Even Hezekiah said you have no need to be jealous of Clem.'

Oliver kissed her tenderly. 'I know, I don't think I'll ever forget a word of what he said. But I can't help feeling sorry for Catherine Lanyon. I know I shouldn't have called her stupid, it was unkind of me, but she's never going to be happy married to Clem Trenchard.'

'But he fell in love with Alice eventually, don't forget. Clem has always had a deep love for the women in his life. He asked Catherine to marry him because of his concern over Jessica whom he adores. I don't think he'll be unkind to her.'

'I suppose I should understand that he'll always love you. Who could not? But if she doesn't see sense and refute him after he touched you in front of everyone yesterday, I think he might well find his own reasons to wriggle out of the marriage. It will be the best thing to happen to her. I wish I could advise her but it's not my place.'

'It's not anyone's place to interfere, except perhaps Timothy's.' A gleam came into Oliver's dark eyes and Kerensa pulled his face round sharply to look at her. 'Oh, Oliver, you wouldn't?'

'I'd like to but I won't. Timothy will have enough on his hands becoming our son-in-law. I suppose he'll need to have Miss Catherine out of the way at the Parsonage when he takes his bride there. I'll have to spend some money on that Parsonage, make it fit for Olivia to live in.'

Polly appeared with the tea and when she had gone they spent a happier time making plans for the future. A slow shuffling and grunting was heard making for the room. The couple smiled knowingly at each other and Beatrice came in, clutching a wide pewter mug under her huge drooping bosom.

'Smelt un bein' made,' she rasped, nodding at the teapot. 'Do 'ee mind if I join 'ee in a sup?'

'Of course we don't, Bea,' Oliver said, leading the old crone on her shaky legs to a chair by the fire.

Kerensa took the mug and filled it to the brim with strong black tea and plenty of milk. 'Here you are, Beatrice, just as you like it,' making sure Beatrice had a firm grip of her mug before she let it go.

'Don't go away, young missus, I want to 'ave a good look at 'ee.'

Kerensa complied by standing in front of the old woman like a little girl awaiting inspection before being allowed in the presence of genteel parents. 'You looked me over yesterday, Beatrice, several times. I'm a bit shaken but apart from that perfectly all right.'

'Mebbe, mebbe not, there's somethin' I'm goin' to tell 'ee, though 'ow come thee never knaws yerself—' Beatrice stopped as Oliver laughed loudly. 'What's the matter with 'ee then? Laughin' at an ol' woman! What've I said to start un off screechin' like a banshee? What're 'ee both gawpin' at me fer!'

'She knows, Beatrice. I told her myself this time.'

'Could've told me then! Some strange little baby this one's goin' to be.'

'Oh, don't say that, Beatrice. I've got enough trouble with the children I have now,' Kerensa said, laughing happily, the ordeal of the day before temporarily forgotten.

—

Olivia led Timothy up to her studio, her arm tucked comfortingly inside his. She had cried a lot since the harrowing incident of the day before and the brighter light made her blink rapidly and she rubbed at her eyes.

'You aren't going to cry, are you, Olivia?' he said, full of concern.

'No. Not now you're here, Timothy.'

'But if you want to cry, I have two good shoulders you can do it on.'

'I'd like it if you held me again,' she said, able to smile at last.

They embraced again, she revelling in his warm strength, he in being her comforter.

'I feel really honoured that you would have agreed to meet me secretly, Olivia,' he said, caressing the red hair falling over her slender shoulders.

'I've been so afraid that you would feel badly about me when you found out. I know now you wouldn't have suggested anything of the kind, but I was just so full of hope…'

'I could never feel badly about you, Olivia,' he said, his words caressing her hair. 'And I've been full of hope that you might care for me. You do, don't you?'

She took her arms away from his neck and led him across the room to her painting easel. 'Perhaps this can speak for the way I feel about you.'

On the easel was a picture of the head and shoulders, in profile, of the two of them, facing each other. It was almost finished and portrayed their features with love and tenderness, gazing into each other's eyes.

'Oh, Olivia!' he breathed. 'If you want, my beloved, we could always be like that.'

'I would like that, Timothy. With all my heart,' she answered, her face full of joy.

Timothy clutched her hands and there was a pained look on his face, making his grey eyes wide and bright. 'But what about Sir Oliver? He wouldn't allow you to marry a humble parson. I've got very little money, and not much expectation of climbing high in the Church.'

Olivia stroked his cheek and ran her fingertip along his chin to the small cleft that was so much a part of his charm. She wasn't concerned at all. 'I think that when Papa has had time to think about it he will be only too glad to see me happily married to someone I love, especially after what so very nearly happened to me. Besides, Mama knows how we feel about each other. Remember the way she pulled him out of my bedchamber. If Papa has any objections she'll soon talk him round. She always gets her own way, Papa is really quite soft in her hands.'

Timothy grinned blissfully. 'And I suppose that's how you want me to be, Miss Olivia Pengarron. Soft in your hands.'

She twisted her face to tease him as he took her back in his arms. 'Some of the time.'

'Olivia, you will marry me, won't you? If your father agrees.'

'He will, and yes, Timothy,' she said, raising her face to be kissed, 'I will.'

–

Kane was about to ride over to Trecath-en Farm but Oliver hailed him from across the stable yard. 'I would like a word with you before you go, son,' he said.

Kane dismounted and gave the reins back to Jack. 'Sounds serious,' he said curiously.

'I'm about to check on the animal hut. Walk with me there.'

In the hut a small assortment of birds and animals were recovering from injury or illness. Some were well again but too tame to be freed back into the wild and had become pets of the family for their own safety. Kane picked up a dark brown rabbit which had only three paws, having lost one in a gin-trap. He looked at the rabbit critically as it scrambled up his front and snuggled into him like a human baby, as Meg's rabbit had done only two days before.

'Russet is getting fat because she can't run about. We'll have to cut down on her food ration,' he said.

Oliver stroked the rabbit's soft back and nodded in agreement. Then he turned to his favourite creature in the hut. In a wide cage was a stoat he'd named Samson. He had found it in the middle of a field almost dead. Rummaging around, he had discovered its concealed nest at the edge of the field and saw it was the only survivor of a litter of nine. Oliver had not expected the tiny stoat to live but many hours of hand-feeding had paid off and Samson had grown, though he was still undersized. He had an endearingly ugly, bluntly pointed face, and seemed reluctant to be set free.

Wary of getting a nip from Samson's sharp teeth, Oliver took him out of the cage, holding him firmly and tickling him under his small rounded ears. 'Samson's as long and thin as Russet is fat and round,' he remarked.

'Yes,' Kane smiled. 'But keep him away from us or she'll end up as rabbit dinner.'

Stroking Samson's brown back down to the black-tipped furry tail, Oliver fed the stoat with fruit and berries. He took his time. He was reluctant to speak about Captain Hezekiah Solomon.

Hezekiah's body had been buried within hours of his death, deep in a spot where two cart tracks met and crossed on the outskirts of Penzance. Nothing marked the place, though Oliver doubted if even the body-snatchers who sold specimens to those wishing to further the cause of medical science would want to dig up the murderous dandy's remains. The evil that had marked his life seemed to hover above his final resting place. Only four people had attended the burial: two gravediggers, an official and Oliver, who'd steeled himself for the event. No one had said a single word of reverence or prayer. It would have been a waste of time. Hezekiah Solomon had met his destiny in the hereafter at the point of his suicide and nothing said or done could alter that. And Oliver had no desire to ask the Almighty for mercy on the soul of the man who had so nearly violated and murdered his daughter.

A rotting body on a gibbet close by creaked in the wind and spread its smell of corruption. The hanged tinner, who'd been out of work because of lung disease, had been executed for stealing a sheep to feed his starving family. His sentence had been harsh and merciless, while Hezekiah Solomon had died by his own flamboyant action and had escaped the justice of this world.

'Rot in Hell, Hezekiah,' Oliver had said with feeling before mounting Gereint. He quickly left the spot that would soon be rumoured to be haunted by a terrifying spectre with murderous snake's eyes and long, shiny white hair. It would be a place where it was said no animal would linger, no bird would sing and no flower would grow.

Oliver brought his troubled mind back to the present. 'I want to speak to you about something Hezekiah Solomon said yesterday, Kane,' he said, delivering his words in a slow, low voice.

'About me being prostitute's spawn?' Kane replied, looking for a piece of carrot for the rabbit.

'It's been on your mind too, then.'

'Nothing Hezekiah Solomon or anyone else says to me about my parentage can hurt me, Father. You see, since I've been home I've made some enquiries into what my blood-mother and father were like. I was quite successful and have been waiting for the right time to tell you and Mama.'

Oliver looked a little shaken. He put the stoat back in its cage so he could give his son his full attention. 'Go on.'

Kane gave him a full account of his visits to Frances Nansmere and Meg at the swamp.

Oliver stayed silent for a long time, taking it all in. 'I knew you'd called at the brothel… and I assumed it was for the usual reason. I suppose I should have known that one day you'd ask for yourself, wanting to know more than the little I had found out and told you. It must make you feel better to know that it was Peggy Wearne and this rover who were your natural parents and not that whore and the dreadful sailor your mother had to contend with.'

'It does,' Kane said. 'But I shall always wonder who the rover is – was.' Colour spread up his neck and face as he admitted, 'I thought it could have been Ricketty Jim. He's got brown eyes and… and I asked him.'

A light smile brushed Oliver's face. 'I could have told you it wasn't Ricketty Jim. He's not capable of fathering a child.'

'So he gave me to understand. Well, I suppose there are some things in life we are never meant to know and I must be content with that. Now I'm resolved to get on with my life. I have made up my mind to accept the property at Gulval. I know Mama will be glad I won't be going far away.'

'Yes, she will, and so am I. It's good to see our son grown up and making the right decisions.'

Kane smiled enigmatically. 'Well, there are one or two things that have helped me decide to stay within the Mount's Bay area.'

–

Kane found all the Trenchards, Kerris and Ricketty Jim sitting round the hearth in Trecath-en farmhouse's kitchen. They were looking glum, except for Kenver and Kerris, who shared bright snatches of conversation as they planned their new life together.

Jessica brightened up at seeing him and moved up on the bench she was sitting on so he could sit down beside her. 'How's Olivia?' she asked.

'Very distraught. She wouldn't let anyone but my mother see her for a long time but the Reverend Lanyon was with her when I left the Manor.'

'How's your mother?' Clem asked.

'She doesn't appear to be taking it too badly.'

'That's good,' Clem said, then shut up as though he was in a huff about something.

'We're not in a working mood today,' David said, to explain why they were all sitting around.

'I understand that,' Kane replied, looking at Clem and wondering why he seemed to be ignoring him. 'I'm in no mood to work either.' He glanced at the courting couple. 'The Reverend Timothy is going to be kept busy at the altar, I see.'

Clem grunted and Kane wondered if the tall blond farmer was losing heart for his own matrimonial plans.

'We're hoping to have the wedding here and that you'll come, Kane,' Kenver said, holding Kerris's hand and gazing at her fondly.

'I'll be honoured to,' Kane replied. He looked at Jessica. 'Would you like to go for a walk, Jessie?'

'Yes, I—'

'She's got the meal to get,' Clem said moodily.

'We can manage, Kenver and I,' Kerris piped up.

Clem bit back an angry retort. He went to the door, his face like thunder, his dogs jumping around his feet. 'I'm going out to start some work.'

The twins got up as one. 'We'd better join you,' Philip said.

Kane glanced at Ricketty Jim and received a sympathetic look. Was it only yesterday he had been here asking this man if he was his father? It seemed years ago after all that had happened.

'We'll go for a short walk,' Jessica said to Kane, then added to Kerris, 'I'll be back to help you in a little while.'

'We can manage,' Kerris said, smiling at her man.

'What's the matter with your father?' Kane asked as he and Jessica strolled towards the valley.

'I think it's got something to do with the way Sir Oliver spoke to him yesterday. But he shouldn't have touched your mother like that, he deserved it. It upset Miss Catherine too. She was some quiet on the way home, shouldn't wonder if she won't have him now.'

'I hope our parents' difficulties won't come between us, Jessie,' he said, stopping to hold her.

'I won't let them,' Jessica said, offering him her lips.

After what had nearly happened to Olivia, Kane was restrained. He kissed Jessica gently then they walked on with their arms round each other.

'Have you found us somewhere to go?' she asked.

'I have a place in mind. I'm going to buy a property round the bay at Gulval, Vellanoweth Farm, but I'm beginning to think it would be better to be open about our wanting to be close. After that dreadful episode yesterday, it doesn't seem right meeting in secret. Do you think Clem has any idea we're more than just friends now?'

'No, and I don't think he would like it with these other weddings going on. It would be best to keep it to ourselves for now. I'd like to see your farm.'

'I'll arrange it when all is settled. I'll invite you over properly, perhaps with Kerris, then everything will be above board. When Olivia is over her ordeal and you come to the Manor again, I'll walk you home. It will give us a short time of privacy together and I can't see why anyone should object to that.'

'That will have to do for now, then,' Jessica said, very disappointed. She couldn't see how she and Kane could get closer if they hardly met.

'Something that won't do is the way you're not kissing me right now,' he laughed.

–

Luke and Cordelia rode to the charity school during the morning, glad not to have been involved in Hezekiah Solomon's death. Luke pored over the registers, checking on how many children were attending, while Cordelia taught the alphabet to the five- and six-year-olds. The school met from ten o'clock to two o'clock, giving the children time to work before and afterwards to earn money for their families. Matthias Renfree appeared soon after midday and Luke and Cordelia left.

'What shall we do now?' Cordelia said as they trotted away. 'I feel we would only get in the way at home and I don't really fancy going home anyway.'

'Let's ride on to Marazion and spend some time there,' Luke replied. Then, after mulling over the events at Penzance the previous day, he said, 'I'm glad you're not likely to get involved in any rash adventures, Cordelia.'

'No, of course not,' but she turned her head so he couldn't see her guilty blushes.

Chapter 23

Jessica and Cordelia were amazed that Olivia insisted on going ahead with their smuggling plans in spite of her recent ordeal and the fact that early in the New Year she was to become the wife of the respectable young parson. They were both happy and excited over her good news and felt she should do nothing to risk it going wrong. Jessica had urged that at least she be allowed to postpone the run and arrange with Zack Maynard that it take place at some later date. But Olivia declared she needed the excitement and challenge of the run to purge herself of the foul aftertaste of nearly being ravished and murdered by Hezekiah Solomon.

So the three young women met, as arranged, in Trelynne Cove two nights after the fateful trip to Penzance. But there was one thing hampering their plans and Jessica and Cordelia used it to try to persuade Olivia to change her mind. Despite her pleas, Jack still steadfastly refused to come with them.

They huddled under the shelter of the cliff out of the keen wind and Jessica and Cordelia were all for going home. If Zack Maynard and his men out in their rowing boat did not see a return signal to indicate that it was safe to land the goods, they would abandon the run. Zack Maynard had sternly told Jessica the last time they'd met that this would be their one and only chance and he would not arrange another run if anything went wrong. In the circumstances, she thought it was probably the best thing that could happen. Then Olivia could be safely married and if she and Cordelia still craved adventure, they could seek it by some other means.

'I've no intention of not going ahead!' Olivia said crossly, wrapping the black cloak she wore more tightly against the cold. 'We all agreed to this run and I'm going to see it through.'

'But getting married is in itself an adventure,' Jessica tried to reason with her. 'The Reverend Lanyon wouldn't approve of you being here.'

'It's none of Timothy's business and he won't know anything about it, will he? Anyway, I'm sure he takes in contraband. He couldn't afford those new lace curtains in every room of the Parsonage on his stipend.'

'That may be so, but how can we possibly manage without Jack to carry the heavier things?' Cordelia pleaded. 'It will be hard enough work clambering over the rocks to the hidey-hole with the things we can manage to carry.' She was no more or less frightened than the other two but now they were here, out in the cold and dark of an early October night, she saw it as an unromantic escapade and probably a foolhardy one. The sky was inky-black, the full moon covered by dark clouds. If Uncle Oliver found out, he would be furious at the risk they were taking. As it was, Jessica said she did not trust Zack Maynard and that he gave her the chills, the way he looked at her.

'Then Maynard and his men will have to carry them up the cliff and put the goods on our ponies or take them back to their boat, won't they?' Olivia said defiantly. 'Anyway, we're all healthy and strong. We shall go ahead, or are you two feeling cowardly? I'm surprised that you want to back down, Jessie. You've always been the most wilful and daring of the three of us.'

Jessica thought that perhaps she was a coward, and shouldn't be. If Olivia could brave the night after her recent experience, then surely she could too. 'Oh, all right then. You two stay out of sight,' she said. 'I'll go back up on the cliff top and watch for the signal out at sea and get the lantern ready to signal back. 'Tis nearly midnight and they'll be signalling soon. When I've done it, I'll come down and join you two on the beach. Keep your eyes peeled for trouble, and no chattering. And if we run into any Revenue men, don't panic. If we can't sweet-talk them out of arresting us, we'll bribe 'em. If that don't work, you only have to say who you two are and they'll let us go. They'd rather face the Devil, I'm sure, than Sir Oliver's wrath.'

While the other two girls picked their way down to the shoreline to hide among a large outcrop of black granite rocks, Jessica walked carefully back up the cliff path. She tried not to send loose stones scurrying away from her feet and disturb the night. She muttered under her breath that the Reverend Timothy Lanyon was taking a mighty handful upon himself by marrying the stubborn Miss Olivia Pengarron. It was her stubborn streak that had made her go off to Penzance for a secret meeting without telling anyone where and why she was going, and even if she had, she wouldn't have allowed herself to be talked out of it.

Jessica hoped this run would go well; it might provide her with the means to obtain the necessary silks to clothe herself for the many weddings she was going to attend. Her father's, her uncle's and now one of her closest friends'. Who next? Surely not Cordelia. She didn't seem to like men. She was more content, when not writing her endless letters to her absentee brothers and sisters, to follow where Luke Pengarron led. He kept all unwanted suitors at bay for her; no one could get past his possessiveness and fits of bad temper. Not Cordelia then. Certainly not me, she told herself. It was wonderful dallying with the handsome Kane Pengarron; he kissed so nicely and it was good being close to him. But neither he nor his equally handsome brother would want to marry out of their class. Come to that, neither did she, she told herself. She couldn't see anything permanent coming out of a romance with Kane Pengarron.

Jessica walked gingerly towards the cliff's edge, being careful not to slip on the damp surface or trip over a tuffet of coarse grass or granite boulder. She lit her lantern and kept it out of the draught and out of sight by placing it behind a boulder and kneeling down in front of it. Her excited eyes had barely had time to scan the restless sea for the smugglers' signal when something was thrown over her head, muffling her only scream.

–

Jack had been pacing up and down the cosy living room of his little cottage close to the stables for over an hour. It didn't sit easy on his shoulders that he had had a bad quarrel with the elder daughter of the household. Miss Olivia's wilfulness had shocked him. She had called him many unpleasant names and had unfairly declared him disloyal to the family, taking no notice of the fact that his decision not to go on the smuggling venture was precisely because of the loyalty he felt he owed to her parents. Jack had begged her at least to ask Master Luke or Master Kane to go along with them; they were both at home that night and were used to smuggling in Trelynne Cove. She had bluntly refused his suggestion, saying her brothers would doubtless try to stop her too and she was having none of that. In the end she had tossed her red head and said scornfully that the run wouldn't go ahead because of his selfishness. But now, here he was, long past midnight, worrying that she might not have been telling the truth and that the three unwise young women had gone ahead with the run after all.

Jack grabbed his coat and sped to the stables. There was no one about, but neither were Miss Olivia's and Miss Cordelia's ponies. He stood there gazing at the empty stalls. If he went to the house and asked where they were, and it turned out they had ridden off to spend the night at someone's house on a social visit, he would be seen to be impertinent. Miss Olivia would be absolutely furious. He didn't care. He was more than a servant to this family. They cared about him and trusted him. If the two young ladies had put themselves into any possible form of danger, Sir Oliver and her ladyship would expect him to tell them.

He ran into the house through the kitchens. There was no one about, but he wasn't going to waste time asking if he could be seen anyway. The family were still up. Jack rushed through the house to the parlour where there were lights and he could hear talking.

Red-faced but determined, he knocked on the door and entered after Sir Oliver called out, 'Come in.'

'Jack? What it is?' Kerensa said, standing up in alarm. 'Has there been an accident?'

'Forgive me, m'lord, m'lady, but I have to see you now.'

'Come right into the room then,' Oliver said, rising to his feet, as did Luke and Kane who were also there. 'Get straight to the point, Jack, it's obvious something serious is amiss.'

Jack was confronted by a sea of worried faces. 'It may be wrong of me to ask,' he said anxiously, 'but I have to know where Miss Olivia and Miss Cordelia are. 'Tis very important that I know they're safe. Their ponies are not in the stables.'

'What? They should be in bed. They both retired early. What's going on, Jack?' Oliver demanded, as Kerensa clutched his arm.

'If they aren't in bed then I think they could be in Trelynne Cove, smuggling, sir,' Jack blurted out.

'Luke, run up the stairs and see if your sister and cousin are safely abed. If they're not, and they probably aren't if their ponies are gone, we'll saddle up and go after them.'

'I'm sorry, sir,' Jack said helplessly, and quickly told the story of how Olivia had been badgering him. 'I should have come to see you earlier but Miss Olivia said she wouldn't go in the end because I refused to go with them. I was worried about what might happen to them and Jessica Trenchard. I believe it was all her idea, sir.'

'Those Trenchards!' Oliver spat. 'They're nothing but a blight on my land!'

Kane made to protest at that but Luke burst through the door shaking his dark head. 'There's no sign of them, Father.'

Beatrice, having been awakened from a drunken stupor at the kitchen hearth when Jack rushed through the room, was shuffling up the corridor, curious to see what was going on. 'What's up, Master Luke? Is somebody ill? Is there trouble afoot?'

Luke didn't answer and Beatrice pushed past him into the parlour. 'What's goin' on?' she said, wiping a large drip off her nose and sniffing loud enough to receive momentary attention. ''As somebody died, God rest their soul?'

'Stay with Kerensa until we get back, Bea,' Oliver said, picking the old woman up bodily and dumping her down beside Kerensa.

'I want to come with you, Oliver,' Kerensa said, but he held her back.

'Oh no you're not. Not in your condition. There's enough of my womenfolk in possible danger as it is. Jack, saddle up and go over to Trecath-en Farm. See if the Trenchard girl's there. If not, tell her father to come to the cove immediately and collect her.'

The men were quickly gone and Kerensa and Beatrice were left staring at each other. Kerensa made a quirky face. ''Tis always left to the women to sit and wait,' she complained.

''Cept for those three maidens out there somewheres now,' Beatrice replied, thumping her heavy chest to assist a burst of coughing. 'Shall I make 'ee a dish of tea, me 'an'some?'

'I suppose so. 'Tis what we always do in moments like these. I'll come to the kitchen with you. I'm glad Kelynen has slept through all the commotion or she'd be down here with all her endless questions.'

No sooner had the words left her lips when a large black dog bounded into the room and her sleepy-eyed younger daughter appeared in her nightgown. 'Mama, where have Papa, Kane and Luke and Jack gone in such a hurry? I looked out of the window and saw them riding out of the stable yard.'

Kerensa smiled and held her arms out. 'Come to the kitchen, my love. It's just as warm in there, and Beatrice and I will tell you all about it.'

'Everything seems to be unsettled since Kane came home,' Kelynen said, stifling a yawn, after she'd been told the reason for the abrupt departures. 'Nothing happened for ages and now it doesn't seem to stop.'

'Well, just you be sure to behave yourself, young lady,' Kerensa said affectionately. 'But while we're sitting here waiting anxiously for your sister and cousin to come safely home, I've got some news for you. Something else that's going to happen. I'm expecting another baby early next year.'

'I thought you were,' Kelynen said matter-of-factly. 'What with the way Papa's been fussing over you lately. And you needn't worry about me causing you worry, Mama. I've got Rex to keep me in line.' She patted the broad head of the dog who was dozing at her knee. Then she stifled another yawn. 'I couldn't sleep but I'm tired at the same time.'

'Be better if 'ee goes back to bed, cheeil,' Beatrice rasped, giving the girl a toothless grin. 'Rex'll be able t'sleep better anyway.'

'Yes, you go on back up to bed, Kelynen. I'll come up to tell you straightaway when they've come home.'

'Go on, I'll look after yer mother,' Beatrice said, when the girl looked doubtful.

Kelynen was never inclined to argue like her brother Luke and her errant sister. With a shrug of her slim shoulders, she kissed them both and went back to her room, Rex walking up beside her protectively.

''Tes all part of motherhood, my dear,' Beatrice said, looking at Kerensa shrewdly. 'She'll be a worry to 'ee too when she gits old enough.'

'I know,' Kerensa said resignedly. 'But she is right, Beatrice. Everything's been turned upside down since Kane's come home.'

'You don't wanna read nothin' into that, m'dear! Fate shakes things up fer a little while then it'll all settle down again.'

'But we've had deaths, the unmasking of a murderer, now all these weddings and I'm with child again.'

'And when thee takes it all apart and looks at it every which way yer can, m'dear, ye'll see they were all bound to 'appen.'

'You mean Kane was bound to leave the army and me to have another baby? That Hezekiah Solomon was bound to be found out? Sir Martin was bound to die and Sebastian to choke to death with his eating habits? And the girls to seek adventure?' After a few moments' thought on each event, Kerensa realised the truth of most of it. 'But not Clem marrying the parson's sister,' she said with a smile.

'Naw, p'raps not that, I'll agree with 'ee. 'Ow do 'ee feel about that then?'

'It seems an unlikely coupling but I wish them well.'

'Still 'ave a little love fer 'e, Clem Trenchard, don't 'ee?'

'For Clem? I don't suppose the feelings of love I had for him will ever fade away to nothing. But I love Oliver and I'd like to see Clem happily married, the way he was with Alice.'

'But thee don't think 'e'll be 'appy with Miss Cath'rin'?'

'I think it's unlikely, they're not at all suited. Oliver thinks he'll back out when the time comes. It would be very cruel if he did. I think Miss Catherine finds her spinsterhood something of a shameful condition. But if he does marry her and they end up hating each other, that would be cruel too.'

'Well, we'll jus' 'ave to wait 'n' see. They might git along jus' fine, stranger things d'appen at sea an' it went bring the sky fallin' down. But there's nothin' wrong with bein' unmarried, don't know why maids d'git into such a state over it.'

Kerensa looked at Beatrice with a sudden burning curiosity. 'Did you ever get married, Beatrice? I don't think I've ever heard you mention a man in your life.'

The old woman tapped her fat red nose with a finger. 'Never 'ee do mind, but I've 'ad me moments.'

Kerensa smiled but became anxious again. 'They must be at Trelynne Cove by now. And I don't really believe that Olivia and Cordelia doing this was inevitable.'

–

The Pengarrons and Jack trotted quickly over the familiar tracks through the night, all carrying lanterns, and soon parted company for their separate destinations.

'I wonder how they came up with this idea,' Luke said through the dark to his father and brother.

'From you and your little gang of free-traders I expect,' Oliver retorted. 'Yes, I do know about your little nocturnal activities,' he added on a crosser note.

'And you mind us free-trading?' Kane asked, as they reached the beginning of the cliff paths that would take them to Trelynne Cove.

'Not you, I don't, it's what every Cornish man does and enjoys taking the risk. But it must have been where the girls got their idea from and that I do mind. If the Trenchard girl and her ilk want to risk themselves ending up as prisoners of the Revenue men, then that's up to them, but there are other considerations where Olivia and Cordelia are concerned. They're ladies and are open to different forms of abuse.'

Kane didn't like the way his father was referring to Jessica. He was terribly worried about her and he decided to change the subject before he was stung into saying something he would regret. 'Are you and Mama adding to the family, Father?'

'Yes,' Oliver replied. 'And so far it hasn't been a happy time for her. We were about to tell you when Jack came into the room. Let's hope we can get your sister and cousin back safely. I don't understand how Olivia could take such a risk so soon after her recent ordeal.'

It took only a short time to get to Trelynne Cove. There seemed to be nobody about. They dismounted and ran down the winding path onto the shingle, shouting the girls' names. There was no sign of their ponies and all was quiet except for the roll of the sea and the cry of the winds.

'Do you think they've been here?' Luke said, holding his lantern higher. 'Perhaps they went somewhere different to where they told Jack.'

'No,' Kane said. 'If they've arranged to land a run at the cove, they wouldn't have gone anywhere else. Perhaps they have already met the smuggling party and left.'

'Impossible,' Oliver snorted. 'A smuggling run takes time and it would take three girls even longer to haul goods about. Even if they had gone, we would have met them returning home. But look around. There's no sign of anyone having been here.'

'Perhaps they've gone over to Trecath-en Farm to stay the night there with Jessica for some reason,' Luke said, trying to think of a comforting reason for the girls not being at the cove or at home.

'I hope you're right,' Oliver said grimly. 'I have a bad feeling about this. We'll walk to each end of the beach calling their names. They could be hiding away and are afraid to come out, not realising it's us who's here. We'll go up to Mother Clarry's end first.'

They walked in a row, their riding boots crunching over the shingle, calling loudly with their hands round their mouths. 'Olivia! Cordelia! Jessica!'

When they reached the end of the beach they stopped and looked up at the outline of Mother Clarry's seat, a jutting piece of smooth rock that was rumoured to be the seat of an ancient mythical witch.

'I wish she was up there now, this very minute, to tell us if anything has happened here,' Kane said, his gut in a tight knot.

Oliver cupped his lips and shouted, 'Olivia! Cordelia! It's Father! Answer me!'

But there was no reply. It was chillingly quiet. The clouds had been slowly clearing from the moon which was now circled by a halo of yellow and pink, but nothing could be seen in its light.

'Where are they?' Luke said in anguish, looking upwards. If the moon had witnessed what had happened to his sister and cousin and Jessica, it gave no clue to their whereabouts now.

'We'll try the other end of the beach,' Oliver said.

They retraced their long strides, shouting all the way. There was no sign of the girls.

'What next?' Kane asked.

'We'll clamber over the rocks. Try your great-grandfather's hidey-hole. We should have thought of it in the beginning. If there was any trouble, they might have gone there. In fact they could be in there hiding from us. Leave your lantern here, Luke, we'll go in by the light of mine and Kane's. You'll need your good arm to hold on with.'

Even in the half-dark they quickly located Old Tom Trelynne's hidey-hole, behind which lay a shallow cave hewn out of rock. Kane and Luke had contraband stored in there now, put there on an almost pitch-dark night after the rest of the smuggling party had disbanded. Their hopes soared when they saw a boulder at the entrance had been removed and they made light work of removing more until it was wide enough for a broad man to squeeze through.

One by one they wriggled through, Kane compressing and hurting the tender spot on his stomach and Luke jarring his painful stiff arm. Oliver could just make them out rubbing at their old wounds as they all stood on the other side.

'Are you two all right?' he asked, as if he was talking to two elderly ladies shamming their ailments.

His sons dropped their hands guiltily to their sides.

'Good, then we'll proceed, shall we? We won't shout. I don't want them getting in a panic and falling off the rocks in the dark.'

He led the way, followed by Luke, with Kane bringing up the rear on the narrow, tricky route to the cave. Luke stumbled, and Kane braced his feet and reached out to stop his fall. They came to the entrance of the cave without further mishap and looked inside intently. Nothing seemed to be there but the contraband lying about in casks and bales.

'I thought they'd be here!' Oliver said desperately. 'Olivia! Cordelia!'

'Jessica!' Kane and Luke called together.

One of the bales of silk seemed to move.

'What was that?' Oliver said. 'Did you hear something?'

Then something was pushed aside and two figures rose like ghosts in the eerie lantern light. The men gasped.

'Father! Oh, it's you,' Olivia called out, climbing over contraband and running to him.

Cordelia was on her heels with cries of 'Uncle Oliver!'

The girls hugged the brothers but before any explanations were asked of them, Kane gripped Olivia's wrist tightly and asked with a hiss, 'Where's Jessica?'

'But isn't she with you?' Olivia cried.

Chapter 24

'Where is Jessica supposed to be?' Kane shouted in blind panic, pulling on Olivia's wrist until she cried out and Oliver wrested his hand away. 'Why isn't she here with you?'

'She went up to the top of the cliff,' Olivia wailed, jumping up and down as she always did when distressed, 'to signal back to the smuggling boat. Didn't you see her? Perhaps she's up there hiding or she may have run away home.'

'You were here to take part in a smuggling run,' Oliver said sternly to both girls. 'What made you hide in here?'

'We heard a strange noise from up on top of the cliff,' Olivia began shakily. 'Then we heard a rush of feet running down the cliff path towards us.'

'We didn't know who it was,' Cordelia carried on the tale. 'We thought that perhaps it was the Revenue men. They were shouting, "Get them!" and we thought they could only mean us. We scrambled up the rocks and through the hidey-hole's opening – we'd already moved the rock so we could get through without delay should anything go wrong. We hoped Jessica had found a place to hide away in the dark. She knows the area very well.'

'Did you see any smugglers?' Luke said.

'We saw no one at sea. They could have signalled to us and receiving no signal back sailed away,' Olivia replied, shivering with the cold despite the extra clothes she'd put on.

'So you have no idea who these men were?' Kane asked.

'No. We heard them swearing when they couldn't find us,' Cordelia said, shaking in her boots. 'Then after a long time everything went quiet and we decided to wait until it got light before we came out.'

'You would have recognised them as Revenue men by their uniforms and they would have challenged you in the name of the King,' Luke interjected. 'I have an awful feeling the men were in fact the smugglers but they planned something other than smuggling for you.'

'They could have asked for a huge ransom for both of you,' Oliver said grimly.

'But not for Jessica!' Kane tore back out of the cave and scrambled to the opening of the hidey-hole, his lantern bobbing wildly. He thrashed over the shingle until he was racing up the cliff path.

'Jessica! Jessica!'

When he got to the top he scrambled about looking for her and then he saw her lantern, knocked onto its side, the candle lying on the ground. 'She's gone!' he shouted like a madman. 'She's gone, taken.'

Luke who was behind him grabbed his arm. 'Kane, the girls say that the run was planned by Zack Maynard. He must have taken Jessica. Apparently she saw him at one time going into a gin shop in Marazion. We'll search every drinking hole in the town until we find them.'

'You know this Zack Maynard?' Oliver asked at their backs.

'Yes, he's the man who's been organising our runs here in the cove and other places. We think we may know where to find him and his gang,' Luke said.

'I knew we couldn't trust that man,' Kane moaned, and he felt partly responsible for Jessica's disappearance.

'Luke, escort your sister and cousin safely home,' Oliver said. 'You'll have to take Kane's horse for them. Kane and I will ride together on Gereint to Marazion at once.'

'Why must I take them home?' Luke grumbled.

'It is just as important to escort these miscreants safely home and reassure your mother,' Oliver said in a tight voice that brooked no argument. 'Go with him,' he ordered the girls. 'Go straight to your rooms and stay there. I will have more to say to you both about this, and Olivia, I shall be sending Jack straightaway to Perranbarvah to inform Timothy Lanyon of what you've been up to. No doubt he will have some harsh words for you, and deservedly so.'

'Yes, Father,' she said contritely. 'But please go quickly and see if you can rescue Jessica from that man. From what she said about him, I fear he has the same designs on her as Hezekiah Solomon had on me.'

'Don't worry your mother unnecessarily,' Oliver warned, 'or I'll punish you severely.' Then he and Kane mounted Gereint and left.

They met Clem and Jack a few moments later coming towards them. 'I have some grave news for you, Trenchard,' Oliver said, and he recounted the story.

Clem made a groaning noise and looked as though he was about to burst into tears. 'So it's just my maid who's in danger, is it? My son Philip thinks this might have something to do with a man he and your sons have been smuggling with.'

'Zack Maynard is his name,' Kane said from his perch behind his father.

'Aye, that's the one. Philip usually met him at Painted Bessie's kiddley but thinks he haunts Marazion as well. If he and his gang have taken Jessica and planned to kidnap Miss Olivia and Miss Cordelia, they are more likely to have run for there, to get away on a ship or something,' Clem said fearfully. 'With the kidnapping gone wrong, they know we'll be after them sooner or later. Philip and David have ridden on ahead on the farm home to Marazion. If you intend to help me get my daughter back, Kane, Sir Oliver, I thank you for it but we'd better hurry. It's high tide in an hour and Jessica could end up anywhere in the world.'

They rode quickly to the Parsonage to inform the Reverend Lanyon of the night's activities and to ask him to go to the Manor and stay there until they returned home. Kane took Jack's pony, leaving him to make his way home with the parson. Then he, his father and Clem rode as fast as they dared on their joint errand, the only time in their lives that Sir Oliver Pengarron and Clem Trenchard had put aside their differences.

Philip and David Trenchard were frantically searching up and down the town's street and alleyways. They had already been in three drinking holes but had found no sign of Zack Maynard or any of his gang.

'If I see just one of Maynard's lot I'll break his bloody back if he doesn't tell me the run went ahead all right and Jessica and the others are safe and on their way home,' Philip snarled.

'So will I,' David said, thoughts of his sister's safety taking precedence over his religious scruples. 'Then I'll break Maynard's back for free-trading with them.'

'Even if the run went smoothly, Father will be so damned furious with Jessie he'll keep her cooped up at home for months on end. And about ruddy time too. He should have done it years ago. Pity she's not more like Kerris or Miss Catherine. We'll be the talk of the bay for months after this. Mother would have been worried out of her mind over it.'

They were walking along the main street again, stopping every late reveller or more respectable pedestrian and asking them if they'd seen a man called Zack Maynard, but without any luck. They next decided to try a beer house that verged on the long strip of sandy beach; if they found no one there, they would try all the brothels.

They walked past the houses near the beach and had nearly reached the beer house when they saw two men leave the place.

'Let's ask them if they know Zack Maynard,' David said.

When they hailed the men, the strangers walked quickly on without turning back to answer.

'They think we're out to rob them,' David said as he and Philip began to follow them.

'Maybe, but I want to see who they are.'

The twins increased their pace and so did the two men in front of them. 'Hey!' shouted Philip. 'Just a minute there. We only want to ask you something. We're looking for someone.'

The strangers broke into a run and the twins were quickly on their heels. Because the others had been drinking, they were caught easily.

'We got no money! Got nothing of value!' they cried.

'We aren't going to rob you. We only want to ask you if you know a man called Zack Maynard and where he can be found,' David said severely, shaking the man he had in his grasp.

'Ask fer un in one of the gin shops,' the man said in a terrified voice. ''E's usually in the one in the main street.'

'You know him then?' Philip dragged the man he was clutching by the collar of his rough coat to the light coming from a window of the last house. 'I recognise you. You're one of Maynard's men. What happened tonight? Where is he? Have you been involved in a smuggling run?'

David slammed the man he held captive against the same wall. 'You'd better tell us what we want to know or we'll slit your throats,' he snarled. 'Were you in Trelynne Cove tonight, the place you've brought in goods for Sir Oliver Pengarron's sons?'

'Aye, we were. Jus' got back from there. But there was no run. Zacky reckoned 'e wouldn't smuggle with no women. We went there jus' to frighten 'em. Never to do no 'arm.'

'No harm to who?' Philip demanded, pulling his man away from the house as the occupants threw open a window and demanded to know what was going on. David followed suit.

'To the ladies. We never touched 'em, honest! Couldn't find 'em in the dark. They 'id away from us. We thought they'd slipped past us an' run away 'ome,' Philip's prisoner blubbered.

'Who did?' David said.

'Pengarron's ladies, his daughter an' niece.'

'What about the other girl who was there? Our sister, Jessica Trenchard? Did she hide away with the others? Is she safe?'

When neither man answered, Philip whipped out a large knife and cut his captive's cheek. 'You have two seconds to answer before this goes across your throat.'

''E's got 'er! Zacky!' the man squealed, licking at his blood as it seeped past his lips.

'Where? Where is she? Where's he taken her to?'

'On a ship by now, up at the Mount. They'm sailin' on the next tide.'

'Not if we've got anything to do with it!' David growled. 'Which ship?'

'Dunno, Zacky never said, he wouldn't take we two with un,' the man David was clutching whined. 'Please, mister, let us go. If Sir Oliver catches up with we 'ell 'ave us 'ung fer trying to kidnap 'is daughter 'n' niece.'

'Then good for him. How many men has Maynard taken with him on the ship?' Philip snarled.

'Just two others,' one of the terrified men replied.

The twins laid into Zack Maynard's men with a ferocity that left them lying unconscious on the ground. Shouts made them turn round and they saw Clem, Oliver and Kane running up to them.

'Is one of them Zack Maynard?' Clem asked, pointing at the inert figures on the ground.

'No, they're two of his men. They told us that Maynard's got Jessie on a ship moored up at the Mount. He's planning on sailing away with her.'

'It's what we feared,' Clem said, already beginning to move away. 'Come on, let's get a boat. We'll row across.'

Oliver stopped to prod the two fallen men with his boot. 'They'll be out long enough for us to get back and make sure they're arrested legally.'

The men ran down to the shore and pushed a rowing boat out into the cold, deep-green water. They jumped in and Philip and Kane rowed across to St Michael's Mount. Oliver and Clem sat opposite each other, staring into each other's eyes in the moonlight.

'I hope we get Jessica back all right, Trenchard,' Oliver said quietly.

'Thanks,' Clem said stonily.

'I mean it. I know what it's like to have your daughter in danger.'

'Yes... thank you,' Clem said in a less hostile tone.

'Why did they do it, why did Jessica do it?' Kane said, in an agonised tone. 'What does Maynard want with her?'

'He'd better not harm one hair on her head or I'll tear him from limb to limb, I swear,' Philip said heatedly.

'If you get to him before I do,' Kane muttered under his breath.

David sat quiet, saying silent prayers.

The sea was calm and it only took a few minutes to reach the Mount's harbour.

Oliver said, 'We'll head straight for the ships and climb aboard the first one. There's only five that I can see. No talking from now on, we don't want to advertise our arrival.'

—

A blanket was pulled off Jessica's head and she blinked in fear as the face of her captor loomed up to hers. She was sitting on what she recognised with chilling terror as a ship's bunk, her hands tied behind her back. Zack Maynard was sitting close beside her.

She spat in his face. He smiled cruelly and used her long hair to wipe it off.

'Sorry about having to be so rough with you, Jessica, my dear, but you did struggle a lot,' he said in a mellow voice. He stroked her hair and she tried to move away but he pulled her back by a handful of curls. 'Your hair looks a bit unruly but that's how I like it. Don't be scared.'

'Don't be scared?' she hissed at him. 'It's easy for you to be brave while you have me prisoner with my hands tied behind my back.'

Zack made a patient face then he pulled her in against his body while he untied the rope. Jessica tried not to think about his closeness. She surveyed their surroundings with a feeling of despair.

'What are we doing on this ship?' she demanded.

'I'm taking you on a little journey, Jessica. I'm sure you are a girl who appreciates adventure.'

'Where are you taking me?'

'You'll find out soon enough. The tide is coming in quickly. We'll soon be setting sail.'

When her hands were free, she thrust her arms between their bodies and he let her go without any further advances. She rubbed at her wrists where the rope had burned in her struggles.

'I tied you up very carefully, Jessica,' he said. 'If you hadn't struggled, your wrists wouldn't be hurting you now.'

'Thanks for nothing!' she said ferociously. 'Don't expect me to do anything you want me to do without a fight.'

'You're certainly a wild young beauty, aren't you?' he leered.

'Just what is it you want with me, Maynard?'

He grinned at her. 'I want you to be my woman. If you're good to me, then I'll be good to you. I'll look after you well. But if you're not good to me, I'll dispose of you or put you in some foreign brothel.' When she shuddered, he added, 'I thought you'd see reason, Jessica. You're an intelligent girl. You're too good for some weak-chinned farm labourer. I've got money to spend on you, buy you pretty things, take you to high social functions.'

'You're fooling yourself,' she said acidly, but the night's events filled her mind again. 'Where are my friends? What have you done with them?'

'Couldn't catch 'em. Was going to try for a huge ransom off Sir Oliver Pengarron but they were clever and hid from us. Didn't have time to wait for daylight to find them. Don't worry, my dear, we wouldn't have harmed them. Was going to take them up the coast a little way and when the ransom was paid, set them free. We would have had a good chance of getting away if we left them unharmed because Pengarron wouldn't have rested till he caught us if we'd hurt them.'

'They might have got home by now and raised the alarm. My father, my brothers and the Pengarrons may be coming after us even now.'

'I don't think so. I reckon your friends are still hiding away and will be too afraid to come out till daylight. By then it will be too late to do anything, we'll be well on our way to a new life.'

'Why take me? Why couldn't you leave me alone?'

'It's very simple, Jessica. I want you for myself, always have. Don't worry, I won't share you around.' He put a hand on her shoulder which she tried to push away. 'You're just for me, my dear.'

He made to kiss her and Jessica struggled with all her might as he tried to cover her mouth with his.

'You'll be disappointed,' she spat at him. 'I'm not a virgin. I've been with a man before. Like you said, Zack, I like a bit of adventure.'

'You bitch!' he roared. He slapped the side of her face viciously, leaving a crimson weal and making her scream out. He got up and paced the cabin floor angrily. Jessica curled up in the corner of the narrow bunk, holding her face and trying not to cry. Then he said in cool, nasty tones, 'Never mind. I'll enjoy having you anyway. I'm not sure you're telling me the truth. I'll take you as you come and we'll see the truth of it then.'

'You bloody swine!' Jessica cried.

'Now that's something I don't like, women swearing. Say you're sorry!'

'Go to hell!'

He grasped her cruelly by the throat and banged her head against the wall of the ship, choking her. 'Say you're sorry!'

Jessica was in agony but she tried to shake her head. He tightened his grip until she could bear it no longer. 'S… sorry,' she choked.

There was a knock on the door and a voice called out, 'Cap'n wants to see 'ee, Zack.'

Maynard took his hand from Jessica's throat and she collapsed in a heap on the bunk, gasping and spluttering. 'I'll be back and I'd better find you in a more co-operative mood.'

He locked the door and she got shakily off the bunk. She tried picking up a tankard but her hands were trembling. She tried the door handle but couldn't move it at all. Feeling for the first time in her life that everything was hopeless, she went back to the bunk, sniffing back her tears.

–

Oliver, Clem, and their sons had reached the first ship. Philip climbed up an anchor rope and kept lookout, then quickly and silently the others followed until they were all on board.

'Looks like a French merchantman,' Oliver whispered. 'There don't seem to be many people about so this one is probably not getting ready to set sail. Come on, we're wasting time here, let's try one of the other ships.'

A voice came to them. '*Qui est là?*' They turned to see a sailor with a pistol in one hand, a lantern held high in the other.

'We're looking for a girl who's been kidnapped,' Oliver said in French. 'We are looking for a ship getting ready to set sail.'

'That will be the *Morning Star*, berthed last in line. She's heading for the Tropics,' the sailor said in his own language. 'Who has been kidnapped?'

'This man's daughter,' Oliver said, pointing to Clem. 'A sailor by the name of Maynard took her and he tried to kidnap my daughter and niece too.'

'I know the captain of the ship,' the Frenchman said. 'I will come with you and get you on board. He will have nothing to do with kidnapping.' He turned to Clem. 'Don't worry, my friend, we will get your daughter back.'

Kanc translated his speech to the Trenchards and the gathering followed the sailor down the gangplank and along the pier, passing another four ships until they came to the *Morning Star*.

The sailor stood on the gangplank and shouted permission for himself and his fellow companions to come aboard. There was a scuffling as someone ran for the captain. The men stood about impatiently. Philip wanted to charge the ship but Oliver advised caution. He was afraid if Maynard and his cronies panicked, they would kill Jessica.

The captain appeared a few moments later to greet his French friend and welcome him aboard. Zack Maynard was with him.

Chapter 25

The three younger men who had smuggled with Zack Maynard recognised him and shouted his name together. Maynard took to his heels and Kane made a desperate lunge after him.

'Zack Maynard!' he screamed. 'Stop and fight like a man.'

Maynard didn't heed him. With his mouth set in a grim line, he flung himself down a short wooden ladder and headed for the cabin Jessica was locked in.

When the French sailor told the captain about Jessica's plight, he ordered his crew to find and capture Maynard's men.

Jessica had heard the running feet and the thumps overhead as Maynard's men were hauled on deck and beaten. Fearful for her life, she lifted a lantern off its hook and hid behind the door. As Maynard came rushing through it, a knife held ready to put at her throat with the intent of using her to bargain for his freedom, she smashed the lantern down on his head. He reeled forward under splintering glass, crying in pain as the cabin was plunged into semi-darkness. Kane dived into the cabin and brought his clenched fists down on the back of Maynard's neck. Maynard cried out again and sank to the floor unconscious. Kane kicked him over and delivered a blow to his jaw for good measure.

Clem rushed into the cabin and took Jessica into his arms. She had her eyes on Kane where he stood in the shadows as she said shakily, 'Thank God you came. I was so frightened. He was going to take me overseas.'

'You're all right now, my love. He won't hurt you again.' Clem raised her chin and kissed her tear-wet cheeks. 'Look what he's done to you,' he gasped, horrified at the sight of the angry weal that covered the side of her face. Even in the gloom it was clearly visible. 'I'd like to kill the swine. Did he do anything to you?'

'No, thank God, you got here in time. I just want to go home, Tas. He said Olivia and Cordelia are safe. Is that true?'

'Aye. Master Luke's taken them home.' Clem looked up and listened. All had gone quiet. 'I think your brothers and Sir Oliver have dealt with Maynard's gang.' Clem turned to Kane. 'Thank you for what you did, Kane. He's been worried out of his mind about you,' he informed Jessica.

'Have you?' she asked Kane and moved towards him, his concern for her warming her heart.

Kane stepped forward and she could see him better. His face was black as thunder. 'How could you? How could you put yourself into so much danger, and Olivia and Cordelia too after what nearly happened a couple of days ago? You want horsewhipping, Jessica Trenchard!'

Reeling in shock, the rest of her face turning as red as the angry weal, Jessica sought refuge in her father's arms again, burying her face in his shirt and sobbing. Kane's hostility had come from out of nowhere and blocked out every other emotion she was feeling.

'How dare you speak to Jessica like that!' Clem snarled. 'Have you no feelings, Kane Pengarron?'

Oliver appeared in the doorway, bending down as Clem had had to do to see into the cabin. 'Is Jessica all right, Trenchard?' he asked gently.

'We got here in time, thank the Lord,' Clem said, glaring at the gangleader's still body. 'What about his men?'

'Trussed up like geese for the pot. I'll make sure they hang, every last man of them.'

'Thank you for your help, Sir Oliver,' Clem said. It was only one of a few times Clem had given the baronet his title and spoken to him with respect. He felt he owed him that.

Oliver inclined his head. 'I'm sure you would have done the same for me.'

'Aye, personal feelings don't come into it when there's occasions like these,' Clem muttered, giving Kane an icy look.

'Thank you, Sir Oliver,' Jessica whispered through her tears.

'I'm glad you are safe but your escapade has led us a merry dance, young lady,' Oliver replied sternly.

Jessica hung her head in shame and Clem held her protectively.

'I think, Trenchard, it would be a good idea if you kept your daughter on a tight rein in future. Like you, she has a habit of upsetting the peace of my estate. And I also think it would be wise if she doesn't see my daughter or niece again for a very long time.'

Clem was furious. He could hardly believe he and his daughter were being spoken to like this immediately after her ordeal and with the perpetrator lying at their feet. 'Well, I think it would be a better idea if they *never* see each other again!'

'That's fine by me,' Oliver said, pulling Kane out of the cabin. 'Let's get Maynard and his men off this ship and let the good captain go about his business. I shall see that both the Frenchman and the captain are rewarded for their help.'

Jessica remained numb as she was bundled into a rowing boat and taken back to shore. Somehow news of the drama had spread and a crowd was gathering. Wrapped in the blanket Zack Maynard had used to kidnap her in, she stayed on the beach while the tied-up bodies of the gang were thrown out of another boat, borrowed from the French sailor's ship, and bundled onto the sand. She stayed close to David.

A tall man pushed his way through the crowds. He pulled people round roughly to view their faces until he'd located Jessica.

'Jessica, my dear, are you all right?' Luke said, searching her face in what light he could find. He reached out his good hand and let it hover near her wound. 'I've been so worried for you. Did Maynard do this to you?'

'Aye, Maynard struck her and she's all shaken up but otherwise she's fine, Master Luke,' David said for her.

Luke sighed with relief and for a moment he took her hand. 'I'm so glad to hear that. Let me take you somewhere where you can have a little brandy for the shock.'

'No, thank you, sir,' David said firmly. 'We don't want no fuss, people are looking.'

'Oh, yes, of course. Forgive me.'

After Kane's unexpected brutality, Luke's kindly concern was like nectar to Jessica's desolated soul. She smiled wanly at him, knowing Kane was watching them from his strangely active eyes. 'Thank you for your good wishes, Master Luke,' she said, her voice husky after her ordeal. ''Tis much appreciated.'

'Well, if there's anything I can do…'

Kane was walking towards them. She shot him a cold, hostile look which made him stay his ground, then she said to Luke, 'If I think of something, I won't be shy in asking you.'

Oliver came up and asked Luke if he wouldn't mind riding straight back to the Manor again and informing his mother all was well. 'She's had enough to worry about recently,' he said, sweeping his eyes pointedly over Jessica. 'We might as well allay her worst fears. After all, the girl's mother was once her close and trusted friend.'

Jessica wanted to cry until her heart broke. With her father about to marry again because of her wanton behaviour since her mother had died, the remark seemed needlessly cruel.

Kane watched Jessica being led away by David and put up on the farm's work horse. He wanted to follow and apologise to her. It was only out of sheer terror that she would be raped and murdered as his sister had so very nearly been that he had snapped at her. The thoughts that had gone through his mind since Jack had broken the news and she had been missing from Trelynne Cove had been unendurable. He hadn't planned to be so harsh. It had just come out when he'd seen her standing in her father's arms, looking so small and young, her hair flying all around, her cherubic face marred. He had hurt and upset her – just how much had shown in that terrible look she had just given him. Why couldn't he have been kind and understanding as Luke, who was not known for those attributes, had been? He would ride over to Trecath-en Farm as soon as the situation was cleared up here and put things right with her. But then he suddenly found himself confronted by Clem, who said with a barbed tongue, 'I can't stop you from coming to the farm but I want you to know you are no longer welcome on it.'

Catherine was at Trecath-en Farm when the Trenchards got back. She had been so worried about Jessica, she had implored Timothy to escort her there before he rode to the Manor. Jessica was embarrassed to see her sitting in the kitchen with Kenver and Kerris. After thanking her for her concern, she went straight to her room. It was getting light now and the twins, not bothering to go to bed, said they'd get straight on with the milking of the small dairy herd and be back later for an early breakfast. They knew Clem was dismayed to see Catherine at that moment and wanted to make a hasty retreat. Kenver and Kerris also made a tactful withdrawal.

Catherine stood about uncertainly. She was still smarting at her humiliation on Penzance streets but knew if she wanted to keep her claim on Clem Trenchard, she mustn't show it. 'Kerris, Kenver and I have drunk endless cups of tea while we've been waiting. Would you like some, Clem?'

'Rum, more like it,' he said moodily, running his hands through his hair and flopping down wearily on the settle.

'I'll get it,' Catherine said, looking about to see if she could spy a bottle or jug.

'Sorry, I'm forgetting my manners,' Clem said, in weary tones. ''Tis in the cupboard under the stairs.'

'I don't want you to worry about manners at a time like this,' she said, getting the rum which she found in a huge cloam jug which she could only just carry.

'No, you're not one for standing on ceremony, are you?' Clem said in a vacant voice, as if he didn't care about a thing in the world any more. 'You're a good woman.'

'I'll make a good stepmother,' Catherine said, thinking it an opportune time to mention it.

'Aye, I suppose you will. Tonight proves Jessica needs you more than ever.'

She was pleased to hear that but she thought, I wish you needed me, Clem.

'Eh?' Clem said as if she had spoken aloud.

'I didn't say anything.' She sat down beside him and touched his arm. 'Don't be too dejected, Clem. When we're married things will get better, I promise.'

''Tis those blasted Pengarrons!' Clem cried angrily. 'Sir Oliver and Kane spoke to me and Jessica like we were dirt beneath their feet, though strangely enough Master Luke was kind to Jessica for once. They're always there, Catherine, like grit under a man's fingernails, rubbing salt in his wounds.'

Catherine recalled Clem's hands on the beautiful Lady Pengarron's shoulders. 'I understand.' One of them was always getting in her way too.

'Do you? I wish I didn't have to live on Pengarron's ruddy land.'

'It won't be so bad after we're married. You'll have married a lady whose brother just happens to be going to marry Sir Oliver's daughter. He'll have to show you some respect then.'

'You think so?' Clem said doubtfully.

'I'm sure of it,' she replied, attempting to lay a deeper hold on this moody fiancé of hers. She was still afraid he would change his mind and try to get out of their wedding. She wished now she hadn't asked to delay the ceremony, to be seen to be 'courted'. She could have been safely married by now. She loved him, bad moods and all, and in an effort to claim him as hers for good she thought she'd stir up some basic masculine feelings in him for her. She put a hand on his face and turned him to look at her. In his anger the depth of his summer-blue eyes made her go weak at the knees like the proverbial old maid.

'I promise I'll make a better life for you,' she whispered.

She brought her lips to his and kissed him with as much passion as she could muster. But although he kissed her back, as always, he gave her only a little bit of himself.

–

Timothy was permitted to see Olivia the next morning. She was brought down to the parlour by Polly and they were allowed to be alone. Timothy took her hands and kissed them, then pressed his lips to her cheeks. Retaining her hands, he said softly, 'I stayed the night. Your father wanted me to wait to see you.'

Olivia searched the face of the man she loved and whom she feared she might have lost through her foolish behaviour. 'Are you furious with me, Timothy?'

'I admit I was at first. I'd quite made up my mind to lock you away for good. But not now, beloved, not after a night to think about it.'

'You're not angry at all?' and her heart sang with hope.

'It's not unknown for women to indulge in free-trading and I think I understand why you did it. After your ordeal in Penzance, you needed an exciting memory between that and now. I just ask that you never put yourself in any such danger again because I couldn't bear to lose you.'

'Oh, Timothy, I couldn't bear to lose you either. Thank you for being so understanding. I've had such a miserable night worrying first about Jessica and then that you would change your mind about marrying me. Papa wouldn't even let Cordelia and me spend the night in the same room to comfort each other.'

Timothy smiled and kissed her hands again. 'I think that was your father's idea, the pair of you spending a miserable night.'

'I know that Jessica is safe but do you know how she is? We're not allowed to see her for a few weeks and I'm anxious for her to know it's something Cordelia and I do not wish. She seems to have been blamed for what happened but it was through my stubbornness the so-called smuggling run went ahead. Jack tried to talk me out of it and then both Jessica and Cordelia wanted to abandon it. Will you tell her I'm sorry?'

'Catherine's over there at the moment. I'll look in on Trecath-en Farm when I leave. After all, Clem is to be my brother-in-law and Jessica will be my niece so I owe them my loyalty too.'

'Goodness!' Olivia exclaimed. 'Do you realise that when I'm your wife, Jessica, Philip and David will be my niece and nephews. How confusing.'

'How complicated,' Timothy grinned. 'But people are just going to have to get used to it.'

—

There was a little rap at Cordelia's bedchamber door and she sped across the room and opened it. When she saw it was Luke, she pulled him into the room.

'I'm not supposed to be here,' he whispered. 'Father will be furious if he finds out, so if anyone comes, I'll have to hide away under one of your gowns. How are you, sweeting?'

'Miserable, fed up and embarrassed, and while I don't mind being punished by being confined to the house and grounds for a week, I don't think it's fair that Jessica should take all the blame as the ringleader. It was her suggestion to begin with but Livvy and I were just as eager and last night Jessie and I wanted to call the whole thing off when we found out that Jack wouldn't come with us. But Livvy wouldn't listen. What is unfair is that she is allowed to come and go more than I am because of the Reverend Lanyon.'

'Hold up,' Luke grinned, 'you're prattling on like a runaway horse. I made a point of being kind to Jessica last night, although apparently Kane was beastly to her.'

'I'm so pleased you were kind to her but why was Kane beastly to her, for goodness' sake? Poor Jessie.'

'Anyway, Father will soon forget all about it when he's got over the shock. It did come hot on the heels of that awful business at Penzance. He'll come round and Jessica, you and Livvy will be able to see each other again.'

'Well, I've got an awful feeling that things will never be the same again. They can't be, can they? Livvy's getting married, for a start.'

'Well, you'll just have to get yourself a good-looking parson too, my dear,' Luke said, lifting a piece of intricate lace on her shoulder.

Rooted to the spot by his proximity, Cordelia said softly, 'I don't want one, thank you, Luke. I'm quite happy to keep things the way they are.'

Catherine was sitting on the bed in the main bedroom of Trecath-en Farm when Kerris popped her head round the door to inform her that her brother was trotting into the yard. Catherine had been up and dressed for over an hour. When Kerris had awakened her earlier with a dish of tea and said all the Trenchards, except for Kenver, were in a bad mood, she had thought it prudent to stay out of their way.

Clem had given up his bed for her and she'd stood in her shift, which she had slept in, and watched from a corner of the window as he and the twins had walked off to go about their work. She'd hoped he would turn round so she could see his face but he seemed bent only on where he and his dogs were going.

She didn't mind lingering in the bedroom. If all went well, she would share it with him in less than three weeks. His clothes and personal things were there and she had touched and studied them all. She hadn't minded sleeping in the lumpy bed, between the linen he had slept in the night before and smelling wonderfully of his unique maleness. Now she could no longer linger and went downstairs to see her brother and face Jessica's mood of the day.

Kerris let Timothy into the parlour where Catherine and Jessica joined him. Timothy kissed Catherine and shook Jessica's hand warmly.

'How are things at the Manor?' Catherine asked, seeing that Jessica was in no mood for conversation.

'Sir Oliver is still furious with Olivia and Cordelia, I'm afraid.'

'He's also furious with me,' Jessica said bitterly. 'He and others.'

'I'm sure he'll calm down soon, Jessica. Sir Oliver can be quite stern but he is fair.'

Jessica emitted a loud 'Huh!' and Catherine coloured, praying she wouldn't go into a fit of temper with Timothy here. She didn't want anything to happen that might make her brother doubt the wisdom of her marrying into this family.

But Timothy smiled encouragingly at the girl. 'I'm sure Sir Oliver will calm down in a few days and things will get back to normal.'

'I doubt it,' Jessica said tartly.

'You must want it too, Jessica,' he urged.

She tightened her face and refused to look at him.

'How are you after last night?' he asked.

'I'm just glad it's all over, and don't worry, I don't intend to do anything else of the kind. Certainly not with the ladies of the Manor.'

'They are both anxious for you to know that they're impressing upon Sir Oliver and Lady Pengarron that it wasn't your fault the run went ahead, Jessica. Indeed, Olivia told me that you and Cordelia tried in vain to get her to call the whole thing off, and Jack of course refused to go. I'm afraid that poor individual is likely to get a piece of Olivia's tongue, apparently it was he who told his lordship and the rest of the family that it was all your idea.'

'So that accounts for the way he spoke to me,' Jessica whispered to herself, but it wasn't Sir Oliver she meant. 'Reverend, if you've come to pray for me, would you kindly do it now. I have a lot of work to get on with.'

When Timothy had said a brief prayer of thanksgiving for Jessica's safety, she left the room. He looked at his sister. 'They're a moody lot, this family,' he observed.

'Not all the time and not all of them,' Catherine said quickly in their defence.

'Oh, I meant no criticism, my dear. I find them a fascinating lot and the girl is quite beautiful. I wonder that the younger Pengarrons haven't fought over her, but...'

'But what?' Catherine asked anxiously. 'Please don't say you think there is more trouble brewing.'

'From what I've heard, Kane and Luke spoke to her in different, totally unexpected ways last night. It's obvious that Clem's feelings are running high and Jessica is certainly looking depressed. Her spirits are dampened but if they come to the fore and erupt in ill temper...'

'Don't, Timothy. You're frightening me.'

'Well, Catherine, there are always going to be sparks while Trenchards live on Pengarron land.'

'Then it's time for things to change,' Catherine said determinedly. 'And I'm going to try to do something about it.'

Chapter 26

For days Kane had wanted to go over to Trecath-en Farm and put things right with Jessica and Clem, but he was worried about causing more trouble between his family and the Trenchards. Would Clem ever forgive him for being so horrible to Jessica? Would she? She had been about to come to him, her arms held out for love and comfort, and he had simply heaped more pain on her. It was no wonder that Clem had said he wasn't welcome at Trecath-en, and although as the landlord's son and as a gentleman he couldn't be stopped from going there, he wanted to show Clem respect.

Kane had tried to talk to Jessica when he saw her at Marazion market, at church when she sat stern-faced next to Miss Catherine, and on Ker-an-Mor Farm when she was there visiting her Aunt Rosie. But the strong-minded girl had adamantly refused to speak to him. He would have had to tie her down to get her attention.

Kane knew he loved Jessica now. He loved her wild ways, her beautiful sky-blue eyes, her head of shining bouncy curls, everything about her. He made up his mind he would speak to her if it was the last thing he did. Somehow he'd make her listen. Clem had always been his friend; surely he would be reasonable if he apologised long and loudly enough? If Clem came round, perhaps he would make his obstinate daughter give him a fair hearing. If he explained that his proud father had calmed down and had actually said he missed Jessica's boisterous presence about the Manor, surely that would help. If he said that Olivia and Cordelia were looking to him to put matters right so things could return to normal, perhaps that would help to persuade Jessica to forgive him. They had said they would never forgive him if Jessica didn't come to Olivia's wedding. But Kane had reasons enough on his own account for returning things to the way they were before the kidnapping.

But first he had to attend a family luncheon. Kerensa, who loved family occasions, had organised it and he didn't want to let his mother down. So reluctantly he dressed himself smartly and tried to prepare his mind to cope with excited talk round the table about Olivia's wedding and the changes it would bring to their lives with the first child leaving home to get married.

–

Jessica spent most of her time in wretched moods. No one but Clem seemed to notice or particularly care. Kerris and Kenver were too happy planning their wedding which was to be held in the farmhouse in two days' time, immediately after his brother's in Perranbarvah's church. Kenver had saved a reasonable sum of money over the years from the sale of his crafts and this he had given to Kerris. Full of new confidence, her plain face transformed by happy anticipation, she had been taken to Marazion with Catherine, a more subdued bride, to buy new clothes and linen. No longer the quiet, fearful little mouse she had been when she had first entered the house, she chattered happily and took more interest in the household organisation; after all, as Mrs Kenver Trenchard she would be nearly equal in standing with Miss Catherine as Clem's wife.

In the days that followed the kidnapping, Catherine was too worried that something would go wrong at the last minute to snatch her sullen bridegroom away from her, to pay much attention to Jessica's moods. Philip was too elated at the prospect of having a rich stepmother and too busy mentally spending her money. Once Catherine was a Trenchard, and with his father showing her no real interest, he was confident she could be manipulated to his way of thinking. David was too absorbed in wondering how he was going to tell his father he intended to leave Cornwall for Yorkshire with Simon Peter Blake who was due home soon.

Only Clem realised how unhappy his daughter was. He'd been about the farmyard all morning, putting the finishing touches to the lean-to that was being converted for Kenver and Kerris to live in. He'd watched as Jessica angrily washed clothes next to the well, beating the laundry as if she hated it, tipping water over her feet and looking all the time as though she was about to burst into tears. She didn't speak when she'd brought him a mug of tea and only grunted when he'd said brightly, 'Cheer up, my love. You look as if all the worries of the world are on your shoulders.'

'We don't want to see that face at our weddings, do we, Clem?' Kerris chirped, squeezing past Clem in the doorway as she entered to make up the bed fresh for her wedding night.

'I'm all right,' Jessica told them with a wan smile.

'You've got your dress all ready for the wedding, haven't you?' Clem asked her anxiously.

'Yes.'

'And you like it?'

'Yes, Miss Catherine helped me choose the material.'

'Well, you could try to sound a bit more enthusiastic,' Kerris said, smoothing down the bottom sheet over the mattress with long sweeps of her hands. She smiled heartily as she worked; nothing could dampen her spirits.

Jessica wandered away with her head hanging down and Clem followed her into the kitchen.

'You haven't drunk your tea,' she said, looking up from the fire-place where she was attacking the flames with a brass poker.

'Never mind that, cherub. Sit down. I want to talk to you.'

'I'm all right, Tas,' she said, becoming defensive, thinking he was probably getting worried she'd be miserable at the weddings. 'I won't spoil it for you and Uncle Ken.'

Clem sat on the settle and beckoned her to join him. He put his arms firmly round her and she rested her head on his shoulder. 'You're so unhappy, my love, and I hate seeing you like this. I know you're delighted for Kenver and Kerris, that they've found happiness at last and that Kerris will always be here to help with the work. But are you so very unhappy that I'm going to get married again?'

'No,' Jessica stressed. 'I hated the idea at first. I thought it was ridiculous, you asking a lady to marry you. But now I know Catherine

I like her more and more. She's kind and gentle and she's understanding. She's never once tried to play the lady over me or make me feel inferior. And she's told me often she doesn't want to try to replace Mother, she just wants to be here and help me if she can. I won't mind at all having her around. In fact with her and Kerris in the house, I'll be free to do other things.'

Clem was quiet, momentarily made to think about his bride. Then he asked, 'Then why are you so sad, Jessica? Are you still upset over Zack Maynard kidnapping you? Are you fearful over something? Maynard can't hurt you any more. He'll hang for what he did.'

'It's nothing to do with that,' she said against her father's shoulder, then she tried to get away from him but he held her there. 'I'll be all right,' she protested, bitter tears emerging. 'Just let me get on with my work, Father.'

'It's those Pengarrons, isn't it?' Clem said, anger brewing up. 'They humiliated you. Don't let them upset you so much, Jessica. Forget them, forget all the Pengarrons, and don't take any notice of Luke Pengarron just because he spoke nicely to you. He's nearly as bad as his rotten father. Forget those women, too, and start a new life with Catherine as your stepmother. She'll teach you how to behave more like a lady, then you'll be able to attract a good hus—'

'Stop it, Father! I don't want to marry anyone. I don't want to talk about the Pengarrons or anyone else. I just want to be left alone!' She ripped herself away but Clem followed her.

'Why are you so het up? What aren't you telling me?' He searched her face and she turned blood-red. 'Dear life, you're not... It's Pengarron, isn't it? *Isn't it?*'

'Yes, but it's not what you think.' Jessica grabbed her furious father and tried to explain. 'Listen to me, please!'

Clem pushed her away, the only time in her life he had been rough with her. 'I'll kill him, I swear I'll kill him!'

'Father—'

'Just you stay here, girl!' he shouted, shaking and ugly-faced. 'I'll deal with this and when I come back I'll deal with you.'

He stormed out of the farmhouse and rode out of the yard on Tally without even bothering to saddle her. Jessica ran after him shouting, pleading with him to stop and listen to her.

Kerris rushed out of the lean-to. 'What's going on? Jessica, what's happened?'

'He wouldn't listen to me, Kerris,' she answered miserably. 'I wish the twins didn't have the work horse with them. I have to follow him and I'll have to run all the way.'

As her feet pounded over the ground, her long curls streaming out behind her, Jessica wished she had simply told her father the truth. She was in love with Kane Pengarron and her feelings of hurt and rejection came from the way he had accused her on the ship. She had been about to put herself in his arms and declare her love and need for his protection in front of her father, and then his. But Kane had shouted at her as if he despised her, had no tender feelings for her at all; as if he thought her stupid and worthless, an irresponsible girl who had put his womenfolk in danger. She should have told her father all this, and now, because he'd refused to listen to her properly, he was riding like a madman to the Manor and was about to make things even worse. She prayed no one was at home today.

–

Kerensa was contented to see all her family seated round the table. Olivia and Cordelia chatted happily about Olivia's wedding, careful not to mention the other two marriages due to take place in two days' time so as not to make their father tut and frown. Oliver was happy too, his main topic of conversation being the baby due in the New Year. Luke teased the girls, saying he would be pleased to have one less female about the place. Oliver laughed and said in that case he hoped the baby would be a girl. Kelynen quietly listened to the conversations while Kane ate automatically, withdrawn and silent. Kerensa was sure she knew who he was thinking about.

They were on the last course and Kerensa was suggesting the family take a stroll around the gardens together when shouting was heard.

'What's that all about?' Oliver said, getting to his feet.

The next instant Clem burst through the door, with a worried-looking Polly O'Flynn on his heels. 'I'm sorry, m'lord,' she cried helplessly, 'but I couldn't stop him.'

'I'll take care of it, Polly,' Oliver said sternly, facing Clem in anger. 'You have two minutes to explain why you've violated the peace of my house, Trenchard, before I personally throw you off my property!'

'I'm not going anywhere until I've beaten the life out of your blasted son!' Clem raged, standing his ground.

Kerensa came forward to stand beside her husband. She took in Clem's appearance; he was untidy, his shirtsleeves were rolled up and he had obviously left his work to come here. 'Which of our sons?' she asked coolly.

Clem looked from her to Luke, still seated somewhat stunned with the others round the table. He jabbed a finger at him. 'That bastard,' he spat coldly.

Kerensa flinched. Luke looked utterly surprised, then rather amused as Kane got to his feet. Oliver ordered Kelynen from the room and she went without a word. Then he turned on Clem. 'How dare you come into my house and insult a member of my family and in front of such young ears. What's Luke supposed to have done anyway?'

'What's he done?' Clem said, taking a few menacing steps towards Luke. 'He's got my daughter with child, that's what he's done, the young swine! And he's going to answer to me for it.'

Kane exclaimed in horror. Olivia and Cordelia gasped and got up and moved away from the table, leaving Luke to face the farmer's wrath.

Luke burst out laughing.

'Control yourself, Luke,' Oliver warned, seeing that Clem was about to stretch across the table and lay hands on him. 'This is a serious matter.'

'Did you?' Kane demanded of his smirking brother. 'Did you touch her?'

Luke looked from face to face. The shock on Olivia and Cordelia's faces. The urgent questions and dismay on his parents'. The amaze-

339

ment on Polly's as she stood in the doorway. The outrage and challenge on Clem's. And the blind, jealous fury on Kane's.

Very, very slowly, Luke put his fingers into a breast pocket and produced from it a long golden curl tied tightly in the middle. He grinned wickedly and twirled it between his finger and thumb. Then, gazing into Kane's startled brown eyes, he drawled, 'I suppose one should not lie.'

'You bastard!' Clem exclaimed and went to pounce on the jeering young man. But something in Kane's voice made him halt.

'Where did you get that?' Kane hissed.

'You do recognise it then, brother? Didn't she give you one? What a pity. She gave me this when we spent one delectable afternoon together, alone, in Trelynne Cove.'

Kane gave a howl of rage and jumped on the dining table. Plates, glasses, cutlery and a bowl of flowers were sent flying. Kerensa cried out and grasped Oliver, who looked as if he couldn't believe what was happening before his eyes, under his roof, between his sons. Olivia and Cordelia clutched at each other and moved further back. Clem was rooted to the spot where he stood, his eyes wide, his expression one of utter bewilderment.

Luke leaned back in his chair in a lazy manner as Kane crouched before him with his hands held like claws in front of his throat. 'I've done something to annoy you, brother?'

'She wouldn't go with you! Tell the truth or I'll be the one to beat you to pulp! You're lying, you're lying, aren't you? Aren't you?'

Luke held the curl under Kane's nose. 'Then why did she give me this?'

Kane slapped the curl out of his brother's hand, then roared, 'You're lying! She wouldn't go with you and you have no right to say so.' He clutched Luke's collar. 'Outside! I'm going to beat the life out of you just for saying it. You won't get away with your spiteful tongue this time, brother.'

'No!' Kerensa lurched away from the others and pushed Clem out of her way. 'Stop it! I won't have you fighting each other.'

'Keep out of this, Mama,' Kane said, through clenched teeth. 'This time he's gone too far and he's going to pay for it.'

Kerensa looked helplessly at Oliver and pleaded silently with him to do something. He came to her and Clem moved aside, feeling he was quite forgotten. 'It's their fight,' Oliver said quietly, and pulled her away.

Luke jumped to his feet, casting his chair aside. He looked triumphant. After years of being taken pity on as a cripple, someone was treating him like a man at last.

'But Luke has only one good arm,' Kerensa muttered.

'He's an equal with the sword,' Oliver said. 'They can fight as gentlemen.'

'No!' Kerensa screamed. 'I won't have it.'

'Kane can fence with one arm tied to his side to ensure absolute fairness,' Oliver said, his voice grim as he overruled his anxious wife and took charge of the situation. 'I trust them not to kill each other. The winner will be the one who first draws blood or gets the other to yield. Is that agreeable to you both?' he asked his sons.

Kane jumped off the table and nodded, his face still dark with rage. Luke smiled, his eyes glimmering with excitement, and nodded too.

Oliver looked at his wife and then at his daughter and niece. 'You ladies stay in the house. This is men's business.'

'We will not!' Kerensa held his eyes defiantly. 'At least I will not. If my sons are going to fight and try to hurt each other, then I shall be there to watch it.'

The company, including the two younger ladies and Polly who felt it was her duty to stay close to her child-bearing mistress, trooped outside to the back of the house and took up positions on the lawn. Other folk about the Manor were sidling up behind, and on receiving no orders from their master to go away, they resolutely joined the family, standing in a semicircle. Jack was there and Conan and Michael, the stable boys. So were the gardeners, Ruth and Esther King, and Nathan O'Flynn, who much to Polly's disapproval was holding their son, Shaun. Kelynen came rushing up with Cherry, both holding on firmly to Rex's collar. Beatrice shuffled up last, rasping breathlessly, ''Ere, wait fer me. I don't want t'miss this.'

Oliver tied Kane's left arm flat against his body, and then his sons, who had collected their fencing weapons on the way outside and removed their coats and neckcloths, faced each other. Oliver warned them that he wouldn't hesitate to step in and stop them if things got out of hand.

Another person turned up to watch the fight. Having obtained no admittance at the front of the Manor, Timothy Lanyon had wandered round the back of the imposing house. He raised his eyebrows, greeted his future parents-in-law in whispers, then went to hold his fiancée's hand.

Kane and Luke locked eyes. Kane's were full of latent fury, Luke's brimming over with excitement and enjoyment, and this made Kane angrier. They moved about the grass, Kane stalking, Luke strutting.

Kerensa clung to Oliver, but she was furious with her menfolk. Clem was looking at her and caught her eye. She stared back with a face of immobile hardness. Clem's head was full of anguished thoughts. Kane had kept insisting to Luke that Jessica 'wouldn't go with you'. Did that mean she had lain with Kane and he had sired her child? He wasn't concerned about Oliver Pengarron's reaction to his bursting in at their meal table, but Kerensa looked at him as if she despised him. He hated that. He thought of Alice, his late wife. She had dreaded the thought of Jessica getting with child out of wedlock; she would have been distraught over this. Clem had failed his late wife and his beautiful, spirited, beloved daughter.

Kane lunged at Luke's right shoulder but Luke's blade was up and foiled the move. Luke thrust hard at Kane's left side. His blade was stopped and their swords pointed to the ground, steel grinding on steel.

Timothy whispered in Olivia's ear, 'Why are they fighting?'

She whispered back with a little sob of emotion in her voice, 'Clem Trenchard burst in on us with the news that Jessica is with child. Kane became furious and this is the result.' She shrieked as steel clashed in a flurry of darting movements as her brothers fought for supremacy, both on the attack, but equally matched. They moved apart to size each other up again.

''Aven't seen nothin' like this fer years 'n' years,' Beatrice said joyfully, her piggy eyes following each thrust and withdrawal, her

342

head rolling and arms extended as she followed the fencers with her own movements. 'Come on, me 'an'some!' she shouted to both men.

The swords met and clashed for several minutes, the fencers gaining and losing the advantage in equal measure, their feet scoring the wide, short-cut lawn. Luke leapt up onto a low wall that divided some flowerbeds and Kane swept up his weapon in an effort to unbalance him. Luke was confident and completely steady and with one mighty swipe of his sword succeeded in sending Kane's flying from his hand. Luke smiled blissfully. He pointed his blade to the top of the wall so his brother could retrieve his weapon. He didn't want to finish yet. He was thoroughly enjoying himself and had two advantages. Kane's fury was making him just a little less cautious, and Luke, having had the use of only one arm for so long, was used to the restriction where Kane was not.

Kane turned his back to fetch his sword. He knew that despite Luke's deviousness, he would not take unfair advantage. But win or lose this match, he would wring the truth out of his brother somehow. He would not have Jessica's reputation sullied.

When Kane's sword was back in his hand, Luke sauntered over to him, close to the spectators. The dancing for position started again. Kane slashed out rather wildly to unhand Luke's sword and the movement left him vulnerable. Luke made a short, sharp movement with his expert hand and with a cry from Kane a thin red line appeared across his chest.

Kerensa screamed and Luke shouted in triumph. Kane said ungraciously, 'You win, brother,' and threw his sword down.

The two brothers expected a hubbub of voices to break out and discuss the points of the fight. They expected their mother to ran up to them and declare, 'Thank God you're both still alive!' But all eyes had suddenly turned to someone they had not noticed before, standing silently alone, ashen-faced, against the backdrop of the Manor house.

In silence they watched as Jessica Trenchard came forward. She went up to the fencers. 'Were you fighting over me?' she asked, her voice icy.

Luke glanced at the ground, unable to meet her eyes.

Kane stepped towards Jessica and explained, 'Your father said you were with child by Luke. Tell them both it's not true.'

'It isn't,' she said, loud enough for all to hear while staring at Kane.

'Then it's you!' Clem shouted. 'I thought I could trust you, Kane Pengarron.'

Before Kane could speak, Jessica turned on her father. 'I am not with child! I wouldn't allow myself to get into that condition. I promised my mother I wouldn't. She told me all about how she was expecting the twins before she married you and how she suffered for it. How unkind you were to her at the beginning of your marriage because you were in love with someone else. You may have been happy and in love when she died but she never forgot how she'd suffered. She begged me never to do the same, she couldn't bear to think I might suffer the same pain she had. And I vowed to her and myself that I would never go with a man unless I married him and I swear on her grave that I haven't! I may be unladylike and rather wild at times, but I've always lived under a mother's influence, my own mother's influence. There is no need for you to marry again to protect my reputation, Father!'

Clem hung his head in utter shame. 'Jessica, I'm sorry...'

She moved away from him and spoke to the whole gathering with a stricken face. 'How could you believe that I was with child? By Luke or Kane? I hate you all.' She turned on her heel and walked off.

Olivia tried to go to her but Timothy held her back, saying, 'Now is not the time.'

Kane ran after Jessica. He wanted to tell her he had not believed for a moment she was with child, that he knew she was still pure and untouched. She had done nothing other than kiss him and he would never believe she'd gone further with anyone else. She heard him running and turned momentarily to face him. The look on her face stopped him in his tracks.

She said, as if her tongue was poisoned, 'I hate you most of all.'

344

Chapter 27

Unaware of the drama that had been going on at Pengarron Manor, Catherine Lanyon and Nancy Wills were in the parlour of the Parsonage putting the final touches to some of the wedding clothes. Nancy had persuaded her coy mistress to have white sequins sewn down the stomacher of the bridal gown and she was stitching these in herself. Stopping to study her handiwork, Nancy carried the ivory-coloured gown over to the window to get a better light.

Catherine paused in her own needlework. 'What does it look like?' she said anxiously.

Nancy laughed and brought it over to her chair. 'See for yourself. It's beautiful. Bet you're some glad I talked you into letting me do it for you, aren't you now? Just because you're a little bit older than the average bride doesn't mean you can't have a really beautiful dress on the most important day of your life.'

Catherine delicately touched the sequins and smiled with a satisfied sigh. 'You're right as always, Nancy. I was just afraid it would be a little too much. I've been dreading the thought of walking up to the altar and seeing Clem cringe at the sight of me.'

'There's no danger of him doing that. You'll be as beautiful as any other bride and I'm happy to tell you that being in love 'as made you blossom from having a sweet pale face to one of glowing beauty. You can take it from me, Miss Catherine, Clem will truly appreciate you.'

The glow that Nancy spoke of spread all over Catherine's face. 'Do you really think so? I must say I can't wait to live on Trecath-en Farm; I feel that I belong there already. I wish I could take you with me, Nancy, but you'll have to stay with Timothy and soon it will be Miss Olivia who will be your mistress here.'

'Well, I daresay the Reverend Tim won't mind me coming over to visit you but I'm sure I'll prefer the smell of salt and even fish from the village below to those of a farmyard. 'Tis some exciting, all these weddings. After yours and the reception here, it'll be straight over to Trecath-en Farm to witness Clem's brother and Kerris getting married. I can't wait to see her, after all this fuss with the murders, that Peter Blake character and that evil little sea captain. I thought there was something passing strange about he, he gave me the creeps the day he came here to see the Reverend Tim, and that was only to further his evil plans.'

'Don't, Nancy,' Catherine said, unable to repress a shudder. 'Don't talk of anything horrible. I just want things to be happy from now on.'

Nancy sat down and they worked in silence until she had sewed in the last sequin. 'There, that's finished. I'll hang it up away from prying eyes. Miss Catherine…' Nancy unnecessarily threaded a needle and kept her eyes on it. 'I hope you don't mind me bringing up the subject of the, um, the wedding night, but as you haven't got a mother alive—'

'I have no qualms about that, Nancy,' Catherine said, keeping her own eyes firmly on the new shift she was sewing. 'I have seen far too many illegitimate babies enter the world and helped their unfortunate mothers not to know how they arrived in that condition… I will be all right, I'm sure, in that respect.' Catherine wasn't totally sure what 'that respect' entailed, but she was looking forward to lying warm and comfortable in Clem's arms.

Timothy Lanyon arrived home soon after the dust had died down from the Pengarron brothers' sword fight. He sought out his sister immediately and found her and Nancy in the parlour. Catherine's heart gave an uncomfortable lurch at the sight of his grave face. She laid aside her sewing.

Nancy Wills rose and made to leave the room. 'I'd better make a start on the evening meal,' she said tactfully.

Catherine could not look at her brother. 'Is Olivia all right? You look troubled, Timothy.'

'Yes, Cathy. Olivia's fine.'

'She hasn't got up to any more ill-advised adventures?' Catherine gave a brittle laugh. 'Is all well at the Manor?'

'I arrived to find the family and servants assembled at the back of the house and I'm sorry to say Luke and Kane were preparing to fence swords over a fierce altercation,' he replied.

Catherine sighed with relief. She had thought her brother's gloominess somehow concerned her. 'Oh dear, so that's why you're so maudlin. Her ladyship must have been most upset.' Then she looked up with concern. 'She hasn't become so distressed that she has lost the child she is bearing, has she? That would be too awful after her losing her last infant son.'

'No, Catherine. The younger Pengarrons were fighting over Jessica. Apparently Clem was under the misapprehension that Jessica had got with child. Luke intimated that he was the father and it sent Kane into a violent temper – hence the sword fight, which Luke won by drawing blood.'

'And then? There must be more to this story judging by the dour expression of your face. Was somebody else hurt?'

'No. Jessica turned up. She had run over to the Manor although we didn't notice that she was a witness to the fight. She was in a terrible rage. She turned on Clem and told him she had promised her mother she would always stay chaste. She was hurt and furious that anyone could think she was with child, especially after her mother apparently was as a bride. Most of her hurt was directed at Clem but she told all of us that she hated us.'

'Poor Jessica, I would feel just as outraged if someone questioned my virtue in that way,' Catherine said warmly. A niggling panicky feeling was filling her stomach and she wished Timothy would air all he wanted to say. 'But Timothy, there is something about your manner that suggests this somehow concerns me. Do you not wish me to marry Clem now because he got his first wife with child before the wedding?' Timothy crouched down and took Catherine's hands in his.

'What I'm trying to say, my dear, is that because of what Jessica said to Clem, because of her assertion that she knew her duty with

347

regard to her virtue because of her mother's love and teaching, he must realise that his daughter does not really need a stepmother. The girl said as much to him… I'm very sorry.'

Catherine felt a shocking numbness spread through her. 'But… but that does not necessarily mean he won't…'

Timothy gave a long, deep sigh. 'Clem's a loner by nature, my dear. He won't take on anything… that's unnecessary in his life. A wife would be a huge commitment and he was—'

'Only doing it for Jessica's sake?' she challenged him. 'How do you know he hasn't taken a fondness for me? How do you know he will break off our betrothal? Did he say so? Did he tell you to tell me this?'

'I didn't get the chance to speak to him after Jessica left. There was so much else going on. But Catherine—'

'I love him, Timothy,' she sobbed, tears of despair falling down her face. She knew her brother was right, she only had to recall the way Clem held back from her when they kissed. 'It's not just the shame of being a spinster at thirty-one years of age. I love Trecath-en Farm and don't consider it a come-down from a parsonage and I'm fond of Jessica and the twins. I get on well with Kenver and Kerris and she seems to rely on me and my decisions. I was looking forward to being some sort of mother and hopefully a friend to them all. I could have told Clem long ago that Jessica is sensible enough not to need the kind of training he thought she did. I'm even fond of Ricketty Jim… we were going to be one big family… and now…' She cried wretchedly and Timothy held her.

'I'm sorry, Cathy,' he said tenderly, stroking her hair which had fallen out of its careful arrangement. 'There was no easy way for me to tell you. I only thought to soften the blow before Clem tells you himself. Would you like me to send Nancy in to you?'

'No… I'd rather be alone.'

–

When Clem got home, riding droopily on his plodding mare, there was no sign of Jessica. Kerris was on the way to the well to draw water and stopped to tell him Jessica had gone off to be alone, taking Gracie with her.

'Was she very upset, Kerris?'

'Aye, she told me and Kenver all about it. She's very upset and deeply hurt. If only you had listened to her, Clem. Then you wouldn't have gone off in a huff and none of that business at the Manor would have happened. She was humiliated in front of her friends, the two young ladies, on top of what she's gone through already.'

Clem ran anguished hands through his hair. 'Oh Lord, I feel terrible. I only wanted to help her, cheer her up out of her despondency, then when we were talking I got the wrong end of the stick and now I've made things worse. How will she ever forgive me for what I believed of her? I should have known better. But Luke Pengarron is a blatant womaniser and he spoke so kindly to her on the day of the kidnapping. I thought there had been something between them. It was typical of him to pretend he was responsible for what I'd accused him of. Then I accused Kane. I should have known I could trust him, of all people. I've liked and trusted him since he was a small boy. By his reaction today it's obvious he's in love with Jessica. Now I wonder if she was about to tell me she loved him too before I went charging off like an angry bull. She must have been miserable over the way he spoke so harshly to her at the kidnapping and I told him he's not welcome here. Oh, it's all such a mess, Kerris. I've made a mess of everything this year. Somehow I've got to start putting things right.'

Kerris put a hand understandingly on his shoulder. 'You've only got a couple of days to do it in, Clem.'

'Yes, I know.'

Clem stalked off dejectedly. He couldn't forget his daughter's stricken face as she'd left the Manor. He'd stood in a daze as the servants went back to work and the family dispersed, all except one. Oliver had nudged his arm.

'Are you all right, Trenchard?' he'd asked in a flat tone.

'What? Aye… I owe you an apology. I'm…'

'You're stunned,' Oliver summed up for him. 'Yes, you do owe me an apology but the matter wouldn't have got so out of hand if Luke had told the truth at the beginning. I won't tolerate people bursting into my house but I don't condone my son's behaviour either. I shall be talking to him.'

Clem blinked heavily and shook his head as if he was trying to adjust his hearing. 'I didn't expect you to be this calm, Sir Oliver. I thought you'd be threatening to thrash me by now.'

Oliver shrugged. 'I think I understand how you feel. If I'd thought someone had deflowered one of my daughters or my niece and left her with child, I would have behaved in a similar manner.'

'Well, I am sorry. I'm man enough to offer you my apologies and to ask you to pass them on to your family, particularly… your wife.'

Oliver looked at Clem curiously. He had not referred to Kerensa as his wife before now; he'd always infuriated him by calling her Kerensa in an intimate manner.

'There's no real harm done to my family. Kane's only got a flesh wound. It's Jessica you need to show how sorry you really are. In fact we've all done her a grave disservice.'

Clem had nodded wistfully. 'It's going to be damned difficult to make it up to her after this.'

Clem went into Kenver's workshop-cum-bedroom. Kenver was sitting at his workbench with half a dozen nails hanging out of his mouth as he hammered the soles onto a pair of shoes he was making for Kerris. Clem sat down dejectedly on his bed 'At this moment I wish I was you,' Clem told him mournfully.

Kenver took the nails out of his mouth. 'Why's that then?'

'Because your life is so uncomplicated.'

Kenver tapped in another nail. 'Yours doesn't have to be complicated, Clem.'

'So it's all my fault it's complicated, is it?' Clem asked his calm-faced brother.

'Aye.' Kenver banged another nail into the brown leather.

'You're right,' Clem sighed. 'What am I going to do, Ken?'

'Only you can decide that.'

'I feel so bad about what I've done to Jessica. All these months I thought I was doing right by providing her with a stepmother and all the time she had her own strength to live her life decently on her own.'

Kenver left his work and wheeled over to Clem. 'You were always fearful of Jessica getting into Alice's condition out of wedlock, weren't you?'

'I've never forgot how horrible I was to Alice when we first married. At one point I even wished her dead... so I could be free for Kerensa again, in case Pengarron died. I couldn't bear to see Jessica treated in the way I treated Alice.'

'Jessica has always lived by what Alice taught her. And of all the unlikely people to choose to keep Jessica on the straight and narrow, you had to pick the parson's sister to marry you.' Kenver shook his head hopelessly.

'Aye,' Clem replied, giving a short laugh.

'Clem, have you ever thought,' Kenver said carefully, 'that if you stayed a widower, and if one day Kerensa is widowed, you'd both be free again? Sir Oliver is a lot older than she is.'

Clem got up and looked out of the window, leaning heavily on the sill. 'I had to face something today, Kenver. The fact that Kerensa will always be Lady of the Manor. She stood up against me at her husband's side. At that moment I never felt so lonely in all of my life, not even when Alice died. Kerensa will always be Pengarron's, as his wife, or as his loyal grieving widow and mother of his children. After all these years, my hopes have finally come to an end. Kerensa is totally his.'

'What will you do now?' Kenver asked gently.

'I know one thing, Ken.' And Clem shuddered. 'I don't ever want to be that lonely again.'

He moved to the kitchen and helped himself to a large tot of rum. He took it outside and drank it as he went round the yard with his two male dogs following at his heels, thinking over the events of the last few months. He was angry at himself for upsetting Jessica so much, desperate to see her and put things right. But for once he was putting his own feelings first.

A few hours ago he had asked Jessica if she minded him marrying Catherine Lanyon. He had thought that was the reason for her melancholy. If that was what had been making her so unhappy, then out of his love for her, and the fact that he didn't really want to get married again anyway, he would have called the whole thing off. He had been rather surprised at Jessica's replies about his bride-to-be. She had said she liked Catherine, that she was looking forward to having her here with Kerris so she could do the things she preferred. His marriage would in fact suit Jessica, and Philip and David for that matter.

But would it suit him? Jessica had said Catherine was kind and gentle and understanding. He thought about those words and realised he agreed with them. Jessica had said she didn't play the lady or try to make her feel inferior. It was true. Catherine had a way of making him feel important, that he really mattered to her, that she was putting his feelings before her own. And probably the strongest point that Jessica had said in Catherine's favour was that she had no wish to replace her mother. Clem did not want a replacement for Alice.

He did not want a replacement for Kerensa either. He swigged back the remains of his rum and bent to pat Halwyn and Gawen. Gawen had a silky, pure white blaze on his head and it reminded Clem of Catherine's soft snowdrop-white skin. He thought about her physical attributes as the dogs nearly bowled him over in their eagerness to be made a fuss of. Her hair, the colour of nature's earth, was now always arranged in gentle, feminine styles. There were the few times they had kissed, when he had held her or touched her, when she had touched him. He thought about them and realised she felt as good to be near as any other woman. In fact she felt remarkably soft and tender and he only now realised her shyness, her hesitancy as a maiden unused to men, and of late her responsiveness to him and slight possessiveness. Clem was suddenly overwhelmed. Ordering his dogs aside, he ran indoors.

'Kenver!'

'Yes, what is it?'

'I'm going out.'

'If Jessica comes back, where shall I say you've gone?'

'Tell her I'm going over to the Parsonage.'

—

Catherine was in the parlour standing looking out of a window when Clem came up behind her. She knew he was there, she saw his reflection, but did not turn round. She held her wedding veil twisted round her hands.

'I know why you've come, Clem,' she said in a tight voice.

He moved up close behind her. He wanted her to turn round and look at him but could see she was holding her body rigid. He knew what she must be thinking, what she believed to be true. Nancy Wills, who had let him in, had coolly told him the Reverend Lanyon had spoken to his sister and he needn't be long about his business!

'I've come to tell you I don't need a stepmother for Jessica,' he said quietly.

'I know.'

'You don't know what I want to say.'

'But I do. Timothy's spoken to me. Please go, Clem,' she pleaded, her eyes brimming. 'This is very painful for me.'

'I don't think you understand, Catherine. Folk will call me a louse if I call off the wedding.'

'They'll understand. Everybody knows you were only marrying me for your daughter's sake... and that now you don't need me. Timothy told me what happened at the Manor.'

'It changes everything, Catherine.'

'I know,' she murmured, and silent tears fell down her cheeks. 'I understand.'

'You'll think me a selfish man, but putting Jessica aside, I've realised that I don't want to spend the rest of my life alone.'

'Well, you can marry another... a farmer's daughter or widow perhaps, someone more suitable.'

'But I've grown to like and trust you, Catherine. Alice wasn't a farmer's daughter and we were happy at the end.'

Catherine turned round slowly. She left her tears unchecked. Clem moved a step closer.

353

'What are you saying?' she whispered. And hope was surging through her soul.

'I'll be honest with you, Catherine. I want you not as a substitute mother on the farm but as my wife, for me alone. Will you take a chance and see how marriage works out between us? Will you give me the chance to love you, honour you, all the things we'll say in the vows in two days' time?'

She cried openly and he took her into his arms. She was soft and yielding to him now and he caressed her and kissed the top of her head.

'Does this mean yes?' he asked gently.

She took her face away from his body. 'Oh, yes, Clem, yes. I love you so very much.'

'Do you?' He was surprised; he had not realised that before. Overjoyed, he smiled deeply into her eyes. 'Well, I've loved all the women in my life.' Then he pulled her to him and kissed her as a lover should.

Chapter 28

As she was Timothy's fiancée, Oliver relented and allowed Olivia to attend the Trenchard wedding. When she came face to face with Jessica afterwards in the Parsonage they both felt awkward.

'Catherine looks beautiful, and your father seems to be very happy,' Olivia commented.

'He is,' Jessica said, looking at Clem who was proudly holding Catherine's arm on his and conversing with her sister, the mother of young Thomas. 'He's quite at home with Catherine's family.'

There was an uneasy pause then Olivia said earnestly, 'I'm sorry about what happened to you on the night of the smuggling run, Jessie. It was all my fault, I shouldn't have insisted on going ahead with it. My father doesn't blame you any more than he does me and Cordelia.'

Jessica sipped from a glass of wine and nibbled at the food. Her face was serious. 'I'm just glad it's all over. Has it occurred to you, Livvy, that Zack Maynard might have gone ahead with his plans to kidnap us even if we hadn't gone to Trelynne Cove that night?'

Olivia shivered. 'No it hasn't. I won't be doing anything of the kind again. I don't want to put Timothy through any more worry.' She gazed lovingly at the young parson who was entertaining Philip and David, then added, in an embarrassed voice, 'I'm sorry about what happened afterwards too. I didn't believe what your father thought about you, nor did Cordelia.'

'It will soon be your wedding day,' Jessica said, smiling and taking her friend's arm. 'Let's forget the past and look forward to the future. Are you coming over to the farm for Uncle Ken and Kerris's wedding later? You're very welcome.'

Olivia glanced doubtfully at Clem but received a friendly smile back. 'I'd be delighted to.'

'You must send for Cordelia. It will be good to get back to normal again, the three of us doing everything together – at least until your marriage.'

Olivia looked carefully at her friend. 'Shall I ask if anyone else would like to come?'

Jessica turned away and made a pretence at pouring herself more wine. She knew who Olivia had meant. The last person on earth she wanted to see was Kane. She and her father had managed to get back onto good terms – Catherine had been a great help, explaining that he had only reacted in the way he did out of fatherly love and worry, and because he'd never been sure of what was the right thing to do about her – but her hurt over Kane went too deep. 'Just Cordelia,' she said quietly.

–

Three weeks had gone past since his family's weddings and Philip Trenchard was in Marazion facing the Barvah Giant in the wrestling ring. Philip had never felt more confident of winning. He had a rich stepmother, by his standards, and she was already spending money on her new family. Despite their objections, Catherine had showered Jessica and Kerris, now the supremely happy Mrs Kenver Trenchard, with new clothes. She had bought Philip and David and Jessica a fine horse each. Kenver had received tools for his workshop. Ricketty Jim had blushingly accepted a new hat, a shirt to keep for best, and a pipe. She hadn't bought clothes for Clem. That would have embarrassed him. She had presented him with equipment for the farm and Clem had surprised his family by thanking her and kissing her tenderly in full view of them each time. And Philip had other plans, bigger plans for what else Catherine could spend her money on.

Part of his plan meant asking Catherine to merge her money with his own. He had managed to save £100 over the years, by betting, smuggling and the amorous services he gave to wealthy ladies. Today he had bet that sum of money on a ten-to-one wager with a gentleman. If he won, he'd receive the princely sum of £1,100. If he lost, he would probably be able to turn to Catherine to bail him out. Philip looked at Matthew King and raised his head in a cocky movement. 'But today, my friend, you lose,' he whispered.

Kane Pengarron was one of those gathered round the straw-covered ring in the biting-cold weather. He was standing next to Paul King and the rest of the fisherman's family. He was not there to see the wrestling; he was hoping to see Jessica. Clem, David and Matthias Renfree were standing in a group with Jack and Nathan O'Flynn, but for once Jessica hadn't come to watch her brother. Kane was disheartened but decided to stay in case she turned up later. Someone pushed in beside him and for one heart-stopping moment he thought it was her, but he looked down on the quiet face of Simon Peter Blake.

'Good morning, Pengarron,' Simon Peter said briefly, then looked at the wrestlers who were warming up their bulging muscles.

'Back home, are you, Blake?' Kane said disinterestedly.

'Only for a short time,' Simon Peter replied, keeping his eyes on the ring. 'I've come to take someone back to Yorkshire with me.'

They said no more. Philip Trenchard and the Barvah Giant were shaking hands and no one wanted to miss a minute of the match, not even Kane now. An atmosphere of great expectancy hung in the damp, chilling air. The betting had never been as heavy as it was today, the anticipation as fraught. Not a sound was to be heard outside the ring. It seemed as if the busy market town and sea port had come to a sudden standstill.

The crowd were of one hope, that the wrestlers would take their time and give them a long match to savour and remember afterwards. Matthew King looked as confident as he always did, but Philip had a stronger grip on himself today, more control over his movements, an utterly determined glint in his blue Trenchard eyes as he waited for the Giant to make the first move.

Kane looked anxiously at every eager face in the crowd but still there was no sign of Jessica. Was she well? It wasn't like her to miss Philip's wrestling.

Nearly fifteen minutes passed. A child coughed and Matthew King checked the movement he'd been about to make and a ripple like the sound of a rushing stream went round the crowd, then it fell silent again.

Clem felt Kane's eyes studying his face and he looked back at him, gazing steadily for a moment, then he lost interest. His hopes were high and his fists were clenched for his son. He knew Philip felt he was going to win today and Clem's guts were churning for him, just as a father's do when he desperately wants to see his son succeed at something as a small child. If Philip won, Clem wouldn't be able to wait to get back to the farm and proudly tell Catherine what her stepson had done. And to give her the little gift he had bought for her, a tiny bottle of perfume whose purchase had cost him a much embarrassed soul.

Philip paced the ground, patient and in control, waiting for the Giant to do something. They could stay here all day and all night and it wouldn't bother him.

Two latecomers joined the crowd and the man's great height ensured them a swift passage to the front of the ring. Sir Oliver and Kerensa, Lady Pengarron, took up position somewhere in the middle between their elder son and Clem and his group. Oliver nodded at Kane and a few acquaintances who couldn't miss him and momentarily gave him their attention. Kerensa watched the wrestlers to get a feel of how the match was going. Then she looked around the crowd and caught Clem's eye. He looked back for just a moment. It wasn't a particularly friendly acknowledgement and she thought he must still be angry over Jessica. He looked different. Proud and upright, in control of himself, a bearing in him that she hadn't seen for twenty-two years, not since the days of their betrothal, before he had lost her. Marriage to Miss Catherine Lanyon had certainly changed him. His shows of attentiveness over her at church were not for nothing then. Kerensa suddenly, desperately, wanted to speak to Clem.

At last the Barvah Giant made his first move, trying his favourite forehip. Philip calmly and ably countered it; he kept his ground and warded the Giant off by holding his forearms up then pushing him away with them.

The crowd cheered with a sound like a hurricane. They fell quiet when the wrestlers resumed their pacing, facing one another like bulls pawing the ground. A cold wind got up and whistled round the ring of tense spectators, but no one heard or felt it.

David noticed Simon Peter squeezed in, practically under Kane's arm, and smiled quietly to himself. He was praying that Philip would win his heart's desire today. His twin would be happy, as happy as his uncle and Kerris were, and his father and Catherine seemed to be. Then perhaps it would be easier to tell his family – those who had no inkling what was on his mind – that he intended to go away with Simon Peter and become an itinerant preacher. Matthias Renfree had taught him, as he had all the family, to read and write, but he'd also given him extra lessons on the Bible and David knew it through and through. He wanted only to give his life to its teachings and he hoped his father would understand. If Clem let him go with his blessing, then there was only Jessica to worry about.

His sister seemed happy enough these days and responded with affection to her new stepmother. Jessica had looked beautiful in her new dress on the double wedding day. She had behaved with perfect decorum and the family had been proud of her. It was not her day, of course, and no one would have expected her to look as radiant as the two blissfully happy brides but she seemed to have suddenly grown up overnight and had showed an astonishingly calm maturity that gave her a delicate, ethereal beauty. Now all she had to do was to mend her broken heart.

David glanced at the tall, commanding but gaunt-faced figure of Kane Pengarron. Or have it mended, he thought. And then his sister could take away the despair in those eyes so deep and dark they could be clearly seen across the ring. She was supposed to have come to watch Philip fight. Their father was looking for her among the expectant crowd now. Was she deliberately staying away because she knew Kane Pengarron would probably be here?

Philip had never felt so happy in all his life. He was almost light-headed with the certainty he was going to win this match. He decided to make a move and went for a 'crook'. He got a good grip on the

Giant's sash and pulled one of his feet off the ground. Then pivoting round to face the same way as his opponent, Philip passed a leg inside one of the Giant's and crooked his foot above a thick ankle. Then he pulled the Giant's head and huge shoulders against his chest and, lifting the foot he was crooking higher, he attempted to throw the Giant over and drop him on his back. It was in desperation more than by his brute strength that the Giant managed to rip himself free and send Philip hurtling away.

The crowd went wild and Oliver clutched Kerensa to him to keep her safely on her feet. He watched Philip Trenchard crow his pride to the crowd and wondered if Clem was feeling justly proud of his strapping son. Clem looked animated enough. And Oliver noticed the same changes in him as Kerensa had. Their eyes met, and for the first time there was no challenge in Clem's. In fact he bowed his head in respect to Oliver's station before looking away and happily cheering on his son. Oliver was amazed. What had happened? Surely the parson's sister had not wrought such a change in this moody individual, and so soon. She was more than an agreeable-looking woman and possessed a pleasing character. Indeed, if she had been available years ago when he was looking for a suitable lady merely to take to wife to mother his children, he would have been glad to choose her. Then he wouldn't have been outwitted, in a bargain over Trelynne Cove, into taking the owner's sweet young granddaughter as his wife. Then Kerensa would have married Clem instead of him and… Oliver chuckled at his musings and Kerensa looked up at him curiously. He hugged her tight and whispered under his breath, 'Thank God Catherine Lanyon wasn't around then.'

It was now more than an hour since the wrestling match had started and the crowd was nicely warmed up to it. The odd mutter went round its ranks as the betting changed heavily in Philip's favour. The skies suddenly opened up and rain fell in a steady rhythm but Matthew King was sweating like an ox on a hot summer's day. He wiped at the moisture over his eyes.

The tension got the better of Paul King and he shouted, 'Get on with it, Matt!'

'I'm doing me ruddy best!' Matthew bawled back and a roar of laughter went round the crowd.

The wrestlers got back to business. Philip could sense the Barvah Giant was getting tired and he decided to take advantage of it. He went for a flamboyant counterattack on the Giant's next hitch, a throw only a very strong man could attempt. Matthew had his hefty body turned into Philip and was trying to throw him over his hip. Philip lifted him up on his own hip and, gripping the Giant's sash, pivoted him round and dropped him heavily on his back. Matthew King could not keep both hips off the ground and Philip Trenchard got a 'back'. He had beaten the Barvah Giant.

Kane didn't want to fight his way through the jubilant crowd and congratulate the victor, who already had his family and numerous women vying to shake his hand, hug him, and paw his muscular body as the rain skimmed off his blond hair. Kane only wanted to find Jessica and try to talk to her.

His parents were at his side. 'I'm taking your mother to the Commercial Inn out of the rain. Are you coming with us?' Oliver shouted above the noise.

'No, thank you. I'll see you later at home,' and before his mother could protest, he kissed her wet cheek and moved away.

He was looking around, wondering where Jessica was most likely to be if she'd come at all, when a hand touched his arm.

Simon Peter said, 'Will you come to the coffee shop with me, Kane? I would like to talk to you.'

'Not now,' Kane replied gruffly. 'I have business to attend to.'

'That's what I want to talk to you about,' Simon Peter persisted.

Kane looked at him stupidly. How could he possibly know what he had on his mind?

But Simon Peter did, for he next said, 'I want to talk to you about Jessica Trenchard.'

The coffee shop was filled to capacity with rain-drenched gentlemen who had watched the wrestling; the place resounded with their excited post-mortem of the event. Kane and Simon Peter found a quieter corner. Kane did not wait for their coffee to be served before demanding from the other man exactly what it was he wanted to talk about.

'My parents have told me about all the things that have happened to Jessica in the time I've spent away from Cornwall,' Simon Peter began. 'I was amazed. But that apart, I understand she's very unhappy.'

'Why are you telling me this, Blake?' Kane demanded impatiently.

'I'm going back to Yorkshire soon. I would dearly like to ask Jessica to come with me – as my wife.'

Kane gasped and reddened.

Simon Peter went on, 'In her present mood she might accept.'

'Are you going to ask her?'

'I only wish I could. I've asked her often enough but she has always turned me down. Even my mother asked her to consider me and that didn't work. I love Jessica very much but...'

'But what?'

'I think she'll only ever marry for love and she's not in love with me.'

Kane looked at Simon Peter with a mixture of extreme irritation and curiosity. 'What are you trying to say, man? And how can you possibly know what you're talking about anyway? You've only just got back to Mount's Bay.'

'I've listened carefully to all the talk. The bay is still full of it where you Pengarrons and the Trenchards are concerned. I know Jessica very well.'

'Oh, for goodness' sake, Blake, where is all this getting us?' Kane exclaimed, making other coffee drinkers look at them. He lowered his voice. 'I shall leave the very next minute if you don't explain.'

'Well, apparently Jessica said she hated you more than anyone else, and I understand she has kept up her resentment against you. Well, mayhap she cares very deeply about things where you are concerned.'

'You think Jessica cares for me?' he asked incredulously, as a waiter put their coffee in front of them. He toyed with the cup's curved handle and waited for Simon Peter to continue.

'I said mayhap. Her behaviour is not typical. She usually blows hot one moment and cools down the next. You remember what she was like as a child.'

'She's no longer a child,' Kane pointed out, but he was avidly interested now.

'That's the point. If she can be so intransigent now it must mean it goes deeply with her.' Simon Peter stirred his coffee then looked Kane straight in the face. 'She's worth fighting for, don't you think?'

'You're damned right!' And Kane had to lower his voice again. 'Simon, you are a good man not pestering Jessica again, especially as she might accept you just to get out of her unhappy situation. Thank you for thinking of me. I suppose if you're in love with a woman you recognise when someone else is too. Actually I was just on my way to track her down in the town when you insisted we come here. You have given me heart to approach her.'

'Then don't allow me to waste any more of your time,' Simon Peter said.

Kane got up and shook Simon Peter's hand firmly. 'Thank you, you've proved yourself a good friend and a true gentleman today. Was it Jessica you came home to take back to Yorkshire with you?'

'No, that was someone else but I'm not at liberty to say who.'

'I wish you well,' Kane said, and he was soon shoving his way hurriedly out of the coffee shop.

–

Luke Pengarron was also in town. He had witnessed the last moments of the wrestling match; he had inherited his father's height and was able to watch it from the back. He'd put two hundred guineas on the Barvah Giant and felt quite sporting about his loss, but he hoped Philip Trenchard would soon get his face rubbed well and truly in the mud.

He felt at a loose end today but had no wish to join in the crush in the coffee shop. He no longer had Sebastian Beswetherick to accompany him when it suited him and since the sword fight with Kane, his brother had shunned his company, hardly speaking to him when he dragged himself away from his farm at Gulval and came home for short intervals. Luke knew why. Kane was obviously in love with Jessica Trenchard and it would take him a long time to forgive him for lying that he had got the girl with child. Mind you, Luke thought, as he strolled along under the gloomy sky, it's an easy task for a man to fall in love with Jessica Trenchard.

Luke spent an unnecessary half-hour at his barber's having the ends of his long black hair tidied. He heard no gossip that entertained him and stepped outside in a dismal mood, his head down, but at least the rain had stopped. A small, well-clad foot appearing out from under a good-quality cloak and dress stopped in front of him. Thinking a lady acquaintance was about to brighten his afternoon, he looked up expectantly. 'Jessica! It's good to see you. How are you?'

'Do you care?' she asked coolly.

'Yes, of course. Yes. Oh, let me explain about what I let everyone believe about you and me. I am sincerely sorry for your distress. I... didn't think of it from your point of view and I beg you to believe that I didn't purposely say it to sully your reputation.'

Jessica eyed his earnest face, as dark and handsome as ever. 'Well, I never thought I'd live to see the day the great high and mighty Luke Pengarron, heir to the Lord of the Manor, would not only apologise to me but grovel as well.'

She walked on past him and he followed her. 'Please, will you give me a chance to explain, Jessie? I was going to write to you but I thought you'd look on it as a lame attempt to avoid explaining things to your face. And knowing you, you'd probably have torn it up before reading it and hate me more.'

'What makes you think I hate you?' she asked casually as she stopped at a dressmaker's shop.

'You said so, at the Manor that day. You said you hated us all and I took that as me in particular after what I'd said. Please don't go in there. Talk to me, just for a little while, Jessie.'

Jessica sighed. 'Oh, very well.'

The rain had held off for a few minutes but there were still lots of people milling about. 'Let's go somewhere quieter,' Luke said, offering his arm. 'There's a house nearby that belongs to a friend of the family. She isn't at home at present but we're always welcome to use her parlour. You have my word of honour you will be perfectly safe. Her maid will be there and she is a strict Methodist.'

'Just for a little while then,' Jessica said firmly, shivering despite the thick, soft wool of the new cloak Catherine had given her. 'The wind is cold. I'll be glad to get warm.'

The house was a small Palladian building, quite new and painted pastel pinks and blues. Jessica was impressed by its elegance and tasteful furnishings. The 'strict Methodist' maid looked friendly enough. She showed them into the parlour which housed a welcome roaring log fire and departed to fetch a tray of tea.

Jessica refused to have her hat and cloak removed but allowed Luke to show her to a chair near the wide marble hearthside. They spoke little until the tea was brought in and the maid had left, leaving the door a little ajar.

Luke poured the tea and Jessica was grateful for its warmth.

'You must be very proud of your brother for winning his match against the Barvah Giant,' he said conversationally.

'That's right, I am. He might not be too pleased with me though. I didn't watch it,' she admitted.

'Oh?' Luke raised his black eyebrows in surprise. 'Why was that?'

She looked down at the flames flaring and twisting on the blackened logs. 'I know it sounds silly but I just didn't want to.'

Luke felt concerned. 'But why not, Jessica?'

She shrugged her shoulders and her golden curls fell about them. 'I don't really know. I suppose…'

'Yes?'

'I don't know why I'm telling you this, but… against all the odds my father seems happy married to Miss Catherine. My Uncle Kenver is happy married to Kerris. David is planning to go away and start a new life and will be happy doing what he's always wanted to do the most. If Philip got his heart's desire…' She looked forlornly at Luke. 'I couldn't have faced him being so happy as well, with me being so miserable deep inside.'

'Dear Jessie. I'm partly to blame for your misery. You must think me very cruel to have used your curl of hair and said what I did. If I explain, perhaps it will cheer you a little.'

'I will be most interested in what you have to say,' she said. She looked as if it was unlikely she would believe him.

'That day we were sitting round the dining table. It was just an ordinary family meal and life seemed its usual ordinary, boring self. Then from out of nowhere your father burst into the room hurling accusations at me. My father sprang up in fury and they were quarrelling and somehow they looked ridiculous. It didn't seem real. Then I was laughing and taking out the curl you'd given me. It was your father I was trying to hurt, not you, Jessie.

'Then Kane leapt on the table in front of me shouting furiously at me. I wanted to hurt him too. Him with his perfect body, an army career behind him that should have been mine. I wanted to hurt him, not you, never you, Jessie. I deliberately provoked that sword fight with him because I wanted to prove I was as masculine as him, that I could leap about and show off and not just be the brother with only one good arm. Do you understand? Do you believe me?' He was beside her now, looking down at her out of intense dark eyes.

'Yes, I think I do.'

Luke smiled a deep, beautiful smile. He knelt and took her cup and saucer away. Then he produced her curl. 'I'm going to make a full confession to you. That day in Trelynne Cove I asked you for this with one intention only. The hair for Cordelia's doll was only an excuse. I'd always intended to seduce you, Jessica. I'd made a wager with Sebastian Beswetherick that I would have my way with you and I was going to use this as proof that I had.'

Jessica could easily believe that this young gentleman could have planned such a despicable thing. But his confession spoke of a different outcome. She wondered why. 'You could have told Sebastian Beswetherick that we had been together. You had the proof.'

He took her hand. 'I couldn't do that to you, my dear, and I swear you are dear to me.'

Jessica gazed back at him and thought that she would not mind if this handsome young man kissed her. She was in great need of comfort, of warm physical contact. As she did not pull her hand from his, Luke stood up and raised her gently to him. Then he put his arms round her waist and she put hers round his neck and they kissed softly.

'I shall be satisfied with just that,' he said lightly.

It was good but it was all she could give him. 'It will have to do for the rest of your life,' she told him quietly.

Luke detected a movement where the door was ajar and recognised the colour of the cloak Kane was wearing today. He still had Jessica in his arms and as Kane pushed the door open, he gave her another small kiss on the lips.

Kane's gasp of horror made Jessica whirl round and Luke lazily dropped his arms. Luke made a deliberate act of looking surprised. Jessica turned bright red and Kane a deathly white.

'Do excuse me,' he said in a voice that sent icy tingles down her spine. 'I didn't realise I would be interrupting something.' He turned and left the house.

Cordelia entered the parlour a short time later loaded down with parcels to find Luke in an exceptionally good mood. He was alone and singing to himself over a glass of fine brandy. He held out an arm to her and she went to him to be hugged and kissed.

'You are very happy,' she remarked, fussing with the packages. 'Did you put a large wager on Philip Trenchard? It's all around the town how well he won the wrestling.'

'No, actually I lost two hundred guineas on the Barvah Giant. Have you been shopping again for Olivia's wedding?'

'Yes, do you want to see? Why are you so happy then?'

'Come here, my dear,' he said.

'Well?'

He put his arm round her and held her close. 'Well, some people can't have what they want most in the world,' he said, recalling Kane's stricken face. 'I don't suppose any of us can,' he added, moving his rigid arm. 'But there are always compensations.'

'I suppose you're right,' Cordelia agreed, not really understanding what he was going on about.

He kissed the top of her small dark head. 'Well, I'll always have you, won't I?'

She gazed up at him with adoration written over her little sparrow face, and said, 'It's all I've ever dreamed about.'

Chapter 29

Kane rode straight and fast to Frances Nansmere's brothel. The rain had started again and came down on him in a deluge and the wind howled and tormented him. He was soaked through to the skin when he hammered on the brothel door. He was admitted by the maidservant who showed him into a room where several scantily clad prostitutes were lolling around on plush furniture. Kane took in their appearance with one moody sweep of his eyes as they automatically turned on their charms to attract him. They were all younger than Frances Nansmere, most were prettier and had better figures, but he had no interest in them. He swept out of the highly perfumed room to saucy giggles and disappointed comments.

'Get me Mistress Nansmere,' he ordered the maidservant harshly, making her blink, curtsey, mutter an apology and rush up the winding stairs with a clatter of shoes.

He threw off his wet cloak and hat and paced the hallway impatiently until Frances Nansmere came floating down the stairs alone.

'My dear sir. My dear Kane.' She stretched out an arm and fluttered her fingers awhile before she reached the bottom step. 'How wonderful to see you again. It is an honour to have you here again. My apologies for Annie showing you into the girls' room before calling for me. I have brought in some new ones, they are all very good. Some new to the profession but willing to please, some highly experienced. I take it you are not interested in any of them?'

Kane took her hand as she alighted the last step, kissed it firmly, then said bluntly, 'I want you.'

'Oh, good. I shall enjoy a little talk with you. There is a nice cosy fire burning in my parlour. Shall I lead the way?'

Kane still had hold of her hand. He said, quite forcefully now, 'I want you in your bedchamber, Frances. Is it convenient?'

'Yes, yes,' she said in delight and he immediately put his foot on the stairs and they climbed up together.

Frances's bedchamber was a mixture of the exotic and the refined. The bed was massive, draped in filmy silks and covers. Pictures of every description, some extremely erotic, covered the walls. Silver candelabra and a gigantic crystal chandelier, Chinese vases and pots of dried, scented flower petals lent atmosphere and beauty to the room.

Frances had noticed his strained features and that he looked drained of energy. He would need something to revive him. She went to a table laden with liquor.

'What can I get you, my dear?' she said in a silky voice. 'Champagne, red wine, white wine, brandy?'

'A large brandy, thank you,' he said quietly, sitting on the edge of the bed.

She poured brandy for him and white wine for herself while he pulled off his boots and half lay, half sat against the many plump, silk-covered pillows at the top of the bed.

'You look rather tired, Kane. Have you been busy of late?' She gave him his drink and positioned herself beside him. She stroked his arm and hair, caressing his cheek then running a soft finger along his lips, waiting patiently for him to reply.

At length, he said, 'Yes and no. I've taken my time getting used to being home and looking over the changes in the parish. But I've also recently signed the deeds for a property at Gulval, Vellanoweth Farm.'

'Then we won't be too far away. I'm so pleased. I hope you will come here often.' Frances finished her wine then began to take off her dress. Kane slowly sipped his brandy, gazing at her soft white flesh as it was revealed to him.

'I don't want to waste time talking,' she said, casting aside her stays, 'but I'm curious to know how things went with the old woman Meg. Have you found out what you wanted to know about your parents?'

'I found Meg most interesting,' he said, smiling a little at the memory of her. 'A great animal lover. She's left the swamp now. I hope she's set herself up in a nice little cottage for herself and her cats and rabbits and the rest of what she calls her family.'

Kane told Frances the full story of Peggy Wearne and how it was impossible to know who his real father was.

'But at least it wasn't that sailor you thought it was,' Frances said, moving her hands about his thigh. 'Are you pleased?'

'Yes. I've got the past into perspective but before you say any more, I don't want to talk about the future.'

'Or the woman you love?' she asked, knowing it was daring of her but curious as to why he wanted this change of service from her today.

Kane threw his glass angrily across the room and it smashed into a myriad tinkling pieces against the wall. Frances's eyes followed its passage but then Kane pulled her roughly into his arms and kissed her long and ardently.

'Mmmm,' she murmured, 'you kiss as excitingly as you get into a sudden temper. I like to listen to you talk. What else are you good at, I wonder.'

Frances untied her silk shift and let it fall to reveal what little there was left to reveal. Kane looked momentarily then gathered her back to him and they kissed again. Frances moved her trained hands about him. To undo his breeches, to pull out his shirt, to touch, to stimulate. But he kept bringing her arms back round his neck and after several minutes they had progressed no further than kissing. Then he sighed.

'You're tired,' she purred. 'Lie down and leave things to me.'

He did as she bade but his body was tense and after a few moments more, she lay down beside him. He put an arm round her exquisite bare shoulders and she rested hers over his middle.

'Are you nice and comfortable now?' she asked softly.

'Yes. You're right, Frances. I am tired. I feel as though I want to sleep for the next week. We'll leave it till later.'

'Some men can take a mistress while they're in love or married,' she said softly, 'even if they deeply love their wives, simply for the hour's pleasure or because they need more than what they receive from their wives.'

370

He lay still, just listening.

'I've recently acquired a local gentleman like that who comes occasionally when he absolutely has to. But not you, Kane. You can only give yourself to the woman you love. All I could give you is cold comfort and you can't allow yourself to relax and accept that.' She stayed silent for a while, then said carefully, 'Would you like to talk about her? Usually I hate being made a confidante over a man's love but I would be most interested in yours.'

Kane stared thoughtfully at the lustrous canopy above them for some time. Then he said, low and huskily, 'She's as beautiful and free as the summer sky, as wild and unpredictable as the sea. I've known her since we were small children but it's only a short time since I knew I loved her. We used to be good friends but we've quarrelled a lot since I've been home. Then there was a thunderstorm and she was terrified and I comforted her. Oh, how I like to hold her – it's like holding something vital to my very being, something which is badly missing when she's not in my arms. I think she cared for me deeply too. Then she was in great danger but when I knew she was safe, instead of taking her in my arms and telling her how relieved I was, I just bawled at her. I wanted to tell her that I loved her and couldn't bear to lose her but instead I was cruel and upset her. Later there was another incident and she told me she hated me. She won't ever forgive me, Frances.'

'You can't be sure of that,' Frances said gently.

Kane shifted his position and got comfortable again. 'Anyway, it's too late now. She's lost interest in me. Just before I came here I found her in my brother's arms. They were kissing.'

'I see,' Frances said, raising herself to look down into his wonderfully sad, sad eyes. 'And that's why you came here?'

'I think I just wanted someone to hold me.'

'Well, I'll hold you for as long as you like.'

'There's plenty of money in my pocket. Can I stay here all night?' he whispered.

'Of course. But Kane, what will you do tomorrow?'

'I'll go home long enough to tell my parents I'm going to stay on my farm for good. I'll plunge my time and energies into getting it working the way I want it to be, try to forget my golden-haired, beautiful… try to forget Jessica.'

'Jessica. So that's her name. Kane, I know your brother. He comes here often. He's not ready to settle down, not for several years. Jessica probably doesn't mean anything to him. Don't give up hope.'

Kane made a disheartened face. 'Luke was beastly to her too yet she's forgiven him and soon found her way into his arms. She looks at me as if I was dirt.'

'But—'

'Leave it, Frances. Someone else urged me to try a short time ago but it was all for nothing. It's too late. Now stay with me or give me the brandy bottle, but please don't talk any more.'

Frances settled herself against him and he drifted off into a long, hopeless sleep.

–

Two days had passed since Philip had won the wrestling match. A ballad was being sung locally about him and Jessica was humming it softly as she milked the goats in the barn. She did not realise someone was watching and listening to her.

'What a charming scene and what a pleasant voice,' he said at last.

'Oh, Simon Peter!' she exclaimed, jumping up from the stool. 'It's wonderful to see you after all this time.' And she ran into his embrace. 'Why haven't you been over before? David said you've been home for days. I tried to see you but couldn't find you anywhere.'

'I tried to get away before, but my parents have been monopolising me. You look as beautiful as ever. How are you, Jessica? And how are you getting on with your stepmother?'

'I'm fine and Catherine has settled in well. It's as if she's been here for years. I still miss my mother of course but Catherine's good to have around. How are things in Yorkshire?'

'It's a beautiful county, full of hills, dales and moors, vastly bigger than Cornwall and almost as beautiful. I've done some open-air preaching and I think I was well received.'

'Good for you. You're not going back yet, are you? I want to see a lot of you.'

'I'm going back in a few days and I'm hoping your father won't object to David coming with me. Is Matthias Renfree here yet? He said he would come over to lend moral support.'

'Aye, Uncle Matthias has been here for about twenty minutes. I thought he was looking rather sheepish. So that's what it's all about. Father's checking the boundaries to see if they'll withstand the winter's storms, but he should be back soon.'

'How do you think he'll take it, Jessica?' Simon Peter moved aside so she could get to the next goat and passed her the bucket when she was sitting comfortably. 'I know your father is rather possessive over his children.'

'He'll soon come round. Everyone's got their own life to live, he'll see that. After all, he married Catherine against most folks' advice and it seems to be working out very well. Anyway, it's not as though you're both going away for ever.'

'What about you, Jessica? You've got your own life to live. Haven't you got some news for me?'

'What are you talking about, Simon Peter? What sort of news?'

'Well, I rather thought there'd be some concerning you and Kane Pengarron.'

'What?' Jessica yanked on the goat's teat and made it bleat in protest. 'Have you gone off your head? I hate the man. Why should I have anything to do with him?'

Simon Peter was taken aback. 'But didn't you see him after the wrestling match? I had coffee with him and he told me he was going to seek you out and make things up to you.'

'I saw him briefly, that is he saw me and Luke briefly.'

'And he didn't ask to speak to you?'

'No,' Jessica said defensively. 'Kane thought he was interrupting something and went off in a huff.'

Simon Peter frowned. 'Interrupting what, for goodness' sake? Jessica?'

Blushing, she admitted, 'Luke and I were kissing.'

'Kissing? You and Luke? You're not... *Luke?* Jessica, what were you thinking of?'

'It didn't mean anything. He was being honest with me and I was going to leave and we just kissed. It didn't mean anything, Simon.'

'But Kane obviously thought it did.'

'What if he did? It's none of his business. I'll kiss who I like.'

'But Kane is in love with you, Jessica.'

She went as white as the goat beside her and shivered as though an awful truth had dawned on her. 'Wh... what makes you think that?' she got out in a gasp.

'He told me. He was going to find you and explain how he felt. Oh, Jessica, that little kiss you shared with Luke has ruined everything. Kane will think it most odd after his brother had said he'd got you with child and then to find you kissing him.'

'I don't care,' Jessica said, turning away. ''Tis none of his business what I do with Luke. No one understands how we feel about each other. We're sort of friends and that friendship is our business.'

Simon Peter lowered himself to her side and put his hands on her shoulders. He could feel her shaking gently as she cried. 'You love Kane too, don't you, Jessica?'

She nodded miserably. 'It... it just seemed to grow with us... but I had no real hopes about it. He's a gentleman and I'm just a farmer's daughter. Worse still, I'm a Trenchard and his father wouldn't want him to marry me for that reason alone.'

'You know Kane better than that, Jessica. If Sir Oliver had any such objections, Kane wouldn't care about them.'

'Well, things can't be put right now, it's all such a mess.'

'Jessica, Kane is living on his farm for good now. I was hoping he had put things right with you and asked you to marry him. I thought he'd gone away to prepare a home for you to live in.'

Harsh, bitter tears ran down her face. 'Will you leave me alone please, Simon? I'll come in when Father comes home.'

When he'd gone, she threw herself on the bales of straw and cried as if her heart was breaking.

Clem looked at the sea of faces all gazing anxiously at him. The whole family was crammed into the kitchen with Matthias Renfree and Ricketty Jim and, most unusual, Simon Peter Blake. Clem thought it must be something serious because the men looked solemn and Jessica had been weeping and Catherine had an arm round her.

'What's the matter?' he asked Catherine. Since their wedding day he always spoke to her first.

'It's nothing serious, Clem,' she replied, 'Well, it is, but nothing terrible has happened. David has something to tell you.'

David was grateful to his charming stepmother for giving him this opening. Clem looked straight at him. 'Well, son?'

'I want to go back to Yorkshire with Simon Peter, Father,' David plunged straight in. 'To become a preacher. When I've learned how to proclaim the Gospel up there, I hope to be allowed to come back and work for the Lord in Cornwall. I want you to let me go and give me your blessing.'

Clem gazed from face to face. Behind the assortment of expressions, he could see everyone was on David's side, ready to plead for him if need be. He turned to Matthias. 'Do you think he can do it?'

'I'm sure of it, Clem. We've prayed long and hard and believe it's the Lord's will for him. It's up to you now. "Honour thy father" – he won't go unless you say he can.'

Simon Peter was next to be asked a question. 'And you're prepared to take care of my son while he's away?'

'Yes, sir,' Simon Peter replied respectfully. 'He will share my lodgings with me. They are warm and spacious and comfortable. The Society will help support him in all his needs.'

Clem took in Catherine, Jessica, Philip, Kenver and Kerris and Ricketty Jim in one sweeping look. 'And I take it none of you mind him going?'

'It's what he's always dreamed of,' Catherine said.

'Please, Father, give him the chance to do what he really wants to,' Jessica pleaded.

'I've got what I've always wanted and I'm hopeful other plans I've got will be realised soon,' Philip said, putting a muscular arm round his red-faced twin. ''Tis David's turn now.'

Kenver spoke for himself and Kerris. 'We think he should be allowed to go, Clem.'

Lastly it was Ricketty Jim's turn to air his opinion. 'I'm proud to be included in the family's decisions. I believe it's only right and proper for him to go. Like the others, I don't mind putting my hand to the extra work without him.'

It seemed the whole company held their breath as they waited for Clem to make his decision, He beckoned David to him. 'Are you sure this is what you want to do, David?'

'Aye, Father,' David said eagerly. 'Since I was a littl'un.'

'Why haven't you said anything before?'

'I was going to but there's been so much change and excitement going on lately I thought it wouldn't be fair to worry you.'

'I don't want you to go,' Clem said, and David's face fell. 'No man wants to see his children leave home. But it seems a higher authority them me has a say in this. You must do what your heavenly father wants you to.'

David could only gasp his thanks and hug his father as a cheer echoed round the kitchen. The barrel of bootleg rum was brought out and a toast was drunk to David's health and future while, ironically, the three staunch Methodists, David, Simon Peter and Matthias, drank tea.

When Matthias returned to Ker-an-Mor Farm and the family were off about their work, Catherine said to Clem, 'It was wonderful, the way you gave David your blessing.'

'Aye, but I shall miss him. Of my three children, he is the quietest and I suppose I've taken less notice of him. He was the only one not inclined to moods and tempers and I'll miss his calming influence.'

'He won't be gone for ever.'

'What was the matter with Jessica?'

'I think it was something that Simon Peter told her. Kane Pengarron has left the Manor to set up his farm. I suppose he won't be seen much around the estate any more.'

'Oh, I see.'

'You liked Kane, didn't you, Clem? I think you'll miss him too.'

'Aye, I suppose I will. But not as much as Jessica, eh?'

Philip came back into the kitchen and lingered about. He didn't look his usual cocky self. Clem watched him.

'I suppose you'll be the most lost without David around. Twins are usually very close.'

'It's not about David, Father,' Philip said with a nervous cough.

Catherine took her husband's arm and steered him to sit down. 'Philip has something to say to you, Clem. In fact we both do.'

–

It was a bitterly cold December day. The sky was stark and grey overhead, the sea swept in on gigantic rollers and spray hissed and cascaded thirty feet high over the jagged black granite rocks. The undercurrent dragged everything back the way it had come in its awesome strength. The wind came from every direction and mercilessly bit into everything in its wake. It was too cold for wildlife to hop and fly or lull about, but Kerensa could be found at any time of the year in Trelynne Cove. And Clem knew that sooner or later, if he went there often enough, he would find her there alone.

Today he was in luck.

He saw Kernick, the second chestnut pony she had given that name, down in the cove and he rode Tally cautiously down beside him and dismounted.

Kerensa was up the end of the beach where Mother Clarry's seat was situated. She was thinking of Clem. Yesterday, while at the Parsonage to see how the changes Olivia was making were coming along, she had met Catherine Trenchard. Catherine didn't look pleased to see her. Ever since the day Kerensa had seen her preparing to go over to Trecath-en Farm for dinner with the Trenchards, she had seemed eager to avoid her. Kerensa thought the reason was probably because Catherine felt uneasy, or perhaps jealous, of her past love for Clem. But now she wanted to face Catherine over her aloofness. She studied Catherine's child-like face; she looked years younger since her marriage to Clem, softer, prettier. Kerensa thought with a tinge of regret that this was how a woman in love and married to Clem Trenchard would look.

She cornered Catherine alone in the dining room. 'It must seem strange to you, all these changes, Catherine,' she said, trying to sound friendly.

'I approve of Miss Olivia's taste,' Catherine returned, only glancing at Kerensa. 'The Parsonage has been greatly changed for the better with the generous funds Sir Oliver has made available for it. I think she and Timothy will be very comfortable here.'

'And how are you finding things in your new life?' Kerensa asked.

Catherine lifted her chin and said in challenging tones, 'I'm very happy indeed.'

'I'm pleased to hear it.'

'Thank you, m'lady. Miss Olivia and Timothy are inspecting the extension to the parlour, if you were wanting to see them. I was just looking over the improvements in this room.'

'I'll see them a little later. It isn't often we get the chance to talk nowadays. I hope that just because you're married to Clem you don't feel you can't call at the Manor as you did before.'

'Like his first wife did, you mean? She was your closest friend, I understand.'

Again that challenge. Kerensa sighed. 'Catherine, I don't mind that you've married Clem. I'm sure Alice wouldn't either. I only want to see him happy and Alice would have felt the same way. You see me as a threat, don't you?'

Catherine had paled. She sat down heavily at the new dining table, made of the finest Pengarron oak. 'I think he'll always love you. Do you love him?'

Kerensa came forward and put her arm round Catherine's shoulders. 'The only feeling that Clem and I have for each other is as friends, a soft spot if you like. It's no more than that, I promise you. I'd like for us to be friends too, Catherine. You don't have to duck your head when our eyes meet in church, you know.'

'I've only been married a few weeks and I simply couldn't bear to lose Clem,' Catherine murmured.

'I know how you feel. It's exactly how I feel about my husband. Now, why don't we look critically over the changes to this house? And if we don't like them, as ladies of standing and experience in such things we will say so.'

Catherine Trenchard was a most reasonable person, ready to live in harmony with those around her. They had inspected her old home in minute detail, finding the odd fault and voicing their views, much to the consternation of Olivia and Timothy who saw the Parsonage only through a rosy glow. Catherine had told Kerensa she wouldn't come to the Manor, feeling it wouldn't be quite right as Clem would never be invited there, but had agreed that she and Kerensa could be friends when they met elsewhere.

When Kerensa saw Clem coming towards her in the cove, his tall blond figure easily recognisable, she walked quickly to meet him.

'Hello, Clem. It's good to see you. I was just thinking about you. I met Catherine yesterday, did she tell you?'

'Yes, she did. It's a long time since we were here together, even longer since we were here alone.'

'Are you well?'

'Aye. Are you?'

'Yes, thank you. Is there… any particular reason that you're here? Not that you're not welcome,' she added hastily on account of his stern face.

'I've been this way quite often lately hoping to see you alone. I want to talk to you and this is the best place to do it.'

'I see, good. Shall we find somewhere more sheltered? The wind's cutting across here. How about under Mother Clarry's rock? It's always sheltered there.'

She returned to the witch's seat with Clem striding silently beside her, their feet crunching over the shingle. She looked at him often but he had his face set ahead. She sat down on a boulder and wrapped her cloak round herself.

'Are you cold, Kerensa?' he asked, and he looked concerned.

'No, not really, I'm well wrapped up. Why don't you sit down beside me, Clem?'

He did, but not close, as he would have done once without hesitation.

'You look serious,' she said. She wasn't sure if in his present mood she should talk about Catherine but she was curious to know about their life together. 'How's Catherine today?'

'She's fine. She's settled down to farm life very quickly. Course she doesn't do any of the heavy work,' he said, as if he was stressing his new wife's position was similar to Kerensa's. 'She's a real asset to the farm and the family are very fond of her.'

'I'm glad for you. I hear David's just left for Yorkshire. You must miss him. With Olivia about to get married and Kane away on his farm, it seems we are beginning to lose our children, Clem.'

'Mmmm.'

Kerensa looked down at her gently spreading middle. 'You can probably see that I'm starting another baby, a second family.'

'Me also. Catherine's just realised she's with child.'

'Oh, Clem, that's wonderful. Are you pleased?'

'Of course I am,' he said moodily. 'I've always liked children, you ought to know that.'

Kerensa's heart was cast down. She put a hand on Clem's arm. 'I didn't think there would ever be bad feelings between us, Clem.'

He studied her hand but did not seek to remove it. 'I can't forget the way Jessica was treated by the men of your family, Kerensa. Even you were willing to believe that she was pregnant by one of your sons. Is it because I got Alice like that that you think all the Trenchard women are tarred with the same brush? Alice wasn't cheap and common, even if she wasn't a virgin on our wedding night, and neither is Jessica. She's suffered cruelly at the hands of your menfolk, even Kane. I feel very bitter about it.'

'I'm very sorry, Clem. But in all fairness you thought Jessica had lain with Luke too. It was the reason you came rushing over to the Manor.'

'Only because I thought he'd got her drunk or something, but I admit, thinking about it, even he wouldn't have done that.' Clem went silent and gazed at the sea.

'It's upset you deeply, hasn't it?'

'All the way over to the Manor I kept thinking, what if Luke was responsible and he actually offered to marry Jessica and she accepted him? I would rather have seen her in her grave beside Alice than married to Oliver Pengarron's son, to have my daughter as the next Lady of the Manor, after you, the girl who was stolen away from me.'

'And Kane? What if there had been a baby and it had been Kane's?'

'I wouldn't have minded that too much. Kane's not a Pengarron by blood and I've always liked him. He won't inherit anything of the Pengarron property, and somehow I think of him as belonging only to you.'

'I see. Then have you forgiven him for shouting at Jessica on the night of the kidnapping? He only acted so because he was so worried about her.'

'Maybe, but he ought to have said he was sorry. Even Luke's told Jessica he's sorry for saying he'd got her with child. Why hasn't Kane said he's sorry?'

'I rather think he's tried to but without success. It's more difficult for them.'

'Well, it's all over now, in the past, and I suppose that is where it should stay. Kane's got his farm and a new start and Jessica is about to start a new life with her stepmother and me.'

'Oh?' Kerensa was startled.

Clem looked her full in the face. He swallowed hard as if he had great difficulty with what he had to say. 'Kerensa, we're leaving Trecath-en Farm and the Mount's Bay area. All the family are going and Ricketty Jim's coming with us.'

'No, Clem, no!' The last thing on earth she wanted was for Clem to leave the estate. She clutched his arms as if she would forbid him to go.

He held her shoulders firmly and spoke as she shook her head in disbelief. 'As you know, Catherine has her own income, not a lot by Pengarron standards but she's saved most of it over the years and it's become a goodly sum. Philip approached her and asked her to put her money with his. He'd taken a huge chance on a wager when he wrestled the Barvah Giant and made over a thousand pounds. They came to me next and offered to buy a farm between them. It took them a long time to persuade me because I've got little money of my own, but that was only pride and I've had to put it aside. It's not been easy living on Pengarron land over the years, especially after my father died and I became the tenant and Sir Oliver my landlord, knowing he's got the right to ride over it any time he chooses and if he wanted to be difficult he could easily find a way of throwing us off. But the events of the past few months have made things intolerable, for me and Jessica, and it will never be easy for Catherine knowing you are the landlord's wife and how I've always felt about you.

'We're going to have our own farm, up at St Cleer on the Bodmin moor. We'll be our own men, Philip and I. He'll take care of the land and I'll deal with the animals and that way we won't clash. The farmhouse is much bigger than Trecath-en's and there'll be plenty of room if Philip marries and has a family and if Catherine and I have more children. There are two houses on the land so Kenver and Kerris will have their own place with a big room for his workshop.'

It was a hard task for Kerensa to take this in. She said shakily, 'I... I'm very pleased for you, Clem, but...'

'But what, Kerensa?' and he gazed at her deeply.

'Will I ever see you again?'

'I don't know. I realised that day at the Manor when I charged in that you're totally Pengarron's now. I'm sure he'll be glad I'm leaving his land. I'm finally going away after all these years to start a new life. I wish you well with your new child.' He removed her desperate hands from his arms, held them tightly for a moment, then got up. 'Goodbye, Kerensa.'

'Goodbye, Clem,' she uttered, just managing to hold back her tears.

She watched him walk away from her. The tall blond man she had been going to share her life with on Trecath-en Farm. And now he was going away from her forever.

'Clem!'

He'd only walked a few paces and came straight back to her. In an instant she was being held tightly in his arms. They looked into each other's eyes and they were back in the days of their youth, a girl of seventeen, a young man of nineteen, very much in love and looking forward to a future together.

They kissed longingly… and then it was time to come back to the present.

Kerensa lowered her arms from his neck and he took her hands, kissing them both tenderly, and they looked at each other with tears falling from their eyes.

'I'll always love you, Kerensa.' She went to speak but he put a finger to her trembling lips. 'Remember me with affection.'

Then he left Trelynne Cove and Kerensa alone with her thoughts. She walked to the shoreline, not feeling the cold that struck her face and tried to sweep off her hat. Clem the boy had gone many years ago; her enforced marriage to Oliver had seen to that. In the years since, they had both reared a family, known much sorrow, heartbreak and joy. More than once, circumstances had thrown them together and they had nearly given themselves to one another. But fate had always stepped in to forbid it.

Now fate was stepping in again, and Clem the man was going away from her, possibly forever. Kerensa felt lost and lonely but knew it was the best thing to happen. She would think of Clem Trenchard all of her life, and it would be with more than affection.

Chapter 30

While her husband was absent, presumably off on one of his long quiet spells, Catherine was ruthlessly discarding things the Trenchards would not take with them to St Cleer. Kerris and Philip were carrying them out to the bottom of the vegetable patch at the back of the farmhouse, and Jessica was throwing the items now deemed rubbish onto the high twisting red flames of a huge bonfire.

Kerris held up a pair of curtains, faded but with plenty of wear left in them, and showed them to Jessica. 'I'll put these into the charity pile. Somebody will be glad of them. Miss Catherine is certainly having a good turn-out.'

'My mother chose these,' Jessica said, fingering the material. 'She saved up for ages to buy the cloth. I remember sitting on her lap as a little girl while she sewed them.'

'Oh! Shall I tell Miss Catherine? She probably didn't realise they meant something to you. I said they would do for mine and Kenver's house but she's insisting on us having new throughout.'

Jessica picked up her fork and poked the bonfire to get a better blaze on the furniture burning in front of her. A cupboard, pocked with woodworm and so old that no one was sure of its origins, crackled for a few moments then shuddered and disintegrated into small pieces. Kerris was watching Jessica's face.

'Shows how dry that wood had become. Put the curtains into the charity pile, Kerris. I've been through the house and put aside everything I want to keep. It's good to think some of my mother's and grandmother's things will help the needy of the parish. I don't blame Catherine for wanting to make a fresh start. 'Tis the best way to go about it.'

'Aye, I think Miss Catherine is more excited than I am. She'll be able to hold her head up more when we move away. She'll be the prominent lady of the area, the wife of a landed farmer, not just a tenant's wife. I must say though, Kenver and I think your father is a brave man to let Miss Catherine and Philip spend their money like this on a new farm. Must have been a blow to his pride; certainly Kenver had to think hard about agreeing to it.'

'Perhaps it was brave of Father, but there's nothing here for him now and everything is so difficult. It's the same for me.' Kerris jumped back as Jessica slammed the fork down so hard it threatened to put the bonfire out. ''Tis a shame about that, but things have a way of working out, Jessie.'

'Aye,' Jessica said, attacking the bonfire once more, 'but not for the best for everyone.'

–

Round the bay, up on high ground at Gulval on Vellanoweth Farm, Kane was half-heartedly wandering through the twelve large square rooms he was living in. Most of the rooms were completely empty; the room he slept in contained only a mattress. His footsteps echoed around him. He had no heart to choose the furnishings to fill the house and resolved to ask his mother for help; he was sure she would be delighted to do it for him. It would give her all the excuses she would need to come over often and mollycoddle him, exhort him to eat proper meals and make sure his clothes were kept up to standard.

Stopping at a bedroom window, he put his head outside and looked out across a wide patchwork of bleak fields, many of which would be growing his wheat, oats, barley and animal feed in the New Year. He tried to picture the crops swaying in their splendid colours in the breezes, awaiting a band of harvesters to swathe them down and make him richer and successful. He hoped he would have something to feel happy about then.

This year he had left his regiment, settled the question of his true parentage, bought the farm and land he'd dreamed about in the pain and heat of the Tropics, but… he wanted someone to share his new life with him. To share the joys and worries of farming life, to take on the fickle weather with him that affected so much of its success, to mourn with him when they were beaten by it and laugh with him when they'd triumphed over it. To comfort him in moments of grief, like when he'd learned that the ship *Rockingham Castle* had sunk on its way to Ireland with the loss of many of his friends from the 32nd Foot. He wanted that someone to fill this large empty house with lots of babies, with joy and laughter… and a little wildness.

He moved to another bedroom, the largest one, evidently meant for the master and mistress of the place. The windows here looked out to St Michael's Mount in the green waters of the bay. He swept his eyes round to Cudden Point, sprawled out in the sea, and could see his father's estate stretching back from the cliffs behind it. Drawing his eyes nearer home across the fields, he saw the strong tower of Ludgvan Church, and round to his right the parish church of Gulval, with Penzance as a backdrop. These last sights held no interest for him and moodily he swung back to Pengarron land again, where somewhere, on one little spot, lived the girl who had given him more trouble than anyone or anything else in his entire life. A girl with hair as wild and as free as her nature and as golden as the cornfields, with laughing summer-blue eyes, and an utterly stubborn will.

You should be here with me, Jessica Trenchard, he thought miserably. Then you could choose the furniture to put in this place, what curtains to put up at its windows. You should be feeding your own chickens here in the yard below me, waiting for me to come home from the fields, sometimes working with me in them, and always loving with me wherever we are. Kane hung his head. He'd had nightmares about his past and had purged them, but now he had bad dreams about his future.

A voice hailed him from down in the yard. He had not realised that a cart had pulled up in it. Kane had acquired some staff. On a byway of Mount's Bay he had come across the legless Jacob Penberthy and his son Ben looking for work. Now the old soldier who had been so helpful to Clem when he was looking for clues to Kerris's identity up the hazardous life of begging and live in a cosy little cottage while his son worked on the farm. Knowing the Penberthys had worked on Trecath-en Farm and had met and spoken to Jessica made Kane feel a little closer to her.

He made his way downstairs. This was what he had to do now, work hard and see to his men, and try to forget how much he yearned for Jessica Trenchard.

Oliver was in his study when Kerensa arrived home. He got straight up from the letters he was writing at his desk and she went to him to be cradled in his warm arms. He took her to the fireplace and rubbed her arms to bring some warmth to her shivering body.

'You should not stay out in this weather so long, beloved,' he gently chided her. 'I wouldn't like you to catch a chill, especially in your condition.' He placed a gentle hand on her middle and felt their baby kicking. He smiled happily, but her face caused him concern. 'Is everything all right? You're very quiet and you look as if you've been crying.'

'Oliver, I was in Trelynne Cove and Clem came there to talk to me, to tell me something.'

Oliver's face darkened. 'How dare he! What did he want? Won't that man ever leave us alone? Damn him!'

'But that's why he came to see me, Oliver. To tell me he's leaving the farm.'

'That's the best news I could possibly hear – but he should have told me first.'

'Don't be angry, my love. He wanted to tell me to my face rather than let me hear it from someone else. Catherine and Philip have put up the money, most of it, and they've bought a farm at St Cleer. The whole family, and even Ricketty Jim, are going. Clem said it's intolerable for his family living on Pengarron land after all that has happened over Jessica, especially with Jessica and Kane being in love and seemingly hating one another. It must be hard for Catherine too, being the wife of a tenant farmer when she's gentry born and bred.'

'And knowing he'll always hanker after you, the landlord's wife.'

'But if he was still feeling like that, Oliver, he wouldn't have agreed to leave Trecath-en Farm and Mount's Bay. St Cleer is a long way away, we'll probably never see him again. It must have cost him dear to swallow his pride and allow his wife and son to buy a farm for the family. He could easily have refused and Philip would still have had enough money to buy a smaller farm for himself so he wouldn't have been letting his son down.'

'Well, whatever the reason, I'll be eternally grateful that Clem Trenchard is leaving my land,' Oliver said. 'I shall breathe easier after twenty-two years of having him hanging about. Since he took up with Miss Catherine, he's even been in our church every Sunday. And it will make things easier for Olivia to settle down with Timothy. '

'There was never any chance of anything between Clem and me, Oliver. You do believe that, don't you?'

'Yes, but I could never forget you had once been in love. Now we can bury that in the past for good. I… wish him well, I suppose.'

'It will mean Jessica leaving too, taking her even further from Kane,' Kerensa said.

'I regret that. I can see how much Kane loves her. He'll always love her, always mourn her, no matter what he does with his life.' Oliver suddenly laughed. 'Dear Lord, I've just described the way Clem Trenchard must have felt about you.'

'You sound as though you don't feel too badly about him now,' Kerensa said hopefully.

'I don't know about that. Well, I admit to understanding something of how he's felt over the years. I know how I would feel if I lost you. I would be desolate. And now Kane has well and truly lost Jessica.'

'The terribly sad thing about it is that it doesn't have to be like this. I'm sure she loves him just as deeply as he loves her, and there's no one to take her away from him, nothing but their own stubbornness.'

Kane, who had come home to pick up some of his things, overheard the last two sentences. He came into the room and stared at his parents.

…rd?' Oliver said.

'I did. There's no point in people going on about us being stubborn,' Kane said heatedly. 'Jessica and I can never sort out our differences. Too much has been said and done. I wish you would just forget it.'

'Jessica's leaving Mount's Bay, Kane,' Kerensa said softly.

'What?' He sprang forward. 'Is she going to marry Simon Peter Blake?'

'No, but she might as well be as far as you are concerned,' Oliver told him bluntly. 'The Trenchards have bought their own farm at St Cleer, Bodmin. She'll be miles away from you and it would serve you right if she forgets all about you.'

'But Mother said she loves me. Why should she forget me?'

'Well, that rather depends on you. I would never let your mother go as easily as you have her.'

'I…' For a moment Kane looked as if he was going to swear and Kerensa gave him a mother's warning look. 'That girl's not going anywhere unless it's to Vellanoweth Farm with me!'

Oliver laughed and hugged Kerensa as their elder son rushed out of the Manor house.

'Do you think he'll convince Jessica?' Kerensa asked between his kisses.

'My dear, I have an awful feeling I'll be facing Clem Trenchard across the church at a wedding.'

Kerensa snuggled in against her husband's warm, broad body. It was wonderful to be this much in love and she said a little prayer that Kane would be holding the girl he loved in his arms like this soon.

–

Kane trotted into the yard of Trecath-en Farm and knocked on the kitchen door. Catherine opened the door and immediately invited him in. He was embarrassed to find the only other person there was Clem.

'I… I've come to see Jessica.'

'She's seeing to her chickens,' Clem said.

'Do you mind if I go and talk to her, Clem?' Kane asked uncertainly, his hand hovering near the door latch.

Clem put his arm round Catherine's shoulders, then he answered Kane with a friendly smile. ''Tis all right by us, but don't you go until you get the matter settled, do you hear me, Kane Pengarron?'

'You can stake your life on it,' Kane said determinedly.

Jessica saw him coming and stared coldly at him for a few moments. She wasn't pleased to see him. She was getting used to the idea of moving to St Cleer and starting a new life so many miles away. There would be a new sister or brother next year to look forward to and she had made up her mind to throw herself into some new interests, charity work or something – Catherine could tell her how to go about it. She had scattered corn for her chickens and she had been standing in front of the cone-shaped coops planning how to expand her little business and now this Pengarron oaf with the cruel mouth was coming to torment her again. She wished she had kissed a dozen men for him to see and not just his brother. Get back to your own farm, she thought angrily, and leave me to get on here. What are you doing here anyway? Come to boast about your new property? To make us feel how small ours is?

She didn't dare to hope that he was here for what she really wanted and she turned her back on him, hammering in a nail to fix the fencing on the bottom of a coop to fortify it against attacks from predators.

Kane tightened his features at her unfriendly gesture but he wasn't deterred.

'I want to talk to you, Jessica,' he almost bellowed, going round to face her stooping figure.

'What do you want?' she said in an offhand manner, dropping the hammer and turning away from him again to pick up the second laying of eggs.

'I'm not here to pay a social call.'

'I gathered that!'

Kane sighed heavily and drummed his fingers on the wood above but she refused to look up from the nesting boxes.

'Will you please turn and face me? I have some things I want to explain and I have no intention of talking to your back!'

Jessica picked up all the large white and brown eggs in the coop she was stretching into. Only then did she face him. 'Well? I can't stop you and I suppose I should be grateful that at least you said please.'

Kane looked at her irritably. Must she make it so damned difficult?

'I know I upset you after you were rescued from Zack Maynard and I've neglected to apologise for it. Don't you realise how frightened I was for you, Jessica? It was only days after Hezekiah Solomon had held Olivia prisoner and he was going to rape her, humiliate, torture and murder her. I was terrified Zack Maynard was going to do that to you before I could reach you.'

'Well, I'm very sorry to have frightened you, Mr Kane Pengarron. I should have remembered to put your feelings before anyone else's. You men want us women to be quiet and meek, don't you? You don't like it if we step out of line from the expectations and rules you put on us, and when we do you hate it.'

'You were very nearly murdered, damn it, Jessica! Don't you see or are you too stupid?'

'I can see you don't like it that I wanted a bit of adventure! Why should you men have all the excitement and we women have to stay meekly at home waiting for one of you to do us the dubious honour of making us your wife and having us at your beck and call! Go away, I never want to speak to you again.'

Kane looked at her calmly and coolly. 'Do you really mean all that, Jessica Trenchard?'

She flung up her head, making her curls bounce. 'Yes, I do.'

'Very well. I hoped you would see reason, but...'

He walked quickly away and Jessica's heart plunged to her feet. She stared after him. 'But what, Kane?'

She was still there moments later when he came charging through the yard on his horse, scattering her squawking hens in all directions.

'What on earth—'

He snatched her up and put her on his horse, imprisoning her in front of him. Her basket of eggs fell from her hands, breaking all over the ground. She screamed and struggled and got a glimpse of her father and stepmother laughing at a window as they galloped past.

Kane rode up to the top of Trecath-en valley with her struggling and protesting all the way. He pulled her off his horse and pushed her into Ricketty Jim's shack then stood in front of the doorway to block her escape.

Jessica shook her dress and cloak down to cover her legs and raged at him, 'And what do you hope to achieve by this, you… you…'

Bending towards her in a mocking fashion, he said, 'So you want adventure, do you? How about this, Jessica? I've just kidnapped you. Is this adventure enough for you?'

'You're mad!' she shouted, tossing her head and making her hair swirl about her shoulders. 'You think you can do anything you like. Riding like a fiend through somebody's yard, breaking their eggs, frightening their chickens. My hens probably won't lay for months now and it's all your fault!'

'Never mind your ruddy chickens, this is more important.'

'Oh, of course it is. Everything a gentleman like you does is far more important than anybody else's life.'

'I tried to speak to you reasonably, calmly and sensibly but you wouldn't have it. It's your fault we're here like this!'

Her heart was pounding in her chest. Must he look so wild and handsome when he behaved like this? She mustn't look into his beautiful sad brown eyes or she'd be lost. She was drinking in those eyes and had to turn away from him.

'Why don't you look at me?' he demanded. 'Look at me when I'm speaking to you.'

'Why should I?'

He lowered his voice to a husky softness. 'Why don't you look at me, Jessica?'

'It's… it's your eyes.'

'What about my eyes?' he asked, totally puzzled.

Jessica was finding it impossible to stay angry with him. She was ⟨…⟩s gesture of 'kidnapping' her, his determination to make ⟨…⟩ him this time, and she knew with a joyous freedom in her heart what he was going to say to her at last. She was smiling blissfully and couldn't stop doing it as she answered him. 'I find them… irresistible.'

He moved round her and raised her chin with a gentle hand. 'When I look at you like this?'

'When you look at me at all,' she whispered back.

He reached out and picked up two handfuls of long golden curls, then he bent his head towards her face but she was already making to kiss him. They kissed with heat and passion and a wild abandonment, hungry for every sensation, for knowing each other's lips and souls completely.

When he finally broke away, he said softly, 'You must know that I've bought my own farm, Jessica.'

'Everybody seems to be doing it these days,' she murmured, remembering how he had just made her feel and how she had enjoyed it so very much.

'Would you agree with me that the best woman to become a farmer's wife is a farmer's daughter?'

'Mmmm, I suppose I could.'

'You're a farmer's daughter,' he murmured, kissing her shining curls.

'That's true,' and she kissed his chin.

'You'd make a good farmer's wife.'

'It has been said before.'

'I'm no longer a soldier but a farmer.'

'Vellanoweth is a good farm, so I've heard.'

'It is, except for one thing.'

'Oh?'

'It lacks a mistress, a good farmer's wife. You could be that wife, Jessica. How do you feel about giving that poor overworked parson, my future brother-in-law, some more work?'

'I think I could be persuaded,' she said dreamily.

'And how do I do that?'

'You could try looking into my eyes.'

393

He gazed at her longingly, and as he saw the love and passion she held for him in the depths of her eyes, the sad startled effect that had been in his for so much of his life drained away. A new radiance was there, glowing with love, joy, hope, and fulfilment. And this would be the way he and Jessica would look at each other for the rest of their lives.